AN AMISH CHRISTMAS WEDDING

AN AMISH CHRISTMAS WEDDING

Four Stories

Amy Clipston
Kelly Irvin
Kathleen Fuller
Vannetta Chapman

ZONDERVAN®

ZONDERVAN

An Amish Christmas Wedding

Requests for information should be addressed to:
Zondervan, *3900 Sparks Dr. SE, Grand Rapids, Michigan 49546*

Library of Congress Cataloging-in-Publication Data

Names: Clipston, Amy. Evergreen love. | Irvin, Kelly. Holiday of hope. | Fuller, Kathleen. Wreathed in love. | Chapman, Vannetta. Christmas prayer.
Title: An Amish Christmas wedding : four stories / Amy Clipston, Kelly Irvin, Kathleen Fuller, Vannetta Chapman.
Description: Grand Rapids, Michigan : Zondervan, [2020] | Summary: "From bestselling authors of Amish fiction come four delightful stories perfect for celebrating love, joy, and the everyday miracles Christmas brings"-- Provided by publisher.
Identifiers: LCCN 2020018908 (print) | LCCN 2020018909 (ebook) | ISBN 9780310361398 (paperback) | ISBN 9780310361404 (epub) | ISBN 9780310361411 (downloadable audio)
Subjects: LCSH: Amish--Fiction. | Christmas stories, American. | Christian fiction, American.
Classification: LCC PS648.A45 A348 2020 (print) | LCC PS648.A45 (ebook) | DDC 813/.6080334--dc23
LC record available at https://lccn.loc.gov/2020018908
LC ebook record available at https://lccn.loc.gov/2020018909

Printed in the United States of America

20 21 22 23 24 LSC 10 9 8 7 6 5 4 3 2 1

Contents

Glossary*

ach: oh
aenti: aunt
appeditlich: delicious
bedauerlich: sad
bopli/boppli: baby
boplin/bopplin: babies
brot: bread
bruder: brother
bruders: brothers
bruderskinner: nieces/nephews
bu: boy
buwe: boys
daadi/daddi: grandfather
daadihaus: small house provided for retired parents
daddi haus/dawdi haus: grandparents' house
daed: father
danki: thank you
dat: dad, father
dochder: daughter

dochdern: daughters
dummkopp: moron
Dummle!: Hurry!
Englischer/Englisher: non-Amish person
eppies: cookies
familye: family
fraa/frau: wife
Frehlicher Grischtdaag: Merry Christmas
freind: friend
freinden: friends
froh: happy
gegisch: silly
geh: go
gem gschehne/gern gschehne: you're welcome
Gmay: church district
Gott/Gotte: God
Gotte's wille: God's will
grandkinner: grandchildren
grossmutter: grandmother
Gude mariye: Good morning
gut: good
Gut nacht/Gut natch/Gute nacht: Good night
haus: house
hund: dog
Ich liebe dich: I love you
in lieb: in love
jah: yes
kaffee/kaffi: coffee
kapp: prayer covering or cap
kichli: cookie

kichlin: cookies

kind: child

kinner: children

krank: ill

kuche: cake

kuchen: cakes

kumm: come

liewe: love, a term of endearment

maed: young women, girls

maedel: young woman

mamm: mom

mammi: grandmother

mann: husband

manns: husbands

mei: my

mudder: mother

naerfich: nervous

narrisch: crazy

nee/nein: no

nix: not

onkel: uncle

Ordnung: written and unwritten rules in an Amish district

rumspringa: period of "running around" for Amish youth before they decide whether they want to be baptized into the Amish faith

schee: pretty

schmaert: smart

schnee: snow

schtupp: family room

schul: school

schweschder/schwester: sister

schweschdere/schweschders: sisters

seltsam: strange

sohn/suh: son

vorsinger: song leader

Was iss letz?: What's wrong?

Wie geht's: How do you do? or Good day!

wunderbaar/wunderbarr: wonderful

ya: yes

Yankee: non-Amish person

yer: your

yers: yours

yerself: yourself

youngie: teenaged to young adult person

*The German dialect spoken by the Amish is not a written language and varies depending on the location and origin of the settlement. These spellings are approximations. Most Amish children learn English after they start school. They also learn High German, which is used in their Sunday services.

Evergreen Love

Amy Clipston

With love and appreciation for Zac Weikal
and the members of my Bakery Bunch

FEATURED CHARACTERS

MARIETTA (DECEASED) AND MENNO BONTRAGER
Lorene
Emma Grace

VERNA AND RUFUS LAPP
Joyce m. Elias Zook
Ryan
Jonathan

RENAE M. ROBERT BYLER

ANN M. JAY LAPP
Peter
Lily

JOYCE M. ELIAS ZOOK
Maranda
Barbiann

1

LORENE LIFTED HER HEAD AFTER A SILENT PRAYER AND surveyed the supper table, set with her father's favorite meal. *Mamm* had made breaded pork chops, mashed potatoes, green beans, and homemade applesauce for *Dat* almost weekly, and for the last four years, Lorene had believed continuing that gift of love was the right thing to do.

But now *Dat* looked at her with a familiar sadness, and for the first time, she had second thoughts.

"*Danki* for making all this, Lorene." He was only in his late fifties, but he seemed to have aged at least a decade since they'd lost *Mamm* to a bad case of flu. His brown hair and beard were threaded with gray, and the wrinkles around his eyes and mouth seemed even deeper lately. This was only mid-October, but perhaps he was already struggling with how challenging celebrating

Thanksgiving and Christmas had proved to be without the woman he loved.

"Gern gschehne." Lorene forced a smile, then glanced across the table at her younger sister. Emma Grace always reminded her of *Mamm*, in part because she'd been blessed with their mother's reddish-brown hair. Lorene had instead inherited fiery-red locks. She'd been told her coloring matched her maternal great-grandmother's, but that didn't mean she wasn't a little envious of her sister's more toned-down looks. Silly, since at twenty-four, Emma Grace was six years her junior.

Emma Grace shifted in her seat, and then instead of filling her plate, she began folding and unfolding her paper napkin.

Dat halted his reach for the platter of pork chops. "Emma Grace, are you all right?"

"Ya." She pushed the ties from her prayer covering off her shoulders and then sat straighter before looking at him. "It's just time for . . . an announcement." She looked at Lorene with hesitation in her deep-brown eyes.

Lorene set her fork on her plate and then divided a look between her father and sister, suddenly feeling as if she'd been left out of some secret. "What announcement?" She lifted her glass of water and took a drink.

"Well . . . Jonathan and I are engaged."

Lorene gasped, then choked. Setting down her glass, she coughed and coughed, working to regain her composure.

"Take a deep breath." *Dat* tapped her back.

Lorene wiped her eyes and settled herself before staring at her sister. "Did you say you're engaged to Jon?"

"That's right. And I'm so *froh*." All hesitation gone, Emma Grace displayed a wide grin, and a faraway look appeared on her face. "We've chosen the Tuesday two days before Christmas for our wedding. You know Christmastime is my favorite season. I can already envision Christmas *kichlin* at the reception."

Lorene's mind spun as she studied her sister's face for any sign of a lie. If she was lying, she'd become a good actress. "Is this a joke?"

"No." Emma Grace frowned, then looked at *Dat* as if for his confirmation. When he gave a little nod, Lorene gasped again.

"So you've known about this," she said to him. She heard the accusation in her tone, but she couldn't seem to help it.

Dat blinked. "Well, of course I have. I had to give Jon my blessing."

Emma Grace's smile wobbled when Lorene returned her gaze to her sister.

"You're marrying Jonathan Lapp."

"*Ya.* I am."

"Jonathan Lapp from our church district." Lorene said the name slowly, trying to wade through what this meant for them all—for her.

Now Emma Grace narrowed her eyes. "*Ya.* Why do you keep repeating his name? It's not like you don't know him or that we've been dating."

Lorene tried to swallow against her suddenly dry throat. Emma Grace was planning to marry her ex-fiancé's younger brother. The room started to spin, and she took deep breaths in an effort to calm her stampeding heart.

Emma Grace tilted her head. "Are you all right, Lorene?"

Lorene shook herself from her panic. How could her sister ask such a question? She had to know how much this news would throw her even after all these years. That's why she'd been hesitant to tell her, right?

"But you've been dating only since April." She counted off the months on her fingers. "That's six months. Why are you in such a hurry?"

Now Emma Grace lifted her chin as though offended. "We're in love, and we're *froh.* We've also prayed about this, and a short engagement feels right. I'm twenty-four, and he's almost twenty-five, and we're ready to settle down and have a family. Why wait? Again, it just feels right." She gestured at their father. "*Dat* has given his permission, as have the bishop and deacon."

"But this still seems awfully rushed. Where will you live?"

"Here." Emma Grace pointed toward the floor.

"What?" Lorene turned her eyes to *Dat*, and he nodded again. Then she looked back at Emma Grace. "You and Jon are going to live here?"

"*Ya.* When Jon told his parents he planned to propose, they said we could live with them. First, they have plenty of room since Elias and Joyce live in the *haus* Elias built for her on their property. And second, because then Jon could continue running the dairy farm with his *dat* and Elias."

Lorene pressed her lips together. She was perfectly aware that Elias Zook, just before he married Jon's older sister, Joyce, had built a house for her—on the land where Ryan was supposed to build a house for Lorene. But Ryan never got around to building it, and then . . .

Her stomach twisted, and she had to work to keep a flood of memories from pulling her under.

"But then," Emma Grace continued, now talking a mile a minute, "our parents helped us work through a new plan. If Jon works this farm with *Dat* instead, he can take it over when *Dat* retires. That means Elias can take over the Lapps' dairy farm someday. After all, Ryan moved away and started a new career, so he's not in the picture when it comes to the farm."

Lorene stilled at the mention of her ex-fiancé's name, questions swirling through her mind. Last she'd heard, Ryan was still working for his uncle's shed company in Gap, a nearby town. But was he married with a family? Or at least engaged? No one had ever told her either was the case—not that she'd asked. But that didn't mean he wasn't.

She closed her eyes for a beat and willed herself to stop thinking about the man. Ryan's business was his, not hers. Then she gritted her teeth and pushed on, determined to convince her sister to change her mind—or at least slow down.

"Have you truly thought this through? We'd have barely two months to plan the wedding. Why don't you wait . . . maybe until spring?"

Emma Grace's eyes misted as she turned back to their father. "You said she would support me, *Dat*. That it would all work out, the way Jon and I believe God intends. But she's trying to—"

Dat placed his hand on top of Emma Grace's. "Don't worry. It will all be fine." But his eyes had moved to Lorene.

"No, it won't." Emma Grace sniffed, then glared at Lorene. "I was afraid of this. At first I thought this might be hard for you because of Ryan. But now I think you're just jealous because you've never found anyone else in the five years since you broke up with him." She caught her breath as her eyes narrowed. "You don't want me to be *froh*! You want me to be lonely and *bedauerlich* like you!"

Emma Grace jumped up, then practically ran for the stairs.

Her heavy footfalls echoed from the stairwell, followed by the loud slam of a door.

Lorene stared at her plate as a suffocating silence filled the kitchen. She reached for the bowl of green beans but then withdrew her hand. Her appetite had evaporated. She cringed at the thought of Emma Grace marrying into Ryan's family, but how could her sister fail to realize the full extent of the challenge this marriage would present for her?

"You were awfully hard on her." *Dat*'s voice was soft, but his words were heavy.

"*Ya*, I was, but her attack on me was quite pointed, and . . . Jealousy isn't the issue, *Dat*." Her throat seemed to close as guilt threatened to strangle her, but she didn't want *Dat* to know how much she was struggling. "I just don't want her to rush into this and then regret it later. They've dated such a short time."

Dat's dark eyes grew warm even as she fudged the truth. "Lorene, we've known the Lapps for years. They're a *gut* Christian family. I'd like to stop hiring farmhands for the help I need, and Jon's being here will allow that. Also, rather than sell the farm someday, I'll be able to hand it over to one of *mei dochdern* and her spouse."

Lorene pressed her lips together. She had to come to grips with reality. She might have been that daughter, but now she never would. She'd just failed to let herself imagine anything like this could happen. How foolish! What had made her think Jon and Emma Grace's relationship would never blossom into love?

"Emma Grace and Jon grew up together," *Dat* continued, "and your *mamm* and I were childhood *freinden*. Our marriage was *froh*." He paused, his eyes now nearly pleading with her. "I want *mei kinner* to stay in the faith and be *froh*. Jon is not only a *gut* Amish man, but he makes Emma Grace *froh*. He's also offering her a life on this dairy farm, the place she's always known and loved. It's a tough life, but it's a *gut* life."

He gave a sad sigh. "What more could I possibly hope for her? After all, we never know how long God has planned for us to be here, do we?"

Lorene nodded as his eyes misted. It was obvious he was referring to *Mamm*. Now shame grabbed her by the throat, stealing her words.

Dat gave her shoulder a gentle squeeze. "Trust God to lead your *schweschder*."

Lorene sniffed as tears formed. How could she stand in the way of Emma Grace having a happy life? "I know you're right, *Dat*."

He gave her a wistful smile. "Your *mamm* would be so *froh* to see Emma Grace settling down."

Lorene wiped at her eyes. *Especially since I'm thirty with no viable prospects for a husband.* She stood. "I'll go apologize, then ask her to come back to eat with us."

"Danki." Dat reached out and touched her hand. "We need to support her."

"Of course. You go ahead before the food gets cold."

She rose from the table and strode to the staircase, then climbed to the second floor. A crisp breeze filtered through the open window at the top of the stairs, sending in the scent of logs burning in neighborhood fireplaces.

Lorene stood outside her sister's closed bedroom door for a moment, saying a silent prayer.

Lord, please give me the right words to apologize and earn mei schweschder*'s forgiveness. Also, please soften my heart toward the idea of her marriage to Jon Lapp.*

Then she knocked.

"Go away."

"I'm coming in." Lorene pushed the door open and found her sister lying on her bed, facing the wall. "I'm sorry."

When Emma Grace remained silent, Lorene sank onto the desk chair and nervously brushed her hands over her black apron, peppered with spots from cooking. "I should have been more encouraging, and I sincerely apologize. If Jon makes you *froh*, then I support you fully."

Emma Grace craned her neck to look over her shoulder. "You mean that?"

"Absolutely." Her voice sounded strained to her own ears, and she hoped Emma Grace wouldn't notice.

"I'm sorry for what I said too. It was mean and hurtful. I *was* afraid this might be hard for you, but then—"

"It's okay." Lorene shrugged even though her sister's words had stung. "When did Jon propose?"

"Last week, after he spoke with *Dat*." Emma Grace sat up. "We met with the deacon and bishop the next day. Then Jon told his parents, and that's when the plans for where we would live started to develop. Elias and Joyce don't know about this yet. Jon's going to tell them at a family supper tomorrow night."

Lorene smiled as her eyes filled once again. "I really am *froh* for you."

Emma Grace nodded. Then her eyes grew misty too. "And I really *am* sorry. What I said about Ryan was a cheap shot, and you didn't deserve it. I never wanted to hurt you with any of this."

Lorene was suddenly unable to speak. Part of her wanted to

ask Emma Grace questions about Ryan, but she couldn't form the words. She had to admit the truth, though—at least to herself. She'd longed to know what Ryan's life was like in Gap ever since her sister announced she was dating Ryan's younger brother.

She fingered the hem of her apron as his handsome face filled her mind. She could still envision his pale-blue eyes, naturally curly light-brown hair, inviting smile . . .

No, no, no!

She'd had no choice but to break off their engagement. Leaving their relationship had made sense, and she couldn't live in the past. She was certain Ryan had moved on, and she would continue to do the same.

Emma Grace's dark eyes warmed as she reached out and touched Lorene's arm. "Are you all right?"

"Ya." Lorene forced her lips into a smile. "We need to start talking about wedding plans. We don't have much time to pull them all together."

"I know, but it's going to be so much fun. Like I said, I want Christmas *kichlin*—a whole Christmas theme with evergreen branches, candles . . ." Her expression turned serious. "But most of all, I want your blessing. You're *mei schweschder.* You're important to me."

"You have my blessing." Lorene pulled her into a hug. "I was just surprised. But I'll be supportive from now on. That's a promise."

She'd been more than surprised, but she'd have to get over it.

"Danki." Emma Grace's smile was nearly as bright as the fall sunshine streaming through the front room windows as they'd cleaned them that afternoon.

"I have something to ask you," Emma Grace said, again

hesitant. "Jon's invited the three of us to his *haus* for lunch on Sunday. Will you come?"

"Of course I will."

Emma Grace bit her lower lip. "Ryan might be there."

Lorene's stomach dropped.

"Will you still come?" Emma Grace's eyes were hopeful, reminding Lorene of a puppy dog. "For me?"

Lorene nodded, but her body tensed. "Of course I will. And I'll be fine."

"Danki." Emma Grace hugged her.

"Why don't we go downstairs? We can discuss wedding plans while we eat."

"Okay." Emma Grace popped up and started for the door. "We have so much to talk about."

As Lorene followed her down the stairs, her mind spun with both excitement and dread. She really was thrilled to see her sister happy, but she cringed at the idea of this new connection to Ryan Lapp. The two of them would soon be related through their siblings, though, and she'd have to beg God for the strength she'd need to see her through.

2

AFTER HIS DRIVER DROPPED HIM OFF, RYAN BREATHED IN the cool evening air and climbed the back steps to his parents' home. He'd been surprised when his mother called and insisted he come for supper on Saturday night, explaining that Jon wanted the entire family together. When he'd asked her why, she'd just mumbled something about how she really couldn't say.

Curious.

Until she called, he'd planned to stay late at work so he could finish building a large shed that had to be delivered next week. But thankfully his uncle Jay believed a family supper took priority. Ryan would make up the time on Monday.

When he reached the back porch of the large, white, two-story farmhouse, he glanced behind him, toward his father's rolling pasture and row of three red barns. Beyond them he spotted his older sister's two-story home. No lanterns glowed in the windows, indicating that Joyce and her family were most likely already at their parents' house.

He lifted his hand to knock on the door, but then he shook his head, smiling as he recalled his mother instructing him to never knock. "You might live in Gap now, but you're still our *sohn*," she'd told him.

Ryan stepped into the mudroom and was immediately drawn to the familiar aromas of his mother's baked chicken and freshly baked bread as well as the familiar voices filtering from the next room. He removed his boots, straw hat, and jacket, then padded into the kitchen to join his family. *Mamm* and Joyce were carrying food to the table, where *Dat*, Jon, and Elias already waited. His nieces were there too. At three and thirteen months, Maranda and Barbiann were the light of their parents' lives, to say nothing of how special they were to their uncles.

"Ryan!" Joyce called as she set a large bowl of egg noodles in the center of the table. "It's about time you showed up. We thought we'd have to start without you."

"I got here as quickly as I could." Ryan nodded a hello to everyone.

"*Onkel* Ryan!" Maranda exclaimed as she held up her hand.

"How are you?" Ryan strode to her booster seat and tousled her dark braids.

"I'm *gut*," she announced with a wide grin.

When Barbiann squealed, Ryan smiled and touched her nose. "And how are you, Barbi?"

The toddler blessed him with a wide grin and a wave.

Ryan chuckled to himself as he crossed to the sink, then began washing his hands. "Did I miss anything important?" he asked, looking over his shoulder.

Elias shook his head. "No, but Joyce was getting antsy because you were late. You know how your *schweschder* gets about being on time." He shot his wife an innocent expression when she narrowed her eyes at him.

Ryan laughed to himself as he dried his hands. He'd always thought his brother-in-law had the patience of Job when dealing with his high-strung sister. While Joyce tended to panic when the simplest things went wrong, Elias always remained levelheaded and soft-spoken. But their contrasts didn't end there. Joyce had inherited *Mamm*'s light-brown hair and pale-blue eyes, but Elias had dark-brown hair and hazel eyes, coloring he'd passed along to their daughters.

Mamm patted Ryan's hand as she reached for a pitcher of water sitting on the counter. "It's *gut* to see you. It's been too long."

Guilt weighed on Ryan's shoulders. "I'm sorry, *Mamm*. I need to visit more often." Living ten miles away, he did miss his family. He just never relished returning to where . . . He shook his head. Family suppers like this were special, and he intended to enjoy every minute.

"We'll hold you to that, *sohn*." *Dat* winked at him from the head of the table.

"Rufus! Don't make him feel worse," *Mamm* said, scolding him.

"I'm only kidding, Verna." *Dat* pointed to the seat beside him. "Sit, Ryan."

"Are we ready to eat?" Jon called over their nieces' voices. Maranda hummed while she chewed on a piece of bread, and Barbiann sang a song with gibberish words as she swung her piece of bread into the air.

"*Ya*, I think we are." Joyce sat down beside Barbiann and shushed her.

Ryan took his place beside *Dat* and bowed his head in silent prayer. Then he joined everyone in filling their plates.

"How's work?" *Dat* asked him.

"*Gut*. I'm building a twelve-by-twenty shed that has to go out next week."

"What does it look like?"

"The gentleman who ordered it asked for vinyl siding, a loft, and a garage door in front. No windows."

"Really?" *Dat* asked. "Makes you wonder what he plans to keep in it."

"Right." Ryan laughed. "How are things here on the farm?" he asked as he sliced a bite of his chicken.

"The same." *Dat* shrugged. "The work never ends with cows."

Elias pointed his fork at *Dat*. "That's the truth."

Ryan smiled, enjoying the conversation. But something was up. Each time he glanced across the table at his younger brother, he found him grinning from ear to ear. Jon seemed different somehow—happier than usual, his eyes bright. Jon was almost twenty-five, seven years younger than Ryan, but Ryan had frequently been told they definitely shared a family resemblance. They both had pale-blue eyes and light-brown hair, but Ryan had somehow been blessed with unruly curly hair like *Dat*'s while Jon's was straight.

"Hey, Jon," Ryan said, his voice raised above the din of the conversations around them. They immediately dwindled. "I heard you called this family supper."

Now Jon's smile seemed to brighten. "That's right."

"What's the occasion?" Ryan lifted his eyebrows.

"*Ya*, what is it?" Joyce said with a demanding tone. "I've been trying to get you to spill it."

Elias's mouth pressed into a straight line. "And she's been talking about it ever since *Mamm* invited us over."

Everyone chuckled. And out of the corner of Ryan's eye, he spotted his parents exchanging knowing glances, telling him they knew exactly what Jon was going to say. Now he was more curious than ever.

Jon cleared his throat and took a trembling breath. "Well, I'm getting married in December—a Christmas wedding."

Joyce squealed and clapped her hands.

Elias patted Jon's shoulder. "You are? That's great!"

"I didn't even know you were dating anyone seriously," Ryan said. "Who's the *maedel*?"

Something unreadable flickered across Jon's face as he met Ryan's gaze. "Emma Grace Bontrager."

Ryan stilled as the name twirled through his mind. He must have heard Jon wrong. He knew only one Emma Grace Bontrager in Bird-in-Hand, and she was his ex-fiancée's sister. Jon couldn't be marrying her. "Who?"

Jon hesitated as a sheepish expression spread across his face. "Emma Grace Bontrager."

"*That* Emma Grace?" Ryan kept his words measured, but it wasn't easy.

Jon nodded. "*Ya*, that's right."

The air in Ryan's lungs seized, and then his heartbeat sped into a wild gallop.

Joyce jumped up, then raced around the table and hugged Jon. "I'm so excited. I had a feeling you and Emma Grace were heading down this road. When did you propose? How close to Christmas will the wedding be?"

As Joyce's questions and Jon's answers became background

noise, Ryan found himself drowning in memories of Lorene. Her gorgeous fiery-red hair. Her rosy lips. Her deep-brown eyes. Her long neck. He could still envision her laughing at one of his jokes and then running away as he chased her.

Lorene had been the love of his life, the woman he'd planned to marry—until she broke up with him, citing his not building their house. Then she'd angrily turned her back on him without another word and stalked inside her farmhouse. His several attempts to get her to talk to him over the next few weeks failed. She never gave them a chance to work things out, an opportunity for him to explain. She'd just left him with nothing but heartache.

And that heartache finally drove him to move away from his family and church district, especially when his uncle reached out to the family when he needed extra help to keep his shed business going. Taking the job helped him cope with the crushing anguish Lorene had left in her wake.

Ryan's appetite disintegrated as he tried to comprehend what was happening now. He was confused. He'd always believed he and Jon were close. On many occasions, Ryan had confided in Jon, especially when Lorene broke up with him. But Jon had kept his dating Emma Grace a secret. Why? The fact that his brother had done so sent disappointment and hurt shooting through him.

But then he realized Jon probably didn't want to stir up painful memories for him prematurely. He must have asked everyone else in the family to keep his dating Emma Grace a secret, too, just in case he and Emma Grace eventually broke up anyway.

When he sensed someone was watching him, he turned to see his father giving him a concerned look. Ryan tried to smile, but he knew he'd pulled off only a grimace. He looked back at Jon, still fielding a barrage of questions from their sister.

Then the full reality hit Ryan—like a ton of hay tumbling from the loft in his father's barn. Jon was going to marry Emma Grace Bontrager. That meant he'd have to face Lorene sometime soon. How would he manage to see her again without reliving the heartbreak that had haunted him for five years?

"Why don't we serve dessert now?" *Mamm*'s question crashed through Ryan's thoughts. Soon he stared down at the large hunk of chocolate cheesecake Joyce had placed in front of him. He broke off a piece of it, but he had to force the bite down his throat because his stomach had tied itself into a knot. Then he sipped his coffee, hoping it would have a settling effect.

He also tried to make eye contact with Jon, but his brother quickly turned away after a glance.

Ryan was grateful when Joyce and *Mamm* began clearing the table, but when his mother lifted his plate, her brow furrowed. "You don't like the cheesecake?"

Ryan managed to make his lips curve into a smile. "It's fantastic. I'm just full."

Mamm seemed unconvinced, but she let go of his plate and continued gathering dishes. "Huh. Well, I'll put some in a container for you to take home."

"Danki." Ryan stood, then followed the other men to the mudroom for their jackets and boots before stepping out to the porch with a lantern. He sank into his favorite, well-worn rocker. He pushed it into motion and listened to the swish of its movement. Then he breathed in the crisp evening air, all the farmland scents washing over him, hoping the rhythmic feel of the chair would calm his nerves.

Dat and Elias stepped to the railing, and Elias pointed toward the far end of the pasture. "We need to get that back section of the pasture fence repaired before the winter weather sets in."

"*Ya*, we do." *Dat* gestured toward the largest barn. "And I'm concerned about the barn doors. Those hinges need to be replaced soon. I was thinking about a fresh coat of paint too." He smiled at his son-in-law. "But with Jon moving to Menno Bontrager's farm once he's married, and knowing you'll be taking over this farm someday, I want your input now more than ever."

Jon was moving to the Bontrager farm? He was sure that made sense somehow, but he must have missed more of the conversation than he'd thought.

Ryan looked at Jon, who still seemed to be avoiding his gaze. He was chewing his lower lip, his arms crossed, standing by the back door and studying the toes of his boots.

Heaving a sigh, Ryan looked toward his sister's house. The Zook home stood on the same plot of land where Ryan was supposed to build Lorene a house. His shoulders tightened as he again recalled the day she announced she was breaking off their engagement. He leaned forward and rested his elbows on his thighs and tented his fingers in front of his face as he shoved away that memory.

"Why don't we go look at those barn doors now?" Elias said. When *Dat* agreed, Elias pulled a flashlight from his pocket, then started down the steps with *Dat* following.

Ryan turned toward Jon, who was now staring out toward the barn, his jaw clenched. Ryan could almost feel the anxiety coming off him in waves. He couldn't stand the awkwardness.

"You can sit," Ryan said.

Jon faced him, his expression pained as he sank into the rocker beside Ryan and folded his hands. "You're upset with me, and I don't blame you."

Ryan shook his head. "I'm not upset with you. I'm just . . . surprised." He rubbed at the stubble on his chin. "I was just wondering why you didn't tell me you were dating Emma Grace." A new thought hit him. "Do you not feel as close to me since I moved to Gap?"

Jon's headshake was emphatic. "No. That's not it. I just didn't want to upset you because of Lorene. No one in the family did."

Ryan nodded. "That did occur to me. But I want you to be *froh*. And if Emma Grace makes you *froh*, then I'm satisfied."

Jon's shoulders visibly relaxed. "*Danki*. Will you be my attendant at the wedding, then?"

Ryan smiled. "I'd be honored."

But then his smile flattened as another thought struck him. Lorene would no doubt be Emma Grace's attendant, and that . . .

Then another thought hit. Had his little brother really thought this through? Was he rushing into marriage?

"Have you been dating Emma Grace long?"

Jon held up his hands. "I know what you're thinking. Only for six months, but we've prayed about it. We're ready, and God seems to be leading us. Like I said, we'll live with her *dat*, me helping him with his dairy farm, and then I'll take it over when he's ready to retire. Everyone is supportive."

"That's great."

Ryan stared out toward where *Dat* and Elias stood talking by the barn doors, and Lorene's face filled his mind again.

Four years ago, he'd attended Marietta Bontrager's funeral, offering Lorene a solemn nod when she looked his way. He'd expected her to at least respond, but she'd looked right through him as if he didn't exist. That had hurt.

Since then he'd made sure he stayed out of her way, never even attending a church service in Bird-in-Hand. And as much as he'd longed to know about her, he'd never asked his family for information. No wonder they didn't want to tell him Jon was dating Emma Grace. Being in the same church district, though, they had to know how her life had turned out.

Was she married? He hadn't seen a man comforting her at the funeral, but that didn't mean she hadn't married in the four years since then. Lorene was beautiful, funny, and except for the day she summarily broke off their relationship, sweet. She'd also wanted a family more than anything. Most likely, quite a few men vied for her attention once she was free.

His heart clenched as he imagined Lorene raising a family with another man, and suddenly the questions he'd held back bubbled to the surface. He turned to Jon. "How is Lorene?"

Jon sat back, looking as though he'd expected him to ask. "Fine, I think. Emma Grace has never said otherwise."

"Gut." Ryan gave a stiff nod. He wanted to know if she was married, but he didn't have the courage to ask, and his brother didn't offer.

After a few moments of silence, Jon leaned forward in this chair, again hesitant. "You heard *Mamm* say the Bontragers are coming for lunch tomorrow, right? This will be the first time we're getting our families together. Will you come?"

Ryan stilled. No, he hadn't heard that either. "Are just Menno and Emma Grace coming?"

"No. Lorene too."

Ryan was still trying to believe his brother was really marrying Lorene's sister. Now he wanted him to be in the same house with Lorene—*tomorrow.* "I don't know . . ."

"Please." Jon folded his hands as if begging. "If you and Lorene could at least get along—"

"Get along?" Ryan closed his eyes for a moment. "She's the one who ended our relationship." He pointed to his chest. "She won't want to see me, Jon."

Jon held up his hands. "I know it won't be easy. But if you could just try . . . for my sake."

Ryan sighed. "Of course I can."

"So you'll come, then?"

Ryan rubbed at a knot on the back of his neck. *"Ya."*

"*Danki.* This means so much to me."

Ryan suddenly felt the need to retreat to the solace of his own place. "I should get going. I'll call my driver."

Pulling his flashlight from his pocket, he strode out to the phone shanty and made the call. Then he stepped back into the house and kissed his nieces' cheeks in the kitchen.

Mamm handed him the chocolate cheesecake she'd packed. "Will we see you tomorrow?" He couldn't help but see the concern in her eyes, the same concern he'd seen in *Dat*'s out on the porch and now mirrored in Joyce's eyes as well. He gave both women a smile, realizing *Mamm* must have been worrying about him.

"*Ya.* Don't worry. I'll be fine. Really."

He didn't have to wait long for his driver, and after saying good-bye to the men in the family, Ryan climbed into the van, then glanced at his sister's house again as they motored down the driveway. What would life have been like if he'd built Lorene a house there and married her? He would never know. But now he had to prepare his heart for facing her in less than twenty-four hours. He just hoped it was strong enough to stay intact.

Minutes later his shoulders tensed as the van sped toward Gap. Why hadn't he asked Jon—or Joyce and *Mamm*—if Lorene was married? If she was, her husband would no doubt be with her tomorrow, maybe a child or two as well. And if not a family, maybe a boyfriend. Joyce and *Mamm* probably assumed Jon had told him what to expect, and maybe Jon thought he knew.

Now he'd just have to brace himself for whatever was coming next.

3

LORENE GAZED AT THE FAMILIAR HOUSE, VAST PASTURE, and row of red barns as *Dat* guided his horse up the Lapps' rock driveway. She'd visited this farm for church services many times since breaking up with Ryan, and she'd taken each visit in stride.

But today dread crept in. Emma Grace had confirmed that Ryan would be coming when she talked to Jon at church that morning, and for the first time in five years, she'd be face-to-face with her ex-fiancé. How would she manage to keep her emotions in check while trapped at a supper table with the man who'd crushed her heart, her dreams, her future?

As she gripped the cake saver on her lap, she closed her eyes and breathed in big gulps of air, trying in vain to ward off the memories that swarmed her mind. Walking around the pasture holding Ryan's hand, laughing as he chased her toward the barn, stealing kisses with him on the porch swing . . .

Stop, stop, stop!

Dat halted the horse by the back porch. After he climbed out of the buggy, Lorene followed, her eyes focusing on Joyce's house across the pasture. That could have been where she and Ryan shared a home and raised a family. But he hadn't loved her enough to make their future a priority or a reality, and that truth still felt like an ice pick stabbing her heart.

"You okay?" Emma Grace appeared at Lorene's side.

"Ya." Lorene glanced toward the road, and once more since Friday, she opened her mouth to ask if Ryan would be bringing a girlfriend. But she still didn't want Emma Grace to realize how hard this was for her, spoiling her sister's day.

She did assume Ryan wasn't married. If he were, Emma Grace would have mentioned that Jon had a sister-in-law. But he could still have a serious girlfriend, and that idea sent a mix of trepidation and envy rushing through her. She stood taller, though, steeling herself against the heartache of seeing Ryan with another woman.

She needed to be strong. She'd been so angry and hurt when she called off the engagement. It had taken years to manage both of those feelings. But once Emma Grace made her announcement, the hurt had made a strong comeback—much stronger than the anger.

Emma Grace raised an eyebrow. "You sure you're okay?"

"Of course." Lorene started toward the porch steps, where *Dat* stood waiting for them. "Let's go inside." She followed her family into the Lapps' house, finding Jon, his parents, and Joyce and her family all gathered in the large kitchen. No Ryan.

"Hello!" Verna gave Lorene a hug before reaching for the cake saver. "What did you make?"

She handed her the container. "It's a lemon *kuche.* I just had an urge to make one yesterday."

"Oh, I love your lemon *kuche*!" Joyce hugged her too. "You always used to bring those—" Her eyes widened as she gave an awkward laugh.

Lorene's cheeks heated as she realized what Joyce had started to say. Because she knew they were Ryan's favorite, Lorene had often brought lemon cakes to the Lapps even before he'd asked her to be his girlfriend. She and Joyce had been close friends then, and she'd harbored a secret crush on Ryan. The cakes were her way of trying to subtly win his attention.

Lorene wanted to throw the cake into the trash can. Why hadn't she baked a chocolate cake instead of running the risk of giving Ryan the wrong impression?

Joyce turned toward the doorway as Maranda and Barbiann scampered in carrying cloth dolls. "Can you say hello to Lorene?" she asked the girls.

"Hi!" Maranda gave a wave, and her sister squealed.

Lorene smiled down at them. *"Wie geht's?"*

Maranda giggled as Joyce scooped Barbiann into her arms.

"Rufus, what do you think of these two getting married?" *Dat* asked Jon's father.

"Dat!" Emma Grace whined as Jon took her hand in his.

"I think it's a *gut* idea." Rufus smiled. "We think the world of Emma Grace."

Verna turned from where she'd set the cake saver on the counter. "We're delighted. Two of our *kinner* will be settled down."

Lorene stilled at her words. Now she knew for sure that Ryan still wasn't married or even engaged. She backed up against the sink, then glanced out the window, crossing her arms over her middle, trying to stay calm as she awaited his arrival.

"We have a lot to do before the wedding," Emma Grace said. "I love Christmas, so I do want a Christmas theme. Red tablecloths with matching candles. Christmas *kichlin*. And wouldn't it be perfect if it snowed?"

Lorene's body went rigid when a horse and buggy came up the driveway, then halted. The buggy door opened, and her knees wobbled when Ryan's face came into view. She held her breath, waiting to see if a woman climbed out of the passenger side. But Ryan just closed the door, then unhitched the horse and walked it to the barn.

He was alone. Maybe he was still single too—like her. But what did it matter? Nothing would ever happen between them again. "Lorene."

She spun toward her sister's voice to find everyone looking at her, and her cheeks felt as if they might burst into flames. *"Ya?"*

"I was going to ask you earlier, but I've been so excited . . . Will you be my attendant at the wedding?"

She tried her best to smile. "Of course I will."

"Ryan agreed to be my attendant," Jon said.

Lorene froze at the words. That meant she'd have to walk down the barn aisle with Ryan, hold his hand, sit facing him during the long service, and spend the day at his side. *Could this whole situation get any worse?*

But of course Ryan would be Jon's attendant. He was Jon's only brother.

Then Ryan stepped into the kitchen. Lorene clutched her hands together, trying to steady herself as she watched him smile and greet his family.

He was even more handsome than in her memory. He was older, of course, but he also seemed more mature. And his eyes looked bluer than she recalled, a bright contrast to his gray shirt. He also seemed taller, and although his waist was just as trim, his shoulders looked broader than she remembered.

His light-brown hair was a curly mess, most likely from sitting under his straw hat during the ride over. Then her eyes found his lips, which shot more memories through her mind. She looked down at her shoes and then back up again, willing herself to stop staring at him.

Ryan shook her father's hand and greeted her sister. When his eyes moved to her, her lungs felt as if an invisible hand were squeezing all the air out of them. The room fell silent, and Lorene knew everyone was watching her.

Ryan licked his lips, and a muscle flexed in his jaw. "Hello, Lorene."

"Ryan." She managed a nod, hugging her arms to her chest as if guarding the cracks he'd left in her heart.

A moment passed as they looked at each other, and her skin started to itch under his stare. Surely everyone—including Ryan—could hear her heart hammering against her rib cage. She wanted to rush out of the house and run all the way home just to escape the weight of everyone's stares.

"Let's get ready to eat," Verna announced, and Lorene jumped with a start.

For the first time, she noticed the table was already set. She turned to Verna. "What can I do to help?"

"You'll find two containers on the top shelf in the refrigerator. One has macaroni salad, and the other has potato salad."

Between them, the four women brought out lunchmeat,

chips, pretzels, and rolls along with the salads. Lorene set an extra pitcher of water on a counter, then turned toward the table. The other women had already taken their places, and when she realized the only empty chair was beside Ryan, she inwardly groaned.

"Have a seat, Lorene," *Dat* said with an encouraging look.

Lorene walked around the table and sank onto the chair. As she pulled it in, her leg brushed Ryan's, and she felt him flinch. She bowed her head and tried to concentrate on a silent prayer, but his nearness sent her senses spinning. How was she supposed to ignore the familiar spicy scent of his aftershave?

When everyone had prayed, Ryan scooped a pile of macaroni salad onto his plate, then passed the container to Lorene. She muttered a thank-you, and soon conversations swirled around the table. Lorene kept her head down as she made a sandwich, but out of the corner of her eye, she caught Ryan glancing at her.

"How's the job, Ryan? Jon told us you work for your *onkel* now." *Dat* bit off a piece of the pretzel in his hand.

"Gut." Ryan nodded. "I like working there."

"*Ya.* Ryan decided he'd rather spend time with sheds than cows," Rufus said, winking at his son. That surprised her. Hadn't Rufus been disappointed when Ryan left the farm?

"I can't say I blame him." *Dat* chuckled. "Sheds are less temperamental."

Everyone laughed, and Lorene enjoyed Ryan's deep, warm laugh. Had she missed that sound? Yes, she had. She stole a glance at him and found his eyes full of mirth.

"Emma Grace," Joyce began from the far end of the table, "did *mei bruder* surprise you when he asked for your hand?"

Lorene caught a tender look passing between the young couple. The love her sister and Jon obviously had for each other sent a jolt through her. It was hard not to lose faith that marriage and a family was God's plan for her. Ryan had looked at her like that once, but would another man someday? The few men she'd dated since Ryan hadn't cared for her the way he had—or the way she thought he had. And none of them had warmed her heart the way Ryan had warmed hers.

Emma Grace nodded at Joyce. "He did surprise me. He took me on a ride to our favorite park, and when we sat down on a bench, he proposed." She gazed up at Jon, and they shared another intimate look.

Lorene tried to ignore how her heart began to ache for the happier times she'd spent with Ryan. She wondered if he recalled those times with fondness or if his memories formed a different picture.

But five years ago she'd realized she'd rather be alone than with someone who balked at going forward with their future. Upon their engagement, Ryan was supposed to build her a house on the Lapp property his father offered them, but then he'd invented excuse after excuse for not doing it, let alone setting a wedding date.

First, he said he wanted to save more money, and that seemed reasonable even though she knew the Lapp farm was quite successful. Then he said he didn't have time to think about a house because he was helping his father teach Jon more about running the business. He was, but that went on for months. Last, he said he should probably get someone else to draw up the plans, but then more time went by without his taking any action.

When she finally confronted him, he said he just wasn't sure if it was the right time.

That was when she finally realized Ryan would never marry her, that their engagement was nothing more to him than a dating relationship he felt comfortable extending indefinitely. That splintered her heart. He didn't love her enough to take that step toward their marriage.

She pressed her lips together as the familiar despair squeezed her lungs. No, it had never fully dissipated. Perhaps it never would.

For the remainder of lunch, Emma Grace and Jon answered questions about their plans, but she hardly listened.

"Why don't we have our dessert?" Verna announced as she lifted the platter of leftover lunchmeat and an empty roll basket. Lorene rose as well, along with the other two women. Joyce gathered several plates and started toward the counter. "I'll put on *kaffi*."

Lorene did her best to avoid Ryan's eyes as she retrieved drinking glasses from the table.

"I made a carrot *kuche*." Joyce carried it to the table, then set it alongside the cake saver Verna had just placed there.

Verna opened it. "And Lorene brought a lemon *kuche*."

"Oh, that looks fantastic." Elias rubbed his hands together.

Dat nodded. "My oldest *dochder* makes the best lemon *kuche*."

Lorene made the mistake of glancing toward the table just as Ryan looked at her.

"I remember that." Ryan's eyes focused on her, sending a tremor through her body.

She looked away and turned off the water, then reached for the dish soap.

"Lorene," Verna said as she carried clean plates to the table, "we'll worry about the dishes later. Would you please get the sugar and milk for the *kaffi*? Joyce is finding clean plates."

Soon Lorene took her seat next to Ryan, careful not to brush his leg or arm as she ate the only cake she could stomach—Joyce's.

Verna turned to Emma Grace. "May I be a part of the wedding planning? I promise I won't interfere. I would just like to be involved."

Lorene glanced across the table and found tears sparkling in her sister's eyes.

"I would like that." Emma Grace's voice shook a little. "With *mei mamm* gone, it would be nice to have your help." When she sniffed and wiped at her eyes, Jon patted her back and whispered something in her ear.

Lorene felt a sudden crush of grief, and she tried to clear her throat against a sudden knot. Losing her mother had been a devastating blow from which she would never fully recover, and moments like these made that especially clear.

When she spotted Ryan looking at her again, she turned her gaze toward her half-eaten piece of carrot cake. She didn't want his pity.

"I would love it if you and Lorene came here to plan the wedding, as well as to make preparations," Verna continued. "Then Joyce can help, too, if she wants to."

"I do!" Joyce said. "Especially if *mei dochdern* can nap here. *Mamm* and I could help with the sewing and writing out the invitations."

"I love that idea," Emma Grace said. "What do you think, Lorene?"

When Lorene looked up, she sensed all the eyes in the room once again on her, including Ryan's. "That sounds fine."

She knew what would be more than fine—Ryan gathering outside with the other men when they finished dessert so she could catch her breath.

4

RYAN COULDN'T TAKE HIS EYES OFF LORENE. EVEN AFTER all these years, he was captivated by her beauty—her red hair peeking out from under her prayer covering, her eyes that reminded him of dark chocolate, her long neck, her pink lips . . .

From the moment he'd walked into the kitchen, he'd felt as if an invisible magnet was pulling him toward her. And he had to admit how relieved he'd been not to see her with another man. But why did his heart still crave her after the way she'd left it in shambles? That his attraction to her hadn't faded after all this time made no sense to him whatsoever.

But attraction wasn't the only thing plaguing him. He'd also longed to console her when Emma Grace mentioned their mother. Almost physically feeling her grief, he'd had to stop himself from touching Lorene's shoulder.

He was losing his mind!

"Let's get the kitchen cleaned." *Mamm* lifted the remnants of the lemon cake and stood.

Had Lorene made that lemon cake for him? He couldn't even count how many of them she'd made before they started dating and even after they became a couple. It had been his favorite dessert and her signature cake. He longed to ask, but he couldn't bring himself to form the words.

Lorene reached for his coffee mug, and he blocked it with his hand, causing her fingers to brush his. She quickly pulled her hand away as if he'd bit it, and he pressed his lips together with annoyance. Was he truly that repulsive to her?

"I'm sorry," she muttered, turning her attention to his father's mug.

"It's okay," he said. "I'm just not finished. I'm going to take this *kaffi* out to the porch."

She nodded without meeting his gaze, then turned away. But he'd thought he'd seen her blush. Or had her cheeks just heated with the same resentment she'd made clear the day she broke his heart? He didn't know, but he recalled how she'd blushed the night he asked her to be his girlfriend. How had she gone from loving him to despising him so? Spending any time with her would be a nightmare—and this was only the beginning.

Lifting his mug, Ryan stood and followed the other men out to the porch. Christmas had always been a wonderful time for him and his family, but he couldn't wait for this wedding to be over. The sooner he could get away from Lorene, the better.

Lorene stationed herself at the sink to wash the dishes while her sister dried. Behind her the conversation hovered around wedding plans. Lorene looked out the window toward the porch, where the men all sat in rockers.

"I have this *schee* green material you might want to look at for your wedding dresses," she heard Verna say. "It would be so Christmassy and go well with the red tablecloths and candles you mentioned earlier."

"Oh *ya*!" Joyce chimed in from her place sweeping the floor. "Green would look lovely with your reddish hair—and Lorene's hair too."

"I would love to see it. I'll pay you for the material," Emma Grace said.

Verna stepped beside her, dropping a wet cloth next to the sink. "Don't be *gegisch*. You can have it if you like it."

Lorene scrubbed a large serving spoon harder as if trying to erase Ryan's face from her mind. She longed to go home, but she had to wait for her family to finish visiting. Maybe Ryan would decide to go home soon. That would relieve her anxiety.

A wail sounded from the high chair, and Lorene turned just as Maranda, who'd been sitting on the floor playing with her doll, jumped up and hurried to her baby sister.

"Mamm!" Maranda hollered over the sobs. "Barbi is crying."

Joyce seemed amused as she joined her children. "*Ya*, I know, honey. *Danki*." She looked at her mother. "May I put the girls down for a nap in your room?"

"Of course. Do you need help?"

"No, but *danki*." Joyce gathered Barbiann in her arms and then led Maranda toward the downstairs bedroom.

Once again Lorene found herself wondering if she and

Ryan would have had children of their own by now if they'd married.

Stop torturing yourself!

"Could I see the material when we're done?" Emma Grace asked Verna.

"Of course."

"Why don't you go look now?" Lorene said.

"But we're not finished." Emma Grace pointed to the two serving bowls still sitting on the counter, waiting for their leftovers to be put away.

"I'll finish up." She waved them off. "Go on. I've cleaned up after meals before."

Verna gave a little laugh. "Okay. *Danki*."

Emma Grace and Verna headed up the nearby staircase, most likely to the sewing room, and Lorene breathed a sigh of relief. Finally, she had a moment alone to collect her scattered thoughts. She scooped potato and macaroni salad into containers, and then as she washed the serving bowls, she found herself stuck on the intense look Ryan had given her just before he went outside. Most of his looks that evening had been hard to decipher. Did he despise her? Did he want her to leave as much as she longed to go?

She rinsed the bowls before drying them, then set them in the cabinet where she knew they belonged. She pulled the plug from the sink, and when she turned around, she swallowed a gasp. Ryan was leaning on the doorframe to the mudroom, his jacket still on.

She pressed her hand to her chest as she worked to calm herself.

"I'm sorry." His lips twitched as he stepped toward her. "I didn't mean to startle you."

"It's okay." She held out her hand for his mug. "Do you want more *kaffi*?"

"No, *danki*." He studied her, his eyes again intense, and she thought they might bore through her skin. "You look *gut*," he finally said—with no apparent loathing in his expression.

"Danki." She shifted her weight on her feet, feeling off-balance by the compliment.

He walked past her, then set the mug on the counter. "How have you been?"

"Fine." She shrugged as she grabbed the wet cloth Verna left to wipe down the sink, not looking at him. "You?"

"Fine."

She racked her brain for something to say. Only when she came up with a question did she dare look into his eyes. "Do you like living in Gap?"

"I do." He leaned against the counter.

"And you like working for your *onkel*?" Her questions were lame and redundant since he'd already answered them during lunch, but what else could she say?

"I do." He looked like he might say more, but instead he tilted his head. "What have I missed in your life?"

She stepped away from the sink and rested her hip against a kitchen chair, then fingered the corner of the table. "I've just been busy taking care of *mei dat* and *schweschder*." She paused, suddenly thinking of her mother. "I wish *mei mamm* could know Emma Grace is getting married." Her voice cracked, and she tried to swallow back the sudden emotion.

His expression filled with sympathy, catching her off guard again. "I'm sorry about your *mamm*. She was a *wunderbaar* woman."

"Danki." She looked down in an attempt to avoid his warm expression.

"*Mei mamm* told me when she passed away. I was at the funeral, but I didn't get a chance to talk to you."

Stunned, her gaze snapped to his. "You were there?"

He blinked, looking surprised. "*Ya.* You looked at me at one point, but you didn't . . . seem to see me."

"*Ach.* I was a mess that day. I don't remember much of it." She shouldn't be surprised that he'd come to the funeral. After all, her mother had treated him like a son.

An awkward silence developed as they stared at each other. So many unspoken words seemed to be floating between them.

Lorene suddenly needed to keep her hands busy. She grabbed his mug, then focused on washing it. But she could feel his stare.

"It was *gut* seeing you." His voice was close to her ear, sending a shiver through her.

She looked up at him, and butterflies swept through her stomach as she took in his expression. "*Gut* to see you too."

As he walked back into the mudroom, she gripped the edge of the sink. How was she going to make it through this wedding?

Back on the porch, Ryan sat next to Menno while he and Jon talked about the Bontrager farm. He tried to listen, but his mind was beset with thoughts of Lorene.

As much as he'd longed to avoid her, he was overcome by curiosity when he found her alone in the kitchen. He was struck by how she spoke about taking care of her father and sister, as though that was all she had in her life. Did that mean she was single? Not even a boyfriend?

For a moment, Ryan considered asking Menno if Lorene was seeing anyone. But he dismissed the idea. He didn't want to seem too nosy or make him uncomfortable.

"It will be nice to have Jon's help," Menno said, turning to him and *Dat*. Elias had gone inside to check on Joyce and the girls. "I've been paying a couple of farmhands to help me for a few years, and I thought I might have to sell my land when I retire. But now I can keep the farm in the family."

The back door opened, and Emma Grace stepped out to the porch, followed by *Mamm* and Lorene.

"I think we need to get going, *Dat*," Emma Grace announced. She looked at Jon. "Would you please walk me out to the buggy?"

"Of course." Jon stood and took her hand.

Emma Grace said good-bye to Ryan, Elias, and *Dat*, then turned toward *Mamm*. "*Danki* again for having us for lunch today."

"*Gern gschehne*," *Mamm* said. "Let's get together soon."

"I look forward to it." Emma Grace seemed to glow as she and Jon descended the steps.

Lorene held the cake saver—tightly, he noticed. "I enjoyed lunch, Verna." Then she looked at *Dat*. "It was nice seeing you, Rufus."

Dat nodded. "Nice to see you too."

When Lorene looked at Ryan, his heart thumped.

"Take care," he said.

"You too," she responded before heading down the steps.

"Well, Ryan," Menno began as he stood, "I suppose we'll be seeing each other."

Ryan swallowed as he stood, then shook Menno's hand. "Seems so."

Menno said good-bye to Ryan's parents and then left to hitch up his horse.

Ryan rested his hands on the porch railing as Lorene climbed into Menno's buggy. When she looked back at him, he lifted his hand in a wave. She nodded, and for a moment, he thought he saw a little warmth in her gaze.

But back in the kitchen, he'd almost told her he'd built himself a house in Gap. And what if he'd confessed he'd kept something important from her all those years ago? What would he have seen in her eyes then?

5

RYAN KNELT ON THE FLOOR OF THE SHED HE NEEDED TO finish, and the frustration he'd experienced off and on since Saturday night surged through him. He slammed his hammer on a nail as hard as he could as visions of Lorene flashed through his mind.

"*Gude mariye*," his uncle Jay called as he approached. Jay was only fifteen years older than Ryan, and he was easy to talk to and had a great sense of humor. Ryan considered him one of his best friends. "You're here early on a Monday morning."

Ryan sat back on his heels and swiped the back of his hand across his sweaty forehead. "I didn't sleep much last night. I finally figured I should just come in and get started."

Jay pursed his lips as he studied Ryan, then pointed at him. "You seem tense. What's going on?"

"Nothing."

The older man shook his head and grinned, his hazel eyes narrowing. "I doubt that. Did something happen at your parents' *haus* Saturday night?"

"You could say that." Ryan sighed. "I found out Jon is engaged, and I didn't even know he was dating someone."

"Whoa. No kidding." He held up his hands. "When's the wedding?"

"Christmas, and then he's going to move to his fiancée's farm and work it with her *dat*. Jon will take it over when he retires."

"*Gut* for him." Jay tilted his head and pulled on his beard. "Is that all?"

"Ya." Ryan shrugged, then continued hammering for a few moments. But he stopped when he realized Jay was still staring. "What?"

"Seems like there's more on your mind."

Ryan sat back on his heels again. "Jon didn't tell me he was dating because he was dating Lorene's *schweschder*."

Jay flinched. "Lorene *Bontrager*?"

"*Ya*. He's marrying my ex's *schweschder*." Ryan pointed the hammer at him. "Lorene and her family even came to my parents' *haus* for lunch yesterday, and Jon asked me to be there."

"How did that go?"

At first Ryan shrugged as if it weren't a big deal. But then he decided to admit the truth. "It was maddening."

"Why? Is she married?"

"No. And I don't think she has a boyfriend either." Ryan blew out a shaky breath. "She's still the most *schee maedel* I know. And she was sweet." *At least by the end of her visit.*

He slammed his hammer down, causing a loud crash.

"Is everything okay back there?" Jay's son, Peter, called from somewhere up near the office. At fifteen and just out of school, he was fast learning the business.

"*Ya*, it's fine!" Jay called before looking at Ryan. "Calm down."

"I'm sorry. I'm just frustrated." Ryan clenched his teeth. "She broke off our engagement five years ago and broke my heart. She wouldn't even give us the chance to work things out. But I couldn't stop staring at her. What's wrong with me?"

Jay rubbed his beard. "I guess you still care about her."

Ryan pushed both hands hard through his tangled curls. "And *mei bruder* had to fall in love with her *schweschder*, so now I have to see her at every family event."

Jay gave him a hopeful expression. "Maybe you and Lorene can forge a friendship, put the past behind you. After all, you'll be family."

Ryan shook his head, but then a calmness settled over him. "You know, that's a *gut* way of looking at this situation."

Jay patted his shoulder. "I think so. Now, get back to work," he said, teasing as usual.

Ryan turned his attention back to his task. Maybe he could be Lorene's friend, but he'd have to ask God for help.

Lorene knocked on Renae Byler's back door Wednesday afternoon, holding a loaf of banana bread and shivering in the cold. While she waited, she scanned the property, taking in the two large cinder block buildings that housed a shop and showroom. The furniture Renae's husband, Robert, and his employees made was popular and expensive, leading to a comfortable lifestyle for his family.

Then she looked up at the large, two-story brick home Robert had built for Renae. Renae had always seemed happy with her life, and Lorene tried to tamp down her secret envy.

The back door opened with a whoosh, and Renae grinned as she pushed open the storm door. With golden-blond hair, bright-green eyes, and a pretty face, Renae had never had any trouble finding dates. "I was so excited when I got your message saying you were going to stop by today." She rested one hand on her protruding belly, and Lorene experienced a familiar longing. Renae had waited a long time for this baby, but Lorene might never be a mother.

"I'm sorry it's been so long." She held up the bread. "I made your favorite."

"You remembered! *Danki!*"

Lorene laughed. "It's been your favorite since we were in school. How could I forget?"

"Come in." Renae beckoned her inside, and Lorene followed her to the kitchen.

Lorene glanced around the large room, taking in the long walnut table and six matching chairs Robert had given Renae as a wedding gift, and she once again felt a slight pang of self-pity. Renae had everything Lorene had ever dreamed of—a good marriage, a home, and a baby on the way.

Don't think about that now.

"How are you feeling?" Lorene asked as she filled the teakettle.

"I'm feeling big." Renae reached into a nearby cabinet for mugs. "And I'm starting to get uncomfortable, especially when I try to sleep. But I'm fine."

"It's so exciting that you're due just before Christmas." Lorene set the full teakettle on a burner on the propane stove, then turned to grab plates and a knife.

"*Ya.* Robert is working on the crib." Renae looked at her. "How are you?"

"Well, I got a shock last week. Emma Grace announced she's getting married around the time your *boppli* is coming."

Renae spun toward her. "Is she marrying Jonathan Lapp?"

"*Ya.* And they've been dating only six months. Can you believe that?" Lorene shook her head.

Renae shrugged. "Well, I guess that happens sometimes."

Lorene carried a tray with the bread, plates, knife, and butter to the table. The kettle whistled, and Renae poured water into the two mugs before taking them to the table. They both sat down, then bowed their heads in silent prayer.

Lorene sliced the first piece of bread. "There's more. We went to the Lapps' for lunch on Sunday, and I saw Ryan."

Renae gasped. "You did?"

"Yup. First time in five years."

"And . . ." Renae leaned forward as Lorene put the bread on a plate and gave it to her.

"He's still the most handsome man." Lorene cringed after her admission, then sighed. "And he doesn't have a beard, and he came alone, so I don't think he has a girlfriend." She sliced her own piece of bread, then quickly bit into it as she looked across the table. Renae had lifted her eyebrows.

"Maybe you two could work it out."

Lorene stared at her. "And get back together? Never."

"Why not?" Renae gestured around the kitchen. "You and

Ryan were so *froh* together for a while. Maybe you could start over. God could be granting you a second opportunity. Could you even consider giving Ryan another chance?"

Lorene stared at her mug. *Could I?* But then reality crashed over her. "No. I could never trust him again. He made every possible excuse for why he couldn't even start building a *haus* for us on his father's land. I waited and waited, not even asking for a wedding date. But then I finally had to face the truth. His excuses proved he didn't want to marry me. He didn't really love me, at least not enough."

Renae looked like she wanted to say something, but then she shook her head and looked out the window.

Lorene sighed. "Just say it."

Renae hesitated. "I haven't wanted to press you about this, but did you ever consider that something else held him back from building the *haus*? Something that had nothing to do with you?"

"Like what?"

"I don't know." Renae shrugged. "I just always believed he truly loved you."

Lorene shook her head. "He never gave me any real reason for dragging his feet. If he had loved me, we'd be married now—and maybe expecting too. Now I'm just alone."

Renae reached over and rested both her hands on Lorene's. "Don't lose faith. I believe God has the perfect plan for all of us." She lifted the knife and reached for the butter. "Now, while I eat this *appeditlich* treat, tell me all about Emma Grace's Christmas wedding."

Lorene took a sip of her tea and let Renae's words settle in her mind. She was trying not to lose faith, still hoping God's perfect plan for her included marriage. But only time would tell.

Lorene sat in a booth at the Bird-in-Hand Family Restaurant across from Verna and Emma Grace the following Wednesday afternoon.

"I'm so excited about the shade of green we found for the dresses," Emma gushed as she held up the bag of material she'd just purchased at the nearby fabric store. "I liked the material you offered me, Verna, but I think this shade of green will look even more fabulous with Lorene's red hair."

Lorene shook her head. "Don't worry about me. This will be your day."

"I think that shade is very Christmassy." Verna divided a smile between them. "*Danki* for inviting me to go shopping with you. Today has been so fun. Let me pay for lunch."

"That's not necessary, but *danki*." Lorene touched Verna's hand.

"We're just glad you wanted to come," Emma Grace added.

The waitress delivered their food, and they all bowed their head in silent prayer before they began to eat.

Lorene picked up a section of her club sandwich and took a bite.

"I can't believe the wedding is less than eight weeks away," Emma Grace said as she lifted her chicken salad sandwich. "Time is flying by, and I have so much to do."

Verna swallowed a bite of her grilled ham and cheese. "We need to talk about the menu." She dabbed at her lips with a paper napkin.

Emma Grace looked at Lorene. "I also want to make sure we keep our Christmas traditions while we're preparing for the wedding. Making our Christmas cards, decorating, baking . . . Plus, I need to reorganize my room before Jon moves in. It's all coming so fast."

Lorene tried to smile, but a new dread had begun to wash over her. Frankly, she was surprised Jon wasn't building them a house, but maybe it made more sense for her and *Dat* to move into a *daadihaus*. When Jon moved in, the couple could come to think of her as an intruder. A nuisance. *Dat* would be a partner on the farm, but she'd be a spinster sister in the way.

"Ryan is coming for supper tonight," Verna suddenly said. "I'm making something special for him when I get home."

Lorene looked away as her thoughts moved to Ryan for what seemed like the hundredth time since she saw him at the Lapp farm last week. As much as she tried to forget him, memories of his smile and gorgeous blue eyes still taunted her.

Lorene looked up. "How *is* Ryan?" The question rolled off her tongue too easily, but she couldn't help it.

Verna smiled as if pleased by the question. "He sounded well when I spoke to him Monday."

"Gut." Lorene nodded. "So what are you thinking about the menu, Emma Grace?"

As her sister talked about lasagna and garlic bread, Lorene caught Verna watching her from the corner of her eye. Why on earth had she asked about Ryan? She didn't want to give Verna the wrong idea—or support the one she might already have.

"That sounds *gut*," Verna said when Emma Grace took a breath. "And now that we have the material, we need to start making the dresses next week. Again, you two are welcome to come to *mei haus* to sew. I have that big sewing room with two machines."

"That's nice of you to offer." Lorene looked at her sister. "You should go. I can handle the chores at the *haus*."

Emma Grace frowned, sticking out her lower lip. "But I want you to come too. You need to be a part of this."

Lorene looked at Verna, who nodded in agreement. "Okay."

"Great." Emma Grace rubbed her hands together. "So . . . Jon's birthday is on Monday, and I'd love to have both families at our *haus* for a surprise party Friday night, a few days before so he'll never expect it. I'll come up with an excuse for him to come over."

"How thoughtful of you," Verna said. "May I invite Ryan?" She glanced at Lorene as she asked.

"Of course," Emma Grace said, and Lorene nodded.

She closed her eyes as Emma Grace unpacked her party plans. She would have to see Ryan sooner than she'd hoped. But no matter what she did, he was once again becoming a fixture in her life—just not how she'd once believed he would.

6

"HOW DOES THIS LOOK?" EMMA GRACE TOOK A STEP BACK from the chocolate cake she'd just finished icing.

Lorene breathed in the sweet chocolaty smell, then held out her finger, pretending she was going to swipe a bit of the frosting. "It looks perfect, but let me just sample a little of it—"

"Don't you dare!" Emma Grace laughed as she swatted Lorene's hand away. But then tears filled her eyes. "What would I do without you? I'm so glad you're here to help plan my wedding."

Lorene clucked her tongue. "Where else would I be?" Then a familiar worry hit her, but the sooner she faced it, the better. "Unless you think I should leave after you're married. I could ask *Dat* about building a *daadihaus* for him and me so you and Jon have privacy."

Emma Grace blanched as if Lorene had struck her. "Are you kidding? Why would I want that?"

Lorene gestured around the kitchen. "I'm thinking about

even more than your privacy. You're going to be a *fraa*, and then you'll be a *mamm*. You'll deserve to run the household, and I'll just be in your way."

"No." Emma Grace hugged her. "You're *mei schweschder.* You belong here, and so does *Dat.*" She looked up at Lorene. "I want us to always be close."

Lorene nodded. "Fine. But I want you to be honest with me if it gets too crowded here. You deserve happiness with your new husband."

"Danki." Emma Grace looked at the clock on the wall. "Oops. It's time to get the steaks ready. I want to marinate them the way Jon likes them." She looked at Lorene. "*Danki* for letting me invite Ryan. It's important to Jon and me that we remain close with our families after we're married. I appreciate that you're trying to be *freinden.*"

Lorene gave a little snort as she took the cake saver from the pantry. "I doubt we'll ever truly be *freinden*, but I'll always be civil to him."

"You never know," Emma Grace sang as they loaded the cake into the container.

Lorene did feel a little flutter at the idea of seeing Ryan again tonight. Then she dismissed the thought. "Where are those steaks?"

Ryan stepped into the front office at the shed shop and found Jay sitting at his desk. Peter was perched on a nearby stool. "That shed is finished, and I need to head out. My driver is here."

"Where are you going?" Peter asked.

"To Lorene's *haus.*" Ryan stilled when he realized he'd said Lorene's house instead of Emma Grace's house. Why did it still feel natural to refer to the Bontragers' home as Lorene's?

Jay's brow knitted. "Why are you going there?"

"Emma Grace is throwing a surprise birthday party for Jon, and *mei mamm* begged me to go."

Pete wrinkled his nose. "Why don't you want to go? Sounds like there will be *kuche.*"

Jay turned to his son. "You were too young to remember, I guess, but Ryan was engaged to Lorene about five years ago."

"Wait a minute." Pete held up his hand as if he were answering an arithmetic question at school. "Jon is marrying your ex-fiancée's *schweschder?*"

Ryan nodded and felt a bit uneasy.

To his surprise, Pete laughed. "That's awkward."

Ryan grunted. "That's putting it mildly. I'll see you." Then he gave them both a little wave before heading to the parking lot.

As he walked toward his driver's waiting van, Ryan tried not to think about the surprise party Lorene threw for him years ago. But the memories still formed in his head, and he realized just how much he still missed her.

"Surprise!" Lorene called along with the rest of the crowd.

Jon laughed as he stepped into the family room, then joined Emma Grace. "This is why you were so *naerfich* when we talked last night."

Emma Grace grinned. "I wanted everything to be perfect."

"And it is." Jon kissed her cheek.

Lorene's heart clenched as she once again watched the love pass between her sister and her fiancé.

Jon scanned the crowd. "Is Ryan here?"

"He should be on his way," Verna said.

Lorene hoped Ryan hadn't stopped to pick up a girlfriend on the way. Then she scolded herself. She had no right to be jealous of a girlfriend when she was the one who broke their engagement.

"Let's eat!" Maranda announced, and everyone laughed.

Elias got Barbiann settled in her high chair and Maranda in her booster seat while *Dat* and Rufus took their seats at the long table. Then Lorene helped the women serve the meal, all Jon's favorites—steak, baked potatoes, green beans, and homemade rolls.

When everyone was seated, Lorene looked at the empty seat between *Dat* and Rufus, wondering if Ryan had seen enough of her at his parents' house and didn't want to come tonight. He probably told his mother he'd be here just to satisfy her, all while planning to come up with an excuse for his absence.

"Brot!" Barbiann moaned. *"Brot!"*

Joyce pivoted toward her and whispered something as she handed the little girl a buttered roll. The toddler took the roll and bit into it, sighing as she ate. The tenderness between mother and child warmed Lorene's heart and sent longing through her.

Joyce was the same age as Lorene, and like Renae, she had everything—a loving husband, a home, and children. Suddenly Lorene's loneliness squeezed her chest so hard she felt as if she couldn't breathe. She needed to get out of there.

"Lorene?" Verna leaned over and touched her hand. "Are you okay?"

"Ya." Lorene tried to smile, but it wouldn't come. "I just need to get some air. It's hot in here."

"Are you *krank*, *mei liewe*?" *Dat*'s voice was full of concern.

Lorene pushed back her chair and stood. "No, no. Please just excuse me for a moment."

Lorene made her way through the mudroom, then stepped onto the porch and sucked in the cool evening air, taking in deep breaths. Beautiful streaks of orange and yellow lit the sky.

Leaning forward on the railing, she tried to imagine how life would change when Jon moved in. Even though Emma Grace insisted Lorene should still live there, she wasn't convinced. She'd no doubt interrupt intimate conversations in the kitchen and hamper their ability to be themselves.

Her thoughts were interrupted when she heard the hum of an engine and headlights bounced up her driveway. Ryan had made it!

Lorene's stomach dropped, and she considered fleeing into the house to avoid another awkward conversation alone with him. But her feet didn't move. It was as if they were cemented to the porch floor as a van came to a stop. Ryan climbed out of the vehicle, spoke to the driver, and then started for the house.

As he approached the porch, he looked up at her, a tentative smile appearing on his face. He stopped short of the steps, holding a brown bag.

"Hi. I'm sorry I'm late. I had to finish a shed before I could leave. It's being picked up for delivery tomorrow."

"It's fine. We haven't had any *kuche* yet. How are you?"

His brow furrowed for a moment, and then his expression relaxed again.

"I'm fine. Just busy at work." He lifted his straw hat with his free hand and pushed back a few of his curls, a mannerism she'd seen so many times when he was nervous. "How about you?" he asked.

"I've been busy too. Emma Grace and I were cleaning all day, then making supper." She smiled, shaking her head. "She was scattered, worrying everything wouldn't be perfect for Jon tonight."

Ryan suddenly grinned, and his genuine smile sent a shock wave of heat through her veins. "Remember the surprise party you threw for me when I turned twenty-five?"

Lorene couldn't stop her bark of laughter. "How can I ever forget that disaster?" Then she counted off the infractions on her fingers. "I burned your *kuche*, I didn't make enough food for the guests, and Emma Grace spoiled the surprise by asking you what time you planned to arrive."

Resting his foot on the bottom step, Ryan leaned forward. "But it was fun. Definitely the most memorable birthday I ever had."

"I'm sure it was."

They both fell silent as they stared at each other, and the intensity in his eyes sent a tremor through her. She suddenly longed to have an honest conversation with him as questions filled her mind. *Do you still care about me?*

Then she shook herself. She had to face the truth—again. What went wrong between them could never be fixed.

She turned toward the door. "Come inside. I'm sure the food is still warm."

"Danki." He appeared behind her, holding the door open as she walked into the house.

"Ryan!" Joyce called when they entered the kitchen. "I didn't think you were going to make it."

"I was worried you forgot how to get here," Jon quipped, and everyone laughed.

"Very funny," Ryan deadpanned, but a smile played on his lips as he handed his brother the bag. "Happy birthday, baby *bruder*."

"Danki."

Lorene sat down between Verna and Joyce as Ryan took the empty seat across from her and bowed his head for a silent prayer.

"Still busy at work?" Rufus asked Ryan after he'd looked up.

"Ya." Ryan began cutting the steak he'd just plopped on his plate. "I'm late because a shed had to be ready for delivery tomorrow."

As he fielded questions about his work, Lorene struggled to keep her gaze off his attractive face, trying in vain to hold back memories of their time together. How she missed him! Her feelings for Ryan had never disappeared, no matter how hurt and angry she'd been when she broke their engagement.

Once everyone had finished eating, Lorene helped the other women clear the table and pile the dirty dishes next to the sink.

Emma Grace stepped to the refrigerator and removed the cake saver. "It's time for *kuche*." She gazed at Jon. "I made your favorite." She took the cake out of the saver and brought it to the table, and everyone gasped.

"Wow." Jon smiled up at her. "It's perfect."

Lorene stepped to the percolator to make coffee.

"Let's sing," Verna announced, and everyone stood to gather around Jon.

Lorene sensed someone watching her as she sang "Happy

Birthday." She gazed across the table to find Ryan looking at her. She smiled at him, and when he returned the gesture, she was sure her cheeks were turning red.

Emma Grace cheered when they finished the song, and then she began slicing the cake.

Lorene pulled dessert plates from a cabinet, grateful for a moment to look away from Ryan.

She couldn't help but wonder if Ryan still felt something for her. Or was she just imagining the attraction that seemed to radiate between them?

Ryan sat on the porch with *Dat*, Jon, and Menno after they'd eaten the cake and watched Jon open his gifts. Three lanterns illuminated the porch in the darkness.

Jon turned to Ryan while the others were engrossed in a conversation about the trials and tribulations of running a dairy farm, their usual topic of conversation.

"I was only kidding when I said I thought you forgot your way here," Jon told Ryan while keeping his voice low. "I didn't mean anything by it."

"It's okay. I thought it was funny." Ryan stared out toward the dark pasture, recalling the conversation he'd had with Lorene earlier on the porch. He couldn't stop thinking about the way she'd laughed when he mentioned the surprise party she'd thrown for him. She seemed relaxed, perhaps even eager to share their memories together.

Soon he found himself lost in memories of her—holidays, birthdays, church socials. He missed her so much that his heart ached. He'd dated a few women in Gap, but none of them had come close to Lorene.

Closing his eyes, he silently prayed.

Lord, I'm confused. Why would Lorene appear in my life again when I can't have her? What are you trying to teach me?

Opening his eyes, he turned toward the kitchen windows and spotted her talking to *Mamm*. He marveled at her beauty, then shook his head. Why hadn't one of the bachelors in her church district won her heart and married her?

Then a fleeting thought sent a thrill shuddering through him. Did she miss him too?

No, she couldn't. After all, she was the one to end their relationship. She was the one who'd stomped on his heart and left him over an unbuilt house. She was the one who never gave him the opportunity to explain. He had to keep reminding himself of that.

The back door opened, and Elias walked out, cradling a snoring Barbiann in his arms. Joyce followed, holding a yawning Maranda's hand.

"We're heading home." Elias grinned. "The *kinner* have had it."

After saying good night, Elias and Joyce ferried the children to their waiting horse and buggy. Ryan waved before the horse pulled the buggy down the driveway toward the street.

Emma Grace stepped out onto the porch, touched Jon's arm, and then held up a flashlight. "Could we go for a walk before you leave?"

"Of course." Jon took her hand, stood, and then steered her down the steps toward the path that led beyond the largest barn.

Ryan watched them walk away, their outlines turning into silhouettes in the dark. Jon leaned in close and said something to

Emma Grace before kissing her cheek. The affection sent a pang of longing through him. If he'd made different decisions, would Lorene still have married him?

"It's colder out here than it was last night," *Dat* commented as he pulled his jacket tighter over his midriff. "Winter is on its way, and Christmas will be here soon."

"Ya." Menno turned toward Ryan. "Does your business slow down during the winter months?"

Ryan nodded. "A bit, but some businesses still need buildings in winter. We have enough orders to sustain us."

Dismissing thoughts of Lorene and what he'd lost, Ryan settled into an easy conversation about work.

After a while, the door squeaked open, and *Mamm* appeared on the porch, wearing her jacket and carrying her tote bag. "It's getting late. We should get on the road."

Lorene stepped out behind her. She hugged her arms to her chest, and Ryan took in how beautiful she looked in the green dress and black apron she wore. He'd always admired how green complemented her flaming red hair and ivory skin.

"*Danki* for helping Emma Grace have the party here." *Mamm* gave Lorene a hug, and Lorene patted her back awkwardly. "I'll see you when you come over with your *schweschder* to work on the wedding preparations."

Dat stood and shook Menno's hand. "I guess that's my cue to go." Then he turned to Ryan and shook his hand. "I hope we'll see you soon, *sohn*." He pulled a flashlight from his pocket and flipped it on.

Mamm hugged Ryan and then shook Menno's hand before following *Dat* down the steps.

Ryan peered over his shoulder to where Lorene lingered by

the door. Did she want him to invite her to sit down and visit? Yet she wasn't wearing a sweater or jacket. Maybe she was hoping he'd leave.

But her gaze was pinned on something out beyond the porch. Ryan turned and spotted Jon and Emma Grace walking together, hand in hand, then turned back toward Lorene. Now she was looking at him. His mouth dried as something unspoken seemed to pass between them. He wondered again if she missed him. And if she did, did she miss him as much as he missed her?

"Why don't you have a seat, Lorene?" Menno asked.

"O-okay. I'll be right back."

She disappeared into the house, then reappeared wearing a heavy sweater and sat down in a rocker between Menno and Ryan.

They all sat in an awkward silence for a few minutes, and Ryan finally decided to leave. He didn't want to wear out his welcome anyway.

"I should give my driver a call and get home. I have to work a half day tomorrow to supervise when the crew loads that shed I mentioned." He stood and shook Menno's hand. "It was nice seeing you again."

"You too," Menno said. "You know where the phone is. Help yourself."

Ryan turned to Lorene and held out his hand. "*Danki* for allowing *mei mamm* to invite me. I had a nice time visiting with you and your family."

She hesitated, studying his hand for a moment. Then she grasped it and shook it. The feel of her skin against his sent an explosion of heat zipping up his arm. When he held on to her hand too long, she suddenly pulled it back as if it were on fire.

She stood, her eyes wide. "Take care." Then she spun and hurried into the house.

Ryan stared after her. How he longed to run after her. The desire to ask her if she still cared for him gripped him. But after murmuring good night to Menno, he descended the porch steps and headed toward the phone shanty, feeling as though he were leaving a piece of his heart with Lorene.

7

VERNA STOOD FROM ONE OF HER SEWING MACHINES almost a week later and turned toward Emma Grace. "We made a lot of progress on your dress today."

"We did." Emma Grace smiled as she peered at the green garment. "I love the color. It's so Christmassy!"

"It's perfect." Lorene stood and glanced at the clock on the wall, finding it was almost four. "It's getting late."

"Can you both stay for supper?" Verna turned toward Emma Grace. "I know Jon would love for you to stay so you can visit."

Emma Grace gave Lorene a hopeful smile. "Can we stay?"

"You stay. I need to get home and cook for *Dat*. I just have to call our driver to come and get me. I told him I'd call when we were ready to go. I'm sure Jon will take you home."

"Danki."

Lorene followed Verna down the stairs to the kitchen. Then

she headed outside to call her driver from the barn. She hugged her arms to her waist and shivered as the November chill seeped through her blue dress and black apron. Leaves blew around her feet as she peered up at the large, fluffy clouds in the sky. It would be getting dark soon, another indication that winter was on its way to Lancaster County. She should have grabbed her shawl before she rushed outside.

As she approached the barn, she stilled, and then her heartbeat sped up when she spotted Ryan standing by the fence talking to Rufus. She swallowed back her anxiety and plastered a smile on her face as Ryan turned toward her, then gave her a surprised expression. She waved and kept going, pushing the ribbons on her prayer covering over her shoulders as she continued toward the barn.

"Lorene." Ryan jogged up beside her. "I didn't expect to see you here."

She stopped and faced him. "Your *mamm* invited us over to work on the wedding dresses. We got a lot done this afternoon." She pointed toward the house. "She also invited us to stay for supper, but I need to get home to cook for *mei dat*. Emma Grace will stay, but I'm calling for my ride. *Dat* needed the horse and buggy today."

"I can give you a ride in *Dat*'s buggy. Jay asked his driver to take me to Bird-in-Hand to run some errands for him, and then I had him drop me off here so I could visit awhile. But I'll just bring *Dat*'s horse and buggy back here and then call my driver."

"Oh, that's not necessary, but *danki*." She took a step toward the barn, hoping to avoid being cooped up in a buggy with him. "Our driver is expecting my call."

"Lorene, let me give you a ride." Ryan pressed his lips together as annoyance seemed to flicker across his face. "We're adults, right? Can't we at least pretend to get along for our siblings' sake?"

She studied him, then suddenly felt like a *dummkopp.* He was right; they were adults and should behave like it. "Fine. Let me just get my things and tell Emma Grace and your *mamm* I'm leaving."

His expression relaxed. "I'll hitch up the horse."

Lorene stepped back into the kitchen, where Verna was pulling chicken from the fridge, a box of pasta on the counter. Emma Grace was filling a large pot with water.

"I'm going to head out. *Danki* for a nice day, Verna. I enjoyed being together."

"*Gern gschehne,*" Verna said over her shoulder.

"Tell *Dat* I won't be home too late," Emma Grace said. "Is Todd on his way to get you?"

"No. Ryan is here, and he offered to give me a ride."

Verna turned off the faucet and spun toward her. "He is?" Her expression seemed to fill with hope, and Lorene took a deep breath. Verna would be sadly disappointed if she longed for Lorene and Ryan to reunite.

"*Ya.* I'll see you soon." Lorene retrieved her purse and tote bag before heading out to the mudroom, where she pulled on her shawl.

Outside, she slowed at the sight of Ryan leaning against his father's buggy, talking and laughing with his father and brother. She drank in his gorgeous blue eyes, broad shoulders, and wide chest—and goose bumps raced down her arms.

Stop it!

She pushed herself down the porch steps and adjusted her purse and tote bag strap on her shoulder as she joined them.

Ryan turned toward her and raised his golden-brown eyebrows. "Ready?"

No!

"Ya." After saying good-bye to Rufus and Jon, she climbed into his buggy and felt as if she were stepping back in time.

Ryan slipped into the driver's seat. Then out of the corner of his eye, he saw Lorene sitting ramrod straight, staring out the window, gripping her purse and tote bag on her lap.

The sight disappointed him. She acted as if he were a stranger, as though they hadn't known each other nearly their whole lives and been engaged.

"So," he began, grasping for a point of discussion, "you made progress on Emma Grace's wedding dress?"

She nodded, keeping her eyes focused out the window. "I started on mine too."

"*Danki* for including *mei mamm* in the plans. I know she appreciates being involved."

"Well, we're *froh* to spend time with her." She licked her lips while still looking away from him, and a silence fell over them.

What on earth could he say to ease the awkwardness?

Ryan halted the horse at a stop sign, and Lorene suddenly turned to face him, her expression serious. He braced himself as she leaned closer.

"Can I be completely honest with you?"

He nodded and rubbed his chin. "*Ya*, of course."

"Do you think Emma Grace and Jon are rushing things? I mean, they've been dating barely more than six months. Shouldn't they wait a little longer before they get married?"

He pursed his lips, and a familiar frustration poured through him. "I think if they've prayed about it and believe marrying now is God's plan, then they're doing what's right."

She shook her head, her expression grim. "But they don't even have their own *haus*. They're moving in with *mei dat* and me, and that doesn't seem like—"

He felt a similarly familiar temper begin to flare as he guided the horse through the intersection. "They love each other, Lorene. Isn't that all that matters? *Haus* or no *haus*." He gave her a sideways glance. "I've built myself a *haus* in Gap, and it's just brick and wood."

She blanched as if he hit her, and guilt shook him.

An awkward silence fell over them again, and he sighed. "I'm sorry."

She snorted. "It's a little late for that."

"What does that mean?" He halted the horse at a red light, then turned toward her and pointed to his chest. "In case you've forgotten, you're the one who broke up with *me*."

"You pushed me to it." Her voice was tinged with pain.

He studied her dark eyes and found them glistening. "How do you figure that?"

She gave a sarcastic laugh. "You made every excuse not to build our *haus* so we could set a wedding date." She counted them off on her fingers. "Let's see. Not enough money, you had to help your *dat* teach Jon more about how to run the farm, and then you decided you needed plans but never got them." She gave a sardonic smile, and her words dripped with acrimony. "Last, you just didn't think it was the right time."

Her face darkened. "But you know all that." She sniffed, and her voice thickened. "And then I realized the truth. You didn't love me enough to build a *haus* and start a life with me. Too bad I didn't realize that sooner. Sometimes I think I wasted those years with you." Her voice broke.

Ryan pressed his lips together. Her words were like a hammer to his heart. "I'm sorry, Lorene. I—"

"No, you aren't." She spat the words at him, wiping at her eyes. "You moved away and started a new life. And you even built yourself a *haus*." She faced the windshield once again. "You moved on—while I took care of *mei dat* and *schweschder* and watched *mei freinden* get married and start families."

He blinked as the answer to his burning question came into clear focus. "So you're not dating anyone."

Her lips twisted as she kept her gaze focused straight ahead.

"Lorene, why aren't you dating?"

She looked at him. "I have dated a few men, but I'm not dating anyone now." She hesitated. "Are you dating?"

He shook his head. "Not for a while."

Her eyes seemed to widen with surprise, and then she turned away.

They both fell silent again as only the rumble of passing traffic filled the buggy.

When the horse moved up her driveway, Ryan longed to smooth over what had just passed between them, but he drew a blank. He wanted to tell her the truth, but it was too late. She'd only be angry that he'd spent so much time being dishonest with her.

He halted the horse by her back porch, and she spun toward him, her expression seeming resigned. "Look. I told Emma Grace I'd be fine with this. Why don't we just agree to get along for their sake?"

"Sure." He nodded. "That's what I want too."

"Gut." She pushed open the door. "*Gut nacht. Danki* for the ride."

Before Ryan could respond, she was gone, and he wanted to bang his head against the door as she disappeared into the house.

Emma Grace had convinced *Dat* to spend Thanksgiving Day with the Lapp family, and now Lorene gripped the cake saver in the front passenger seat of her father's buggy.

She'd been dreading this day and had considered feigning a bad headache so she could stay home. But she couldn't bring herself to disappoint her family.

As the Lapp farm came into view, Lorene bit her lower lip and tried to imagine what she would say to Ryan when she saw him. Embarrassment gripped her when she recalled how she'd vented her feelings to him in his father's buggy almost three weeks ago. Why had she allowed herself to explode like that?

At least when she and Emma Grace had been sewing the wedding dresses and creating table decorations at the Lapp home on several more occasions, Ryan hadn't been there. What a relief. She'd enjoyed spending time with Verna, but each time she arrived, she worried that her oldest son would pop in for another impromptu visit.

Today would be different, though. She was certain Ryan would join his family for Thanksgiving dinner, and she dreaded seeing him. She owed him an apology. Although she'd resented his twisting her comment about Jon and Emma Grace not having their own house, he'd been tolerant and kind while she berated him, and guilt had been her companion each time she recalled their emotional discussion.

Dat halted the horse at the top of the driveway, where Ryan stood with Jon, Rufus, and Elias. She also recognized his uncle Jay. And the boy at his side had to be his cousin Pete.

Shoving away her worry and shame, Lorene climbed out of the buggy and greeted them all with a smile.

"Happy Thanksgiving," Lorene said to Jay. "It's been a long time since I've seen you."

She shook Jay's hand, then turned to Pete, who'd been so short and rotund when she'd last seen him. Now a teenager, he was tall and slim like his father, and he also shared Jay's coloring. "You were only about ten the last time we spoke. You're all grown up now."

Pete looked embarrassed as he shook her hand. "It's nice to see you too."

Lorene turned toward Ryan, and she gave him a hesitant smile. "Hi."

"Hello." He nodded toward the cake saver. "Tell me that's a lemon *kuche.*"

She held it up. "It is."

"Gut." He rubbed his hands together.

Some of the tension released in her shoulders, but she still felt the need to apologize to him. This wasn't the time or place, though. Perhaps they would get a minute alone later.

Emma Grace also greeted everyone as she balanced her portable containers of mashed potatoes and green bean casserole, then nodded toward the house. "We should get the food inside. Plus, it's cold out here." She shivered.

Lorene followed her younger sister into the house and was met with the wonderful aroma of turkey and freshly baked bread, along with several loud, happy voices. She said hello to Verna and Joyce in the kitchen and then peeked into the family room, where Maranda and Barbiann played with blocks.

When Lorene turned around, she greeted Ryan's aunt Ann and cousin Lily. Ann looked just as she remembered her—golden-blond hair and green eyes. Lily, now twelve, shared facial features with her pretty mother, but she had her father's light-brown hair and hazel eyes.

"It's so nice to see you again," Ann told her. "Are you excited about the wedding?"

"*Ya*, I am."

"I can't believe it's less than a month away," Emma Grace said as she adjusted her two containers now on the long table already bursting with food. "Christmas is almost here."

"What can I do to help with the meal, Verna?" Lorene asked.

"We'll get the rest of the food out, and then we'll call the men in to join us."

Soon the food was served, and the men took turns washing their hands at the kitchen sink. Lorene sat between Joyce and Emma Grace, grateful to avoid sitting beside Ryan. But her heart thumped when he sank into a chair across from her, meeting her gaze with a warm smile.

After prayers, conversations broke out around the table. But Lorene kept her attention on her plate. Then she glanced up to find Ryan's bright, intelligent eyes focused on her. She gave him a half smile, and he replied with the same.

She suddenly hated the great chasm that had expanded between them. She wanted a relationship with him. A friendship would be a start, but she craved more. Maybe Renae was right. Maybe enough had changed in the past few years for them to find a way to work out their problems. But even if that were possible, would he consider giving her another chance? Her body thrummed with excitement at the mere thought of being blessed to call him her boyfriend again. But would he ever love her again, enough to make a true commitment to a future with her?

Soon everyone was sharing what they were thankful for, each person mentioning their many blessings, including their families and their homes.

After the meal, the women began cleaning the kitchen while the men took their usual spot out on the porch despite the cold. Conversations about the wedding continued around the kitchen, and Lorene was sure to nod and agree when appropriate even though her thoughts were stuck on Ryan and how her heart longed for him.

After she finished drying the dishes, she stepped into the large family room and glanced around at the familiar furniture—a long brown sofa, its matching love seat, two recliners, two coffee tables, two end tables, and two propane lamps. Her mind spun with memories of all the times she and Ryan had spent together there, visiting with his parents, talking, and laughing. She hugged her arms to her chest as her heart began to hurt.

She missed talking to Ryan, holding his hand, sharing her hopes and dreams, and kissing him. If only she could turn back time. Maybe if she had been willing to talk to him rather than wallowing in her hurt and resentment, they could have worked things out. Her throat felt thick, and her eyes stung with unshed tears.

She turned, then gasped when she found Ryan leaning on the doorframe to the kitchen. His expression was intense, making her nerves hum, but she felt an invisible force pulling them together. Did he feel it too?

This was her chance to make things right. She mustered all the confidence she could find, then took a ragged breath.

"I'm sorry." Her shaky voice betrayed her surging confidence. "I was awful to you the afternoon you took me home, and you didn't deserve it. I hope you can forgive me."

He stood up straight, and then his expression filled with contrition. "I'm sorry as well. I never meant to upset you."

"I need to explain something." She paused, but it was time to be honest. "I didn't break our engagement because of the *haus*. I broke it because when you kept making excuses not to build it, I didn't think you really wanted to marry me. I didn't think you really loved me."

He blinked, and shock seemed to flicker across his face.

"I had to explain that. I'm not so shallow and self-centered that I care only about material things. I hope you know that's not who I am."

He nodded, then swallowed. "I understand. But it wasn't about you, Lorene. I wasn't being honest with you. I didn't want to keep being a dairy farmer, let alone take over the farm from *Dat* as the oldest *sohn*. I'd struggled with that for years. But I didn't know how to tell my family without disappointing them. I was even afraid to tell you. Then when I asked you to marry me, everyone just expected me to build the *haus* and keep working on the farm. At first I thought I could do it, but I was emotionally lost. Yet I should have told you rather than dragging my feet."

He paused. "When you wouldn't talk to me, I finally told *Dat* the truth. Not only did I want to move to Gap to get away, but I wanted the job with *mei onkel* because I needed another line of work. *Dat* supported me, and I was so relieved. I wanted to tell you, too, but . . ."

Lorene's eyes filled with tears. "I wouldn't talk to you. I'm sorry. But I understand."

He blew out a puff of air. "*Danki.* I can't fix the past, but I hope we can be *freinden.*" Then he shrugged. "We have to try for our families' sake."

"Right." She nodded, disappointed. She'd hoped he'd want more than friendship from her, but she'd take friendship if that was all he offered. Even if he had loved her enough to marry her, he didn't now. Nothing had changed.

"Gut." He held out his hand, and when she shook it, she enjoyed the feeling of his warm skin against hers.

Then she pulled her hand away and pointed toward the kitchen behind him. "I need to get back in there. Excuse me."

He stepped aside, and she hurried off.

Later that evening, Ryan sat on the porch between his father and uncle and breathed in the cold air. He jammed his hands into the pockets of his coat and enjoyed the aroma of a nearby wood-burning fireplace. In the distance, traffic hummed on Old Philadelphia Pike and a dog barked. Two lone lanterns illuminated the porch as stars winked in the dark sky above.

Joyce and her family had walked the pasture to their house, and Lorene and her family had gone home too. Ryan moved the rocker back and forth as he tried to evict thoughts of Lorene from his mind.

But he couldn't seem to stop contemplating how pretty she was when she apologized to him.

"So, Ry," Jay suddenly said, "what's going on between you and Lorene?"

"Nothing." Ryan shrugged. "We're just trying to be civil to each other for the sake of our families. Maybe become *freinden*."

"Seems like a lot more than that."

"I agree," *Dat* chimed in. "You seem to be in tune with each other when you're together."

"Do you think you might try again?" Jay said. "You're both young, and you could still get married and have a family."

"No." Ryan shook his head, but deep in his bones he knew he wanted just that. "It's too late for us."

Jay leaned over and tapped the arm of Ryan's rocker. "But you're wrong. God's timing is never too late."

And more than ever, Ryan wanted his uncle to be right. But when he suggested he and Lorene be friends, he'd didn't think he'd seen a desire in her eyes for anything more.

8

Ryan climbed the back steps of his parents' house Sunday afternoon two weeks later. He meant it when he told *Mamm* he would try to visit more often. He should have called to make sure they'd be home, but he'd decided to take a chance. They'd return sooner or later.

When he opened the back door, he was surprised to hear Menno's voice in the kitchen, and his heartbeat sped up. If Menno was here, Lorene would most likely be here, and she'd filled his thoughts ever since Thanksgiving.

He couldn't stop thinking about what his uncle said about God's timing. But as much as he hoped Jay was right, he'd decided it would indeed be best if he was only Lorene's friend. Sticking with a friendship with her would prevent more heartbreak. After all, how could she still have feelings for him after all these years? But he still wanted her in his life, and her friendship would be a tremendous blessing to him.

He found his parents and Jon sitting at the kitchen table with Lorene, Emma Grace, and Menno. They were all drinking coffee, and the room smelled of cinnamon, ginger, and freshly baked cookies.

"Ryan!" *Mamm* said. "What a nice surprise."

"Hello." He waved at everyone. When his gaze landed on Lorene, she smiled and patted the empty seat beside her. He wouldn't have expected a gesture that friendly, but he'd take it.

"Join us," Lorene said. "Emma Grace and I are practicing our Christmas *kichlin* recipes for the wedding."

Ryan's heart warmed as he moved to the sink to wash his hands. "Sounds *appeditlich*."

When he sat down beside Lorene, *Mamm* jumped up and filled a mug with coffee, then handed it to him. As he thanked her, then took a sip, his eyes landed on the variety of cookies arranged on the table.

"I hope these are up for grabs." He swiped a gingerbread cookie and took a bite.

"How do you like it?" Lorene looked hopeful.

"It's so flavorful! And I love the texture."

Emma Grace pointed to the sugar cookies. "I made those."

"They're *gut* too." Jon gazed with pride at his future bride.

Everyone made small talk as they continued to eat. Then his parents and Menno retreated to the family room, and Jon and Emma Grace excused themselves to go outdoors.

Lorene collected the mugs and set them in the sink, then started stacking leftover cookies in containers. Ryan stayed at the table, taking in her face and the stray wisps of hair escaping her *kapp*. She was still the most beautiful woman he'd ever known. How could he have been so stupid, pushing her away because of his own confusion about his future? If he'd only told her the truth, maybe they could have had a life together in Gap.

She looked at him, and her brow puckered. *"Was iss letz?"*

"Nothing is wrong." He nodded toward the table. "Could we talk?"

She hesitated. "What about?"

He smiled. "I just want to ask how you're doing. That's all."

"Oh. Okay." She set the open cookie container on the table, then filled two fresh mugs with coffee before sitting across from him.

"I haven't seen you since Thanksgiving. What's been going on in your life?" he asked.

She sighed, and her shoulders relaxed. "Mostly Emma Grace's wedding plans. The big day will be here before we know it. We have the dresses finished, and we're just about done with the decorations, but we still need to write out the invitations and start all the baking. On top of that, I need to finish making our Christmas cards. Then there's Christmas shopping, decorating . . ."

Ryan rested his hands on either side of his mug as she talked. He enjoyed the lovely sound of her voice, and he noticed she seemed to relax more as the moments went by.

He realized it suddenly felt like old times. They used to sit and talk for hours when they were a couple. They would discuss everything from the weather to friends they knew to their deepest secrets and fears—except, of course what he'd kept from her. Maybe he was romanticizing the past, but he thought of those years as the best days of his life.

"So you really like working for your *onkel*?"

He nodded, then picked out another cookie. "I do."

"Now I know you didn't want to be a farmer, but I never

thought you'd go into construction." She tilted her head as though truly interested.

Ryan set the cookie down. "I wasn't sure. But I felt like I found my passion when I went to work for Jay."

She nodded slowly as if the pieces were coming together in her mind. "Tell me about your *haus*."

He hesitated.

She leaned forward, her dark eyes shining in the propane lights. "I really want to know."

He believed her.

"Well, I built it myself. It took me about a year. I have two bathrooms, three bedrooms, and a wraparound porch."

She smiled. "It sounds lovely."

They were silent for a beat as they both sipped from their mugs. Suddenly courage welled inside him, and he reached over and touched her hand.

"Lorene, I really meant it when I said I want to be your *freind*. We have so much history together, and I want us to feel comfortable when we see each other. Is that possible?"

She swallowed and nodded. "Of course."

"Gut." He relaxed, and something seemed to pulse between them. But he pulled his hand away. "Tell me more about our duties as attendants at the wedding. I haven't been to that many of them."

Ryan lost track of time as they moved from the wedding to chatting about old friends—even times they'd spent together. He was disappointed when Menno walked in and announced it was time to leave.

As Lorene stood, she passed Ryan the containers of cookies. "Take these home."

"Are you sure?" Ryan asked as he stood.

"*Ya.* Enjoy them." She gave him a warm smile that sent heat thrumming through his veins. "I hope to see you soon."

Emma Grace and Jon appeared, too, and Ryan walked out to the porch and waved as the Bontragers climbed into Menno's buggy.

When Jon left for the barn, Ryan turned toward the door and found his mother watching him.

She tilted her head. *"Was iss letz?"*

Ryan squeezed the bridge of his nose as the truth bubbled to the surface of his soul. "I'm still in love with Lorene, *Mamm.* But I'm afraid I've missed my chance of a future with her. I wish I could somehow make things right."

She gave him a bright smile. "You just need to pray for guidance. With God, all things are possible."

Ryan nodded as hope ignited in his heart. And so did an idea for a special Christmas gift he could make for Lorene.

Lorene stared out the windshield of her father's buggy during the ride home. She couldn't stop thinking about Ryan and how easy it was to be with him today. It felt as though they'd never broken up when they talked and laughed together. She knew to the depth of her bones that she still loved him. Her eyes filled with tears as remorse whipped through her. If only she could change the past!

"So you and Ryan talked in the kitchen for a long time," Emma Grace said from the back of the buggy. "Jon even commented on how nice it was to see you two together."

"*Ya*, we've agreed to be *freinden*." *But I want so much more!*

When they arrived home, Emma Grace hurried into the house, but Lorene lingered by the buggy as her father unhitched it. She walked with him as he led the horse to the barn.

"Dat." She could see their breath in the air even inside the barn.

"*Ya*?" he asked as he opened the stall door.

"Do you believe God gives second chances?"

He gave her a knowing smile. "Are you talking about Ryan?"

She nodded as she pushed her hands into the pockets of her coat.

"*Ya*, I do." *Dat* looped his arm around her shoulders. "I have a feeling God has something special in mind for you two. You just need to open your heart and pray."

"I hope you're right."

The following Wednesday afternoon, Lorene and Emma Grace knocked on Renae's door. Lorene shivered in the cold as she held a bag of diapers and baby wipes.

The door opened, and Renae's mother smiled at them. "Hello. How are you?"

"We're fine, Sally," Lorene said as she stepped into the warm kitchen. "How are Renae and the new *boppli*?"

"They're *gut*." Sally seemed to glow, her eyes the same bright-green as her daughter's. "I can't believe little Beth is a week old already."

Renae stepped into the kitchen, holding the baby wrapped in a blanket. Although she had dark circles under her eyes, no doubt from lack of sleep, she still looked radiant. "Hi."

Lorene couldn't help but rush over. "How are you?" But she was already looking at the baby.

"I'm *gut*." Renae bent a littlc and caught her eyes. "Would you like to hold her?"

"Of course." Lorene washed her hands at the sink, then took Beth into her arms. She sank onto a kitchen chair and studied the infant, breathing in the sweet scent of baby lotion.

Emma Grace leaned over Lorene and sighed. "She's so *schee*."

"Danki." Renae sat down beside Lorene and chuckled. "She has a healthy set of lungs."

They all laughed.

"Could I help with any chores while we're here?" Emma Grace offered.

"Would you be willing to help me clean the bathrooms?" Sally asked.

"I'd be *froh* to."

"Your wedding is next week, right?"

"Ya." Her sister couldn't mask her excitement. "I can't wait. And I'll be getting married and celebrating Christmas all in one week!"

The two women left the kitchen, and Lorene returned her gaze to the newborn. She was suddenly overwhelmed with longing. If only she and Ryan—

"Are you ready for the wedding?" Renae asked.

Lorene nodded, but then tears filled her eyes.

Renae touched her arm. *"Was iss letz?"*

"I think I made a big mistake breaking off my engagement to Ryan."

"What do you mean?"

"The last time I was here, I told you what he confessed to

me. If only I had let him tell me the truth back then. And now, as I've been planning this wedding with *mei schweschder* and spending time with him again, I can't help but imagine the life we could have had together. And if God had blessed us, we could have had *kinner* by now too." She looked up at Renae as tears trickled down her hot cheeks. "At least we've become *freinden* again."

"But you still have feelings for him."

"*Ya*. In fact, I still love him. Maybe I never stopped." Lorene looked down at Beth and touched her little hand. "He's the love of my life. And I want this. I want a family. But I want it with him, and I'm afraid it's too late."

"No, it's not." Renae reached over and squeezed Lorene's shoulder. "Maybe God really is giving you and Ryan a second chance. Maybe Emma Grace's wedding is part of that plan too. You can't give up hope. You're only thirty." She laughed. "I know it's unusual, but I just had my first *boppli* at thirty. Ryan's sister, Joyce, was even a little older. There's still plenty of time for you."

Lorene stared at her. "But why would *Ryan* give me a second chance after the way I hurt him?"

Her friend gave her a knowing smile. "Because maybe he still loves you too."

Lorene nodded, but in her heart, she doubted that could be true.

9

"Oh my goodness!" Emma Grace grabbed Lorene's hand the morning of the wedding as they stood in her bedroom. "I can't believe the day is here. I'm getting married."

Lorene gave her younger sister a hug as a whirlwind of emotions rushed over her—happiness, excitement, and nervousness, and then suddenly, overwhelming grief for their mother. She bit her lower lip and held back her threatening tears. She couldn't cry today. She had to be strong for Emma Grace.

"If only *Mamm* were here." Emma Grace's voice was thin as she spoke Lorene's thoughts.

"I know." Lorene touched her chest. "But she's always with us in our hearts, right?"

Emma Grace smiled, then wiped at her eyes. *"Ya."*

"You look so *schee.*" Lorene admired the hunter-green dress Emma Grace wore and then touched the ties on her prayer covering before giving a little laugh. More emotions had bubbled in her chest like water from a spring. She sniffed as tears filled her eyes.

"Don't cry." Emma Grace touched Lorene's shoulder. "And you look *schee* too." She raised her eyebrows. "Just wait until Ryan sees you. I have a feeling you'll be the next bride."

"No, no, no." Lorene shook her head as her stomach fluttered at the thought of marrying Ryan. "Our time is behind us."

"I think you're wrong. I know you haven't wanted to talk about Ryan, but Jon and I both think he's going to ask you to give him another chance."

She almost told her sister she loved Ryan and prayed *she* would have another chance with *him*. But she held back. Now would be the worst time to discuss her problems, taking away from Emma Grace's happy day.

Lorene backed away from her sister and glanced out the window, where a line of horses and buggies moved down the road toward their farm like a parade. She spotted Ryan's cousin Pete and five of his friends from his youth group standing ready to work as the hostlers, taking care of the horses. After the buggy drivers unhitched their horses, the boys would secure the animals in the barns and then feed them around noon.

"Your guests are arriving, so we need to get downstairs." Lorene spun toward Emma Grace and found her fingering her white apron. "You have no reason to be *naerfich*."

Emma Grace scrunched her nose. "Are you sure?"

"Of course." Lorene tilted her head. "What are you worried about?"

"I just keep thinking about what you said about Jon and me having dated for only six months. What if we're not ready? What if this is a mistake?" When her lower lip trembled, Lorene rushed to stand before her, feeling a stab of shame over the reservations she'd expressed.

"*Ach, mei liewe.* I was so wrong." She shook her head and rested her hands on her sister's shoulders. "I can see the love between you and Jon when you look at each other. Jon cherishes you, and God will bless this union. I want you to have the long and *froh* marriage I've always dreamed of."

"Danki." Emma Grace pulled Lorene into a tight hug, nearly squeezing all the air from her lungs. "*Ich liebe dich.* And I'm certain God has planned the same happiness for you."

Lorene sniffed, then started toward the door as she wiped away a tear. "We need to get downstairs so you can greet your guests."

After they'd descended the stairs, she stepped into the kitchen, where Jon's aunt Ann and several women from their church district were preparing the noon meal. Lorene smiled at Ann and nodded at the other women.

Then she entered the family room, and her heart seemed to trip over itself when she spotted Ryan standing with Jon. He was so handsome dressed in his Sunday black suit and white shirt. She hadn't seen him dressed that way in five years. She recalled how they'd shared hundreds of Sunday services together as children and then adults.

Ryan turned toward her, and his eyes lit up as his lips turned up in a warm smile. "Hi."

"Hi." She smiled up at him.

"You look *schee.*" His voice was low and husky, sending a shiver dancing up her spine.

"Danki." And you look handsome.

"Are you ready to marry off our siblings?" He nodded toward where Jon and Emma Grace waited for them by the sofa.

"I guess so."

Ryan made a sweeping gesture. "After you."

Lorene stood between Ryan and Emma Grace as the four of them greeted the guests. She frequently snuck peeks at Ryan, enjoying the sound of his voice and the brightness of his smile. Emma Grace's words about how she and Jon were certain Ryan wanted to try again echoed in her mind. Oh, how she longed for them to be right! But even if he did, her ultimate question remained. After all this time, would he come to love her again—enough to marry her?

Emma Grace and Jon had invited friends from throughout Lancaster County, and she thought the line of guests dressed in their Sunday clothes might never end. But at least everything went along according to tradition. Once inside, the female guests ascended the stairs to deposit their bonnets and shawls on Emma Grace's or Lorene's bed. They also left gifts there, which were usually household items for the bride and tools for the groom. Then, while the women remained inside the house for a while, the men congregated outside.

A few minutes before eight, Emma Grace leaned over to Lorene. "It's time for Jon and me to meet with the ministers." Her words came out in a trembling whisper.

Lorene gave her hand a gentle squeeze. "Everything will be fine." She and Ryan both stood with Emma Grace and Jon. Then she glanced out the window and watched the women who'd been in the house and the men who'd been waiting outside start to file into the barn for the service.

The front door opened, and the bishop, deacon, and minister walked in.

"Are you ready?" the bishop asked Jon and Emma Grace.

They nodded, then followed the three men upstairs to one of the bedrooms. The sound of their footsteps echoed in the stairwell as fading voices signaled the women in the kitchen were leaving for the barn too.

Lorene hugged her arms to her middle as she glanced around the family room, taking in the greenery and poinsettias she and Emma Grace had placed there to decorate for the season.

"Can you believe Christmas is only three days away?"

Lorene glanced behind her as Ryan approached. "No." She shook her head. "I managed to mail out my Christmas cards last week despite all the wedding chaos, but I've been more focused on the wedding than Christmas."

"And the *haus* is decorated"—he jammed his thumb toward the kitchen—"And I know I spotted boxes of Christmas *kichlin*."

Lorene nodded. "That's mostly because Emma Grace wanted a Christmas theme for the reception. Otherwise, I'm not sure we would have had the time to decorate." She stared up into his blue eyes, and she longed to ask him if he still loved her. But her courage fizzled as the fear of rejection took over her soul.

"Jon was *naerfich* when I saw him this morning, but I calmed him down."

"Emma Grace was too. I told her everything would be fine."

Ryan nodded, then seemed to study her. She could almost feel his thoughts turning in his mind. He opened his mouth to say something, but then he just started making small talk, telling her how his mother had been decorating for Christmas too.

"Sounds like they're heading down," he finally said.

Lorene followed him to the bottom of the steps, where they met Jon and Emma Grace as the three men left through the kitchen doorway.

"It's time," Emma Grace told them, excitement filling her pretty face as she looked up at Jon. "I'm ready."

Jon gazed down at her adoringly. "I am too."

Lorene's heart seemed to turn over, and she couldn't stop from turning to Ryan. When he gave her an intense expression, her body tingled with adrenaline.

Ryan held his hand out. "It's time for us to walk down the aisle together."

Lorene's mouth dried as she threaded her fingers with his. The familiar touch of his hand weakened her, and her limbs felt like noodles for a moment. Then she found her strength as they walked together, leading Emma Grace and Jon to the barn where the congregation awaited their arrival.

Lorene's legs wobbled as she and Ryan walked down the narrow aisle as the congregation slowly sang an opening hymn. Four matching cane chairs sat at the front of the barn waiting for them.

When they reached the chairs, Lorene faced Ryan. She folded her hands in front of her and held her breath as her gaze tangled with his. Emma Grace and Jon joined them, and then they all sat down in unison.

Lorene did her best to focus on the ceremony, but she couldn't stop herself from stealing peeks at Ryan. She glanced at Emma Grace beside her and silently marveled at how mature and beautiful she looked. She peered over at Jon and found him gazing lovingly at her sister. She knew in her heart that this marriage was truly right and blessed by God, and she smiled.

She turned back to the bishop as he lectured concerning the apostle Paul's instructions for marriage included in 1 Corinthians and Ephesians. But then her mind wandered, and she imagined sitting in front of this congregation for her own wedding. Would she ever have the chance to be a bride, a wife, a mother?

Her eyes betrayed her, and she looked at Ryan. He turned and looked at her at the same time, and a smile turned up the corner of his lips, sending her heart into a wild gallop. How she longed to know if Ryan was imagining his own wedding day, his own bride. *Her.*

Lorene looked down at her lap as the bishop instructed Emma Grace and Jon on how to run a godly household. She listened as he then moved on to a sermon on the story of Sarah and Tobias from the intertestamental book of Tobit. The sermon took forty-five minutes, and when it was over, the bishop looked back and forth between Emma Grace and Jon. "Now here are two in one faith—Emma Grace Bontrager and Jonathan Lee Lapp."

Lorene held back happy tears as the bishop turned to the congregation.

"Do any of you know any scriptural reason for the couple not to be married?" he asked, then waited for a beat before looking at the couple again. "If it is your desire to be married, you may in the name of the Lord come forth."

Jon took Emma Grace's hand in his, and they stood before the bishop to take their vows.

Lorene glanced at Ryan and found his intense eyes sparkling in the low light of the barn. A chill ripped through her, and she couldn't take her eyes off him.

The bishop addressed Jon first. "Can you confess, brother, that you accept this our sister as your wife, and that you will not leave her until death separates you? And do you believe that this is from the Lord and that you have come thus far by your faith and prayers?"

"Ya."

Then the bishop looked at Emma Grace. "Can you confess, sister, that you accept this our brother as your husband, and that you will not leave him until death separates you? And do you believe that this is from the Lord and that you have come thus far by your faith and prayers?"

"Ya."

Lorene glanced at Ryan and found him still staring at her, sending her senses whirling. What was he thinking?

Then the bishop looked at Jon again. "Because you have confessed, brother, that you want to take this our sister for your wife, do you promise to be loyal to her and care for her if she may have adversity, affliction, sickness, weakness, or faintheartedness—which are many infirmities that are among poor mankind—as is appropriate for a Christian, God-fearing husband?"

"Ya."

The bishop asked the same of Emma Grace, and she responded with a strong "*Ya*."

While Jon and Emma Grace held hands, the bishop read "A Prayer for Those about to Be Married" from an Amish prayer book called the *Christenpflict*. Then he announced, "Go forth in the name of the Lord. You are now *mann* and *fraa*."

Tears trailed down Lorene's cheeks. She was grateful she'd stuck a handful of tissues in her pocket. She wiped her eyes and glanced at Ryan, finding emotion flickering over his face as well. How she longed to read his thoughts!

Emma Grace and Jon sat down for another sermon and another prayer, and Lorene willed herself to not look at Ryan. After the bishop recited the Lord's Prayer, the congregation stood, and the three-hour service ended with the singing of another hymn.

And then it was official—Emma Grace and Jon were married! Lorene thought she might choke on the lump forming in her throat. Her baby sister was Jon's wife! She was so happy for them.

But at the same time, her heart swelled with hope. Maybe she and Ryan had a chance.

10

Ryan felt as if he might explode in a riot of emotions—longing and regret but also hope and, yes, love. He'd spent the entire service imagining what it would be like to stand in front of this congregation and take Lorene as his wife. He knew to the depth of his soul that he wanted to marry her, have a family with her, grow old with her.

But did she want that future with him? Could she love him and give him another chance?

He needed to know, and he needed to know *now*. He'd wasted too many years without her. And he wanted their future to start today, not tomorrow.

Keeping with tradition, younger members of the congregation filed out of the barn first, followed by the wedding party. Ryan held his hand out to Lorene, and she threaded her warm fingers with his. Then they walked together to the barn exit with Jon and Emma Grace close behind them.

When they reached the outside, the cold December air hit Ryan like a wall. He glanced up at the sky and found a bright, crystal-blue sky dotted with white, puffy clouds. Lorene took a step toward the house, and he gently pulled her toward him.

"Wait. I need to talk to you."

"Now?" She squinted up at him, and she looked adorable as other women stepped around her, headed toward the house.

"*Ya*, this can't wait." He knew the men were already converting the benches into tables in the barn, but he couldn't help them. Not now.

He looked toward the pasture. "Can we walk over there? I promise it won't take long. We can go get our coats if you want."

"No. I'll be fine."

Still holding his hand, she steered him toward the pasture. When they stopped, she looked up at him. "What do you want to talk about?"

He took a deep breath, and then his emotions broke free. "Lorene, spending time with you during these past couple of months has been wonderful, and it's made me realize just how much I've missed you." He cupped his hand to her cheek, and she leaned into his touch.

"Lorene, I'm so sorry I let you down five years ago. You had a right to know how I was feeling about staying on the farm, even though I didn't know how to tell *mei dat* how I felt. By not being honest with you, I hurt you, and I let our relationship crumble. If I had just told you, I think you would have understood even then. We could have built a future. It's the biggest mistake I've ever made, and I regret it to the depth of my core."

She heaved out a deep sigh as her eyes sparkled with tears. "I'm sorry for not realizing you were making excuses only because you were going through something. I should have been honest with you about my doubts rather than going on about the *haus* and breaking our engagement without giving you a chance to explain. I'm sorry for hurting you and for giving up on you. You deserved so much better."

"But I'm the one who pushed you away, and then it was too late." He hesitated, and then said, "I love you. I've never stopped loving you. You're the only *maedel* I've ever imagined in my future. I'm ready to beg you to give me another chance." His body went weak as he awaited her response.

She sniffed and touched his cheek. "I've never stopped loving you either. I've missed you all these years."

"Does that mean you'll give me another chance?" he asked, excitement buzzing through every pore.

"*Ya*, it does." She gave a little laugh. "I'm so *froh* you're willing to give our relationship another chance."

"I'm *froh* you're willing too." Leaning down, he brushed his lips over hers, and he thought he must be dreaming. But the heat rushing through his veins was as real as the feel of her lips against his.

As he deepened the kiss, his body seemed to come alive, and at that moment he was certain they belonged together. He needed to talk to her father as soon as possible.

"*Frehlicher Grischtdaag!*" Lorene called when she came downstairs on Christmas Eve afternoon to find Emma Grace and Jon together on the sofa, drinking hot chocolate and holding hands. Lorene smiled as she recalled her sister's wedding.

The past few days had been a blur. After Ryan told her he loved her and wanted to date again, they'd celebrated with their friends and family, eating delicious food and visiting until late in the night. The next day the Lapp family and a few friends helped clean up the barn and house. Then Ryan again stayed late into the night. They'd talked and stolen a few kisses, and Lorene was so happy she couldn't stop smiling.

She slipped into the kitchen and peeked out the window just as a horse and buggy moved up the driveway. Her heart leapt as she grabbed her coat and rushed out the back door.

"Merry Christmas!" she called as she hurried down the porch steps.

"*Frehlicher Grischtdaag!*" Ryan greeted, then pulled her into his arms for a hug. "I have a gift for you." He reached into the buggy and brought out a small bag.

She opened it, then pulled out a trinket box shaped like a small house. She gasped as she ran her fingers over it. "It's so *schee*."

"Open it."

She lifted the lid and found a silver key. She picked it up and ran her fingers over the cool metal. "What's this?"

"It's a *haus* key." Something that looked like nervousness flickered over his face as he took the box from her and placed it on the buggy seat. Then he took her hands in his and swallowed. "Years ago, I was supposed to build you a *haus*. I know it's not the same, but I want to share the *haus* I have now with you. *Mei haus* in Gap."

She gasped, and tears blurred her vision.

"I've asked your *dat*'s permission for this. Lorene, will you do me the honor of becoming *mei fraa*?"

She launched herself into his arms with a dizzying happiness. "*Ya*, Ryan! I will!"

Cupping his hands to her cheeks, he leaned down and gently kissed her. A quiver of desire danced up her spine, and she closed her eyes and enjoyed the feel of his lips against hers.

When they pulled apart, she looked up at him. "A couple of months ago, *mei dat* said we never know how much time God has planned for us here, and he's right. But he always has a plan while we *are* here. I don't think he ever wanted us to suffer the pain of breaking up, but I've realized my family needed me with them after we lost *Mamm*."

"And I realize leaving the farm was the right thing to do for everyone. Elias, for one. And I was able to help *mei onkel* Jay with his business when he needed it." He leaned down and kissed her again, and she melted into him.

When she felt something wet and cold hit her face, she looked up and laughed. Snow fell like pretty glitter. "Look!"

Ryan looked up and smiled. "This is the best Christmas ever. I'm so grateful for our love—our evergreen love." Then he kissed her again.

Closing her eyes, Lorene smiled against his lips. Her heart felt like a flower opening its bloom toward the sun. She was grateful for their love as well. And that God had given them this second chance.

Acknowledgments

As always, I'm grateful for my loving family, including my mother, Lola Goebelbecker; my husband, Joe; and my sons, Zac and Matt.

I'm also grateful for my special Amish friend who patiently answers my endless stream of questions. You're a blessing in my life.

Thank you to my wonderful church family at Morning Star Lutheran in Matthews, North Carolina, for your encouragement, prayers, love, and friendship. You all mean so much to my family and me.

Thank you to Zac Weikal and the fabulous members of my Bakery Bunch! I'm so grateful for your friendship and your excitement about my books. You all are awesome!

To my agent, Natasha Kern—I can't thank you enough for your guidance, advice, and friendship. You are a tremendous blessing in my life.

Thank you to my amazing editor, Jocelyn Bailey, for your friendship and guidance. I'm grateful to each and every person at HarperCollins Christian Publishing who helped make this book a reality.

I'm also grateful to editor Jean Bloom, who helped me polish and refine the story. Jean, you are a master at connecting the dots and filling in the gaps. I'm so happy we can continue to work together!

Thank you most of all to God—for giving me the inspiration and the words to glorify you. I'm grateful and humbled that you've chosen this path for me.

Discussion Questions

1. Lorene's Christmas family traditions include making Christmas cards, decorating, and baking. What Christmas traditions does your family have?
2. Lorene was hurt five years ago when Ryan failed to build the house she expected, causing her to believe he didn't love her enough to marry her. She broke up with him, not realizing the real problem was Ryan's struggle with being a dairy farmer. Can you relate to Ryan's struggle? Or can you relate to Lorene's giving up on him? Why or why not?
3. Lorene's father tells her that God gives second chances. Do you agree? Have you ever experienced a second chance in your life?
4. Which character can you identify with the most? Which character seems to carry the most emotional stake in the story? Lorene, Ryan, Emma Grace and Jon, or someone else?
5. At the end of the story, Ryan and Lorene realize they're

still in love and want to marry. What do you think made them change their minds about each other?

6. What role did the wedding play in the relationships throughout the story?
7. Some people say Christmas has become too commercialized with too much focus on material items and not enough on preparing to celebrate the coming of Christ. What are your thoughts about this? Share them with the group.

Holiday of Hope

Kelly Irvin

To my son Nicholas, whose classroom antics provided fodder for Tommy's story. You've always marched to the beat of your own drum and I love you for it.

Praise be to the God and Father of our Lord Jesus Christ, the Father of compassion and the God of all comfort, who comforts us in all our troubles, so that we can comfort those in any trouble with the comfort we ourselves receive from God. For just as we share abundantly in the sufferings of Christ, so also our comfort abounds through Christ.

2 Corinthians 1:3–5 NIV

1

Henry Lufkin never could have imagined this.

He stared down at the boy. A scowl on his freckled face, his arms crossed, the boy stared back.

The letter said his name was Tommy—as if Henry wouldn't know the name of his best friend's only child. It also said he was ten. Time had flown by so quickly. Tommy was scrawny and looked younger. In fact, he looked like a skinny, bedraggled runt. His dishwater-blond hair needed cutting, and his faded denim pants were too short.

The boy himself had said nothing so far.

They were standing outside the Libby Amtrak train station on this first day of September with its cool breeze and sunshine, not talking, mostly taking turns staring at their boots and the passing cars. The air reeked of diesel, burnt oil, and too many people. It had only been a few hours, but Henry already missed the clean, fresh scent of pine on a breeze wafting from the mountains in Montana's Kootenai National Forest.

Only Dodger, Henry's aging mutt-hound, spoke—if his cheerful barks and enthusiastic tail thumping could be called speaking. Dodger liked trains, and he liked little boys.

His forehead furled in fine wrinkles, Tommy yanked his fisted hands up to his chest as if afraid Dodger would bite his fingers. What boy didn't like dogs?

You agreed to do this. The little angel sitting on Henry's shoulder whispered in his ear. *So get on with it.*

What do you know about raising a child? A widower taking care of an orphan—ha! This has disaster written all over it. That guy was on his other shoulder—a being Henry suspected was of a different persuasion. *You're perfectly happy living the solitary life in the most beautiful place in the world.*

Sometimes a man had no choice. When asked to step up, he stepped up. Henry stuck out his hand. "I'm Henry. The *hund* is Dodger. He won't bite you. He likes you."

Tommy eyed Henry's hand with a sullen expression. He sniffed. Finally, he offered his own. His fingers were sticky, and he had dirt under his fingernails. "I know who you are."

His hand dropped and inched toward Dodger's head. Dodger nudged it with an excited yip. Tommy backed away.

Maybe he'd never had a dog. Every boy should have a dog. "How was the trip?"

"The man in the seat next to me snored." The boy's soft Kentucky drawl roused the usual nostalgic yearning in Henry. He hadn't been home in four years. Tommy likely had never been farther than a few miles from Munsford in his short life. "'Bout broke my eardrum."

"I'm sorry about your *aenti* Anna Mae."

Tommy's shoulders hunched. He ducked his head.

Maybe they should talk about this when they'd had time to get to know each other better. "Are you hungry?"

"I could eat, I guess." The boy's feigned indifference didn't match the way he stared hungrily at the grease-stained bag Henry held up. "It's been a stretch since I ate the sandwiches Doris made me."

Doris was the woman who kept Tommy after Anna Mae died until he could be sent to live with Henry. Tommy talked like a small adult. The story told in the letter lent credence to the fact that Tommy's life had forced him to grow up quicker than most.

"I got us some burgers and fries. And those little fried cinnamon apple pies. I like pie. We'll eat them in the van." Henry waved toward Calvin Little's pristine blue minivan. "Don't forget your backpack. It's an hour's drive to Kootenai."

"What kind of word is Kootenai?" Tommy grabbed a battered gray suitcase and hefted his backpack onto his shoulder. "Does it mean something?"

"It's Indian. One of the tribes here is called Kootenai. It's also the language they speak. Or used to speak. Only a few do now."

The suitcase bumped along the sidewalk as Tommy scrambled to keep up with Henry's long legs. He forced himself to slow down. From now on, he would have to think about another person's well-being. Was the boy hungry? Was he tired? Sick? Did he need clothes? What about school? School started on Monday. And then there would be *rumspringa* and girls and baptism.

What had Henry done to himself?

"Can I ask you another question?"

Did all kids ask this many questions? Henry's beloved quiet evenings filled only with crackling flames in the fireplace during winter and birds chattering outside his open windows in summer disappeared into a murky future filled with endless jawing.

At least Tommy would be in school during the day. The teacher would know how to deal with this new scholar.

Henry slid open the van door and stepped back so Dodger could hop in. "Anything."

"Did you ever get a new *fraa*?"

Almost anything. The boy knew about his first wife. The thought that he and Anna Mae had talked about Henry's loss stung. It was private. No one's business. "After my first *fraa* died, I never thought about marrying again."

"Everybody dies."

Tommy had reason to feel that way. The idea wasn't foreign to Henry either. "I reckon."

"Are you my *daed*?"

"What? *Nee. Nee.*"

Tommy dropped his suitcase on the curb with a thump. "Then what am I doing here?"

"Josiah was your *daed*. You know that."

Tommy's mother died in childbirth. Josiah died of leukemia five years later, leaving Tommy in the care of Josiah's only sister, a teacher who never married. Now she was gone, taken by some kind of cancer.

What was God's plan for Tommy in all of this? Somehow it involved Henry. In God's time they would both see how their lives fit together. In the meantime it was anyone's guess.

"Then what am I doing here?" Tommy's plaintive voice rose. "Why couldn't I stay with my friends Elias or Moses?"

Both families had offered to take him. Plain folks were like that. What was one more mouth to feed? "Because this is what your father wanted." Why, Henry had no idea. The letter from Josiah's sister had arrived the previous week. When Henry called to speak to her, she had already passed. Tommy's one remaining family member was gone. "It's getting late. You've been on the road since yesterday and probably want a good night's sleep before church tomorrow."

"I'm not going to church."

One leg up to climb in the van, Henry paused. "What?"

"I don't believe in *Gott* anymore."

Henry exchanged glances with Calvin. The driver shrugged and grinned. "Now that's something I ain't seen before. An atheist Amish." He revved the engine. "Don't tell me God doesn't have a sense of humor. You got your work cut out for you."

Henry had inherited an atheist Plain boy.

That didn't sound like something the *Ordnung* allowed.

2

Leesa Yoder stared out at a sea of expectant faces. Eighteen pairs of eyes watched her. They'd been waiting for her to say something since she tapped the bell on her desk to signal quiet. She was in charge, but her mind remained blank. A cool September breeze filtered through open windows. Her sweaty palms gripped her fresh pale-blue dress. She inhaled the scent of chalk, fresh paint, and first-day-of-school anticipation.

Her family, the scholars' parents, and the school board thought she could do this. She *could* do this.

She opened her mouth. Her throat closed. No words came out. First-day nerves like prickly burrs pierced her. *Come on, come on. Say something.*

"Teacher, are you going to read some verses?" Her oldest scholar, eighth grader Amy Plank, raised her hand and voiced the question they must all be thinking. "Mercy always started with a devotion."

There it was. Two minutes into her new job as teacher in the West Kootenai parochial school and one of her charges had already reminded her that her younger sister had held this post first. Mercy was tall to Leesa's short. Mercy loved to read, camp, hike, and hunt. Leesa would rather quilt, bake, and can.

They were opposites in every way.

Mercy loved teaching. Now she loved being married.

"*Jah.* Of course." Leesa's voice quivered. She cleared her throat. "We'll start with Psalm 1."

"*Jah*, that's a *gut* one," Diane Moser volunteered. "Mercy helped us memorize it."

Maybe they should start with something else. Uncertainty flooded Leesa. She never should have agreed to take her sister's place. She belonged at home, baking bread, washing clothes, and taking care of babies.

Ian's babies.

Even after almost a year the pain caused by this unwelcome thought hadn't abated one iota.

Her scholars wiggled in their seats. Charlie Moser whispered something to his friend Joshua Miller. Joshua giggled. The first graders, on their first day of school, doodled on their spelling books. One of them, she didn't remember his name, laid his head down as if to nap.

"Teacher?" Amy wrinkled her nose. "Are you sick? You look sort of green."

In a way Leesa did have a sickness. She had a broken heart. Such a silly notion, according to her mother, who said things happened for a reason. It was better to know sooner rather than later that Ian wasn't right for her. As far as Leesa was concerned, it had been later. She'd given her heart to Ian. He'd returned it like a piece of clothing that didn't fit and then made a mad dash to Kansas after wildfires devastated their tiny Montana community.

"Don't dwell on it." Another piece of advice from Mother. She had many of them. It was time to move on. Teaching was one way of doing that. Mother and Father agreed. Leesa had no choice but to go along to get along.

Resolute, she clapped her hands. "No talking unless I ask you a question. And raise your hand before you speak. Those are the rules."

She grabbed a piece of chalk and turned to the chalkboard where she'd dutifully listed the first arithmetic assignments. At the very top, she wrote her new rules.

A steady buzz continued to build behind her.

She whirled. "Stop talking."

The room fell silent.

Esther Mason jumped to her feet and shrieked. "A spider! A spider!"

The boys roared with laughter. Molly Plank climbed onto her chair. Charlie rushed across the room, scooped up the spider, and held it up for everyone to see. "Just a *bopli*, you fraidy-cat." He waved it toward Molly. "He's my new pet. Want to hold him?"

"I'm not a fraidy-cat." Tears trickling down her freckled face, Molly stomped her feet. "I'm *not* a fraidy-cat."

"That's not very nice." Molly's older sister, Carrie, rushed to her defense. "Don't tease her."

"I'm not teasing her." Charlie stuck out his tongue. "I'm sharing with her."

A chorus of high, excited voices filled the one-room schoolhouse.

"Stop. Stop! Everyone hush. Right now!" Leesa lurched into the fray. "Name-calling is also against the rules. Talking is against the rules."

No one seemed to heed her rules.

"What's going on here?"

The deep voice boomed from the back of the room. Leesa tore her gaze from her latest failure to find that Henry Lufkin stood at the back of the classroom, a small boy at his side.

"Nothing. A spider. It's . . . nothing." Her face hot with embarrassment, Leesa raised her voice over the cacophony. "Just a moment."

She clapped her hands. "Silence. Silence! Back in your seats now."

Blessedly, the noise subsided.

Leesa sucked in air. "Third through eighth grade, take out your notebooks and write fifty times, 'I will not talk in class.' Diane, help the little ones practice writing their names. The next scholar to talk out of turn will receive black marks on his or her report card."

To her surprise, they obeyed.

Leesa arranged her face in what she hoped was a teacherly expression and strode to the back of the room. "How can I help you?"

"This is Tommy Bontrager. He's ten. He's new to the area."

Leesa surveyed the boy. He surveyed his shoes. Henry nudged him. "Say hello to the teacher, Tommy."

Tommy's gaze flitted over Leesa's shoulder. He had beautiful blue eyes with long pale lashes. What she could see of his hair under his hat was dark blond. Her fingers itched to give him a decent haircut. "Tommy, my name's Leesa. I'm new too."

Tommy hunched his shoulders. "I can tell."

"Hey, that's not nice." Henry laid his big, tanned hand on the boy's shoulder. "Everybody has a bad day."

As if he knew. Was it simply first-day jitters or the first in a long line of bad days? Leesa kept that thought to herself. "Why don't you have a seat next to David. He's a fifth grader. He's the one with the red hair." Leesa pointed out the scholar. "We're a little behind today, but we'll get started as soon as I talk to Henry."

Tommy clutched his book bag and lunch box to his chest. "Do I have to?"

"We talked about this." Something flashed in Henry's face, but the tone of his deep bass didn't change. "You have to go to church. You have to go to *schul*. Sometimes you have to take a bath. It's what *kinner* your age do."

Scowling, Tommy clomped past Leesa without saying good-bye to Henry.

"I walked with him this morning so he would know his way." Henry shoved his hat back. His expression eased. In fact, he looked relieved. "Maybe you can ask the Schrock *kinner* to guide him to my cabin after school. It's on their way."

"You were late. *Schul* starts at eight thirty." Leesa cringed inwardly. Her words were true, and wouldn't a teacher point this out to a parent? Children were expected to be on time. *"Discipline start to finish."* That's what Mercy had said. *"Start to finish."* Still, Leesa was afraid she sounded surly. "It's important to start off on the right foot."

"I didn't know." Henry drew himself up tall. He towered over Leesa. A frown deepened the lines on his acne-scarred face. "I'm new at this."

So new Leesa had never seen him with a child before. He couldn't have a child. He wasn't even married. Henry was an enigma to Leesa. He and Andy Lambright were good friends. Andy was married to one of Mercy's closest friends. Henry was older than all of them. Maybe twenty-six or twenty-seven. He never went to singings, and he didn't talk much. Mostly he seemed to stare at the mountains with his mournful jasper eyes as if looking for someone or something. "I didn't know you had a child."

"I don't."

Leesa waited for him to fill in the blanks. The silence stretched. *What would Mercy do?* "He didn't want to come to *schul*. It might help me to know why."

"He lived with his *aenti* in Kentucky. She died. So he came to live with me."

"When?"

"Friday."

"So he hasn't had time to adjust. I'll keep that in mind."

Leesa tried to sound sure of herself. She had something in common with Tommy. She hadn't wanted to come to school today either. In fact, she'd pulled the quilt over her head in the dark before dawn and prayed God would give her another choice. Mother's voice urging her to rise and shine had forced her from her bed. Mother had made banana chocolate chip pancakes to celebrate and packed Leesa's lunch for her. Even her siblings Hope and Job, who numbered among her scholars, had cheered her on.

"It'll take a firm hand." Henry's tone left no doubt he saw that as a problem for her. "I didn't know you were teaching."

"Mercy and Caleb got married."

"*Jah*, I guess I didn't make the connection." Now that he had, he didn't seem very happy about it. "Like I said, he'll require a firm hand. They all will."

"I'm capable of maintaining discipline." She drew herself up to her full height. It didn't help that she never grew beyond five feet four inches. "Mercy gave me pointers, and I've read the *Blackboard Bulletin* articles on how to organize the grades—"

"Just don't let them see you're scared."

What did he know about teaching? Or how Leesa felt? "I'm not scared."

"Your hands are shaking, and you're sweating even though it's cool in here. It's September and summer is gone for good."

"Don't you have a job you should be at?"

Henry looked loath to leave Tommy. He clearly didn't trust her.

"I'll make sure he gets home." Leesa waved both hands in a shooing motion toward the door. "Go on."

Henry's eyebrows rose. His steely gaze raked over her. "I'll come by for him."

"You'll make it harder for him to fit in with the other *kinner*."

"Walking home with the teacher won't do the same?"

He obviously didn't remember his school days. "It's considered an honor to walk the teacher home, but most of the kids ride their bikes."

His rugged face filled with uncertainty. "Should I get him a bike? I saw a lot of them out there." He jerked his thumb toward the door. "Now that I think about it, I see *kinner* riding them all over the place."

"That's up to you, but it gets them home faster and they like it. They burn off energy after sitting all day. Don't worry about it today. I'll get him home."

"As you wish."

He was out the door before Leesa could remind him of one basic fact she'd learned over the last year since the wildfires turned her life upside down. Most people didn't get their wish.

She certainly hadn't.

3

"What do you mean 'out of control'?"

"Just what I said." Henry picked up a piece of sandpaper and gripped the bottom rung of the chair he was working on. Caleb Hostetler didn't pause from his work of using a draw knife to peel the outer bark from a lodgepole pine log that would soon be part of a table. Henry's closest friend could talk and build beautiful furniture in Montana Woodwork's warehouse without missing a beat. Henry tried to do the same. "*Kinner* were crying and laughing and talking. I never saw anything like it in a Plain *schul* before."

"It was Leesa's first day." Caleb picked up the pine log and studied it with a critical eye. "Mercy said she was nervous. She'll get the hang of it."

"Tommy dug in his heels and didn't want to go. We were late. She acted like we'd broken the Golden Rule."

Henry had shared Anna Mae Bontrager's letter with Caleb and no one else.

"You're criticizing her for not keeping eighteen *kinner* under control when you couldn't get one small *bu* to the *schul* on time?" Caleb's chuckle wasn't unkind. "It sounds like the plank is in your eye."

"I don't know what Anna Mae was doing with Tommy, but he's not like any ten-year-old Plain *bu* I've ever met." Tommy refused to bow his head for grace before their meals. He balked at taking a bath. Yet this morning he'd made coffee, bacon, toast, and scrambled eggs for both of them before Henry climbed out of bed. He also helped himself to a cup of coffee with more milk and sugar than coffee. "He has some strange ideas about things, but he can cook and he knows how to sew on buttons, so that's something."

"He spent most of his life with a single woman who had no family. Did you ask him about her?"

"He's not talking."

Other than to reject God, baths, and fried eggplant. In that order.

"You two should do well together, then."

Henry ignored Caleb's jab and low rumbling laugh. There was a reason he preferred Dodger's company to that of people. Dodger didn't argue with him about God's existence or complain about his food. He might not be a fan of baths, but he subjected himself to a hosing off whenever he rolled in some dead, stinky critter.

So what if Henry liked hunting and fishing by himself? So what if he was relieved that summer was over and his job as a guide for tourists who wanted to hike and hunt in the Montana mountains had tapered off. He could work part-time at Montana Woodwork and hike, camp, fish, and hunt on his own. Until now.

"What Tommy needs is a *mudder*." Caleb straightened and stretched both hands toward the ceiling. He rubbed his neck and cocked his head from side to side. "*Gott* has a way of leading us to water, doesn't He? Now you just have to drink."

"Here we go again." Ever since Henry revealed to his new friends that his first wife had died in a buggy accident, they'd been angling to set him up with someone new. Four years had passed since Vivian's death. Henry's pain had eased. Memories were more sweet than bitter. A simple contentment with his lot had settled in. Caleb called it inertia. Henry called it life. "Don't presume you know what *Gott*'s plan is. I don't know why Josiah wanted me to care for his *suh*, but I'm willing to stand in the gap for him. I'm not reading anything else into this."

"So what did you think of Leesa, beside the fact that she might not be a *gut* teacher?"

"Did Mercy put you up to this? Leave the matchmaking to her. The role is ill-fitting on your big frame." Henry gently rolled the chair to the opposite side so he could reach another rung. "You've put on some weight since you married."

"I'm eating for two." Caleb dropped the knife and put up both arms like a wrestler. He was a tall man, once lanky, with sandy-brown hair and pale-blue eyes. These days he always seemed to be smiling. A happy marriage did that to a man. "Plus, Mercy's a *gut* cook. She's finally getting used to being at home all the time, but she still bakes more than two people can eat."

"Mercy's the one eating for two. Feel free to bring some of those baked goods to work. You saw at church how skinny Tommy is."

"I did. Stop changing the subject." Caleb inspected his log again. It had a perfect skip-peeled texture created by leaving a layer of inner bark. He laid it aside and picked up another log. "It's been a year since Ian bailed on Leesa and moved back to Kansas. She should be ready to move on."

Ian had been Caleb's roommate in a bachelor cabin that burned to the ground during the Caribou Fire. According to Caleb, Ian led Leesa to believe they would marry and then abandoned her with no explanation to go to Kansas alone. Apparently everyone else thought they would marry too. Everyone except Henry, who worked hard to remain disconnected from the grapevine. He had no idea who dumped whom. Nor did he want to know.

"People recover from heartache at different speeds. If anybody should know that, you should." Henry shook his head at Caleb's glib comment. Like many men, Caleb avoided introspection as much as possible, but Henry's friend had suffered his own woes of the heart on the way to marrying Mercy. "But that's wholly beside the point. I'm not interested in courting."

"You're just going to grow old alone until you dry up and blow away one day while you're out camping. We'll search for you and find an empty sleeping bag and a Coleman lantern."

"I should be so blessed to go like that." Henry had no fear of dying. Living what remained of his earthly life well would be the greater challenge. "I'm sure Leesa's a nice person—"

"Truth be told, Mercy's worried about her. She used to be the bouncy sister who saw the world through rose-colored glasses." Caleb tapped his razor-sharp knife on the workbench. "She never met a person she didn't like. Now she drags herself around like the sky is falling and she needs a boulder to hide behind."

That morning she had looked determined. Resolute. Fierce. Her cheeks had turned crimson. Her dark-blue eyes snapped. She didn't simply walk to meet him. She hustled as if she had no time to waste. "She hides it well."

"From what you told me, you had your moments of darkness and despair too."

Memories crowded Henry. Days when he couldn't pull himself from his bed even though he couldn't sleep. Days when he didn't eat. Days when dark shadows loomed even though rays of sun danced across the floor next to his bed.

"The man she loved didn't die." Just to keep the record straight. "Regardless, you can't put grief on a schedule. She'll find her way through her disappointment in her own time."

"You could help her."

When elephants flew. "She doesn't want my help."

"How do you know?"

"She's not ready for another man. Besides, I don't want to be the B&W ointment on someone's wound."

"You're not getting any younger. There aren't a lot of women to choose from in Kootenai these days."

"Give it a rest."

Caleb flicked bark from his shirt. It landed on Henry's sleeve. "You say you're over it and you're fine. I say if you really were fine, you would've noticed what a *gut* woman Mercy's sister is. Pleasing to the eye too. Not as pretty as Mercy—"

"Let's not compare *schweschders.* It's not nice. Besides, I don't notice women at all." Henry flicked the bark back toward his friend. It landed on Caleb's boot. "You're so good at minding other people's business, so why don't you tell me what to do about Tommy."

"You really don't notice women?"

"Nee."

His face full of mock horror, Caleb shook his head. "That's not normal."

Henry's friend had a one-track mind. "Let's move on. Tommy. What do I do about Tommy?"

"Hose him down like you do Dodger."

"Not about the baths. He says he doesn't believe in *Gott*."

Caleb dropped his knife. His eyebrows rose sky high. He launched into a cross-examination of this piece of information. Just as Henry had known he would.

Henry didn't need a cranky schoolteacher in his life. He had enough problems with his cranky new roommate.

4

MOST KIDS COULDN'T STOP TALKING. LEESA FUMBLED FOR another topic of conversation. Tommy had made it clear he didn't want to talk to her. He also didn't want the teacher walking him home. No matter. She would make sure he made it to his new home. Mr. Henry Judgmental would see that she knew exactly what she was doing.

Raising her face to the late-afternoon sun, she lengthened her stride and cut across an open field catty-corner to the school. The grass was dry from a long, hot summer and crunched under her sneakers. For a short, skinny fifth grader, Tommy moved fast. He didn't want to talk about Kentucky. He didn't want to reminisce about his aunt. He didn't want to talk about the train ride to Montana. And he certainly didn't care to discuss why he refused to play baseball at recess.

"Why don't you use a buggy?"

At last a semblance of interest in something. "I will when

the weather's bad this winter. Sometimes I'll ride my bike, but when the sun's shining, it's *gut* to walk." Those had been Mercy's words of advice. *"Clear your head before you get home and have to help* Mudder *with supper and around the house. No rest for the weary."* "It's nice to breathe fresh air and feel the sun on your face after a long day in the schoolhouse."

"Buggy would be faster."

Which meant less time he'd have to spend with her. Less time for her to probe and get to know him. Ten-year-olds were not known for subtlety. Tough beans. "Why don't you like *schul*?"

"*Schul* is for *kinner.*" His scoffing tone matched the surly look on his face. "I don't need it."

"So you're all grown up?"

He grabbed his backpack straps and picked up speed. His footsteps lifted small plumes of dust in the air behind his scarred leather boots. "I reckon."

Having no family of his own at such a young age might make him feel that way. Leesa's heart thrummed. Not with pity. He wouldn't want that. "Grown-ups can still learn. Did you have a *gut* teacher in Munsford?"

"My *aenti* was the teacher. She was *gut* at everything."

Understanding flooded Leesa. School reminded him of his loss. "It's hard to lose someone you love."

"She was the only teacher I ever had. I don't need another one."

No emotion colored his matter-of-fact statements. He had such a hard exterior, like a tortoise that had tucked his head in his shell and refused to come out. Any sliver of child hidden from sight and sun. "I'm sorry for your loss. Is Henry your *onkel*?"

"*Nee.* He's nothing to me."

Ouch. "He can't be nothing. You're living with him."

Tommy shrugged. "Who knows? I don't."

"It was nice of him to take you in, wasn't it?"

"It's not like he's doing me a favor. I could have taken care of myself back in Munsford."

He was homesick and brokenhearted. Leesa's hands fluttered to her throat. He would never accept a hug from her, but that was what he needed. A prescription of hugs and listening ears and time to heal the wounds he tried so hard to hide.

"Do you like camping? Henry likes to hunt, fish, and hike. Tourists hire him to be their guide when they go hunting. He's *gut* at it."

Tommy's cheeks had turned ruddy in the cool air, and his nose was running. He wiped it on his sleeve. "I don't know. I never done any of that."

Deflated, Leesa cast about for another topic. Naturally a boy living with a spinster aunt in Kentucky would not have experienced those things. However, Henry could teach him. They could get to know each other. Henry might be short on words, but he seemed to have a decent heart. "It's a whole new world, I promise. People move here for the outdoor fun. They move here for a fresh start. That's what Henry did."

"Henry ran away."

"That's a harsh thing to say."

"That's what *Aenti* Anna Mae said."

"Did she say what he was running from?"

"His *fraa* died."

Leesa stumbled over a rock, flailed, and righted herself. Henry Lufkin had been married. That was news. Did Mercy know that? If she did, she'd failed to mention it. "Even more reason not to say such things about him. Losing a wife is sad."

Tommy didn't respond. Leesa pointed north and led him onto the dirt road that would take them to the newly rebuilt cabin where Henry lived.

"How much farther?"

"Not much. Does this look familiar from your buggy ride this morning?"

Tommy looked around and shrugged. "Maybe."

Leesa stopped and flung her arm across Tommy's chest. She pointed with her other hand. "Look."

An enormous moose with massive flat antlers trotted down the road toward them.

"Whoa," Tommy whispered.

"Whoa is right. I reckon he weighs a thousand pounds or more." Leesa backed Tommy away from the road until they stood under the overgrown branches of a maple tree. Gratitude that moose season didn't start for another week washed over her. This animal was too regal to be turned into steak. Her father would laugh at the idea, especially since Leesa loved a good moose steak. "Let's give him plenty of room."

The moose halted in the middle of the road. His large overhanging snout dipped. He sniffed the air. Huge muscles rippled under his dark-brown and black coat.

"What's he doing?" Tommy whispered. "Is he lost?"

"I reckon he's trying to decide where to go next."

The moose's head bobbed. His mouth opened and he bellowed, a sound somewhere between a hound's bay and a donkey's bray. After a few seconds he turned and trotted across the field on the other side of the road and headed toward the mountains. His short tail wagged behind him.

"It looks like he's going back home." Leesa stepped away

from the tree and trudged toward the road. "He just took a detour into town, I reckon."

No answer. She looked back. Tommy hadn't moved. His eyes were wide and his mouth hung open.

"Are you coming?"

Tommy shut his mouth and clumped through the undergrowth. "He was big. Huge!" He scampered ahead of her and turned around so he walked backward. "Does that happen a lot? Do you see moose all the time? What about bears or wolves? Do you see them too?"

Finally. Tommy, the ten-year-old boy, had peeked out from behind the grown-up fort he'd constructed between himself and the world.

He should've gone to pick Tommy up. Henry stood staring at the road from the doorway of the cabin he'd rebuilt with the help of friends after the fire. Tommy should've been here by now. How long did it take for kids to walk from the schoolhouse? It was at least a mile. He rolled his shoulders to loosen tight muscles. It didn't help. A low whine in his throat, Dodger paced between the two spruce trees Henry had planted in his front yard. "I agree."

They probably stopped to play kickball or climb trees. Naw, the other boys knew they had to get home and do their chores before supper.

Where was he?

Movement down the road caught Henry's gaze. Two figures. One short, one shorter. They were headed this direction. Hand to his forehead to block the late-afternoon sun, Henry tromped down the steps and strode to the edge of the yard.

Yep. Tommy. The other one . . . was Leesa.

She'd been serious about walking him home.

"We saw a moose! We saw a moose!" Tommy yelled when he was still several yards away. He picked up his pace and hurtled into the yard. His face red and sweaty, he careened to a stop in front of Dodger, who greeted him with a full-throated bark. "It was in the middle of the road. What do you think of that?"

"They were here first. The mountains belong to them." Stuffing his relief under his hat, Henry smiled at the boy's enthusiasm. Moose were common in these parts. "What took you so long? Did you get lost?"

"It hasn't been that long." Leesa strolled into the yard several paces behind her charge. "I waited to make sure the *kinner* had all their things, and I said good-bye to them. I had to get everything ready for tomorrow and then close up the *schul*."

"You didn't have to walk him home." The words sounded ungrateful in Henry's ears. He tried again. "*Danki* for walking him home, but it wasn't necessary. The Shrock *kinner* live close by."

"I told you I'd make sure he got home safe and sound." Her cheeks were pink from exercise and the sun. The stress and nerves from earlier in the day were gone, leaving behind a pretty woman. "So I did. It gave us a chance to talk."

She was very pretty. Short and curvy. The only physical attribute she had in common with Vivian was her blue eyes. Where had that thought come from? It was all Caleb's fault for planting the seed. Henry did not notice women. He hadn't since Vivian. Sweet, long-legged Vivian with her dark cocoa-colored hair and eyes bluer than a Kentucky summer sky. Her cheeks crinkled with deep dimples every time she smiled at him on those long walks on his parents' farm in Munford. She'd loved to fish, hunt, and hike. She would've loved Montana. He didn't need a photo to remember Vivian. Her face was engraved on his heart. In recent years he'd visited that spot less often. And with less angst.

That's what he got for talking to Caleb. Old memories burbling up from a deep well that was better off stoppered. Henry swept the thoughts aside and forced himself to focus. "Talk about what?"

Her gaze went to Tommy who had dropped his knapsack and settled onto the grass next to Dodger. The dog rolled over on his back and stuck all four legs in the air—his way of communicating that he expected a belly rub. "He's been through a lot. He thinks he's all grown up." Her voice dropped to barely above a whisper. "He's hurting and hiding it. His *aenti* was his teacher, so it makes him feel bad to come to a *schul* knowing she won't be there. He's homesick."

"You got all that in a mile's walk?"

"He's never been hunting, fishing, hiking, or camping." She made a *tsk-tsk* sound. "Can you image? No wonder he was so excited about seeing a moose."

That was wrong. Every child should have good memories of the great outdoors. "I can fix that."

"*Jah*, you can. You have a few months of fall weather before winter sets in." Despite her smile, the words held a challenge. "I'll work on getting him to like *schul* again. The rest is up to you."

"You mean like teamwork."

Her forehead puckered, she nodded. "Do you have a problem with that?"

"Nee." Relief welled up in Henry. Leesa might be new at teaching, but she grew up in a big family. She had to know more about child rearing than Henry did. "No problem whatsoever."

"*Gut.* Make sure he gets to *schul* on time tomorrow."

"I didn't know what time—"

"No excuses. We start devotions at eight thirty sharp."

They hadn't today. No fair. It had been her first day. "He'll be there."

Looking incredibly pleased with herself, she called out goodbye to Tommy.

The boy ignored her. Leesa's pleased look deflated like a punctured ball. "Anyway, *gut natch*."

Her pace brisk, she strode back down the road.

Henry felt immeasurably better. He wasn't alone. He and a woman he had known for four years but hardly knew at all were in this together.

Surely two adults could handle one small child.

5

"Tweet, tweet. Tweet, tweet."

Leesa stood with her back to her scholars. She paused, chalk poised in the air. The schoolhouse windows were open, so it was possible a bird had flown into the classroom, but this didn't sound like a real bird. A brisk breeze wafted through the room, bringing with it the fall scents of fir and earthy decaying leaves. But no actual leaves. And no birds.

This sounded more like a child trying to get her goat. She inhaled, exhaled, and continued writing the geography questions on the board so the fifth to eighth graders could copy them into their composition books. They were to look for the answers in their books and write them down so they could memorize them.

"Tweet, tweet, tweet." The sound was louder this time and full of panache.

A child giggled. Several tittered.

Leesa turned. Immediately heads lowered, the students earnestly attentive to the lessons before them. "Do you not have enough work to do? I can give you more."

No one responded.

Charlie wiggled in his seat. Grinning, he cocked his head toward the older children. Specifically, the fifth graders.

"Do you have something to say, Charlie?"

"Nee." He shook his head vigorously.

"English."

"No."

"Then I suggest you get busy with your reading assignment in the workbook. You stumbled on the oral reading. You don't want to fall behind."

Charlie hunkered down at his desk. "Yes, Teacher."

Once again Leesa returned to writing the questions on the board.

"Chirp, chirp, chirp."

She whirled.

Nineteen faces stared back at her. All nineteen were trying not to laugh and not doing a very good job. Molly raised her plump hand as far as her face and pointed behind her other hand as if no one but Leesa could see her.

Leesa followed the trajectory of the third grader's tiny index finger.

Tommy.

Leesa deposited the chalk on the ledge and brushed the remnants from her hands. Irritation rolled through her in waves. A ten-year-old would not best her. She would not—could not—lose her cool in front of her charges. *Stay calm.* She strode to his desk and gave him her best teacherly frown. "Do you have something to say? Or maybe sing for us?"

"Nee."

"English."

His expression bland, he shook his head. *"Nee."*

"Tommy." She leaned down and put one hand on his desk. "English."

The wooden top gave way and the entire desk crashed to the ground, leaving Tommy in the seat. Leesa flapped her arms like a prehistoric bird and teetered. She came within a lizard's eyelash of falling on her scholar.

His eyes wide with feigned dismay, Tommy crossed his arms and shook his head again. "Now look what you've done, Teacher."

Leesa fixed her fiercest frown on him. "I think you had something to do with it."

Tommy adopted a hurt puppy-dog look. "I didn't touch it. You did."

Breathe. Breathe. If she couldn't handle this one child, how could she manage an entire classroom?

How would she handle her own children? God willing, one day she would have her own. If it was God's plan for her. Why wouldn't it be? *Gott?*

If this—right now, this place, these children—were His plan for her, could she accept that? Could she do her best?

Pain wrapped itself around her heart and squeezed so hard she could barely breathe. She wanted her own children, but right now these little ones needed her. Particularly this rebellious ten-year-old.

Not taking her gaze from Tommy, Leesa managed a smile. "Scholars, it's time for recess. Line up and go outside in an orderly fashion." To her relief, her voice didn't shake with the anger so fierce it rattled her bones. "Quickly now."

"But, Teacher, it's not two—"

"Go." Leesa cut off Diane's protest. "You've earned a few extra minutes of sunshine."

She waited until all eighteen happy campers had exited—with much more whispering and giggling than usual.

"Let's take a look, shall we?" She knelt and examined the desk. All the screws had been removed. "Hmm, all the screws are missing. I reckon that's your handiwork."

"I don't know what you mean." Tommy managed to look hurt. "I was just sitting here."

"Where are the screws?"

"I don't know."

"It's a sin to lie."

"Well, there's no *Gott*, so there's no such thing as sin."

The words were like a scythe slicing through Leesa's skin to the muscle and then bone. "Tommy! You don't believe that, do you? There is a *Gott* who loves you and wants to be your Father—"

Tommy's snort exploded around her. "Like my father who died when I was five? *Nee*, I don't want no father."

Such dejection, such pain, lived in those words. "*Gott* has a plan for you. To prosper, not harm you." Platitudes even a child could see right through. Platitudes Leesa had heard over and over again after Ian's decision to abandon her during one of the worst seasons of her short life. She had survived. So would Tommy. "He brought you here for a fresh start with Henry, who's a *gut* man. He will be a *gut* friend to you."

Maybe even a father, with time.

A morose, silent child looked up at her, his unblinking eyes filled with disbelief.

"You have to be open to the possibilities."

No response. His pale-blue eyes pierced her skin with arrows of disdain and disbelief.

He was only ten and he didn't believe in God. Did Henry know? He had to know.

"I promise you things will get better." She had wallowed in her own doubt and disbelief after Ian left. Her friends and family had tried so hard to comfort her, but she wouldn't have it. Eventually they grew tired of trying. Even Mercy, whose guilt over her own happiness sometimes peeked out from behind her smile, seemed to lose patience. "I haven't had a family member die, but my heart has been broken. It has taken time, but it's on the mend. Yours will heal too."

He sniffed.

"In the meantime you can take your chair and place it next to my desk."

"Huh?"

"It'll give you a fresh perspective. You'll see what I see and must cope with trying to teach a room full of students at different levels and with different strengths. Maybe you'll see your way toward not being so disruptive."

"But—"

"Move your chair."

To her amazement, Tommy did as he was told.

When she rang the bell to end recess, her scholars tromped inside, sweaty and content. Their faces registered surprise and even some amusement at Tommy's new location, but no one commented.

Tommy sat quietly, hands in his lap, for the remainder of the afternoon. Everyone seemed to ignore the broken desk, like a pile of wood kindling, in the middle of the room. Leesa didn't call on Tommy, nor did she ask him to do any more schoolwork.

After she tapped the bell on her desk and dismissed the children for the day, she turned to Tommy. "You can clean the blackboard, sweep the floor, wipe down the desks, and stack your desk at the back of the room. Unless you want to put it back together."

"The other *kinner*—"

"English.

"The other children were supposed to do chores."

"Today you get to do them. What about the desk? Are you putting it back together?"

He stood and edged toward the blackboard. "I can't. I don't have the screws."

"As you wish. Clean the blackboard, sweep, and wipe the desks."

"That's my punishment, then, for something I didn't do?"

"Tommy, every time you lie to me, it hurts my heart. It hurts God's heart. He has a ledger. He's keeping track, and one day you'll be held accountable for your sins."

"If you're trying to scare me, it won't work."

"Get busy. I have papers to grade."

Half an hour later, Tommy's chores finished and Leesa's papers graded, she closed the school door behind them and led the way down the steps and across the playground. "It's a beautiful day for a walk."

"I know my way home." For the first time, a slight quiver ran through the words. "You don't have to walk with me."

"I do. I have to speak with Henry." Leesa shielded her eyes from the sun with both hands. "Maybe we'll see a moose again. My *bruders* saw a bear on Saturday. It took one look at them and scooted into the woods."

"You don't have to tell Henry. I won't do it again."

Tommy's bravado had disappeared. He looked . . . not scared but uncomfortable.

"Won't do what?"

"Whatever you think I done."

"So you won't admit to it and repent?"

"Nothing to repent."

"Let's go."

Unlike their first walk, this one was made in almost complete silence. Leesa stopped trying to engage him in conversation. After a long day indoors, the sun felt wonderful on her face, and the breeze dispelled the cobwebs splayed over her tired, sticky brain.

With each step she prayed. What if Tommy fell ill and died tomorrow? Could little boys go to hell before they had a chance to live long enough to understand the beauty of God's creation, His saving grace, and His love for all His children?

Gott, don't take him yet, please. Give him a chance to be redeemed. Let Henry and me find a way to reach him. Let our community embrace him. We need a bit of time, if You don't mind.

It had been a long time since she prayed for someone else's needs. *Gott forgive my selfishness, my self-absorption, my self-pity, my small-mindedness.*

Soon Henry's cabin came into view. He was sitting in a faded lawn chair in front of the house. Next to him, propped up on a kickstand was a bicycle just the right size for a boy like Tommy.

Leesa waved. He waved back and stood. "I figured Tommy knew his way now."

"He does." She studied the bicycle. It was shiny and blue with the wide tires of a mountain bike. "I need to speak with you."

Tommy's mouth had dropped open. He touched the chrome fender with one gentle finger. "Who's this for?"

Henry scooped up an old blanket from the back of the lawn chair and threw it over the bike. "That depends on what your teacher has to say. Go inside and get yourself a snack."

After one last longing look at the bicycle, Tommy did as he was told. An amazing feat unto itself.

"What did he do?"

Leesa summarized the afternoon's events.

His face a block of stone, Henry paced. Dodger rose from the porch and joined his master in wearing a path in the sparse, brittle grass.

When she finally paused, so did Henry. He mopped his face with one hand and shook his head. "So now you know too."

"You knew he claims to be a nonbeliever?"

"He told me right off. He refuses to pray. I had to drag him to the buggy by the ear on Sunday."

"You need to talk to Noah. As the bishop he's bound to have some good advice, and as a father himself."

"Tommy's ten."

"All the more reason to reach him now rather than later."

Henry lifted his hat and settled it back on his dark hair. "I'll pray about it."

"So will I."

He swiveled and touched the blanket-covered bike. "I

thought it might help if he could ride around like the other *kinner*. Has he made any friends?"

"*Nee.* They think he's funny, but he doesn't play games at recess or talk to anyone over lunch."

"Can I tell you something?"

"You may."

"I don't know what I'm doing."

Leesa breathed a small chuckle. "That makes two of us. Some team we are."

"I'm sorry I wasn't kinder on the first day of *schul*. I can't imagine being in charge of all those *kinner* at once. I'm more of a solitary mountain man."

"I'm more of a kitchen woman."

Despite their dark waters, Henry's eyes were filled with light. He smiled, but an unbearable sadness imbued his face. "I guess we both have our crosses to bear."

"We'll figure it out."

His hand came up and touched her sleeve. The breeze abated. So did sound. She didn't dare breathe. She couldn't move.

His hand dropped. "Sorry—"

"I'd better go. *Mudder* will wonder what happened to me."

"Right."

Say something. Say something. Something kind. At the road she forced herself to stop and turn. "Maybe you could come to supper some night. With Tommy, I mean." She made a stuttered mess of the words. "For Tommy. He could play with my *bruders* and *schweschders* and make friends with them."

She and Henry might even become friends. She didn't add that last part.

"Maybe we could." His expression lightened. "I would like—Tommy would like that."

It didn't seem likely, but then, God had surprised them with His miracles before. "I'll mention it to *Mudder.* Maybe Sunday evening."

The light in his eyes flickered and died, replaced by sudden hesitation. His jaw worked. He ducked his head. "He must be disciplined first. For what he did at *schul* today." He swung his gaze toward the mountains beyond her shoulder, never meeting her eyes. "I must make sure he'll behave himself before I inflict him on your family."

A lot of words for a man who tended to use them sparingly. Deep in her bones, Leesa knew this wasn't about Tommy. Henry was afraid of getting close to someone again.

She studied his angular features and deep-brown eyes. This tall, lanky man feared the same things she did—hurt, loss, and more loneliness.

"That's understandable." She offered him her best smile. "Let me know when you're ready. I mean, when he's ready."

Henry blinked. "I will."

She could feel his gaze on her all the way down the road.

6

Now came the hard part.

Henry stifled a dry chuckle as he stuck the hose in the large aluminum tub in the laundry room and turned on the water. No part of playing father to Tommy had been easy these past three weeks. True, his new housemate made a fine breakfast and he liked to do laundry—both amazing boons for Henry. But every day started with a battle over attending school and ended with a refusal to participate in nightly prayers.

Henry's attempts to draw Tommy out about school were ignored. Today they'd gone hiking in the Cabinet Mountains, roasted hot dogs, and made s'mores. Much of the hike passed in silence, but it was a friendly silence that gave them both a chance to think. Tommy even unbent enough to collect rocks and ask the names of the birds he spotted with Henry's binoculars.

Tiny steps, true, but surely they could be called steps.

Enough steps to take Leesa up on the supper invitation?

Shaking a mental finger at himself, Henry picked up a kettle of hot water and added it to the tub.

He knew better. His decision to ward off the invitation had nothing to do with Tommy. It was about diving into dangerous waters. He liked his quiet, safe world free of heartache and the potential for loss.

Fortunately, school seemed to be going better. At least Leesa hadn't shown up at his doorstep to discuss any more birdcalls or collapsing desks. That was an argument in favor of accepting the invitation, wasn't it?

Nothing had to be decided tonight. Right now the boy needed to take a bath, pray, and go to bed in preparation for church in the morning.

"It's too cold. I'm not dirty." Ignoring the mud on his faded blue shirt, Tommy nudged aside his muddy boots with his toe. He plopped on the chair next to the tub, leaned back, and stared at the ceiling. "Plus, I'm not going to church tomorrow, so why do I have to take a bath?"

Henry added a second kettle of water he'd heated on the kitchen stove and tested the temperature in the tub. It was tepid, but at least it wasn't frigid. Montana had finished with summer, hopped over fall, and settled into winter in early October this year. Tonight they would likely have the first frost. Forecasters were predicting some of the earliest snowfalls on record.

But that didn't excuse anyone from a Saturday bath. When he finished bathing, Tommy could dry off in front of the first fire of the season in their living room. "My answer will not change, so I won't repeat myself. Get in before I toss you in."

Tommy didn't move. "You can't make me."

"Did your *aenti* raise you to speak this way to an elder?"

Tommy's face crumpled. His lower lip quivered. "Don't talk to me about *Aenti*."

"Didn't you go to church with her?"

"She told me *Gott* had plans to prosper not harm me."

"She's right."

"I prayed she would live. She didn't. Nobody listens to prayers."

Not getting the sought-after answer to a prayer was enough to derail many Christians' walks. "Our days in this world are numbered. We're only passing through. Your *aenti* is in *Gott*'s hands now." Henry trotted out all the platitudes that others had offered him after Vivian's death. They hadn't helped him much at the time, but most people simply didn't know what to say. Like his Plain forefathers before him, Henry had squared his shoulders, swallowed his pain, pulled up his pants, and gotten on with life by fleeing two thousand miles across five states to Kootenai. "*Gott*'s plans can be hard to understand, but He always does what's best for us. He expects us to bend to His will."

"*Nee*, I don't think He's there at all. This isn't what's best for me. I want to go home." Tommy hunched his shoulders. He swiped at his face with the back of his dirty hand. "I want *Aenti* Anna Mae to be in her house, making stew and apple pie."

"We don't always get what we want." They were back at square one. Henry had been where Tommy was now. Explaining to a ten-year-old the honing of character required to grow into a strong Christian was beyond Henry's abilities. He barely understood it himself. "Don't give up on *Gott*. He is *gut*. He cares about you. You can't see His plan yet, but someday you will."

Henry was still waiting. Every day he woke up, contemplated his life, stared at the log ceiling, and prayed that today would be the day he understood his purpose in continuing to exist without Vivian and the child she'd carried. And the ones who surely would have come after. Was it only to make furniture for *Englishers* and lead them on hunting and fishing trips in Kootenai National Forest? That seemed too shallow for the God of Moses, Abraham, and Jacob.

"Get in. The water's getting cold."

"Nee."

Gott, give me patience.

"You must do as you are told. Show respect for your elders."

"You're not my *daed*. You told me so."

If Henry didn't establish his authority now, he never would. That was certain. He sucked in a breath and stalked around the tub. "You're right, but your *daed* chose me to stand in for him. So now you must obey me or suffer the consequences."

He grabbed Tommy's collar with one hand and the waistband of his pants with the other. "In you go." He slung the boy into the water backside first.

Legs kicked. Arms flailed. Water splashed.

Woofing, Dodger trotted into the room, stared at Henry with his head cocked, and retreated.

A second later Tommy surfaced. He sputtered and coughed. "I hate you!"

The boy didn't seem to have even a sprig of the humble, obedient, stoic character normally instilled in Plain children from birth. Was Anna Mae to blame, or was Tommy simply a wayward soul shaped by circumstances beyond his control?

"I know the feeling." Henry held out a bar of soap. "Wash your hair and don't forget to clean behind your ears."

Tommy rolled over and attempted to climb from the tub.

Lord give me strength and patience. Henry tugged the boy back on his behind. He dunked the soap in the water and rubbed the bar until his hands were soapy. A bubble floated in the air, landed on Henry's nose, and popped. He sneezed.

"I guess I'll have to wash you like a *bopli*."

One hand on Tommy's shoulder, Henry scrubbed the boy down as best he could, given that he was almost completely covered in sodden clothes. Tommy squirmed and muttered but didn't try to escape.

"Now you can get out."

If looks contained deadly poison, Henry would be frothing at the mouth and keeled over dead in seconds. Tommy stepped over the tub's edge, scooped up a towel, and trudged from the laundry room with all the dignity a ten-year-old kid could muster.

Weary to the bone, Henry sank onto the chair. His shirt and pants were soaked. Water trickled down the tub's sides and pooled on the pine floor. He leaned over and let his head rest in his hands.

Gott, if I can't discipline this one little boy, how can I ever dare to have kinner of my own?

The thought burst into his mind like a sleep-deprived bear awakened from hibernation too soon. Until this moment Henry hadn't entertained the idea of ever being a parent. Not since the morning Vivian died and took their tiny unborn baby with her.

The hope of having his own family had died that day.

Yet, in this moment, he could admit—to himself and to God—that he did want children. He wanted more than dark nights filled with aching, empty silence.

Surely God would understand if he chose to dispense with evening prayers just this once.

The night heavy on his shoulders, Henry shuffled to the living room. The wet towel lay abandoned on the floor in front of the fireplace. He picked it up, slung it over his shoulder, and kept going. The lamp in the second bedroom had been extinguished. The light from the living room allowed him to see enough. Tommy had curled up on top of the bed's quilt, with his back to the door. His bed shirt was inside out and wrinkled.

"Tommy?"

No response.

Henry leaned against the doorjamb. He closed his eyes. *Gott, soften his heart. Give him peace. Heal his wounds. I promise to soften my own heart. I promise to keep trying. I won't give up on him, and I know You won't either. Amen.*

He stood there a few moments longer, staring at the boy's sleeping form. His chest rose and fell. His arm twitched.

Finally, Henry withdrew. Outside he paused.

A small, half-muffled sob drifted through the air.

7

WAS THE GRAPEVINE IN KOOTENAI REALLY LADEN WITH fruit? It seemed more like a long fuse attached to a firecracker. A small piece of gossip lit the fuse, the fire sizzled and crackled its length until it united with the little firecracker, and *boom!* The gossip went flying hither and yon. Everyone was talking about Henry and Tommy. They were watching to see how this bachelor would do raising a boy who had problems. Big problems. Henry might be the best mountain guide in West Kootenai, but what did he know about parenting? All the women were wondering.

These were Leesa's thoughts as she sat on the hard, backless bench between her mother and Mercy, who'd spent most of Minister Lucas Zimmerman's sermon with her hand over her mouth as she tried not to spew her breakfast. It was understandable. The service was at the Yoder house this morning, and Mercy didn't want to spoil her parents' hard work in providing a pristine home for the district's biweekly service.

Don't look. Don't look. Every time she reminded herself not to look, the urge to peek past Mercy at the men's side grew. Henry sat next to Caleb and the older Yoder brothers.

Ever since their exchange that day after school, Henry had popped up in Leesa's brain at the most inopportune moments. When she should be listening to the first graders repeat their alphabet or during the older scholars' spelling practice. Twice Mother had inquired about her hearing after having to repeat herself multiple times during preparations for supper.

Henry had such a penetrating way of looking at her. It was as if he saw all her insecurities, her white lies, and her bitterness. If he did have that power, it would have been so much better for him to have seen her pre-Ian. In those days she thought she had the world on a string like the prettiest pink-and-purple balloon floating over green pastures and majestic mountains.

Not anymore.

Tommy had been doing better in school—somewhat better. His behavior at home must've improved as well. He'd been riding the bike to school—leaving Leesa no reason to walk him home.

Even if she wanted to. Of course, she didn't. Did she?

Mother nudged Leesa with her elbow and glared over the silver-rimmed glasses sitting on her long nose.

What? Leesa mouthed.

Mother's eyebrows rose on their tippy toes.

The sermon. Lucas droned on about Jesus's parable of the seeds that fell on the path, the rocky soil, the thorny soil, and the good soil. What were the seeds? What was the soil, thorny or good? Lucas pondered the thought aloud, then paused so everyone in attendance could do the same.

Was Lucas casting seeds on Tommy? The boy was definitely hard-packed soil on a path from which he might not return.

A thump and a muffled cry sounded behind Leesa. Her mother jumped. A baby squawked. Leesa swiveled in her seat, as did most everyone in the Yoder front room and dining area combined.

With a half-stifled giggle, Tommy scrambled up from the floor. In his haste he knocked over the empty bench on which he'd been sitting in the last row. "Sorry. I nodded off."

The young boys and girls seated toward the back tittered. Withering stares from their parents put a quick end to that.

His face a ruddy beet red, Henry rose and strode to where Tommy was struggling to set the bench upright. Henry grabbed the boy's arm and propelled him out the front door, which he closed behind them with barely a sound.

Lucas looked nonplussed but recovered quickly by moving on to the mustard seed parable. How could such a tiny seed grow into such an enormous plant? What did Jesus want to teach them with these stories?

Leesa tried to concentrate, but truth be told, she preferred passages where Jesus laid out his teachings in a more straightforward manner. Allegories seemed open to interpretation, which was not the Plain way, as Deacon Tobias Eicher had hammered into them during baptism classes. The Scriptures spoke for themselves. They did not need interpretation by folks who thought themselves smarter than God.

Blessedly the one-hour sermon soon wound down, followed by the kneeling prayer and standing for the benediction. The movement helped Leesa fight off sleep, brought on by a night of tossing and turning as her mind revisited the ups and downs of teaching. More ups than downs. The benediction ended. Belatedly, Leesa genuflected and sat only a beat behind everyone else.

She waited for the *vorsinger* to start the final hymn, then peeked past her mother. Henry hadn't returned. Surely he didn't leave. What kind of lesson would that teach Tommy?

Another harder elbow from Mother. Chagrined at her own inattentiveness, Leesa opened her mouth and focused on drawing out each syllable the way she had learned from the time she sat on Mother's lap and played with beads and string.

Fifteen minutes later the song ended.

Her forehead furled in deep wrinkles, Mother stood first and turned to Leesa. "Where was your mind this morning, *Dochder*? It certainly wasn't on Jesus."

"I was listening." Her protest sounded weak in her own ears. "I'm just tired. I didn't sleep well last night."

"I'd suggest more *kaffi*, but you wiggled like a three-year-old as it was."

Heat toasted Leesa's cheeks. Mother never had to chastise her. Mercy had always been the wiggle worm during church. "I'm sorry, *Mudder.* We'd better get to the kitchen and bring out the food."

Ignoring the grin Mercy didn't bother to hide, Leesa squeezed past both women and led the way to the kitchen where they helped spread out fixings for sandwiches, pickles, finger foods, cookies, and pies brought by the women of the district. The men would rearrange the benches to make room for tables.

"So why did you keep looking at Henry?" Mercy snatched a piece of bread from a tray and slathered peanut butter on it.

"Maybe this will settle my stomach. Otherwise, I don't know if I can look at this food long enough to serve it."

Leesa waved her sister away from the table. "There are plenty of us to serve. Go sit outside and get some sun."

"You didn't answer my question."

So much for redirection. The articles she'd read about teaching children said it sometimes worked to turn a situation around. Maybe not as much with adults. "I didn't look at him any more than anyone else. Tommy falling off his bench made everyone look."

"You were looking before that." Her arms loaded with baskets of homemade sliced bread, Naomi Miller paused next to Leesa. They'd been best friends all through school, until Naomi skipped her *rumspringa*, was baptized, and married immediately thereafter in a small, quiet wedding. A few months later little Jennie Lynn made an appearance, but no one openly counted how many months it had been. "Everyone is wondering how he'll ever pull off taking care of a little boy."

"If any single man can, it's Henry. We're working on it together." The words came out of her mouth before Leesa had time to think how they would sound. She had told no one about her discussions with Henry. They were only trying to help Tommy. Yet it seemed like more. What if it only seemed that way to her? "Tommy is a handful at *schul* too. He's having a hard time settling in."

There had been a moment after she walked Tommy home that first day when they seemed to be on the same page. And again the day he took apart his desk. A mutual agreement—or had it been a mutual challenge? Either way, Tommy's well-being mattered to them both.

"Together, eh?" Naomi giggled. "It's about time you moved on from Ian."

"It's not like that."

"What's it like, then?"

"Like a teacher and a parent trying to help a child."

"Uh-huh."

Leesa turned and rearranged the cookie tray. Snicker-doodles, chocolate chip, peanut butter almond, and sugar cookies. All her favorites. Everyone else was probably thinking the same thing about Henry and her. She was, too, if she was honest with herself. But figuring out what to do about it was much harder.

"You'd better get those sandwich fixings out there," Mercy interceded. "All that pontificating will have them ravenous."

Naomi rolled her eyes. "How you do talk, Mercy. Caleb must have married you for your vocabulary."

Maybe he did, Leesa wanted to argue. Would that be so bad? Her sister was a big reader and a big thinker. Caleb thought that was a good thing. They were blessed to have each other.

Fortunately, Naomi sashayed from the kitchen in time to save herself from Leesa's pent-up emotions.

"How is teaching going?" Mercy grimaced and nibbled at the bread. Her pretty face had turned a deeper shade of lime green. "You haven't said much."

What could Leesa say to the former teacher so beloved by her scholars that they still talked about her legendary baseball and volleyball skills? They still recounted how she acted out the stories she read to them on Friday afternoons as a special treat if they'd had a good week.

Leesa was not good at sports. Nor did she act. She liked to

read as much as the next person, but acting out the stories was not one of her talents. "It's going fine."

"I miss it." Mercy managed a wan smile. "I love being Caleb's *fraa*, and I can't wait for this *bopli* to get here. But still, teaching was fun."

Fun wasn't the first word that came to Leesa's mind. *Frustrating*, maybe. But it could be fulfilling. She saw a glimpse of that now and then when a first grader read an entire page without missing a word, or a fifth grader got all the history answers right. And when the kids giggled and bantered but spelled every word correctly in the spelling bee.

"We're settling in. Levi's little *bruder*, Charlie, is a handful. So is Tommy, but I'm getting the hang of it."

"It'll get easier." Mercy's face softened. "I promise, *Schweschder*. I know you. Anything you set your mind to do well, you do well. This will be no different."

Tears stung Leesa's eyes. She and Mercy were so different, but it had never kept them from being close. *"Danki."*

"Go serve." Mercy patted her shoulder. "I'm right behind you."

It felt good to know that her sister wasn't only referring to serving food.

For the next hour and a half, they served, ate, and visited until nary a sandwich or a cookie remained. Leesa answered the same question repeatedly with the same answer. *"How is school?"* "Gut, *very* gut." Several parents mentioned that they would stop by for a visit soon, and Sally Plank offered to bring a hot meal one day for lunch.

The kids would like that. Maybe they would do a pizza day. Leesa wiped her hands on her apron and stepped onto the porch for a breath of fresh air. So many women talking at once made more noise than a bunch of chickens in a crowded coop. The October morning sunshine had given way to gray, low-hanging clouds and a blustery north wind.

Wishing for her sweater, Leesa hugged her arms to her waist and shivered. She loved the change of seasons, but sometimes it came unexpectedly, like a guest who forgot to write ahead. She let her gaze roam across the yard, where several clusters of men lounged at picnic tables, their voices a low rumble compared to the women's high-pitched chatter. Henry had never reappeared. Nor had Tommy.

She looked farther afield. There. Henry stood next to his white gelding with his back to the crowd, his hand smoothing the horse's mane. Tommy was nowhere in sight.

Glancing around, Leesa slipped down the steps and across the yard. No one paid her any mind. She hoped.

"Hey, Henry. You never ate." Food seemed a good enough reason to approach him. Innocent. Leesa slowed, waiting for his response. He didn't turn. "Are you all right? Where's Tommy?"

Henry swiveled. Uncertainty etched lines on his plain face. His eyes burned with an intensity that made Leesa's heart skip a beat. "I gave him a choice. Return to the service or walk home without eating. He chose to walk home. Maybe I shouldn't have given him a choice."

He wanted her to tell him he'd made the right decision. That was obvious. Leesa slipped around to the other side of the horse where she could ground herself by touching the animal's warm, soft back. She studied Henry's face, half hopeful, half fearing condemnation. "We hope *kinner* will make *gut* choices, but we can't always be sure they will. They have to live with the consequences of their actions."

"I'm not sure he even knows the way home."

"He'll find his way."

"He's lost."

"You don't know that."

"I'm not talking about physically."

"I understand, but you'll find him. It might take time, but you'll get through." Leesa smoothed the horse's silky mane. He nickered and tossed his head in appreciation. "He's the same way at school. A time or two I thought I was getting through, but it's only been a few weeks. We both have to give him time."

"He's still talking about the moose."

"That's a *gut* sign."

"I guess so."

"The invitation to supper is still open." A wave of heat rolled over Leesa. Women didn't usually invite men to their houses. But this was different—a teacher inviting a parent and her scholar to supper. "It might help."

"He hasn't made any friends at *schul*?"

"He talks to Job some."

"After his behavior in church, I don't know if I should—"

"If you wait for him to be perfect, it will never happen."

He rubbed his temple. "I knew this would be hard. I just didn't realize how hard."

Exactly Leesa's thoughts about teaching. "Just think about—"

"Are you coming?" Seth, one of Leesa's younger brothers, approached, his expression curious. "*Daed*'s waiting."

"I have to go, but if you need to talk—about Tommy, I mean—stop by after *schul* anytime." Leesa shot Seth a *go-away* frown. "I'm there grading papers most afternoons after the *kinner* go home."

Now would be a good time to extend that invitation again.

Except for Seth's looming presence.

"*Danki.* I'll keep that in mind." Henry glanced at Seth, then back to Leesa, as if he wanted to say something. Instead, he simply nodded.

Leesa scurried after Seth, who grunted. "Huh."

"What does that mean?"

"My *schweschder* is finally moving on."

People kept saying that. "What does that mean?"

"You're courting again."

"Am not. We were discussing his . . . scholar."

"*Jah.* Uh-huh."

Seth could think what he liked, but she and Henry were not courting.

Not yet, anyway. The three little words fluttered on the breeze like butterflies and then flew away.

8

Henry almost made it out of the Yoders' yard. He could've pretended not to hear Noah calling his name, but that would've been dishonest. And right after the Sunday service. He tugged on the reins and halted the buggy.

"I'm glad I caught you. We need to talk." Noah's earnest delivery of those two sentences didn't bode well. Nor did his somber expression. "We could grab a seat at a picnic table. I didn't see you eat."

"My stomach is complaining this morning." This was the truth. So much so Henry had been afraid he might have to miss church. Only his determination to set an example for Tommy had kept him from settling back in bed. "I really need to check on Tommy."

No point in getting into the details of the choice he'd given Tommy or the smirk he'd received in return right before Tommy set out for home, kicking up gravel with every step of his new church shoes.

Noah's smile tightened. "Exactly what I wanted to talk to you about." To Henry's surprise, Noah climbed into the buggy and settled on the seat next to him. He turned up the collar on his coat and rubbed his hands together. "They say winter is coming early. This north wind is proof enough. I'll go with you to talk to Tommy. You can drop me at the house afterward."

A spattering of raindrops spit on Henry's face. A few minutes with Tommy and Noah would know the truth of the child's spiritual malaise. "It's not necessary."

"Given the stunt he pulled during the service this morning, I must disagree. Especially when you consider what I've been hearing."

Here we go. Irritation was wrong. Henry silently counted to ten. Accountability from the community was a staple of their faith. He snapped the reins, and the buggy jolted forward. "What did Leesa tell you?"

"What makes you think Leesa said anything?" Noah paused for a beat. "What has the *bu* done at *schul*?"

Besides birdcalling and destroying his own desk? Those were the least of Henry's concerns. "He's rambunctious, that's all. A high-spirited boy."

"Then why do you walk around looking as if the sky has fallen on your head?"

Henry urged his horse into a canter. The rain came down harder. He scanned both sides of the dirt road that led to his cabin but saw no sign of Tommy. Dealing with the boy's antics challenged Henry, but coping with his spiritual mess was quite another larger swarm of gnats. "His presence was unexpected."

"I reckon that's what they call an understatement."

"He's been scarred by loss. He's been uprooted. He's lashing out."

"A steady, firm hand will rein him in."

It would help, but discipline would not fill the hole in Tommy's heart. Henry picked his words with care. "Or a loving heart."

"Of course discipline must be meted out with love and caring." A gust of wind blew rain into the buggy. The sweet smell of Douglas firs came with it. Chuckling, Noah wiped his face with his wool coat sleeve. "But he doesn't need a friend. He needs a parent. He needs to be reined in before he's completely out of hand."

"With time, he'll settle down."

"Have you considered placing him with one of our Kootenai families? The Planks, the Yoders, or the Shrocks? They have more experience with raising *kinner*."

The idea hadn't occurred to Henry. To have this burden disappear from his shoulders had appeal. To have his quiet, orderly home back. No more waterlogged tussles at bath time. No more visits from a certain teacher.

Nee. What reason would he then have to visit the Yoders for supper?

He brushed the selfish thought aside. Leesa only wanted to help her wayward scholar. She had no interest in the scholar's substitute father. For the first time since Vivian's death, his heart thrummed in a cranky, painful effort to disagree with his head concerning a woman's interest.

There was no interest. Would he like there to be interest?

This was ridiculous. Aware of Noah's piercing gaze, Henry

studied the potholes filling with rain in front of the buggy. He raised his face to the glowering gray clouds. Sweet Vivian's shadowy figure wavered in the distance. She would've been a good mother. She would've known what to do.

So do you, mann. She raised her hand, waved, and disappeared into the foggy, windswept mountains.

Godspeed, my sweet, sweet fraa.

Raindrops blurred his vision. Cold seeped through his damp shirt. Was Tommy out here soaked to the bone, lost and wandering toward the mountains?

Tommy had been uprooted once already. He needed to be able to trust someone. He needed to trust Henry. He kept testing boundaries in order to find out if Henry would cast him aside at the slightest inconvenience.

"Tommy's father left him to me. He's my charge."

"He might be better off with a family that has a *daed* and a *mudder.* Josiah probably thought you would be married by now."

The words were sharper than a finely honed ax. Noah couldn't know how they pierced Henry's heart. "Josiah raised Tommy without a *fraa* until he died. He knew what he was doing. He chose me. I'm honoring his wish."

"Even if it's not what's best for the child?"

"I choose to believe it is for the best."

Noah's grunt was neither assent nor dissent.

They rode in silence until Henry made the last turn and guided the buggy up the muddy, puddle-filled road to his cabin. He pulled into the yard and stopped.

"If he's disruptive during the service again, we'll have to meet with the both of you to discuss punishment."

"Understood."

"He's far too old to act like this. Spare the rod and spoil the child."

"I know." Should he tell Noah about the greater concern? Not yet. Henry would pray. He would work with Leesa. Together they would find a way to reach this hurting child. "I'll check to see if he's inside."

He wasn't. Dodger whined to be let out. No other sound echoed in the tiny two-bedroom abode that still smelled of the bacon and eggs he'd made for breakfast. Probably because the plates of uneaten food still sat on the table. A string of muddy tracks led to Tommy's bedroom. Henry studied the room. The bed was neatly made. A first. The hooks on the wall were empty. Tommy's clothes were gone. His backpack was gone.

Tommy was gone.

Henry left the door ajar for Dodger and retrieved his rain slicker and a large umbrella. Together they left the cabin and he pulled the door shut. *Where are you, Tommy?*

Dodger hopped in the back of the buggy. Henry handed the umbrella to Noah. "He's gone."

"He ran away?"

"It appears so."

His expression perplexed, Noah leaned back. "Maybe you should tell me what happened after the stunt he pulled this morning."

Henry obliged on the fifteen-minute drive to Noah's house. The bishop said little, other than promising to spread the word about Henry's missing charge. They would go out in twos and threes, covering the small community from one end to the other. If necessary, they would form a search party to comb the nearby forest.

"Surely he won't try to walk out of here."

Walk the eighteen miles to Rexford, including the longest-span bridge in the state? "Surely not."

"I plan to talk to the Planks about taking him." Noah's stern tone left no room for argument. "They handled difficulties with their Jonathan well."

"It'll only make it harder for Tommy." Henry argued anyway. "He knows me. He needs stability."

"He needs parents who know better than to give him an option to skip church when that's exactly what he wanted." Noah didn't bother to soften his criticism. "A bad apple can't be allowed to spoil the whole barrel. Whether at *schul* or at church."

"He's not a bad apple."

"He will be if he's not reined in—now. And sharply."

The bishop's logic was infallible. "Let's find him first."

"I'll pray."

"Me too."

9

THE ONE PERSON WHO KNEW TOMMY BETTER THAN ANYone else was his teacher. Henry left Noah's and headed back to the Yoders' house. The skies opened and rain came down in sheets, making it hard for him to see a few feet ahead of the buggy. Lightning tortured the sky, followed by thunder that shook Henry to the core. Tiny hail pinged against the buggy's roof and pelted his face. He had no fear of weather, but neither was he foolhardy. His poor horse didn't deserve this. "We're almost there," he yelled. "Hang in there."

A white lie.

"Tommy. Tommy!" He couldn't help himself. Even knowing the futility of calling the boy's name didn't stop Henry. What if Tommy decided to hike into the woods and hide from Henry's ire? What if he fell? What if he was hurt?

Gott, help me.

A drive that normally took fifteen minutes turned into thirty.

Finally, he reached the Yoder property. He held his slicker-clad arm over his head as if it would protect from the hailstorm and raced to the door. Mercy opened it.

"Henry? What's the matter?"

"Where's Leesa?"

Mercy waved him in and offered a towel while she went to get Leesa from the kitchen. Both sisters returned immediately. "It's Tommy, isn't it?"

"He wasn't at the cabin."

"Where would he go?"

"I hope he knows he can come to me, but he hasn't." Leesa chewed her lower lip. "He has no friends here. We need to find him. When that front comes in tonight, the temperatures are supposed to drop, maybe even to freezing."

"Noah is rounding up the men to start a search party." Henry wiped his face, head, and neck with the towel. Water dripped and pooled at his feet. He was making a mess. In more ways than one. "I can retrace my steps from here, but not in this rain. It'll have washed away any tracks."

He handed the towel to Leesa. Heedless of how wet it was, she clutched it to her chest. "I want to go with you."

"*Nee.* It's dangerous out there. The lightning is fierce."

"We'll go." Leesa's father, her oldest brother, Abraham, and Caleb crowded into the room. "We'll round up the other boys and head out as soon as the rain lets up."

"Much appreciated."

"You're soaked to the bone. At least let me put some *kaffi* in a thermos for you." Leesa whirled and rushed toward the kitchen without giving him a chance to respond. "Don't let him go, Mercy, until I come back."

The men tromped up the stairs to the second floor, already talking about what needed to be done.

That left Henry with Mercy. She smiled. "I know this isn't the time to mention it, but your name has come up in conversation a few times recently."

Warmth flooded Henry despite his best attempt at a neutral expression. "Has it?"

"Christine and Nora think it's a *gut* idea. So do their *manns*."

So the whole world had been talking about him and Leesa. He expected as much from the women, but his male friends? It seemed everyone had talked about it except him and Leesa. Not so much as a buggy ride to date. "They must not have enough work to do if they're talking about me."

"We're your friends." She uttered the words with a diffident smile. "Caleb and I want the same happiness for Leesa that we have in each other."

Now that she was a married woman and a mother-to-be, she could say such things to a single man like himself.

Leesa sailed back into the room. She handed the thermos to Henry and grabbed her coat from the hook by the door.

"You're not going."

"I'll saddle a horse if need be."

In that case she would be safer with him. What would her father and mother think of her hopping in a buggy with him? If the smile on Mercy's face was any indication, they would be happy—as long as he brought her home safely. "I have enough to worry about with Tommy—"

"*Gut.* You needn't worry about me."

She shoved through the door ahead of him. He glanced back

at Mercy. She shrugged and made shooing motions. "Better keep up with her."

If anything, the rain came down harder. The drops pelted his hat and face. Leesa hunched over against the wind. He grabbed her arm to help her into the buggy.

A horn blared.

Startled, he whirled.

A Lincoln County Sheriff's Department SUV pulled into the yard. The overhead lights whirred red and blue for a few seconds, as if in greeting, then stopped.

Tommy? Please, Gott, let him be all right.

Sheriff's Deputy Tim Trudeau slid from the driver's seat. He started to speak, then held up his hand and waited for a crack of thunder that rattled Henry's teeth. "I think I have something of yours."

10

Even with the lightning crackling across the sky overhead, no one moved for a second. Hail pinged on the shingled roof. A whoosh of blustery wind knocked Leesa back against the buggy. Henry grabbed her arm and righted her. She tugged free. Relief mixed with a dose of anger sent heat like her own brand of lightning through Leesa. She dodged Henry and marched into the northern wind toward the deputy.

"Is he all right?"

"It's hard to tell." Tim wiped at his face with a ragged towel as sodden as he was. "Not much of a talker. I stopped at Noah's, and he told me to look for Henry here."

Leesa zipped around the SUV and manhandled the door. Looking like a drowned puppy, Tommy was huddled on the seat under a blue flannel blanket. Tim had left his vehicle running and the heat on high. The truck smelled of wet little boy. Leesa fought the urge to climb in beside Tommy. "Are you all right?"

He hunched his shoulders and nodded.

"Come on, let's get you inside. I reckon some of Seth's old hand-me-downs will fit you."

His face crumbled. "You still want me?"

Leesa took his icy, wet hand. "Nothing you can do will make us not want you."

Head down, he slid from the seat into the cold wind and rain. Leesa threw her arm around him to shelter him from the storm. If only it was that easy to shelter him from life's storms. Henry came up on the other side, and together they scrambled toward the house.

"Tim, come inside and get dry before you start back," Leesa shouted over another long roll of thunder that sounded like a train picking up speed. "The coffee's hot."

Inside, a flurry of activity followed. They hung coats by the fireplace to dry. Mother brought towels and blankets to them. Father stoked the fire. Mercy handed out mugs of steaming hot coffee to the adults and hot chocolate for Tommy, who'd changed into Seth's old pants and shirt.

In that time Tommy offered no explanation. He burrowed under a quilt in the rocking chair closest to the fireplace and sipped his hot chocolate. Henry stood close by, ostensibly warming his hands, but his expression said he feared Tommy would bolt and disappear again.

Leesa's family melted away, claiming chores upstairs or in the kitchen. No doubt Mercy and Mother were straining to hear as they tossed vegetables in a pot of elk stew. The sweet perfume of cinnamon rolls scented the air, mixing with the comforting smell of burning wood.

Leesa turned to Tim, who had settled his tall, meaty frame on the sofa. His lips were blue and his teeth chattered. Leesa scooped up a blanket from the pile Mother had provided. "Take this. Can I get you more coffee?"

"I'm good. I can't stay long. I told Juliette I would come for dinner as soon as my shift's over."

"Where did you find him?"

Tommy burrowed deeper into the quilt. His blue eyes were barely visible. Doodles, the family dog, propped his grizzled snout on the boy's lap. Tommy's hand slipped from under the cover and patted him.

"We got a call from the postmaster—"

"In Rexford?" Henry turned his back to the fire. If he stood any closer to it, the seat of his pants would catch fire.

"Yep. That's the one. He said he picked up a boy who had hitchhiked across the bridge and was asking for a ride to Libby. Apparently Tommy here claimed his car had broken down, his cell phone was dead, and he needed a ride into town to get help. Needless to say, the postmaster saw right through that story."

Tommy settled his mug of hot chocolate on the end table and sank farther into his chair.

"He offered to take a look at the car, but Tommy came up with some more fairy tale. Rather than argue with the boy, he drove into Libby and called the department. I met them at the train station, which it seems was Tommy's actual destination."

"You were going back to Kentucky?" Leesa tried to make eye contact with Tommy. He was having none of that. "With what? How would you pay for a ticket?"

He pulled his hand from the covers and displayed a wad of wet, wrinkled bills.

"My grocery money." Henry scooped the money from the boy's hand. "You stole from me?"

Leesa shot him a frown. *Not now.* She knelt in front of the rocking chair and tucked the quilt tighter around Tommy's body. "Are you warm enough?"

His chin quivered. He nodded.

"I'd better get going." Tim settled his coffee mug on the end table and stood. "No laws have been broken, and this seems like a family matter."

"You're sure you can't stay for supper?"

Tim raised his head and sniffed like a wolf on the hunt. "It smells great, but Juliette will have my hide if I'm late for her mother's Sunday pot roast."

Leesa saw him out. Neither Tommy nor Henry had moved when she returned to take Tim's spot on the sofa. A standoff? She studied the two faces, both morose. She decided to start with Tommy. "Why go to Kentucky? Kootenai is your home now. You have family here."

"I don't—"

"Maybe not by blood, but we are your family because we care for you. Right, Henry?"

Henry edged closer to Tommy. He cleared his throat. "Teacher is right. Just because I get mad at you doesn't mean I'll stay mad. I discipline you because I care about what happens to you. If I didn't care, I wouldn't bother."

"You were really mad this morning."

A complete sentence with no sarcasm or disrespect. They were making progress. Henry squatted next to the rocking chair. He rubbed his fingers on its smooth varnished arm. "What you did was disrespectful. I want only *gut* for you, Tommy, and not only now, but for eternity."

"I'm sorry," Tommy whispered. "I'm just mad. All the time."

Henry patted his knee. "Believe me, I know the feeling."

"Me too," Leesa admitted. Not as much as in those days after the wildfire, but often enough. "All the time."

"Really? Grown-ups feel this way? You get mad at *Gott*?"

"Jah." Henry glanced at Leesa and then away. "After my *fraa* and our unborn *bopli* were killed, I was angry all the time. I wanted to die. I didn't bother to get out of bed for a long stretch. I blamed *Gott* for everything bad. I forgot all the *gut* He had done."

A knot swelled in Leesa's throat. His loss was so much greater than her own. A wife and a baby he never had a chance to meet or hold. She swallowed hard. He wanted to reach Tommy so badly he was willing to lay bare his agony in front of her. She studied her hands in her lap, giving him space to do it.

"How did you get over it?" Tommy petted Doodles, but his gaze was fixed on Henry.

"I didn't. A person doesn't get over something like that." Henry settled back on his haunches. His features had softened with his tone, and lines disappeared from his face. He was lost in memories. "You do learn to go on. We like to say that we're just passing through this world and *Gott* knew the number of days our loved one would be here. Both are true. But it still hurts. I had friends who helped me. The bishop helped me understand *Gott* doesn't make bad things happen. He allows them so we can become better people who can help others in their time of need. Like I'm helping you now. That's what Christians do. That's what your *Gmay* does."

A long speech for a person of few words. Here was a man who cared so deeply for a little boy, he would do anything to ease his pain.

Tommy's forehead furled. His expression grew pensive. "Even after your *fraa* and your *bopli* died, you believed?"

"I always believed. *Gott* never said life would be easy. He said it would be hard, but He already overcame the world. He is always with us."

"It doesn't feel that way."

"It will, one day."

Tommy sighed. "Okay."

"Okay. That doesn't mean there won't be repercussions for running away, stealing the grocery money, and hitchhiking." Henry took a breath. "When I think of you hitchhiking, I just—"

"I know. It was stupid. I'm sorry."

A perfect, perfect apology. "Maybe not too many repercussions," Leesa offered. "He did say he was sorry."

Henry growled. "Of course a child has to learn that actions have consequences." He scrubbed at his face with both hands. "That's what I've been told."

"Noah?"

With a slight shake of his head, he stood. "We'll talk more about that later." He held out his hand to Tommy. "We should get home. You have *schul* tomorrow, and so does your teacher."

"Nee, nee." Leesa hopped up. "*Mudder* makes enough stew for two dozen people. It'll warm you both up. Plus, Mercy's cinnamon rolls melt in your mouth. And it's still raining. You'll get drenched again and catch a cold or worse."

Seth, Job, and Levi stomped to the top of the stairs and peered down over the balcony. "Does that mean we can come downstairs now?" Seth, always the ringleader, called out. "We want to play Life on the Farm. Tommy can play too."

"I guess that means we're staying." Henry backed away to let the stampede of boys through. He landed on the sofa next to her. His face suddenly crimson, he scooted down. "It'll be *gut* for Tommy to spend time with your *bruders*."

"What did Noah say that causes you such concern?"

"He wants Tommy to move in with the Planks." Henry's expression turned somber. "Mind you he hasn't even spoken to them yet, but he says they'll give him the firm hand he needs."

"*Nee*, he needs stability. He needs you." She put her hand to her lips to stymie the flood of words. When they subsided, she let it drop. "It will only make things worse."

"I told him as much. I can only hope we"—his gaze collided with hers—"I can make progress with Tommy that will make Noah change his mind."

"You were right the first time. *We* can help Tommy." She must be light-headed from all the excitement. His dark-jasper eyes staring into hers made it hard for her to think. He wanted her help. He wanted to do this together. "Together we'll help Tommy . . . and each other."

Henry leaned forward, elbows on his knees, and stared into the fire. The flames leapt. The wood crackled and popped. Still its heat was nothing compared to what burned through Leesa as she awaited his next words.

His gaze shifted to her face. "I hear there's been some talk."

"Some talk? About what?"

"About us." He smiled, something he didn't do nearly often enough. It transformed his plain face. Even white teeth, full lips, and dimpled cheeks gave him his youth back. "According to your *schweschder*, everyone thinks it's—we're—a *gut* idea."

"They do, do they?" She floundered, hunting for words suddenly lost in a dense thicket of unfamiliar emotions. Trepidation, uncertainty, anticipation, hope. "What do you think?"

"I think I feel like I'm waking up from a long, deep sleep to find that life has been passing me by." His voice dropped to a low, deep whisper for her ears only. The boys, busy setting up their game, took no heed of his words. "I don't want that to happen anymore."

"The last year's been a hard one for me." Leesa waited for the familiar sting of disappointment and despair. It didn't come. Only a sense of optimism she hadn't felt in a long time. With it came the certainty that there was no need to rush. Small steps were fine. Even better than a mad, headlong rush. "I'm sure you know all about what happened to me. It felt mean and ugly. I feel like I did something wrong. That it was my fault."

"It wasn't."

"*Nee*, it wasn't. But what I want to say is I might be a little skittish."

"You and me both." His hand crept across the sofa's dark-navy material, stopping midway between them. "Maybe we could start with a buggy ride."

Leesa eyed Tommy. He had wrapped the blanket around his neck like a shawl. He was busy counting his livestock and money.

"I might have to come to you."

"That would be nice." Henry glanced at Tommy. "We could sit on the porch after he goes to bed."

Leesa slid her hand toward his. Their fingertips touched.

The cold seeped away. All of it, not just that brought on by the day's rain and wind.

11

Evenings sitting on Henry's porch soon turned into Leesa coming by after school each day to deliver Tommy in her buggy as winter pushed autumn aside and the first snow blanketed the mountains. Then Leesa started staying to fix supper. She discovered Henry's cooking left much to be desired. His cabin also needed a woman's touch when it came to cleaning—not something she dared say aloud. He did the best he could, no doubt.

If Tommy saw anything odd in this development, he said nothing. His behavior at school had improved. He didn't always participate, but he no longer derailed the proceedings.

Nor did her own family say much. Mother, with a smile and a twinkle in her eyes, accepted Leesa's explanation that she was working with Henry to help Tommy adjust to living in Kootenai. Father looked less happy—likely because he didn't approve of her visiting Henry's home alone—but Mother's pointed stare stopped his comment in its tracks. After all, Tommy was always there.

Despite her determination to go slow, Leesa could admit, if only to herself, that she wouldn't mind a few minutes alone with Henry. He measured his words with great care, but sometimes she saw him staring at her with a strange look of wonder. As if she were a deer that had suddenly appeared in his yard and decided to take up residence. He didn't quite know what to make of her, it seemed. He'd made no move to touch her.

Did he want to? The question confounded her at night when she found it hard to sleep, which was most nights despite her long days at school.

So far Noah had agreed to hold off on moving Tommy to the Planks, with the caveat that no further incidents like running away and hitchhiking occurred. The thought had barely crossed Leesa's mind on this cold late-November afternoon when she and Tommy drove into Henry's yard. A buggy with a dapple-gray mare was parked next to the cabin. Noah's mare. The bishop stood on the porch with Henry. White puffs hung in the air as they spoke. Why not talk inside where it was warm?

"What is Noah doing here?" Tommy, who'd been half asleep for the last mile, sat up straight. "What do you think he wants?"

"I think we're about to find out." No way to back off now. Had Noah heard about their rather unconventional courtship? Most couples didn't have to worry about a young child being home alone while they were courting. It was an unusual situation all around. "I'm sure he's just visiting."

"Ha." Tommy punctuated his comeback with a snort. He

might behave himself for the most part, but he still spoke his mind more than most Plain children. "Bishops never just visit."

And he was right. Leesa strode up the steps and joined the men with a quick hello.

"I was hoping you might stop by." Noah waved at Tommy who had stopped to romp with Dodger in the yard. "I've heard you've made it a habit lately."

Leesa smiled at him. Nothing to say to that. It was true.

"Let's go inside. I have a pot of *kaffi* on." Henry held open the screen door. "Leesa brought us some snickerdoodle *eppies* on Monday that are mighty *gut*."

They traipsed inside where Leesa took over hostess duties. Let Noah think what he would. They weren't doing anything wrong.

The kitchen was a mess, but thankfully the bishop didn't traverse that far. Henry had been cooking his one good dish—spaghetti. The sauce simmering on the stove filled the air with a lovely scent of oregano and onion. She had to wash two cups in order to have enough clean ones to serve the coffee. A saucer did the trick for enough cookies for the three of them.

Finally, they settled around the table. Noah took a bite of cookie and chewed. He smiled. "My *fraa* is cutting back on sweets. She says they're not *gut* for us. I disagree." He patted his face with a napkin. "It seems Tommy has been doing better."

Leesa almost missed the change of topic. Henry spoke before she could. "He is doing better. At home and at church." His head bobbed in her direction. "And at *schul*."

"We'll let Leesa speak to his behavior at *schul*." Noah nibbled on the cookie. Crumbs decorated his long, dark beard. "I've heard, though, from one of my own *kinner* that he's on the fence when it comes to *Gott* Himself."

Coffee slopped over the edge of Henry's mug. He laid his spoon aside and sopped it up with a napkin. "He's been talking about that?"

"It seems so." Skinny black eyebrows lifted, Noah looked down his long nose at Henry. "I'm surprised you didn't mention his lack of faith during any of our previous conversations."

"He's only ten." Leesa intervened. "Many *kinner* don't have their faith secured so early."

Noah's frown was probably more concerned with her interruption than the content of her statement. This was a conversation more likely to occur among the men at a *Gmay* meeting. "He mustn't be allowed to taint the faith of others."

"As Leesa said, he's ten." Henry's quick smile in her direction encouraged Leesa. He leaned back in his chair and looked at Noah. "He's suffered much for so young a child. We're working on his faith. Slowly but surely he's learning that suffering doesn't mean that *Gott* doesn't exist. He's learning that often hardship comes from this fallen world we live in. That's a hard concept for adults to understand, let alone *kinner*."

Noah picked at the crumbs on his napkin. He squeezed them together in a pinch and popped them into his mouth. Contemplating the empty saucer, he sighed. "Wise words, indeed. I just wanted to make sure you're on top of the situation and not distracted." His frown at Leesa left no doubt as to his meaning. "If my help is needed to properly instruct him, let me know. Sooner rather than later. How has he been at *schul*?"

"Much better." Not perfect, but no child was. "His reading has caught up to grade five, and his handwriting is much improved."

"I'm not asking about academics."

"I haven't had to single him out for correction."

Not this week, and it was already Thursday.

Noah lifted his hat and scratched his head. "You know my *kinner* like to tell us about their day at the supper table."

No doubt. Leesa's siblings did the same. "There was an incident on the playground one day last week."

"Uh-huh."

"All the younger boys were involved. Not just Tommy. Even my *bruder*, Job."

"Who threw the first mud ball?"

"No one gave up the instigator."

Instead, they had given the school's interior a good scrubbing at the end of the day. It seemed only fitting, given how muddy their boots, clothes, and hands had been after the mud fight, which had ended with the boys rolling around in the puddles during the afternoon recess.

"My *kinner* weren't involved."

"Nee." As the children of the bishop they undoubtedly carried a heightened sense of the need to set an example. "None of the girls either."

Noah lowered his hat back on his head. "If you feel you've handled it adequately, I'll let it lie. For now."

Leesa breathed.

"I've heard talk."

Her lungs constricted once again.

"About what?" Henry took a large bite of cookie and chewed slowly. His tone was neutral, but color suffused his face.

"I'm aware that yours is an unusual situation, Henry." Noah pursed his lips as if sucking on a lemon. "The elders and I have concerns, though. Courting is one thing. Two people playing house prematurely is another. Great care is required to make sure lines are not crossed."

Leesa supposed that was the closest he would come to speaking forthrightly on the subject. Her cheeks burning, she studied the pine table as if it fascinated her. Again this was a discussion between the two men at the table.

"Your concern is unnecessary." Henry's tone was cool. "Be assured that decorum is observed within the proper boundaries of courting."

"And it's not just a project you're working on together?"

"What do you mean?" Leesa and Henry voiced the question in unison.

"It's obvious you both care for Tommy." Noah shrugged. "It speaks well of you both. But by itself, that's not a reason to court."

"That's not what's happening here." Henry sounded sure of himself. He grinned at Leesa. "Not for me. You?"

"Nee." Certain her skin would turn to ash, such were the flames burning her face, Leesa managed to shake her head.

"*Gut*. See to it that it isn't." With that, Noah's face broke into a broad grin. "Also know that there are those of us who wish only the best for both of you."

Surprise nearly knocked Leesa from her seat. Their bishop saw beyond convention to the hope for happiness. He hadn't forgotten how sweet romance could be.

Henry looked equally taken aback. Rather than try to respond, he simply nodded.

"Well, I'd better get home before my *fraa* sends out a search party." He stood. "She's making an enchilada casserole. It smells like your supper may be burning."

"*Ach!* I'll get it."

Leesa dashed to the kitchen, leaving Henry to escort Noah to the door. She stirred the sauce with a wooden spoon and lowered the flame. A small taste confirmed it was only slightly singed. She filled a large pot with water for the noodles and set it on the stove.

Hands slid around her waist and tugged her back. Henry's scent of wood and soap drifted over her. His lips nuzzled her neck. "Henry." She should pull away, but she didn't. She allowed her body to lean against his. "Didn't you hear Noah just now? Proper decorum."

"I heard him say people only want the best for us. Which means they want us to be together."

"That may be stretching his words a bit." Leesa turned in his arms so she could lean her head against his chest. She fit perfectly in this spot, like her body had been waiting for it all along. "People want us to be happy."

"I'm happy. Are you?"

She raised her head to look up at him. "I am."

Emotion sparked in his eyes. His head inclined, then paused, his mouth inches from hers. "Are you sure? I don't want to push you. I know you've been down this road—"

Heart pounding in her ears, Leesa stretched up until her lips met his. They were warm and soft and sure. She wrapped her arms around his neck. He lifted her from the ground. She might be flying. Soaring.

Gently, her sneakers touched the ground once again. She opened her eyes, and he smiled. "I've been waiting for that."

"Me too."

"Not too soon?"

"Nee."

"I didn't want to rush you."

"*Danki* for that."

"Any regrets?"

"*Nee.* None. I can either stay in the past and miss wonderful, glorious kisses like that, or I can move forward, knowing that I have to take a chance at getting hurt."

Henry smoothed her cheeks with his thumbs. "Same here."

The feel of his hands on her skin was almost too much. She inhaled and gathered her wits. "We should—"

This time he didn't stop midway. He kissed her softly at first and then more deeply. The past disappeared into a dark, dense forest of soon-to-be-forgotten hurt and loss. Henry offered her his all. She offered him her everything.

"Eww. Gross."

At the sound of Tommy's disgusted voice, they stumbled apart. The staggering drop was much like jumping from the tree branch over Lake Kooscanusa on a gorgeous, hot summer afternoon. Leesa was suddenly immersed in cold water with no air to be had.

"Uh, sorry." Henry recovered first. "We were just . . . We're just . . . making the spaghetti."

Tommy chortled. "I never seen anyone make spaghetti like that before."

"Just hush and go feed Dodger. Then wash your hands and set the table."

Still chortling, Tommy did as he was told.

"We'll have to watch out for that." Despite his words, Henry grinned. "I don't want to set a bad example."

"There was nothing bad about that." Leesa grinned back. "But I agree. Slow and steady remains the best course of action."

"If you're talking about kisses, I prefer slow and long. Would you like me to show you?"

"Henry, he'll be back any minute."

"Sixty seconds is better than nothing."

He proceeded to prove it.

12

SLOW AND STEADY HAD ITS PERKS. LEESA SMILED TO HERself as she stoked the fire in the wood-burning stove. It gave Henry and her plenty of time for kisses, hugs, and sleigh rides with their knees almost touching under thick fleece robes as they dashed over snowdrifts.

She glanced around the schoolroom. The single-sheet, handwritten Christmas programs had been distributed to the desks before the children left school on Friday. The older children had decorated the chalkboard with colored chalk and written WELCOME across the top. The boys hung cotton sheets across the front of the room to serve as stage curtains. They also set up card tables along the far wall awaiting the sweet treats that would be shared after the program.

Any second her scholars and their families would begin to pour through the door.

Leesa was ready. She'd made it halfway through her first school year.

The door swung open. Tommy tromped in with a wrapped package under one arm. A big basket in his gloved hands, Henry followed. Much stomping of feet on the rug mingled with their greetings.

"You're the first to arrive." Leesa rushed to relieve Henry of his burden. She peeked in the basket. Mandarin oranges, apples, and bananas. A perfect offering from a widower who hadn't mastered the art of baking. "I love mandarin oranges."

"This is for you, Teacher." Tommy held out the box wrapped in brown paper. "Open it, open it!"

"You don't want me to save it until Christmas Day?"

Tommy and Henry were invited to the Yoders' for the day. If the weather was bad on Christmas Eve, they would go early and spend the night.

"*Nee*, you're opening all the presents from your scholars now."

"Just let me set this down." Leesa deposited the basket on one of the tables and ripped the paper from the package to reveal a small wooden box on which crude flowers had been carved. "It's beautiful."

"I made it." Tommy volunteered. "Henry showed me how. He let me use some of the machines at the furniture shop. I carved the flowers by hand. It's for your hairpins and your combs and brushes."

"You did a *wunderbarr* job." Leesa hugged him, and he returned the embrace. That he allowed such a display of affection spoke to his steady improvement over the past few months. He no longer fought going to school or church. He even bowed his head during prayer. Henry was still working on the boy's weak faith. Slow and steady would win the race. "I can't wait to go home and put my hairpins in it."

"You really like it?"

"I do. *Danki.*"

"Open the top!"

Leesa opened the box. Inside she found a pile of screws. It took only a few seconds for understanding to dawn. "Your desk?"

His cheeks crimson, Tommy nodded. "I'm sorry I made my desk fall apart, and I'm sorry I lied."

"You're forgiven." Leesa set the box aside and hugged him hard. "Thank you for telling me the truth," she whispered in his ear. "I know you'll do better in the future."

He pulled away and grinned. "What did you get me?"

"Tommy!" Henry squeezed his shoulder. "It's not proper to ask."

"It's not actually Christmas yet, either, you know." She touched his cheek, and Tommy looked up with eyes full of anticipation. She almost relented. She'd splurged on a set of carving tools. Tommy wanted to do everything Henry did, and this would help. For Henry, she'd scrimped until she could afford a new tool belt, including a few new tools. "You'll have to wait until then."

"Aww."

"Are you nervous about your part in the program?"

He shook his head. "Henry helped me practice for hours and hours."

"That's a bit of an exaggeration—"

A whoosh of cold air blanketed the room. Leesa glanced

toward the door. The Beachys, the Rabers, and the Mosers had arrived and were busy removing coats. Happy chatter filled the room. "I need to start gathering the *kinner* behind the curtain—"

"Wait." His back to the others, Henry took a step closer. "I'd like to take a ride after the program. So I can give you your present from me."

Embarrassment swept over Leesa. She hadn't brought Henry's present. "Aren't we waiting for Christmas? I'll have to visit with all the parents and clean up. It'll be suppertime before I'm done. You're still coming for Christmas Eve dinner tomorrow, aren't you?"

"*Jah*, but this can't wait. We'll help you clean up." He grinned like a little boy about to burst with the effort of hanging on to a secret. "Tommy is going to the Beachys' after the program. He and Solomon want to build snowmen. I'll drop you off here afterward to get your buggy, then go pick him up."

He had it all planned. Resisting an offer of time alone was impossible. Leesa nodded. Wilma Beachy bustled toward them, carrying an enormous sheet cake. "We'll talk after."

The Christmas program went like clockwork. The children prepared it all on their own. First came the skits, and then they sang. The older grades recited poems they'd written in English. The middle-age students recited the Christmas story in High German.

Then it was Tommy's turn. Leesa couldn't help herself. She peeked from behind the curtains. Dressed in a long robe made from burlap sacks, he grasped a wooden staff in one hand and a small wrapped gift in the other. He began to tell the story of Jesus's birth from the perspective of a wise man. He'd written it himself in English.

"We saw a big star in the sky, and angels told us about the birth of the baby Jesus. My friends, who were shepherds too, and I followed the star to the place where the baby Jesus was. We were so happy when we saw the baby Jesus with his mother, Mary. We bowed down and worshiped him. We opened the presents we brought: gold, incense, and myrrh. That's a spice and it wasn't cheap. I brought the gold because you can buy stuff with gold. I know they're funny gifts to give to a baby, but life was different then, I reckon."

Chuckles from the crowd filled the air. Leesa sought Henry. He was sitting near the back, grinning from ear to ear. He didn't even try not to look proud. Pride was wrong, but Tommy had come so far in four short months. She couldn't blame Henry for feeling a sliver of it.

"Anyway, I had a dream that told me not to go back to King Herod because he was an evil man who wanted to kill the baby Jesus. So we went back home a different way. Pretty smart, right?" He lifted the staff high in the air. "And that was the first birthday party for Jesus. That's why we give each other gifts on Christmas Day." His voice rising, he pumped the staff and shouted, "Happy Birthday, Jesus!"

He bowed his head and scurried from the stage. Leesa had just enough time to pull her head back behind the curtain before he charged into her space. "How did I do?"

"Wunderbarr." She hugged him. He was no longer a skinny runt. Between her mother's and Leesa's cooking, they'd managed to fatten him up. "You make a very *gut* wise man. Now get ready to sing."

"I love Jesus."

"You do?"

"*Jah*. I may not get everything I want, but sometimes things work out."

Wise words from a child. *Danki, Gott*. "I love Jesus too. Go sing."

Grinning, he rushed to join his classmates on the stage.

The program ended with more traditional Christmas hymns. Leesa peeked out again. The families joined in the singing with laughing, happy faces.

The last singsong note of "Silent Night" ended. *Englishers* probably wouldn't recognize the hymn, sung in the traditional Plain a cappella manner of notes held over the space of ten minutes. The children scattered from the improvised stage and rushed to their families, where much hugging and smiling commenced.

She'd survived her first program as a teacher.

Leesa followed the children, intent on making sure there were plenty of paper plates and plasticware for the refreshments.

"Teacher, Teacher." Molly headed up the cluster of students bearing gifts. "*Mudder* and me embroidered hankies for you."

"You're not supposed to tell." Samantha elbowed her classmates. "You're supposed to let her open the present."

"It's okay." Leesa patted the little girl's cheek. "I'm so pleased you took the time to make something for me. It's very special."

They'd done a gift exchange at the end of the day on Friday. Every child received a gift through the drawing of names. Leesa had given each student a small illustrated storybook of Christmas from the Gospel of Luke. This evening, one by one her scholars presented her with potted plant holders, kitchen towels, and a variety of small, useful gifts. She would need extra bags to carry them home.

"And one more." Harley Beachy spoke as he and Jack Moser

skirted the cluster of children, carrying a blanket-covered gift between them. "From all the parents. We appreciate how hard you have worked with our *kinner* during your first semester of teaching."

Tears pricked Leesa's eyes. "*Danki* for allowing me to teach them."

With a flourish Jack removed the blanket to reveal a large chest made from pine. A simple pattern of leaves covered the hinged lid. "It's beautiful. Just what I needed."

"The boys made it." Jack cocked his head toward the older scholars. "The girls made something to put in it."

Inside she found a Country Hearts quilt.

Such generosity and caring overwhelmed her. Leesa dispensed hugs to the younger children, her head bent in hopes that the others wouldn't see how much the sentiments behind the gifts meant to her. She hadn't dreamed of doing this job. She hadn't wanted it. But one look at Tommy's cheeky grin as he gobbled his third or fourth frosted sugar cookie told her this had been God's plan all along.

"Here, Teacher, *Mudder* made these gingerbread-man *eppies*." Charlie squeezed between his classmates to offer her the cookie clutched in his plump hand—no napkin included. "I put the eyes on and the mouth."

"*Gut* job." She took the cookie. It fell apart in her lap. Charlie's lower lip quivered. "It's okay." She plucked a piece from her apron and popped it in her mouth. "Mmm!"

Giggles followed. A sweet contentment she once thought impossible swept through her. Henry stood near the thermoses of coffee and hot chocolate, watching.

She smiled at him, and he returned the favor.

An hour later the crowd had cleared after mothers and daughters made quick work of cleaning up while the fathers and sons returned furniture to its proper spot.

"Do you want company on the ride home?" Mercy wrapped a thick woolen shawl over her enormous belly. Her coat no longer fit. "Caleb and I are coming over for supper. I can ride with you."

"*Nee*, that's okay. I still have a few things to do here." Leesa forced herself not to look at Henry, who was slowly folding the last card table and stacking it against the wall. "Don't wait supper for me."

"Be careful. It'll be dark soon." Mercy swooped in for a quick hug. Her voice dropped to a whisper. "I told you that you would be a *gut* teacher. And *gut* things come to those who wait."

The old Leesa would've said something bitter like, *How would you know?* Instead, Leesa leaned into the hug. *"Frehlicher Grischtdaag, schweschder."*

Finally, everyone was gone. They exited the building and got into the sled. Henry slid under the sled robes after her and tucked them around their knees. "Ready?"

"Where are we going?"

"You'll see."

What Christmas gift required a sleigh ride? The gift itself didn't really matter. The time spent alone with Henry during this busy holiday season would be gift enough for Leesa. She leaned back and inhaled the crisp mountain air scented with pine and fir. Henry's horse tossed his head and snorted. White puffs of breath hung in the air. The sleigh skimmed over the packed snow. Soon they were beyond the last Kootenai home at the outermost edge of the tiny community.

"Whoa, whoa." Henry, who had said nothing on the drive, pulled the buggy to the side of the road and stopped next to a barbed-wire fence. "Here we are."

An empty, snow-covered field. "Where would *this* be?"

He tied the reins to the bar and slipped his thick leather gloves from his hands. They disappeared under the blanket and found Leesa's. "This is—*was*—Dale Shaeffer's property."

"The doctor who used it as a hunting lodge until it burned down during the wildfires?"

"That's the one. He retired. He and his wife decided to buy an RV and travel around the Midwest visiting their four children and twelve grandchildren. That's why they never rebuilt. They decided to sell instead."

"It sounds as if you've been visiting with him."

"I have. Juliette's dad came into the shop a few weeks ago." Henry's warm fingers tightened around Leesa's. "He mentioned the property was for sale."

The pieces began to fall into place. Leesa's heart pounded. Her breath came more quickly.

"I bought it."

"You bought it?"

"All twenty acres. A single man living alone doesn't have a lot of expenses. I've saved almost everything I've made in the last four years."

"It's a beautiful piece of property."

"With plenty of room for a house." He slid closer. His leg touched hers. He put his arm around her shoulders. He felt warm and solid against her body. "Our house, I hope."

With Henry so close Leesa found it difficult to connect two dots, let alone two thoughts. "Our house?" She sounded like a parrot who could only mimic his words. She cleared her throat. "You and me?"

He leaned closer and brushed her lips with his. "What do you think?"

"No fair. I can't think with you so close."

"Will you marry me?"

Those words she'd waited so long to hear were sweet and clear as an angel's song on the starry, bright night. "*Jah*, I will."

He sighed. "Whew!"

"Did you really think there was a chance I'd say no?"

His arm tightened. He kissed her forehead, her nose, and her lips. The kiss turned a December early evening into a balmy July afternoon. Caught in his embrace, Leesa slid her arms around his neck to capture a warmth that would never fade and never grow old.

Much later Henry leaned back. "How do you feel about slow and steady now?"

"As long as we're in it together, I have no need to rush willy-nilly into anything." She had begun something she needed to finish. Once married, her days as teacher would be over. A current that had nothing to do with the cold ran through her. A wife with babies couldn't divide her time between family and vocation. That would be her someday soon. Overwhelming gratitude filled her to the brim. "I'll always have you to hold my hand. That's all I need."

"Gut." He rubbed his fingers over hers. "It will take some time to save the funds to build the house. And time to build it."

"I like teaching. I want to finish what I've started this year."

"I'm so happy you've found contentment in teaching and

learned it's not just a fallback for a woman who felt jilted and had no other choice."

"*Nee*, it's a vocation, a calling. I love my scholars. I want to see the eighth graders graduate." Leesa kissed his fingers, one by one. "This must be a bittersweet moment for you as well."

"*Nee*, only sweet." He smiled. "Vivian would've wanted this. She was a generous, kind soul who wanted only happiness for those she loved. It must be strange for you to know I've loved another heart and soul, but believe me when I say my first marriage showed me how *gut* life can be when you give all you have to another person. I am who I am because of what I shared with Vivian."

"It must be equally strange for you to know I gave my heart to another first."

"Only strange because he threw away such a sweet gift." Henry shook his head. "I'll never understand that. His loss is my gain."

"Together we'll finish what we started with Tommy."

"We'll have our hands full." He laughed, the sound like music in Leesa's ears. "He will be the envy of all your scholars because he may lose a teacher, but he'll gain a *mudder*."

"I'm the one who is blessed to have him in my life." She planted another kiss on Henry's knuckles. "We'll adopt him, then?"

"As soon as we're married, we'll make it official. My boss is helping me look into how that works. Lawyers and such. More money to be saved."

"We'll figure it out. Together."

Leesa leaned her head on his shoulder. He tucked the sleigh

robe around her. A snowflake meandered from the sky and landed on Henry's nose. "Look, *schnee* again." She laughed and brushed it away.

More snowflakes, each unique, each perfect, floated down and landed on her face. Her life would be different from anything she could've imagined. But God had imagined it for her. The story of a widower, an orphan, and a reluctant teacher who would become a unique, far from perfect, but loving family.

Henry pressed her close to his chest. His heart beat in her ear. "We'll simply have to snuggle closer to keep warm."

What a lovely plan.

"One year from today, we'll marry. That will be our Christmas gift to each other."

"One year from today." She snuggled closer. *"Frehlicher Grischtdaag."*

"Frehlicher Grischtdaag."

Amid snowflakes that sparkled and spiraled from the sky, they sealed the vow with a kiss.

13

ONE YEAR LATER

HER NERVES WERE SHOWING. LEESA TRIED FOR THE third time to pin up her hair with fumbling, shaking fingers. Loose strands tickled her warm cheeks and neck.

"Let me do that for you." Mercy tucked her sleeping baby under a crib quilt in the middle of the bed that would soon belong to Henry and Leesa, husband and wife. The service was set to begin in a few minutes. Savannah did everyone a favor by napping while they prepared for this unusual December wedding. "You're making a mess of it. Your cheeks are so red, you look like you're about to melt into a puddle."

"That would be *wunderbarr.*" Leesa let her sweaty hands drop to the lap of the opal blue dress she'd sewn for the occasion. "I can't see straight."

Nerves and lack of sleep both played a role in her current

state. The last two days had been spent putting the final touches on the new home she and Henry would share with Tommy. They borrowed chairs and tables from family and friends. Mother and the other women did the cooking in Leesa's new kitchen.

It would be a small wedding. Four feet of snow and more on the way saw to that, but Leesa and Henry agreed this was exactly what they wanted. He had only two brothers and a smattering of cousins, aunts, and uncles in Kentucky and Tennessee. None planned to make the trek. The majority of Leesa's family lived in nearby Plain communities. They were accustomed to Montana winters. A measly blizzard wouldn't stop them from attending.

"Why are you nervous? You've been waiting for this forever." Mercy tucked and smoothed Leesa's unruly hair under her prayer covering with expert fingers. "It's about time, isn't it?"

"I'm not nervous about marrying Henry." Leesa's nerves calmed under her sister's ministrations. "But standing up in front of everyone . . ."

"It's only five minutes, tops. You know everyone in the *Gmay*. They're family and friends. Just pretend they're your scholars. You stand in front of them and talk all day long."

Good advice, but hard to take. "Do you think Henry's nervous?"

"Everyone is nervous on their wedding day. Caleb said Henry hit his thumb with a hammer twice in the last week. Nothing shakes Henry, but this has." Mercy stood back and cocked her head at Leesa. "There. All done. You're ready."

Ready or not, here I come.

She'd been ready for months, but the house had not. First they had to scrape together their earnings and save every penny they could. Then Henry and their friends laid the foundation and erected the framework. A fierce windstorm in July destroyed their first efforts. A second round had proven to be longer lasting. Once the frame was boxed, they had worked through rain, sleet, and snow.

Leesa sewed curtains and made quilts with her family and friends. Henry built their bed and a new table and chairs for the kitchen. Caleb contributed matching rocking chairs to be placed in front of the fireplace. Leesa's dad built the kitchen cabinets. Everyone had a hand in the final product.

Today all the preparations were done. Nothing else was needed except the exchange of vows.

"Go on, go." Mercy nudged Leesa toward the door. "Christine and I will be right beside you."

Her witnesses to the best day of her life.

So far.

The living and eating areas of their new house were crowded with long benches set up like the typical church service. In a way it was. Almost all of the three-hour ceremony would consist of the usual series of hymns, prayers, and sermons. Only the last few minutes were dedicated to their vows. How would she manage to wait that long?

Somehow, she did. Every one of her scholars was present, their faces as shiny and expectant as they had been the first day of school a year and a half ago. They had a new teacher. They were in good hands.

When the moment arrived, Leesa rose on legs with muscles like vanilla pudding. She peeked at the congregation for one last look at Tommy, who sat with her brothers. He grinned and waved. Encouraged, she took a long breath and staggered to the spot where Noah stood. Vaguely she was aware of Mercy and

Christine behind her. Andy and Caleb stood near Henry. Then her vision narrowed. She and Henry were alone in their new home with only the bishop between them.

His expression somber, Noah nodded once and began. He didn't need a book. They'd all grown up listening to these words and knew them by heart.

"Are you confident that this, our sister, is ordained of God to be your wedded wife?"

Henry's deep bass echoed through the room. *"Jah."*

"Are you confident that this, our brother, is ordained of God to be your wedded husband?"

Leesa stifled the urge to turn and shout to the world—or at least her *Gmay. "Jah."*

The next question, the same for the both of them, asked before God and the church that they would never depart from each other, always care for and cherish each other, regardless of sickness or circumstance that a Christian husband or wife must be responsible to care for, until God would separate them from each other.

Indeed. No doubt. Leesa hazarded a side glance at Henry. His eyes were bright, his face crimson, his expression determined. *"Jah."*

He took her right hand in his. His fingers were warm and strong. Noah placed his hand over theirs. "So then may I say, the God of Abraham, the God of Isaac, and the God of Jacob be with you and help you together and fulfill his blessing abundantly upon you, through Jesus Christ. Amen."

They were husband and wife. No applause rang out. No cheers. They simply returned to their seats, Henry on the men's side, Leesa with the women, for the final hymn. Mercy and the other women slipped out to prepare the food.

Leesa was now a married woman. Two years ago she never would have imagined that would be possible.

Oh ye of little faith.

Sorry, Gott.

The hymn ended, and Leesa stood with the others. Few words were spoken, but the hugs flew so quickly she barely had a chance to breathe before the next one came.

Finally, she stood face-to-face with her new husband while the other men rearranged benches and brought in tables for the meal.

Henry grabbed her hand, tugged their coats from a hook by the front door, and gently nudged her out to the front porch.

She tried—if only half-heartedly—to pull away. "Henry!"

He put one finger to his lips. "Shush!"

Frigid December air greeted them. Sunlight turned the snow into a brilliantly sparkling meadow so bright Leesa had to squint and raise her free hand to her forehead.

"Quick, kiss your husband."

She had a husband. The thought dumbfounded her. Leesa flew into his arms, and he lifted her in the air and whirled her around. *"Frehlicher Grischtdaag, mann."*

"Frehlicher Grischtdaag, fraa." Henry kissed her and set her back on the porch. "I couldn't ask for a better gift."

"We'll never be able to top this gift, no matter how long we're married."

"I don't know about that. Wait until we have *boplin* of our own."

Joyful anticipation filled her so fiercely Leesa had to look down to make sure her feet were still planted on the porch's pine slats.

She pulled Henry to her for another kiss.

Bam-bam. Something smacked hard against the wall over her head.

Bam-bam. Another one and another one.

"Hey!" Henry moved to block the icy snowballs bombarding them from the front yard. "Tommy Bontrager, you're in for it now."

Soon to be Tommy Lufkin.

"Promises, promises!"

Bellowing with laughter, Henry grabbed Leesa's arm and propelled her down the steps. "We've been challenged."

"I was a *gut* pitcher in baseball."

Leesa scooped up a mound of snow and molded it into a firm ball. She let it fly.

Tommy ducked but not quick enough. It caught him square in the chest.

"Hey, *Mudder*! That's not nice."

Mudder. The word was like the sweet smell of fresh-cut grass in spring. She had been Tommy's teacher. Now she would be his mother forever. "*Suh*, you had it coming."

He hurled another, bigger snowball. It grazed her *kapp*, spinning it sideways. "Now you're in for it!"

The snowballs zipped back and forth, fast and furious. Leesa laughed so hard she couldn't breathe.

Their raucous shouts brought others piling out the door. Soon they were joined by sisters, brothers, cousins, friends, and family.

Gasping for air, her cheeks and hands frozen, Leesa paused for one second.

Danki, Gott.

He had a plan, one she never could have imagined. He wanted her to know:

This is what love sounds like.

This is what love feels like.

Merry Christmas, Gott, Merry Christmas.

Discussion Questions

1. When Tommy's aunt gets sick with cancer, he prays that God will heal her, but she still dies. Tommy loses faith. He's mad at God. This is a tough outcome to prayer for adults to understand, let alone a child. How would you explain "unanswered" prayers to a child?
2. Henry comes to recognize that God has put him in Tommy's life to help the boy find his way back to his faith. Has God ever put people in your life who need comfort from someone who has been through similar life experiences? How did you respond?
3. Henry tells Tommy that God can take any situation and use it for his good, a statement based in Scripture. But Henry also knows what it's like to doubt God's plan. Have you ever doubted God's plan for you? Have there been times when later you were able to see God's hand in the outcome of your situation?
4. Henry and Leesa decide to work together to help Tommy overcome his anger and pain at losing his aunt and moving to a new community to live with

a stranger. Do you think it's a coincidence that they too are in need of healing? Leesa didn't want to teach. Henry didn't feel suited to be a father figure. How did each of the three benefit from their unwanted, unexpected circumstances?

Wreathed in Joy

Kathleen Fuller

To James Fuller. I love you.

PROLOGUE

Mary Wengerd lowered herself onto a wooden park bench as flakes of snow floated around her. She shivered, then glanced up at the dusky sky. It was way too cold to be sitting outside in this weather, but she couldn't go back home. Not until she talked to Jakob.

This had been their favorite spot to meet ever since they were young children. The small park was within walking distance of both their homes in Middlefield, but right now it was empty of visitors. That didn't surprise her. Who would be enjoying a park on a freezing December evening two days before Christmas?

Sighing, she rose and started to pace. Although she wore her warmest coat, boots, gloves, and tights—her muffler tucked tightly around her neck and her bonnet securely over her *kapp*—she was still cold, more so on the inside than out. Her stomach turned. She'd been dreading talking to Jakob all day. But she couldn't put off this conversation any longer.

"Mary."

She turned at Jakob's familiar deep voice, and for some strange reason she remembered the day she noticed it was changing. One day when they were both fourteen and the best of friends—which their other friends thought was odd, though that had never mattered to either of them—his voice had squeaked while reciting his English homework to the class. She was the only student who hadn't laughed. Now that voice was rich and warm, but it didn't reach her heart. And that was the problem.

"Hi, Jakob. *Danki* for meeting me here."

He glanced up at the sky, and a few snowflakes caught on his blond eyelashes. "It's not a *gut* night for meeting here," he murmured.

"I didn't realize it was going to snow when I left a message asking you to come." She sat back down on the bench, and Jakob joined her. She assumed he would reach for one of her hands to hold, just as he had so many times before. But this time he didn't. He wasn't even looking at her.

"I've got something to tell you," they said at the same time, then looked at each other. Mary was sure his surprised expression mirrored her own.

"You do?" she asked.

He nodded, now staring at the ground. Snow was gathering on his broad shoulders, dusting his coat with white powder. "But you *geh* first."

"You can *geh*," she said, eager for the few minutes' respite even though she had no idea what he was going to tell her.

"You're the one who wanted to meet." He glanced at her, and she didn't see the usual twinkle in his dark-gray eyes. The combination of gray and blond was unique, and she'd never seen a man who looked quite like Jakob.

She pulled her gaze away from him, forcing herself to focus, then said a quick prayer before taking a deep breath. "I don't think we should date anymore," she blurted.

He slumped against the bench. "That's such a relief."

Her head snapped back to look at him. "What?"

Jakob waved his hand. "I didn't mean that the way it sounded." But even in the dimming light of sunset, she could see the relief in his eyes. "It's just . . . Well, I was going to say the same thing."

"You were?" She felt a flash of hurt at his words even though she knew she was doing the right thing. "If you were unhappy with how it's been between us, Jakob Mullet, why didn't you say something sooner?"

"Why didn't you?"

"Because I didn't want to hurt *yer* feelings." She angled her body on the bench so she could look at him directly.

"I didn't want to hurt *yers* either." He paused. "Have I?"

She wasn't about to admit she'd felt that quick flash of rejection. This was what she wanted. "Of course not. I just find it *seltsam* that we're on the same page."

"For once." He blew out a breath, and a cloudy puff hung in the air. "It seems like we haven't been on the same page ever since we started dating."

She nodded. Six months ago, after years of friendship and encouragement from their friends and family, they'd begun a new relationship. But dating Jakob had never felt right. It felt forced, and nothing romantic had developed between them other than holding hands. Just the thought of kissing him—a show of affection neither had pursued—unsettled her. This wasn't what love was supposed to be like, and it got to the point where she'd started to dread being with him. That had never been the case before. "I miss *mei* friend," she said, half to him and half to herself.

"Me too. Our relationship was easier when we were just friends." He rubbed his bare hands over his pants legs, then stuck them in the pockets of his coat. "We shouldn't have listened to everyone telling us we were meant to be a couple."

"They never understood our relationship."

"Exactly." He looked at her, then rubbed his thumb over her cheek. "Snowflake," he said before jamming his hand back into his pocket.

And this was a prime example. Shouldn't she have felt something when he touched her cheek? Shouldn't she have butterflies in her stomach? Shouldn't she want him to move nearer, put his arm around her, and draw her close? But she didn't want any of that, and it was a blessing he felt the same way.

Still . . .

"Where do we *geh* from here?" she asked.

"Back to the way things were, I guess." He got up from the bench. "I don't know about you, but I'm freezing." He started to reach for her hand, then retreated. "Do you want me to walk you home?"

She shook her head. "I think I'll sit here for a little while."

He frowned slightly, then nodded. "Make sure you don't stay out too long."

"I won't."

He hesitated, and she couldn't decipher his expression. Then he turned and headed home, in the opposite direction of her house.

She settled back against the bench. The snow fell harder now, but she still didn't leave. Jakob's words echoed in her mind. *Back to the way things were.* They'd been friends since they were six, best friends since they were ten. They'd dated for only six months, but considering the awkwardness of the relationship, she didn't consider that official dating. So returning to their friendship wouldn't be too hard . . . would it? And she'd feel nothing but relief in no time . . . wouldn't she?

"Of course it won't, and of course I will," she said, standing. Positive that everything between her and Jakob would now be right, she headed home—ignoring the niggling doubt in her heart.

1

Early December, one year later

Mildly curious about why a car was parked in their driveway, Jakob drove his buggy toward the Wengerds' house. Other than attending church here the few times Mary's parents had hosted a service, he hadn't visited the family's home for nearly a year. Or rather, he hadn't visited Mary specifically.

Even though he'd spent most of his free time with her for years—hanging out with her and her family, her three older siblings having included the two of them in their activities even after they'd all married and moved into their own homes—it seemed so strange to be here.

Yet he smiled at the memories—only to frown at the thought of how he and Mary had ruined everything by dating.

But he wasn't here to see her. At church the previous Sunday, her father, Wayne, had asked him to come over. He'd made a point of saying what day and time, but when a friend approached him and interrupted their conversation, he'd stopped short of specifying a reason. Jakob had hoped to discreetly ask him if Mary would be there, but he'd lost his chance.

Looking back, he realized the question would have been awkward between them. Everyone had to be dumbfounded that he and Mary had failed to resume their friendship, and he couldn't blame them. After all, they'd told close family and friends that was their plan. Well, at least he had. But he'd rarely mentioned her to anyone now. For some reason, returning to just friends had immediately proven impossible. Even seeing each other at church had been painfully tense.

What had really bothered him was how Mary seemed resentful toward him, and before long he felt resentful toward her too. After all, she'd wanted the breakup as well.

He'd dated two other girls since their breakup, but neither relationship had worked out. And he'd tried not to pay attention to what Mary was doing with her social life. But even in a larger district like their own, word got around. He'd heard she dated LeRoy Yoder for a while. He had to admit he'd been glad they'd broken up. LeRoy was all wrong for her. He could have told her that . . . if they were talking to each other.

He shook his head. He was overthinking this. Wayne needed to see him in his home for some reason, and if Mary was here, they'd just avoid each other as much as possible—like always.

He hitched his horse to a post, then put a blanket over him for warmth against the frigid December air before climbing up to the Wengerds' front porch. He knocked on the door, and when it opened, Mary's mother stood there.

"Jakob," Maria said, her brow lifting in surprise. Then

confusion filled her green eyes, which were so much like Mary's. She pushed up her silver-rimmed glasses. "I didn't know you were coming today."

Wayne hadn't told her he'd invited him to be there? He wasn't sure what to say now.

"Well, don't just stand there. Come inside." She opened the door wider and motioned for him to enter.

He stepped across the threshold. "Is Wayne around?"

"I expect him home soon. He must be running late at work." She tilted her head. "He's the one you're here to see, then?" Now she looked curious too.

"Ya." Jakob put his hands behind his back.

"Oh. Okay. Let me take *yer* coat."

For a moment Jakob strained to see if he could hear Mary's voice. But then he quickly slipped off his boots while shrugging out of his coat. *"Danki."*

Maria, her expression uncertain, said, "*Geh* on into the kitchen to wait for Wayne. And help *yerself* to some hot chocolate. I just made some for our other guest."

"Oh. Okay. *Danki*."

When she didn't say who the guest was, he assumed it was some *English* friend of the Wengerds', someone with a car. He also assumed Maria would join them shortly. Still hoping Mary was out somewhere, he strode across the wide living room and entered the kitchen, then halted.

Mary was seated at the table with her *English* friend, Quinn Butler.

His gaze met Mary's, and he saw both surprise and suspicion in her eyes. Those beautiful green eyes, he noted, which were on a very pretty face, framed by black hair peeking from under a *kapp*. Regardless of their relationship—or lack of one—Mary was still the prettiest girl he'd ever met. That would never change.

But everything between them had.

"Hey, Jakob."

Mary stared at him in near shock and then at Quinn in consternation. Her friend had risen from the table and was giving Jakob a big hug. That greeting wasn't unusual for her. She was about that friendly with everyone.

Jakob returned the hug with a smile.

"Long time no see," Quinn added, sitting back down. She pointed at the chair opposite Mary, completely missing her glare. Ugh, her friend could be so thickheaded sometimes—although she quickly had to admit this wasn't one of those times.

Quinn had lived next door their whole lives—until she moved to Madison only last year—and she was still her best Yankee friend. She'd also been one of the driving forces behind her and Jakob shifting their relationship "to the next level," as Quinn had labeled it. But although the two women had stayed close, Mary had managed to conceal the fact that she and Jakob rarely even spoke to each other after the breakup. Quinn probably assumed he still visited her on a regular basis, that their friendship had been saved.

It hadn't.

"What have you been up to, Jake?" Quinn asked.

"The same old. Working in the woodshop, making cabinets and such." He sat back in his chair, and Mary studied him.

When he'd first come in, he'd seemed . . . well, a little taken aback. Because Quinn was there? Or because she was? But now he was behaving as though he'd just been here yesterday, and the day before, and the day before—like he used to be. Well, nearly that often.

Mary threaded her fingers together under the table. Maybe he was just *trying* to seem relaxed in front of Quinn. But if this was for real, how could he be so blasé about being in her home after all this time? Then again, Quinn also had a way of putting people at ease, and now she was telling Jakob about her upcoming wedding. The wedding she no doubt thought he already knew about.

What was he doing here, anyway?

"I know it's unusual to plan a wedding for Christmas Eve. Not only did we want a short engagement but Tanner and I thought it would be easier on our extended family to marry when we're all gathering for the holidays anyway." Quinn smiled, her vibrant blue eyes filled with delight. Then she looked at Mary. "Besides, Mary and I have always dreamed about planning our weddings for Christmastime."

Mary felt her cheeks heat, then glanced away. The last thing she wanted was for Quinn to bring up their childish dreams. But the dream wasn't so childish anymore for Quinn. It was coming true.

"Is that right?" Jakob said. "I had no idea."

"Oh yes. Christmas is our favorite holiday. Both of us."

"I did know that."

Mary couldn't help but glance at him, but thankfully he was still looking at Quinn. In fact, it was as if Mary weren't even there. That didn't set right with her either, but her mother would still expect her to show the man some hospitality.

"Would you like some hot chocolate . . . Jakob?"

He turned to look at her then. "I would. Thanks."

"Anyway," Quinn said as Mary stood—turning her eyes away from him—"I came over to ask Mary if she would make our wedding cakes. I wanted to ask her in person."

"Cakes? Plural?" Jakob lifted a brow. "How many people are you expecting?"

"Oh, it's a small wedding, but traditionally at Yankee receptions, we have a bride's cake, which is a larger one, and then a smaller groom's cake."

She turned to Mary as Jakob accepted the mug she handed him without looking into his eyes again. Quinn smiled, but then she sobered a little as she turned back to Mary. "I couldn't think of anyone I'd rather make the cakes, but I don't want it to interfere with you spending Christmas Eve with your family. I know how important that is to you."

Mary had always spent Christmas Eve with her entire family, all gathered here at her parents' house. Her father read the story of Jesus's birth from the book of Luke in the Bible, and then they munched on gingerbread cookies and popcorn balls she and her sisters made. They also drank freshly pressed cider made from apples they'd picked at her brother-in-law's orchard in the fall. Then they exchanged simple presents, and Mary always delighted in seeing her nieces' and nephews' faces lit up as they played with their new toys, especially the girls with their dolls.

But while Christmas was a special and beautiful time for her, Quinn was important to her, too, and she wouldn't miss the chance to do something special for her wedding. She'd also been invited to attend the ceremony after she delivered the cakes, and she really did want to see Quinn get married. "I told you, I'm happy and honored that you asked," she said, smiling.

Quinn returned her smile, clasping her hands together. "I know they'll be perfect and delicious."

"I'm sure they will be," a deeper voice said.

Stunned, Mary turned toward Jakob. While she'd been thinking about Christmas, she'd forgotten about him. She met his gaze to determine if he was being sarcastic, but she shouldn't have been surprised to see genuineness in his eyes. Jakob didn't have a caustic bone in his body, and he didn't give out compliments unless he meant them. But the way things had been between them the last year, she couldn't have been sure.

He was leaning back in his chair, an ankle crossed over one knee, his gaze still directly meeting hers as he took a sip of his hot chocolate. She flinched as his eyes held hers—as if she were the only person in the room—and she felt like it was . . .

She had no idea what it was.

Jakob turned back to Quinn, and they started talking again.

Mary put her hand over her fluttering stomach, trying to figure out what just happened. She couldn't remember a time he'd ever looked at her like . . . *that*. Surely it wasn't what she thought—attraction. Jakob had simply paid her a nice compliment just now. No big deal, especially since her baking skills were fairly well-known in the district. His backing up Quinn's assertion that she would do a good job with the cakes wasn't out of the ordinary.

However, the tiny flip in her stomach was. Yet attraction on her part wasn't likely either. Jakob was handsome, no doubt about that. But she'd been down the supposed road of romance with him, and the trip hadn't been worth the pain.

She had to get these thoughts out of her head.

"So, Jakob, I didn't expect to see you this afternoon. What brings you by?"

He shifted in his seat. "Well, *yer daed* asked me to come—"

Her father strode into the kitchen, still wearing his boots and coat. "Sorry I'm late, Jakob." Then he looked at Quinn and smiled. "Hello. Maria told me that's your car outside. How are the wedding plans coming?"

"Great now that Mary's agreed to bake the cakes." Quinn checked her watch, then rose from her seat. "Sorry I have to run," she said, gathering her purse and the magazine she'd brought to show Mary a photo of her wedding dress. "I'm supposed to meet with the florist at four, then with the caterer at seven." She sighed. "I think the Amish have it right when it comes to planning weddings. What I wouldn't do to have a huge group of people helping me with the preparations." She blushed. "I'm having fun, of course. But trying to put all the pieces together . . ." She shook her head. "Anyway, thank you, Mary."

"I'll walk you out," she said, getting up.

Quinn turned to Jakob. "It was good to see you."

"Same here." He grinned.

There went the flip again. She frowned as she accompanied Quinn to the front door, yet she was relieved her mother was somewhere else in the house so she couldn't stare her down with questions about Jakob in her eyes. Then again, Mary certainly had a question for her father. Why did he ask Jakob to come here?

She held Quinn's belongings as she slipped on her winter coat. Then they both stepped outside on the front porch. A blast of cold air hit them as Mary quickly shut the door.

"Thanks again," Quinn said, giving her a side hug. "I'll be back in two weeks to taste test your samples."

"Samples?"

"Oh yes. That's tradition too. You make a few small sample cakes, and then Tanner and I tell you which flavors we like the best." She frowned. "Unless that's too much trouble."

"Of course it isn't." Although she'd never heard of such a thing, it wouldn't be difficult to make a few small cakes. "What's Tanner's favorite flavor?"

"Chocolate, but why don't you surprise us—or at least me? I've planned this wedding down to the last detail. I'd like to have at least one surprise."

Mary nodded, forcing a smile. "I understand." She wasn't about to admit that she didn't like having so much pressure put on her. What if Quinn and Tanner didn't like what she made? Or worse, what if their wedding guests thought her cakes were awful—at least the way they were decorated? She'd have to do some research at the library, then bake some trial runs—and practice decorating too. She was sure her family wouldn't mind being taste testers.

"I'd better let you get inside before you freeze." Quinn headed down the steps, only to turn around when she reached the bottom. "Hey. Are you sure there's, um, nothing going on between the two of you?"

Crossing her arms against the chill, Mary said, "What are you talking about?"

"You and Jakob. I thought I saw a spark in there. More than friendship."

Mary let out an awkward chuckle. "Trust me, there wasn't a spark. I think your head is too full of romantic notions right now. With good reason, of course."

"Oh." Quinn frowned a little, then shrugged before slinging her purse over one shoulder. "I'm sure you're right. Tanner's already tired of me talking about the wedding. I think he's ready to elope, but he knows Mom and Dad would string him up if we did." She grinned and waved with her free hand, then got into her car and drove away.

Mary shivered as she watched her friend leave. It bothered her that Quinn had picked up on something she'd noticed—no, felt—herself. But anything romantic between her and Jakob was impossible. Not only would they never be a couple again, but she was sure their friendship was over for good. That still saddened her. When they broke up, she'd told herself they could return to what they'd had before.

But she couldn't have been more wrong.

"I hope you don't mind talking out here. When I asked you to come, Maria and Mary had plans to be away from the *haus* this afternoon. I didn't know those plans had changed until I got home just now."

"This is fine," Jakob said, shaking his head as Wayne led him to the back of the barn. Whatever the man had to talk about, he clearly didn't want his wife—and maybe not his daughter—to know about it.

Wayne sat down on a hay bale and gestured for Jakob to sit on another one across from him. "I'd like to ask you to make something special for Maria, a Christmas present. This is our thirtieth Christmas together, and I want it to be memorable for her."

Jakob hid a smile. So Mary's father had a romantic side to him. *Apparently that gene missed Mary.* He shoved the thought away. He didn't need to be thinking about her in the context of romance, especially after he'd gazed at her in the kitchen. He'd meant to just glance at her, but when he looked at her after complimenting her baking skills, which were excellent, he couldn't look away. She was so pretty, and a spark of feeling he'd thought was long dead had sprung to life—at the worst time. Besides, he and Mary were over in more ways than one.

He focused on Wayne's request. "What were you thinking of?"

"Well, I have an example of *yer* fine work right here." He looked toward the barn door, apparently to make sure neither Maria nor Mary had followed them, then withdrew a small keepsake box from his pocket. "I bought this from you for *mei frau* a couple of years ago. She loves the design, and I wonder if you have enough time to make her a cedar-lined hope chest like it. *Nix* fancy, of course."

"How big do you want the chest?"

"Enough to hold several quilts. Her *grossmutter* died three years ago, and she inherited several. She treasures them, and she's been keeping them in the linen closet. I think she'd like to have a special place for them all their own."

"I don't think it will be too difficult to make it in time for Christmas. What day do you want it delivered?"

"I'll pick it up, so don't worry about that." Wayne paused. "I don't want you to have to be bothered coming back here." He sighed. "If I'd taken the box to *yer* shop, Maria would have realized it was gone. She uses it every day, and I'm sure she'd miss it. Then I'd have to explain everything. I don't want to spoil the surprise. As it is, I don't know how I'm going to explain *yer* being here today." He shrugged, smiling half-heartedly. "I might just have to tell her this isn't the right time of year to ask questions, it being so close to Christmas and all."

"So you're gonna tell her to mind her own business?" Jakob grinned.

Wayne chuckled. "I know better than that."

"I don't mind bringing it to you," he said. This was Mary's father, and it didn't sit right with him that he would have to pick up the gift. "Just let me know what day and where you want me to unload it, and I'll make it happen."

Wayne nodded. "*Danki*, Jakob." He rose from the hay bale and shook his hand. "Too bad things didn't work out with you and Mary. I really thought they would."

So had he, at least early on. *How wrong I was.*

"Anyway," Wayne continued before he could decide if he should respond, "I know *mei frau* will be happy with this gift. Happy wife, happy life, *ya*?"

"Ya." Not that Jakob had any experience with a wife, happy or not. And the way he was going, he wouldn't.

Jakob rose from the bale, and they left the barn. Outside, a surge of frigid wind cut through him. Thanksgiving had been just last week, but from the cold temperatures they'd been having, winter seemed determined to set in early this year.

"I suppose you wouldn't want to stay for supper?" Wayne asked. "We're having roast beef and mashed potatoes."

Jakob shook his head. "*Mamm*'s expecting me home. But I appreciate you asking."

Wayne nodded. Jakob was surprised he'd invited him, let alone mentioned Mary. More than likely he'd extended the invitation out of politeness, not because he expected him to accept.

They walked to the driveway, and Jakob said good-bye. Wayne waited while he removed the horse's blanket and unhitched him from the post, and then he turned toward the house. As Jakob climbed into his buggy, he heard Mary calling to her father and turned to look at her.

"*Mamm* wants you to bring in a bushel of apples from the cellar," she said from the front porch.

Jakob couldn't help but stare at her from behind the buggy's winter shield. She had her arms wrapped around her chest, wearing only a thin blue sweater. It didn't make sense for her to put on a coat when she was only delivering a quick message, but he didn't like her being unprotected against the chill. A crazy thought entered his mind. He should run over and give her his coat, just like he had so many times over the years when she'd been cold.

He checked himself. Some habits were hard to break, but he'd broken just about every one of them when it came to Mary. Funny how seeing her today brought back memories of her huddled in his coat—always two sizes too big for her no matter how old they were. He'd worked hard not to think about their lost relationship. He had no way to turn back time, no reason to dwell on what would never be again.

The best way to avoid thinking about it now was to leave. He tapped on the horse's flanks with the reins, then pulled out of the driveway and pushed Mary out of his mind, just the way he had ever since their friendship failed to return.

2

"Mary? Mary, did you hear what I said?"

Mary looked at her mother and nodded, even though she had no idea what *Mamm* had been talking about. They had already made apple cobbler from some of the apples *Daed* brought in before supper, and now they were peeling apples for apple butter. She loved apples and never tired of them. Their shiny deep-red color reminded her of holly berries, which reminded her of Christmas, which made her think of Quinn's wedding, and then of all things, of Jakob.

"Humph." *Mamm* set down her paring knife and looked at her. "You've been preoccupied ever since Quinn and Jakob were here. You almost burned the bottom of the rolls, and you never do that." She paused and smiled a little. "They were delicious, by the way."

Mary nodded her thanks, then said, "I'm sorry, *Mamm*. What were you saying?"

"I want to ask you something."

Oh no. Was she going to ask about Jakob? To her surprise, neither of her parents had said anything about him at supper. Or . . . If her mother tried to get *Daed*'s secret out of her, she might have a hard time resisting. She almost wished *Daed* hadn't told her about the quilt chest, but when she inquired why he'd asked Jakob to come over, he didn't have much choice.

"Do you really think you'll have time to make Quinn's wedding cakes?"

She held back a sigh of relief. This was about Quinn, not Jakob. "Why shouldn't I have time?"

Mamm picked up the knife again. "Did you forget you said you'd make six dozen Christmas cookies for the school program?"

Oh. She had forgotten that. She cringed, wondering how she was going to manage baking the cookies—decorated Christmas ones no less—in addition to figuring out Quinn's wedding cakes, all while she was working with her mother as a seamstress for their Amish and Yankee customers. Ever since the holiday season had started back in November, she and *Mamm* had been sewing even more for Yankees than Amish, especially making quilted pot holders, aprons, and other items that could be gifts. It was a blessing to have brisk business, but that meant an extra-busy Christmas season. She was determined to meet her commitments, though.

"I'll have to manage *mei* time well, but I can do it." She glanced at her mother. "I can't say *nee* to Quinn. Not about this."

"I know." *Mamm* sighed and turned back to the apple she'd been peeling. "Quinn is like *familye* to us, and that's the only reason *yer daed* and I are fine with you missing out on Christmas Eve here. I do wish you could be with us, though."

"Me too." Although she was finding it harder to be the only single woman around her family at Christmas. She'd dated one other man since the breakup with Jakob, but she'd never had a beau on Christmas Eve. Last year she and Jakob had ended their dating relationship the day before.

A sudden warmth came over her as she thought about him. Only a few hours ago, he'd been sitting in the same chair she was in now. The effect he was having on her after all this time was so strange.

"I wish I could help you," *Mamm* said, "but you know how our orders are piling up."

"I promise I won't let you down. You don't have to worry about me missing out on work to do *mei* baking."

"Oh, well, I think there's a little wiggle room there." She smiled. "Let's finish these apples and get them cooking. We'll let them cool overnight and then make the apple butter in the morning."

Mary thought that was a great idea, and she and *Mamm* made quick work of peeling the rest of the apples. After the fruit had cooked in *Mamm*'s large stockpot, they put it in two big metal bowls and covered them with foil.

"That's enough for one day." *Mamm* yawned and arched her back, then pushed her glasses up on her nose. "I'll see you in the morning, Mary. *Gute nacht*."

"Gute nacht." After her mother left, Mary pulled a pad of paper and a pencil from a kitchen drawer and sat down, this time in a different seat. Pushing Jakob out of her mind, she first considered the Christmas cookies. Each year the school gave a program, and now two more of her nieces and nephews were old enough to be in it. That was one reason she'd agreed to make so

many cookies when one of the teachers asked. "*Yer* cookies are the best," Juanita had said. "I know six dozen is more than you'd normally contribute, but they would really be appreciated."

"I'd be glad to," she'd said. Of course, that was before Quinn's request for the cakes. Still, making cookies wasn't that difficult. She had her own special cookie dough recipe, and she had Christmas cookie cutters. A few sprinkles of red and green sugar on top of each cookie, and they would be good to go.

Feeling confident that she could handle that task, she turned her attention to the cakes. She'd made scores of cakes since she started baking at age ten. But Quinn's cakes had to be extra special and delicious, and now she couldn't be sure she'd find the time to go to the library to research. She skimmed through two cookbooks and three boxes of recipe cards, then decided to make four sample flavors—chocolate because Quinn had said that was Tanner's favorite, then Italian cream, yellow, and strawberry.

She set down her pencil and rested her chin on her palm. She'd *have* to find time to go to the library. If she didn't, she'd never figure out the best way to decorate the cakes. Maybe she could do that on Monday. The Christmas program was next Thursday evening, so the cookies would have to be done by then . . .

One day at a time.

She froze. That was Jakob's favorite saying. Once again, she was thinking about him. The saying was a common one, and she'd heard other people use it. But whenever either one of them had felt overwhelmed, he'd always say, "One day at a time. That's all we have to get through."

Frowning, she rose from the table. All these thoughts about Jakob were temporary. By tomorrow she'd be so focused on her responsibilities that she'd forget all about him. Nodding to herself, she turned off the gas lamp in the kitchen and climbed the stairs.

As she dropped into bed fifteen minutes later, she realized Jakob certainly wouldn't be thinking about her. *He wanted the breakup, too, remember?* And he'd avoided her just as much as she'd avoided him all this time. Their meeting today had just been accidental, with no other result than being civil in front of Quinn.

But as she closed her eyes, her mind drifted to the warm look he'd given her at the kitchen table—and how wonderful it had made her feel.

Jakob pulled on clean broadfall pants and a fresh shirt—then at the last minute, a blue pullover sweater, too—for the school Christmas program. Two of his nephews and three of his nieces were in it, and he hadn't missed a single one since the first child was old enough to attend school. He looked forward to hearing the kids sing—and to the invariable gaff one or more of them would make during the program. Afterward came the social part—eating the treats the women of the community made for everyone to snack on while they all visited with one another.

He combed his hair, then went downstairs to the kitchen, where his mother was putting on her black bonnet. "*Daed*'s hitching up the buggy," she said, tying the black ribbons beneath her chin.

"I was going to hitch it for him," Jakob said, frowning.

"*Yer daed* was ready early, and you know he gets antsy." She glanced at the doorway leading to the mudroom and clucked her tongue.

"I'll *geh* out and help him."

His father was almost finished, though. Still, he was glad he'd stepped outside ahead of his mother. Snow had started to fall, and he didn't want her to slip on the porch steps. So he quickly swept them clean with a broom they kept propped near the back door in the winter.

On the ride there, he noted the temperature seemed to be dropping, and once they were at the school, he was glad the coal stove in the basement had already warmed the main floor.

This was the same place he and Mary had attended school. Memories of the Christmas programs he'd reluctantly participated in when he was a student washed over him. He glanced around, and on several of the older boys' faces he saw the same forlorn look he supposed he'd worn then. He couldn't help but smile. Right now singing in front of most everyone in the community might seem like torture, but someday, when these boys' own children were in the Christmas programs, they would come to appreciate the event.

Family. Someday he wanted a wife and children of his own, God willing. At one time he thought Mary might be part of that future, but not anymore.

He pushed her out of his thoughts and looked around again. The school was one huge room with a divider in the middle that split the lower and higher grades, but tonight the divider was pushed back, along with most of the desks. Folding chairs for the audience were on one side of the room, and two folding tables laden with all the desserts had been set up on the other side. As he usually did before the program started, he moseyed over to see what kinds of treats he could enjoy later.

His gaze landed on a large platter of sugar cookies in the

center of one of the tables. Although it was surrounded by other cookies, cupcakes, brownies, and homemade candy, he smiled. Those sugar cookies had to be Mary's, and everyone knew her cookies were the best.

Jakob lifted his gaze and spotted her coming in through the back door, carrying another platter of cookies. She looked tired, and he almost joined her to ask if she needed help. He stopped himself when her gaze met his, and he saw only a coldness there. Fine. So much for civility. She didn't want his help, so he wouldn't offer it.

He turned to grab a seat in the audience only to find every chair filled. That was fine too. He could stand. But so many others were standing as well that the only place he could find was against the back wall. And the only space there was near the tables.

He didn't look at Mary as she slipped in right next to him, obviously her only choice. But when he noticed her craning her neck to see the students, he couldn't help himself. He tapped her on the shoulder, then gestured to switch places so she could see better. She paused, then gave him a curt nod. Boy, was she in a mood. He'd seen moods like this over the years both when they were friends and when they were a couple. Experience told him the best thing was to just let her stew about whatever was bothering her. She'd get over it eventually. Still, he couldn't help but wonder what had made her so cranky.

He focused on the program, which as usual was enjoyable. Some of the students forgot their parts, and others not only sang out of tune but drowned out the other students. The older boys mouthed the words, something Jakob had done too. Then he caught his youngest niece's attention. She was six, and she wasn't shy about waving at him when he gave her a smile.

When the program was over, everyone gathered around the tables and filled small paper plates with the treats he'd checked out earlier. He'd been right about which cookies were Mary's. Jakob let everyone else go before him, but he managed to get one of her cookies before they disappeared. Then he spent some time talking with a friend before turning toward the rest of the crowd to find most everyone already gone.

"Jakob."

He turned to his father and saw the concern on his face. He was already wearing his coat and boots. *"Ya?"*

"The roads are getting slippery. We need to leave before it gets too difficult to travel in a buggy. Most families have already gone home."

He nodded, then glanced at Mary. He'd noticed she'd played hostess the entire time, making sure everyone who wanted a cup of cider received one and giving the two teachers time to visit with their students' families. But now the teachers were already cleaning the classroom, and he knew they wouldn't leave until the place was put back together and spotless. "I think I'll stay and help Juanita and Tabitha."

"You'll have to walk home," *Mamm* said as she joined them, wearing her cape and bonnet.

"That's fine. I'll be warm enough, and I have *mei* flashlight." He didn't mind a walk in the snow.

"All right." *Daed* nodded and backed away. "We'll see you at home, then."

Jakob joined Tabitha, the teacher who taught the younger grades. "I'll get these chairs for you," he said.

"*Danki*, Jakob." She looked up at him from lowered lashes. "That's very kind of you."

Tabitha was single, and by the way she was looking at him, he realized she might be interested in him. But he wasn't interested in her. Turning, he started folding chairs, then stacking them on two carts. He rolled the carts one at a time to the back of the classroom, and when he'd finished, Tabitha was shoving the last of the desks into place. Juanita must have left without his noticing.

He was about to see if the two dessert tables were ready to be folded when he felt a tap on his shoulder.

"I really appreciate *yer* help," Tabitha said, smiling up at him.

"You're welcome." He took a step back. Yep, she was definitely interested. She was a nice girl, pretty in a nondescript sort of way, and only two years younger than him. But there was no attraction or spark there, and he wasn't going to let her think there was. "I should be going now—"

"Would you like to come to *mei haus* for a while? I have marshmallows and some homemade hot chocolate, and we're just two doors down. Then if the weather gets really bad, I can take you home in *Daed*'s sled. He won't mind."

"Jakob's already promised to help me carry *mei* platters home," Mary said, coming up beside him.

Jakob looked at her, bewildered. Then he felt her pinch his arm. A light pinch, which had always been her signal that they'd talk later about whatever was going on. In other words, he needed to go along with her.

"Oh, that's right." He slapped his forehead in dramatic fashion. "How could I have forgotten that?"

Tabitha looked from him to Mary, then back at him. "I didn't realize you two were still together," she said, looking disappointed.

"We're not," they said at the same time.

Mary smiled, but the gesture seemed strained. "It's just that no one else was still here to ask. Everyone was in a hurry to get home, including *mei* parents."

"Understandable, because of the weather." Jakob wasn't too thrilled she'd felt the need to say he was her last resort at the same time she was helping him out. Maybe he'd ask her about that.

The bigger question, though, was why she would help him at all.

3

Mary stood there wondering why she'd come up with a fib to help Jakob. She could have just let him deal with Tabitha, who clearly had a crush on him. *Who could blame her?* She clenched her hands together. Where had that thought come from? More importantly, why hadn't she minded her own business?

"I see." Tabitha gave Jakob a good-natured smile. "Maybe some other time, then?"

"Maybe," Jakob mumbled as Tabitha stepped away.

Mary knew he wouldn't be unkind enough to turn her down in front of anyone, but from the light that had shown in Tabitha's eyes, it was clear she intended to take Jakob up on his hesitation.

She turned her mind back to the task at hand. Usually, plenty of people stayed to help with cleanup, but tonight families wanted to get their children home right away when they heard the roads were getting slick. When her parents had been ready to leave, Mary told them she wanted to stay and help, that she didn't mind walking home in the snow. Besides, she had warm clothes and boots, as well as a flashlight in her bag.

Noting that Jakob's parents had left, too, she shouldn't have been surprised to realize he'd stayed to help as well.

"What was that all about?" Jakob asked in a low voice.

"What?" Mary said nonchalantly—or at least she tried to. Her voice cracked as she spoke. She immediately crossed the large room to the dessert tables, then placed both her empty platters and purse in a cardboard box. She didn't need any help lugging the box home, which made her fib even more ridiculous.

"Don't play dumb." He'd followed her.

"Mary, would you mind locking up?" Tabitha called from the window across the room, now wrapping a scarf around her neck. "I know I live close by, but it looks like it's getting bad out there."

"Not at all." Mary waved to her.

"Danki." Tabitha paused before opening the front door. "I'll see you soon, Jakob."

He cleared his throat. "Um, *ya*."

A woosh of cold air, snow, and wind blew inside the schoolroom as Tabitha left, prompting Mary to go to the window and watch Tabitha's flashlight until its light bobbed up her porch steps. But it was getting harder to see through the falling snow. "*Gut*. She made it home."

Maybe she'd made a mistake not leaving with her parents. She hurried to where her hooded coat and scarf hung on a rack and her boots sat on the floor. She'd better leave now.

"You can also stop ignoring me." Jakob had followed her again.

"I'm not ignoring you." She turned and faced him. "If you haven't noticed, it really is snowing harder."

He paused, frowning, then grabbed his coat and scarf and pulled a stocking cap over his hair. "Hang on a second," he said. Then he stepped out the back door, closing it behind him. He wasn't gone for more than a few seconds. "We can't *geh* out there," he said. "Not when it's like this."

"What?" She dashed to the back door and opened it. Immediately the cold air took her breath away, and now the snow was blowing sideways. She shut the door and turned around. "But we can't stay here."

"Why not? We can ride out the storm—and it is a storm now. It's plenty warm enough, and if we have to, we can light up the stove again. I did it when I was a student here."

Mary remembered. When he was in sixth grade, Jakob started helping the teachers light the stove, even coming early before the school day began. By the time he was in eighth grade, he was lighting it by himself, the task an unofficial job. But that was Jakob. Kind and helpful, which made it easy for her to lie about him helping her take her platters home. That was something Jakob would do without a thought.

But none of that was helping now. "I don't want to stay here," she said, going to the window. She silently offered a quick prayer, asking the Lord to stop the storm. But the wind rattled the windows.

"You just don't want to stay here alone with me."

She whirled around. "Not everything I do or say has to do with you," she snapped.

"I know that." He held her gaze, his eyes impassive. "But that doesn't change the fact that it's too dangerous to walk home now." He paused. "I'm glad Tabitha got home all right."

A thread of jealousy wound through her. Maybe she'd mistaken Jakob's expression and body language when he was talking to Tabitha. She'd known him for so long that she thought she could read him like a favorite book. But that had been in the past. Maybe he'd changed since their breakup. Maybe he liked Tabitha and was interested in her, and she had interfered with that.

The thread tightened.

"We don't have a choice," Jakob said, taking a step toward her. "Unless you want to risk getting lost and freezing to death before anyone can find you."

"Don't be so dramatic." But she knew that was possible in a storm like this. Besides, knowing him, if she did leave, he'd insist on walking her home and then have to backtrack to his house. That wouldn't be fair to him, and she didn't want him in danger either. "Fine. But the minute we can leave, I'm heading out the door."

"Whatever," he muttered, then strode to the other side of the classroom and sat on the wooden bench against the wall. The bricks and drywall above the seat were both painted white, and a long board with hooks drilled into it for the students to hang their belongings sat right above his head. He crossed his arms over his chest and stared straight ahead.

Even though she was annoyed that she had to stay here with him, she couldn't help but chuckle.

He glared at her. "What's so funny?"

"You look like a *kind* in time-out."

He rolled his eyes. "I do feel like I'm being punished."

His words hit her square in the heart. "Because you're here with me?"

Jakob turned to her, still annoyed. "Look, you're the one who doesn't want to be here with *me*. How is that supposed to make me feel?"

Again, another arrow to the heart, but this time it was accompanied by a dose of guilt. She hadn't meant to make him feel bad, and she frowned, realizing how her response must have sounded to him.

She blew out a weary breath. She'd managed to meet one of her commitments—bringing six dozen Christmas cookies to the program. But she was still trying to figure out how to decorate Quinn's wedding cakes. She'd found time to get to the library to look through a couple of cake decorating books, but photos of the elaborate cakes nearly caused a panic attack. Should she try to make her cakes look like that?

But she couldn't think about the wedding, or about the pile of sewing she still had to do, or about the headache that had been dogging her all day and put her in a foul mood. Instead, she sat down next to Jakob. "I'm sorry. I didn't mean to make you feel bad."

"Well, you did." He relaxed a little, his shoulders not so tense. "I didn't realize being in *mei* presence was such a hardship."

"It's not. It's just . . ."

"Just what?"

She looked down at her lap. She'd draped her scarf around her neck, and the fringe lay against her dress. She started to pick at it. "I didn't want things to be awkward."

"Too late for that," he said, turning his face away. "Things have been awkward for a long time."

Mary didn't reply. What could she say when he was right?

She had no idea how long they sat there in silence, she picking at her scarf while her head pounded, and he staring straight ahead while the winter wind howled outside. In between the noisy gusts of wind, she could hear the ticking of the battery-operated clock on the wall. It was only eight thirty. The storm could last for hours.

Finally, Jakob spoke. "You never answered *mei* question."

She lifted her brow. "What question?"

"Why did you tell Tabitha I said I would help you? Why did you lie to her?"

"Technically, that's two questions."

He rolled his eyes again, but this time a smile played at the corners of his mouth. "You know what I'm referring to."

"You looked like you could use a little help." She straightened her scarf and patted it. "Tabitha obviously has her *kapp* set for you."

He sighed. "I know. But that didn't mean I couldn't handle her."

"I know you, Jakob. You wouldn't hurt her feelings . . ." She looked away.

"Unlike when I hurt *yers*?" He paused. "Is that it? Did I hurt you when we broke up?"

She waved him off and stood. "Whatever happened between us is in the past." She stepped to the window and looked outside. To her chagrin, the snow was still blowing.

"Is it?" She heard the floor creak as he came up behind her. "From the way you've been acting—and still are—I don't think it is."

Jakob was standing closer to Mary than he had since their breakup. Just not as close as he wanted to, but he'd have to figure that out later. Right now they needed to clear the poisoned air between them, separating them for way too long.

He'd seen the look of pain in her eyes when she jumped up from the bench. He hadn't expected that. If she'd been hurting all this time, she'd hidden it well. But now, as she was wont to do, she was avoiding facing whatever was really going on inside her. What was really going on between them.

"I don't know what you're talking about." She moved closer to the window until she was pressed against the wall.

"You do, but as usual you don't want to discuss it." He backed away, literally and figuratively, and sat back down on the bench. It was as if she wanted to melt into the woodwork, and he wasn't going to push her. He leaned his head against the wall behind him, which was cold. In fact, the whole room was getting colder, just not enough for him to go to the basement and start up the stove. He'd do that only if they couldn't stand the chill anymore.

Mary moved to the coatrack and put on her coat. Then she stood by the gas lamp as if the meager amount of heat it emitted would warm her. She put her hands in her pockets and didn't say another word.

Lord knew, he was tired of riding this emotional roller coaster, but he couldn't help it. Despite his annoyance, his heart softened. Mary began to shiver. He rose from the bench, then slipped off his coat and put it around her shoulders, just as he'd been tempted to do last week when she'd stepped onto her home's porch in the cold. He was glad he'd worn the pullover sweater. "Better?"

She turned around. He was close to her again, but now they were face-to-face.

"You don't have to do that," she said.

"I know."

Her brow furrowed, and when he recognized her expression, he felt foolish that he hadn't paid more attention to it earlier. "Headache?"

She nodded. "It's been with me most of the day."

No wonder she'd been so grouchy. Mary didn't get too many headaches, but when she did, they were long-lasting. He'd been so wrapped up in how things were between them that he hadn't noticed she was in physical pain. "You should sit down."

"I don't need to sit down."

But he put his hand on her elbow and led her back to the bench. When she tried to shrug off his coat, he pulled it closed around her. "Did you take something for it?"

"Aspirin." She freed one hand and put her fingertip to her left temple. "It didn't help much." She closed her eyes.

"You've been doing too much, haven't you?" Jakob scooted closer. "That's usually what brings these headaches on."

"*Nee*, I'm—" She sighed, and her shoulders slumped. "You're right. I still can't hide anything from you."

The reminder that they knew each other better than anyone else knew them hit him. That was one reason they'd thought their romantic relationship could work. They didn't have to go through any of the stages designed to get to know each other on a deeper level. But in the end, that hadn't mattered. Their attempted romance ruined everything. "What has you overwhelmed?"

"The wedding cakes for Quinn."

He frowned. "I've never known you to be bothered by baking. You enjoy it so much."

She looked up at him. "Have you ever seen Yankee wedding cakes? They're so fancy and intricate. I saw a picture of one that had pearls and diamonds draped around it." Her eyes grew round. "Can you believe that?"

"*Ya.* But I can't believe Quinn would want that."

Mary glanced at her lap. "You're right. She would want something much simpler."

"And simple yet pretty is what you can do well." He cupped his hands together and blew on them. "Quinn is also a lifelong friend. You know her almost as well as you know . . ."

"As well as I know you." She took off her scarf and handed it to him. "Here."

"I'm okay—"

Before he could say anything else, she leaned closer and wrapped the scarf around his neck. She smelled like sugar and peppermint, and she was close enough that it wouldn't take much effort to kiss her. For some bizarre reason, that was exactly what he wanted to do.

Mary whispered, her hands still holding the ends of the scarf. "I don't understand," she said, her voice sounding small and soft.

"What?" He barely registered her question, unable to draw his attention away from her lips, then her eyes.

"What went wrong between us?"

4

Mary's voice trembled, and it wasn't because she was cold. In fact, she was far from cold cocooned in Jakob's coat, the one he'd worn for years. The familiar scent of woodsmoke and sawdust filled her senses as she held his gaze, her headache forgotten. All she could focus on was him—and grappling with why their relationship had crumbled when she felt like she did now.

He cleared his throat and removed the scarf from around his neck. He handed it to her and stood, then started to pace, his hands in his pockets.

She stared at the scarf, feeling the same rejection she'd experienced the night they broke up. She didn't understand her feelings then, just as she didn't understand them now. Why did she feel hurt when there was nothing to be hurt about? They'd both wanted to stop dating. He didn't have to answer her question about what went wrong, and he didn't have to wear her scarf. He didn't owe her anything.

Jakob stopped pacing and stood in front of her. "I don't know," he said, crossing his arms over his chest. "I just knew things between us had changed too much. I always felt different around you when we were dating. Always . . ."

"Tense?"

"*Ya.* That's a *gut* way to describe it. Things weren't as easy between us as when we were just friends. Everything felt so . . . forced."

She nodded and rose from the bench. "That's exactly how I felt. I wondered when we should hold hands, how close we should sit next to each other, when—or even if—we should . . . you know. Kiss." Her face heated, and she couldn't look at him.

"*Gut* thing we never did." He chuckled, but it sounded strained. "Imagine how weird we'd feel around each other now if we had."

"That would be horrible." She tried to make her tone light, but as she met his eyes again, seeing them darken to a charcoal color, all she could think about was kissing him. Which was crazy. They'd just admitted kissing would probably have been the worst thing that could have happened between them.

No, the worst thing was the end of their friendship. And thinking about kissing must be because she was so tired and had a headache. At least her headache was starting to subside, thank goodness.

Jakob took a step toward her. "Mary, I can't stand that we're not friends anymore. It doesn't seem right."

"I feel the same way."

"Do you think we can try again?" A smile played at the corners of his mouth. "I don't mean dating. We already know that doesn't work. But we do know our friendship did."

Mary nodded, unable to keep from smiling. "*Ya.* It did. I'm willing to try again."

Jakob grinned. "I'm glad to hear that."

She held out her scarf. "Now will you take this?"

He put it around her neck. "Nice and warm." Then he stepped to the window. "I think it's finally settling down out there. We shouldn't be stuck here much longer."

She moved to stand by him, and for the first time in a long time, she felt comfortable in his company. She peered out the window and nodded, then turned to him. "But it's a *gut* thing we were stuck here."

"*Ya*," he said quietly. "A very *gut* thing."

Half an hour later the storm had cleared enough that Jakob thought it was safe to walk home. But as Mary locked the schoolhouse entrance behind him, he was glad he'd pulled his cap well over his ears. The snowfall had lightened considerably, but the temperature had dropped again.

They waded through several inches of snow to the road, and then they both turned toward Mary's house. She focused his pocket flashlight on the deserted road. "Once we get to *yer haus*, you don't have to walk me home," she said, her voice muffled under the scarf she'd wrapped around her face. "I have *mei* own flashlight."

"But you know I will." He grasped the box of platters tighter. "By the way, I got only one of *yer* cookies."

"I'll make you more."

The wind whirled around them, and neither of them spoke as

they trudged onward. When they came to his house, he kept on, not even when Mary paused. She quickened her steps, crunching the snow, then caught up to him.

"You're so stubborn," she snapped.

"And that's why you . . ." He swallowed the last two words. *Love me.* For years they had joked like that, knowing the love between them was only as friends—and on a spiritual level, as brother and sister in Christ. That teasing had gone out the window when they started dating. The strain between them was gone now, but he wasn't ready to go back to throwing the word *love* around. He probably never should have.

If Mary noticed his sudden silence, she didn't acknowledge it. When they reached her driveway, light streaming from a front window of the house, she turned to him and reached for the box. "I can make it the rest of the way myself."

"I know, but I'll carry this to *yer* door."

"Only if you'll come inside to warm up before you leave."

A tempting offer, since the bitter wind seemed to have seeped into his bones. Even so, he didn't want his parents to worry. "Another time. I need to get home."

"I'll hold you to it."

"But I am going as far as the porch."

When they reached the steps, Mary put her hands on the box and peered at him. All he could see were her eyes and the bridge of her nose. Still cute. "Let *geh*, Jakob."

Knowing she would argue with him until Christmas, he handed her the box. She nodded her thanks and turned to go up the steps. Thankfully, someone had recently swept them clear of most of the snow, probably Wayne. He started to turn around to head home.

Suddenly Mary's feet flew out from under her, and she hit the ground. He ran to her. "Are you okay?"

She started to push herself up to a sitting position. "*Ya*—ow!"

He saw her gripping her left arm. "Are you in pain?"

She nodded. "I think I hit *mei* elbow on the edge of the step." She looked at him, wincing.

Jakob moved to the other side of her and helped her to her feet. Emptied out of the box, her purse and the unbroken platters lay in the snow. He'd come back for them later.

He started to help Mary up the steps, but then he spotted a patch of ice at the bottom of the first one. Without hesitation, he swooped her into his arms and sidestepped the ice, then carried her to the door.

5

THE NEXT AFTERNOON, MARY SAT ON HER LIVING ROOM couch, her left arm in a cast, trying to figure out what to do. And not just about Quinn's cakes and her seamstress work, although both were pressing heavily on her mind because she couldn't exactly bake and sew with a broken elbow. No, something was more disturbing than being unable to fulfill her commitments—her reaction to Jakob carrying her into the house.

She was still surprised he'd lifted her that way. He could have simply helped her inside by letting her lean on him. But instead he'd swept her up like she was a princess in one of those fairy-tale books, and for a split second, she'd *felt* like a princess. That alarmed her, because for one thing, she was no princess and had never wished to be. More importantly, though, she'd experienced something with Jakob for the first time—feeling wonderfully safe and secure deep inside, *in his arms*. Being held by him had felt so good. After so many months of everything between her and Jakob being wrong, suddenly it *all* felt right.

And that was a problem.

Mamm came in and set a cup of tea and a pumpkin muffin on the coffee table in front of the couch, then sat down next to her. "How are you feeling?"

Very confused. "All right," she said, staring at the cup of tea, glad neither of her parents had asked questions about Jakob walking her home.

"Are you in much pain?"

"It's not too bad."

After Jakob had lowered her to the couch, *Mamm* examined her swollen elbow and forearm. She suspected she needed an X-ray, and *Daed* called a taxi driver he knew had snow tires on his car. Fortunately, the man had been willing to take her to the hospital. Jakob stayed until the taxi arrived, even watching as she and her parents pulled out of the driveway.

"*Gut*," *Mamm* said, interrupting her thoughts. "Remember you have the pain pills the doctor prescribed if you need them."

Mary nodded, then lifted her gaze, noticing *Mamm*'s treadle sewing machine in the corner of the living room. A pile of fabric and projects sat on the table beside it. "I'm sorry," she said, sighing. "I said I wouldn't let you down, and I have."

"Nonsense. You slipped on some ice and fell. That's not *yer* fault."

Mary knew that, but she shrugged anyway. "I should have been more careful."

A knock sounded at the door, and *Mamm* got up to answer it. "Hello, Jakob," she said, opening the door wider. "Come on in."

Jakob closed the door behind him. "I stopped by to check on Mary."

"She's right here on the couch." *Mamm* stepped aside, then added, "I'll *geh* make you a cup of *kaffee*."

"Danki." As *Mamm* left the room, Jakob turned to her. "How's the arm?"

"Broken elbow." Mary sighed again and gestured to the cast. "I'll be in this thing for six weeks."

Jakob frowned. "I'm sorry to hear that."

"So was I." She moved to lift her cup of tea with her right hand, even though she wasn't interested in drinking anything. She just needed something to do so she didn't have to look at him. Or stare at him, actually, which was what she wanted to do. All these years of friendship, and even when they dated, she'd known he was handsome. But now being with him set her stomach fluttering. What in the world was going on with her? She fumbled with the teacup.

Jakob hurried over and helped her steady the cup. His fingers brushed hers, and the flutter reappeared. Now that he was a few inches away from her, she had to look at him, and this time she couldn't look away.

He cleared his throat, then backed his way to the front door. "Sorry. I made a mess of the floor," he said, slipping off his boots.

"It's fine." Oh great. Now she sounded a little breathless. She took a sip of the tea, which was too hot and burned her tongue. Wincing, she set it back down.

"Does it hurt a lot?" Jakob sat on the chair across from her.

Assuming he meant her arm, she was about to tell him it

didn't, that she was just fine. But he could always tell when she tried to lie. "*Ya.* I have some medicine, but that's only if I can't stand the pain anymore. Right now it's tolerable."

A relieved look crossed his face. "That's *gut* to hear." Instead of sitting back in the chair, relaxed like he used to be when there, he sat perched at the edge. His expression turned tense. Oh no. They had just settled things between them, and now he was going back to being wary of her.

"So what are you going to do about Tabitha?" she blurted, eager for anything to break the tension growing between them. Before they dated, they hadn't shied away from talking about each other's romantic problems. "She's definitely smitten with you."

"Well, *mei schwester* asked me to walk *mei* youngest niece to school this morning because of the deep snow, and I saw Tabitha talking to that guy who used to live here, the one who was at church a couple of weeks ago."

"Mark?"

"*Ya.* That's him. I couldn't remember his name. According to *mei* nosy niece, he's single and came back to the area to see Tabitha. She seemed interested in him too. That makes me wonder just how *smitten* with me she actually is." Grinning, he shook his head, then said, "Never mind about Tabitha. I'll straighten her out if I have to."

"It sounds like you won't have to."

"Which is a relief." He looked at her with some intensity, but not in a bad way. "Do you need anything?"

"Not unless you know how to bake and sew," she said with a weak chuckle. She was glad their conversation had become lighthearted, but that didn't address her problem.

His face brightened. "I can't sew, but I do know a little about baking."

"Very little." She smirked, then added, "I was kidding anyway." She looked at her lap. "I'll have to tell Quinn I can't make her cakes."

"Maybe you won't."

Her head snapped up. "Of course I will. With me out of commission, *Mamm* will be busier than ever with our sewing. So she can't help me. And I might be able to bake a cake with one hand, but I doubt I can decorate one. At least not so it looks like a wedding cake should."

He grinned again. "But with *mei* help, you can."

Her heart skipped a beat at his smile, but she ignored it. "How can you help me?"

"I don't know, but I'm sure we can figure out something. We used to make a pretty *gut* team, remember?"

She did remember, and she couldn't help but smile. When they were school age, they'd paired up in a picnic potato sack race and won first place. They'd also helped each other's families during harvesttime and had come up with their own system for picking some of the crops, often making it into a friendly competition. She knew she could think of numerous examples of the two of them working well together, but she wasn't sure it was possible this time. "Do you know how complicated decorating a cake can be? Even a simple one?"

"*Nee*, but that doesn't mean I can't learn. Besides, I'm just *yer* assistant, *yer* right hand. *Yer* left hand, actually."

Mary almost smiled, but she was still concerned. "You have *yer* own job."

"Which is slow right now."

She quickly looked toward the kitchen, then lowered her voice. "Really? Even with the quilt chest *Daed* asked you to make for *Mamm*? I don't want to put you out."

He sighed and moved to sit next to her on the couch. "If this was going to put me out, I wouldn't have offered to help. Now's not the time to be stubborn." He paused. "Unless you really want to tell Quinn you can't do it. I'm sure she would understand."

Her friend would, but Mary didn't like the idea of letting her down. "All right, but we'll have to come up with a plan. And I'll have to teach you the basics of cake decorating. Plus we have to get the ingredients—"

"Slow down a bit," Jakob said. "I'm sure we'll figure everything out."

"In a week?"

Jakob's brow lifted. "Didn't Quinn say the wedding is on Christmas Eve?"

"*Ya*. But she and Tanner are coming next week to taste the sample cakes I need to make so they can choose which flavors they want. I also planned on decorating them so they could tell me if they'll look all right."

Mamm walked into the room with a mug of coffee, steam swirling from its top. "Fresh brewed," she said, looking at Jakob. "I hope you can stay awhile. *Nee* need to rush off, you know."

Mary thought she saw a glimmer in her mother's eye. Surely it wasn't hope—an expectation that anything romantic could still develop between her and Jakob. She'd have to explain later that, yes, they were back to being friends after a rough year, but that was all.

Even though for some unfathomable reason, her heart seemed to want more.

Jakob took the mug from her mother and smiled. "I've got plans to stay awhile."

One week, one bag of flour, two bags of sugar, and three pounds of butter later, Jakob sat at the Wengerds' kitchen table across from Quinn and her fiancé, Tanner. They were taking in the four small, round mini cakes, and to his surprise, he was a little nervous. He glanced at Mary, who was biting the inside corner of her lip. It wasn't obvious, but he could tell. And now he was paying attention to her mouth, which wasn't the first time he'd done so since he started helping her with the cakes.

Get it together. He didn't need to be indulging his feelings right now, as confusing as they were. He needed to focus on whether Quinn and Tanner liked any of these cakes.

Over the past week, he'd put aside his own responsibilities, including working on Maria's quilt chest, to help Mary. It was worth every minute, as well as the early mornings and late nights he'd had to put in. Setting aside the past year and getting back to his friendship with Mary had felt good.

But for reasons he couldn't comprehend, he was also feeling a new attraction to her. Why, of all times now, he didn't know. But at least he'd had the distraction of working on the cakes to keep his mind off his perplexing feelings. Yet every time he left her house, his heart missed her, and it had all started the evening she injured her arm, when he picked her up and carried her to her couch.

Mary's leg started to bounce up and down, something she also did when she was nervous. Without thinking, he put his hand on her knee under the table. She stilled. Then she grabbed his hand and held on to it. He knew pleasing Quinn was important to her, but he hadn't realized how important.

"I can't believe you two did this for us." Quinn's eyes grew soft. "Mary, you didn't have to make these cakes. I would have been fine with store-bought, considering your accident."

Mary smiled but still held on to Jakob's hand. "I wanted to do this for you, and I'm glad Jakob was able to help me since *Mamm* is just too busy with our sewing orders."

He tried to ignore the warm feeling flowing through him at her touch and smiled at Quinn. "I was glad to do it, although we had quite a bit of trial and error with the decorating. I need to practice making the holly berries a little rounder."

Quinn laughed. "I never thought I'd hear you say that, Jakob." She looked at the cakes again. Each one was a different flavor, but they were all decorated with a white buttercream frosting, green holly leaves and red berries, and some silver sparkly things he couldn't remember the name of but Mary insisted Quinn would like.

"Don't the cakes look delicious?" Quinn said, turning to Tanner.

He nodded, rubbing his hands together. He was a large guy who looked like he enjoyed eating.

"I'll cut them, then." Jakob lifted a small slice from each cake, putting them all on a plate he then handed to Quinn. He did the same for Tanner. They dug in with gusto as Jakob turned to Mary. "Do you want some?"

"I'm a little tired of cake."

"Same here." They had baked and taste tested more cake and frosting than he cared to think about. Even the faint sweet smell of the cakes was turning his stomach.

Tanner and Quinn spent a minute or two savoring each bite. "Wow," Tanner said, rolling his eyes as he took a bite of the Italian cream cake. "I definitely want the chocolate for the groom's cake, but this is amazing."

"They're all wonderful." Quinn smiled at Mary. "I don't know how we'll pick just one for mine."

Mary finally let go of Jakob's hand, her shoulders relaxing. "I'm glad you like them."

Tanner scraped frosting from the plate. "Don't you want the Italian cream, Quinn?"

"Yes. I really like the strawberry, though."

"The strawberry *is* good."

As Quinn and Tanner tried to decide, Jakob glanced at Mary, pleased to see the smile on her face. She was in her element, making someone else happy. And seeing her happy made him happy too.

"Do we have to choose one?" Quinn said. "Would you mind making two different flavors?"

"Or three? I like the yellow too." Tanner grinned.

"Tanner," Quinn said, elbowing him.

"I'm just kidding."

"I can do all four if you want." Mary sat up straighter, all traces of nervousness gone. "We can make each cake with two flavors. Or four smaller cakes."

Quinn frowned. "That's too much work."

"But would you like all four flavors?" Mary asked, leaning forward.

Quinn nodded, as did Tanner.

"Then four flavors it is. Just let me know in what form, and we'll do it."

Quinn and Tanner thanked Mary profusely, and then the four of them talked for a little while. Jakob learned that Tanner was a business analyst in Cleveland, and that he and Quinn had met at a mutual friend's birthday party. "We hit it off immediately," he said. "Sometimes right off the bat you know you've met the one for you."

Jakob thought about Tanner's words as he washed the dishes after the two of them left. Mary's parents were out visiting friends, and outside a light dusting of snow was falling. The house was cozy, wood burning in the stove warming the room. The Wengerds had already decorated for Christmas with pine boughs, holly berries, and plenty of candles, all currently unlit except for one in the kitchen, which emitted an apple cider scent, Mary's favorite.

"Anything else you need me to do?" Jakob asked, turning to Mary as he dried his hands on a kitchen towel.

"Nee." She wiped the rest of the table. "I think Quinn and Tanner are happy."

"They're very happy." He hung the towel and walked over to her. "Are you sure you're willing to bake four cakes?"

She nodded. "*Mamm* has already offered to help with the final cakes now that she's making headway with our Christmas orders, and baking four instead of two won't matter much. She wants to contribute to Quinn's wedding, even in a small way, and she said she'll make time."

Jakob was a little disappointed to hear that. He'd wanted to help Mary with the wedding cakes, but then again, his decorating skills did leave something to be desired. Besides, he had a lot of work to catch up on. He'd received two orders the day after she broke her elbow, and he still had to finish the quilt chest. "I hope *yer mamm* can live up to *mei* decorating skills."

"You gave her a high bar, but I think she'll be fine." Mary smiled. "*Danki*, Jakob. I feel much better about the wedding cakes now."

Jakob's heart leapt. Her smile was so beautiful it could put sunsets to shame. Corny but true. He could stand in this kitchen forever and stare at her, but she would think he'd lost his mind. He was wondering if he had. "Guess I'll be going, then."

She didn't say anything as they walked to her front door. He put on all his outerwear, then turned to her. "If you need anything, you know where I am." Unable to help himself, he took a step closer to her. "Anything, anytime."

Mary nodded, and he sensed something in her expression that made his heart jump again. But before he could contemplate it, she'd opened the door. "Be careful," she said.

Obviously, she was ready for him to go. Which made sense. It wasn't her fault he wanted to linger . . . forever. "See you later," he said, then stepped out into the cold.

"See you later." She shut the door behind him.

Jakob headed down the driveway, glancing over his shoulder at the house, which looked so warm and inviting. He tucked his chin into the collar of his coat and headed home. Maybe the cold air and brisk walk would bring him to his senses. He and Mary were friends, and that was all they would be. It was foolish to think anything else was possible.

When he arrived home, he went straight to his workshop. Not only did he need to work; he needed the distraction. At this point he would do anything to get his mind off Mary Wengerd.

6

"Tell me the truth, Mary."

Mary looked at Quinn, surprised for the second time this afternoon. The first time was when Quinn arrived out of the blue after the successful cake tasting last night. Mary was still relieved that she and Tanner liked the sample cakes—and that her mother had again offered to help make the cakes for the wedding. Mary had pared down her initial decorating ideas when she'd broken her elbow, but *Mamm* was a decent cake decorator anyway. And fortunately, Quinn and Tanner had been fine with the simple frosting decorations.

But she was a little worried about why Quinn was there. "The truth about what?"

"You and Jakob." Quinn leaned forward, her long blond hair falling over her slim shoulders. They were sitting in the kitchen again, and Quinn was getting straight to the point. "Don't tell me I'm seeing things. I noticed how you two looked at each other last night."

Bother. Hopefully Quinn hadn't seen how Mary had held Jakob's hand under the table. What had she been thinking, doing that? She'd been nervous about the cakes, and Jakob knew that. But she had also been growing jumpier around him, which was why she'd rushed him out the door last night. Her feelings were getting harder and harder to hide, and now Quinn had picked up on them.

Oh no. What if Jakob suspected something too? "We're just back to being good friends," she said, rising from the table. Her arm had started itching under the cast, and she resisted the urge to scratch it.

"I can see that." Quinn set down her coffee and stood. "Mary, we've always been open with each other. I told you about Tanner as soon as I met him." She paused. "Don't you trust me enough to tell me about you and Jakob?"

"Yes, of course I do." Mary put her hand on Quinn's shoulder. "I've always trusted you." She dropped her arm, then sighed and leaned back against the counter. "I just don't trust myself. At least not when it comes to Jakob."

"So there *is* something between you."

"Maybe. I don't know." She shook her head, frustrated, then looked at Quinn. "We tried dating—and look how that turned out."

"But you still have feelings for him."

"They're new feelings, though. I have no idea where they came from, or why I never felt them before."

"Maybe you stopped overthinking things for once."

Mary frowned. "What do you mean?"

"Do you trust Jakob?"

"Yes," she said without hesitation. "I do."

"Have you always?"

"Of course I have. He was—is—my best friend." This conversation was starting to sound more like an inquisition.

"Did you trust him when you were dating?"

"I . . ." Had she trusted him?

"Is it possible you were so afraid your friendship would be adversely affected that you never gave him your heart?"

"I don't know. I thought I did. But I'm not sure of anything anymore."

"Here's what I think. You like Jakob as more than a friend." Quinn's eyes took on the dreamy look she seemed to always have lately. "From the looks of it, he likes you that way too."

She wished she had Quinn's confidence. "How do you know?"

"Intuition." She led Mary back to the table, and they both sat down. "The question is, what are you going to do about it?"

"Nothing."

Quinn scoffed. "That's not the right answer."

"It's the only answer." Mary leaned back in her chair, crossing her arms over her chest. The apple cider candle burned in the middle of the table, filling the kitchen with its sweet scent. That usually comforted her, but lately nothing gave her peace. "I've prayed about this, Quinn. And I still don't see Jakob and me together in the future."

After a pause, Quinn nodded. "I felt the same way about Tanner."

Mary's brow lifted. "Really? I thought it was love at first sight for you both."

"It was for him. And I thought it was for me, but I started getting cold feet. You know my dating history isn't the best. But

I realized I couldn't judge the future by the past. And Tanner is a wonderful man. He isn't perfect. No one is. But he has a strong faith, he's loyal and committed, and most importantly, he's patient with me." She grinned. "How could I not love him?"

Mary thought about Jakob. He embodied all the qualities that were important to her—faith, kindness, loyalty . . . Her list was similar to Quinn's, which didn't surprise her. But Jakob also gave her someone she could trust—completely. She trusted him with everything. She always had, except when they were dating. Why had she held the most important part of herself from him?

"I have an idea," Quinn said. "Invite him to the wedding. He can be your plus one."

"Plus one?"

"Your date." She smiled. "And treat it as a date. Maybe all the two of you needed was some space to appreciate each other. Now that you've had it, you can get back together. Maybe even have your own Christmas wedding."

"Now you're talking nonsense." But her heart warmed at the thought. Then she paused. "What if he says no?"

"Then you'll know for sure that you aren't meant for each other romantically." Quinn leaned back in her chair. "But he won't say no. I'm a hundred percent sure of that."

After Quinn left, Mary thought about what she said. She ran her palms over the skirt of her emerald-green dress at the thought of asking Jakob to Quinn's wedding. She was excited about the prospect. Still, something held her back, but she wasn't sure what. She needed to pray about it more, to ask God for clarity. She still had a few days left before the wedding, still time to determine if she could risk his saying no. She didn't know if she could handle that.

The day before Christmas Eve, Jakob was exhausted. He'd spent many hours working in the shop, especially finishing Maria's quilt chest and on a special project he'd decided to do at the last minute. But his mind and heart were never far from Mary.

He yawned as he began work on a small bread box he had promised a Yankee couple would be done tomorrow morning. He'd sand the top, and after ensuring it was completely smooth, he'd apply a coat of varnish to the whole thing. Then he would turn to the special project, hidden under a tarp with Maria's chest. He had the window partway open to let in fresh, cold air, while a small gas stove heated the shop enough that the varnish wouldn't be too difficult to work with.

"Jakob."

He stilled at the sound of Mary's voice, sandpaper in his hand. "Hi," he said, pleased and surprised to see her. He also reminded himself he had to manage his emotions. *Friends, remember.* "Uh, what brings you by?"

She walked into the shop but stopped a few feet from him, brushing the toe of her boot against the floor.

Frowning, he set down the sandpaper and went to her. "Is something wrong?" He didn't like the somber look on her face. "You didn't reinjure *yer* elbow, did you?"

Mary shook her head, lightly touching the top of the cast cradled in a sling. She didn't usually wear that unless she was leaving the house. "It's fine. Other than the itching, that is."

He remembered that from when he broke his ankle when he was eight years old. "Try not to think about it. That usually worked for me."

"All right." But she wasn't looking at him. She was distracted, so he waited. Whatever she wanted to say, she'd say it when she was ready. But he wished she would hurry up already. *One day at a time.* Taking his own advice, he resisted the urge to look back at the bread box he should be sanding right now. Mary was more important.

"I, uh, have something to ask you." She rapidly tapped her finger on the top of her cast. After another long pause, she said, "Quinn's getting married tomorrow."

Jakob chuckled. "I'm aware of that."

"Oh *ya*. Right." She took in a gulp of air, and then the words came out in a rush. "Would you be *mei* plus one?"

His brow arched. "*Yer* what?"

"*Mei* . . . date." She breathed in deeply again. "Jakob, would you be *mei* date to Quinn's wedding?"

There. The question was out there. And getting to this point had been as painful as she'd thought it would be. But she forced herself to look at Jakob, and as she feared he might, he tilted his head and frowned as if she'd spoken a foreign language. She just hoped he wouldn't ask her to repeat her invitation.

"What did you say?"

She cringed. Now she had no choice. "Will you *geh* with me to Quinn's wedding? But I'll understand if you don't want to, especially since tomorrow night is Christmas Eve and you like to spend it with *yer familye*."

"I've spent it with *yer familye* once or twice, too, remember?"

She did. She had great memories of the two of them sitting

next to each other, listening to the Christmas story, then eating popcorn and drinking apple cider. Jakob was always the first to leave so he could get back to his own family, but he never left without giving her a small gift, usually her favorite candy or a small paper bag of apples. In turn, she would give him a baked treat, usually something pumpkin flavored, his favorite at Christmas.

"Mary."

"Huh?" She shook her head slightly, pulling her mind from the past. Then she met his gaze, and the butterflies in her stomach fluttered at peak level. *It's only mei nerves.* But that wasn't true. She was falling for Jakob, and she couldn't deny that.

"I'll be glad to *geh* with you to Quinn's wedding."

She should have been happy with that, but she had to make sure he understood what she was asking. "It would be a date," she said barely above a whisper.

He gave her a soft smile. "*Mei* answer still stands."

Her heart leapt. "*Danki*," she blurted, then wondered if she sounded stupid.

"What time should I pick you up?"

Jakob had just confirmed this would be a date, yet he seemed about as excited as a man agreeing to simply meet a friend for lunch. *Lord, I'm so confused.*

"Can you meet me there? *Mamm*'s helping me take the cakes to the church where they're having the ceremony, then the reception in the church hall. She wants to see Quinn in her dress and wish her blessings on her marriage."

"I can do that."

She told him the time and place, and he said he would arrange for a taxi. "I should probably do that tonight. I imagine they'll be busy on Christmas Eve, especially if the weather is *gut*."

"Is there anything else?" he said, shifting from one foot to the other. She thought she saw him almost glance over his shoulder. Perhaps he just needed to get back to work, but her heart sank. He might have agreed to go only because he felt sorry for her otherwise attending a Yankee wedding alone. Maybe at this point, her idea of "a date" between them and his weren't even close.

It was on the tip of her tongue to ask him, but she stopped herself. It didn't matter why he was agreeing to go. He did, and that was all that mattered right now. Part of her problem when they were dating was that she overanalyzed everything to the point that she mentally exhausted herself. *Trust.* The word repeated in her mind. She had to trust Jakob . . . with everything, including her heart. And for once, she was going to enjoy the moment. "*Nee.* Nothing else," she finally said, unable to stop herself from smiling. "I'll see you tomorrow night, then. Christmas Eve."

"See you then."

She turned and headed out of the barn.

"Mary?"

Turning on her heel, she faced him again. *"Ya?"*

He smiled. "I'm looking forward to it."

Maybe he really was. Her heart racing, she grinned. "Me too."

7

"You look beautiful," Mary said as Quinn twirled around in her wedding dress. They were in one of the church classrooms, where Quinn, her younger sister—who was her maid of honor—her two bridesmaids, her mother, and Tanner's mother were all getting ready for the ceremony, due to start in half an hour.

"I agree." *Mamm* put her fingers over her mouth. "You're a beautiful bride, Quinn. I'm so glad I got to see you before the wedding."

"You're welcome to stay," Quinn said, going to her.

Mamm shook her head. "I need to get back home. In a couple of hours I'll have a house full of family." She turned to Mary. "We'll save you and Jakob some popcorn and cider."

"Thank you, *Mamm*." Last night she'd finally confided in her mother about her feelings for Jakob, and her thanks extended beyond cider and popcorn. Her mother's support meant so much.

She watched as Quinn hugged *Mamm*. Surprisingly, she felt weepy. Over the past few years, she and Quinn hadn't spent as much time together as they had when they were younger, even when Quinn still lived next door. For one thing, Quinn had been away at college for a few years. But after tonight, even though they would always be friends, their relationship would change even more. She was happy for her, but she couldn't help but feel a touch of sadness too.

After *Mamm* left, Quinn carefully sat on a chair before a full-length mirror leaning against a bulletin board that said "Jesus loves you" in large, colorful letters. Her hair and makeup evidently needed finishing touches, and someone draped a sheet over her dress so it wouldn't get soiled. Mary felt a little out of place among the bustle of cosmetics, hair spray, perfume, and fancy dresses. "Quinn," she finally said, stepping next to her. "If you don't mind, I'll *geh* sit in the church now."

"Of course." She reached out and took Mary's hand. "So you asked him?"

Mary nodded. "He'll be here later."

Quinn's eyes gleamed. "I knew it." She smiled. "Tonight's going to be special for both of us."

Mary hoped so, but she didn't say anything as she squeezed Quinn's hand.

She went into the main part of the church—the sanctuary, she thought it was called, with benches called pews. The decorations were simple but had a glittery flair. Three small evergreen trees sat on the stage, decorated in silver, gold, and white. Red bows were tied at the ends of the pews, and the scents of pine and cinnamon filled the air. As she sat down in the back, she wondered if her dream wedding would come true too. And the only man she could picture in that context was Jakob.

A few minutes later, men wearing black suits and gold-and-silver neckties showed up in the sanctuary, and she watched as they escorted arriving guests to one of the two sides of the church, then the other. So far, one side had more people. She didn't know why it made a difference where they sat, and no one asked her to change her seat. She was glad for that since she didn't want to be noticed. It would also be easier for Jakob to find her where she'd landed.

Where was he, anyway? Mary kept looking at the entryway, but with every person who came in, she was disappointed.

Before long, a man stepped onto the stage up front, Tanner and three men wearing black suits and red ties alongside him. Then the women who'd been with Quinn before the ceremony walked down the aisle from the back of the room to join them, one by one. When everyone stood as the music changed—Mary following suit—Quinn and her parents came down the aisle too.

Still no Jakob.

Her heart sank as she tried to focus on the lovely ceremony—and keep her despair in check. Jakob had changed his mind. She'd been afraid of this. It had been a mistake to ask him in the first place. He didn't want a date with her. He'd wanted only the friendship they once had. *I'll be glad to* geh *with you to Quinn's wedding*, he'd said. Not happy. Glad. She could hear the difference now. He *had* felt sorry for her. She never should have listened to Quinn.

"Do you, Quinn, take Tanner to be your husband?"

Mary clenched her hands together. Pain spiked through her arm under the cast, and she relaxed her hands. How could Jakob do this to her? He should have just said no. She clenched her hands again, wincing.

"Do you, Tanner, take Quinn to be your wife?"

Pressing her lips together, she tried to listen to Tanner repeating what the officiant said, but the ache in her heart increased. Until this moment she hadn't realized just how much she'd been looking forward to seeing Jakob. How much she cared about him. How much anguish she could feel at his second rejection of her. Yes, this was different than when they'd broken up. That had been mutual, even though it had hurt. But this—this was almost unbearable.

"Ladies and gentlemen, Mr. and Mrs. Tanner Johnson!"

Snapping to attention, Mary joined the crowd as they all stood and applauded, the pastor beaming as much as the newlyweds. Mary fought back tears as she clapped for her friend amid the radiating joy throughout the congregation. Then she slipped out of her seat.

She rushed into the women's bathroom off the main hallway and grabbed a tissue. She'd seen several women crying during the ceremony—happy tears, of course—and she hoped anyone who came in would think she was happy too. She looked in the mirror as the tears streamed down her cheeks. "He's not worth crying over," she whispered at her reflection. But deep in her heart, she knew he was.

Knowing she couldn't hide there during the whole reception, she wiped her eyes, then tossed the tissue in a trash can next to the sink. She checked the pins holding her *kapp* in place, then pulled her sweater closer to her body and lifted her chin. She didn't need Jakob to be her date tonight or any other night. This time she was through with him for good.

She opened the bathroom door—to find Jakob standing there.

Jakob had known he was in trouble the moment he'd awakened. He'd finished the last coat of varnish on his special project in the shop, then sat down on his old recliner and closed his eyes. Just for a few minutes, he'd told himself, only to wake up three hours later—about the time the wedding ceremony was to start.

Now he was standing in front of Mary and saw how red-rimmed her eyes were. He'd chalk it up to being happy over Quinn's wedding, but Mary never cried when she was happy. Even if he hadn't known that, the coldness in her eyes would have told him she was more than a little upset.

"I'm sorry," he said, blurting the words as she let the door close behind her. Around them people were exiting the main room of the church, wearing fancy dresses and suits. He'd looked for Mary there first, opening the door on the left side, trying to be discreet. When he didn't see her and everyone started leaving, he stepped back and bumped into a man wearing a black suit and a silver-and-gold tie.

"Are you looking for the Amish girl?" the man said.

"Yes. How did you know?"

The man looked him up and down. He was wearing what he usually wore to church—black pants, suspenders, and a white shirt, his coat slung across one arm, his black hat in one hand.

"Call it a hunch." The man grinned and gestured to the

door down the hall that said Women. "I saw her go into the restroom."

Jakob had arrived just as Mary opened the door.

She lifted her chin. "I have to *geh* to the reception." She brushed past him and headed for the back of the church.

"Wait . . ." When she didn't slow down, he grabbed her good arm. "At least let me explain."

"I don't need an explanation. I'm sure you changed *yer* mind, only to feel guilty about standing up a *friend* at the last minute. You didn't need to come and make excuses."

But her defiant chin fell a little as it trembled, and that was all the opening he needed. He grabbed her hand and led her out to the church parking lot, glad she wasn't giving him too much resistance. He stopped when they were under a streetlight and hidden by a hedgerow of bushes.

"It's freezing out here." She rubbed her shoulder with one hand, the cast pressed against her side.

Oh boy. He hadn't thought about that. His mind had been on getting her alone, impossible inside with all the guests there. He put on his hat and whipped his coat around her. When she tried to shrug it off, he kept his hands on her shoulders. "This won't take long."

He knew they couldn't stay outside for more than a short while, so he started talking. "I fell asleep in *mei* shop. I've been so busy and tired lately—"

Her gaze darted to his, and she narrowed her eyes. "You told me you weren't that busy, even with making the quilt chest for *Mamm*. If I had known, I wouldn't have let you help me make the sample cakes."

"I had a special project too." Which was true. He just didn't want to tell her what it was. "I've been working a few late nights, and I guess it all caught up to me."

Mary nodded, but she didn't say anything.

"I'm sorry. As soon as I woke up, I got dressed and called the taxi, which fortunately was still willing to come after I'd failed to confirm earlier. I just got here a few minutes ago."

She nodded again but still remained quiet.

This wasn't a good sign. "You believe me, *ya*?"

After a long pause, she relaxed her shoulders. "*Ya.* I do. But it doesn't matter. It was stupid of me to ask you out in the first place. I realize that now."

"Because I fell asleep?" He couldn't believe she wasn't giving him a minute of grace for his mistake.

"*Nee.* Because we've been down this road before. Maybe the fact that you fell asleep was God's way of letting us know we . . ." She swallowed. "That we're a mistake."

"I don't believe that." He took a step closer to her. "I think God is giving us a second chance. The question is, are you willing to take it?"

8

Mary couldn't take her eyes off Jakob's as her heart hammered. She believed his story about falling asleep, believed now he really had thought of this evening as a date. But being so upset when she thought he'd stood her up had scared her. Jakob was more important to her than she'd ever realized. Even if they started over, she wasn't sure she could handle it if they broke up again.

"I should be at the reception," she said, finally tearing her eyes away. "Quinn will wonder where I am."

"Quinn is too busy being happy. You and I both know that."

She shivered, and although she tried not to, she looked into his eyes again. Under the light of the streetlamp, she could see a warmth there that reached to her soul. "I don't think I can do this."

"Why?" His grip tightened on her shoulders, as if he knew

she was ready to bolt. "Tell me the truth, Mary. Let down *yer* guard for once."

She wanted to tell him they were better off as casual friends, lie to him to protect her heart. But he deserved the truth. "I'm scared." There, it was out in the open. She was afraid, and she'd been afraid the first time their relationship changed. "I don't want to get hurt."

He ran the back of his hand over her cheek. "I'd never hurt you."

"You would if you decided you didn't want to be with me again." That sounded a little childish, but it was the truth. "*Mei* heart would break if that happened."

"Ah, Mary." Jakob gave her a half smile. "That's why you were so distant with me."

"We'd broken up."

"I don't mean then." He stepped closer to her. "I mean when we were a couple. The minute we decided to date, you changed. I've thought about this, and it was as if you put a fence between us. Then you kept making it higher and higher until I couldn't bear trying to climb over it anymore."

She averted her gaze. "I didn't mean to."

"I can see that now. We do strange things when we're afraid." He lifted her chin and tilted her face toward him. "And since you're being honest, I will be too. I was afraid. A little."

"Just a little?"

"Well, I guess I was more interested in romance all along, so that helped. But yeah. I thought about how it would affect our friendship if we broke up—but not too much." He ran his thumb across her cheek. "I was too busy thinking of us together than apart."

"Which I should have been doing." Her breath caught in her throat.

He nodded. "Like you said, we've been down this road before. But it doesn't have to be the same journey. Our relationship has changed in the last few weeks. *We've* changed." He lowered his voice. "Can't you feel it?"

"*Ya*, but what if—"

He put his fingertip over her lips. "Don't borrow trouble, Mary. Just enjoy."

"Enjoy what?"

"This." He leaned down and kissed her.

The fence came crashing down. The fear that had held her back for so long disappeared, warmth and love taking its place. She was in Jakob's arms once more, but not like when he'd swooped her up after her fall. Now, cocooned from the Christmas Eve chill, everything between them finally felt just as it was meant to be.

"Wow," he whispered after they parted.

"*Ya* . . . wow." Her heart full, she smiled.

He angled his head, his brow slightly furrowed. "What are you thinking about?"

"Kissing you again." Her cheeks heated, but she kept her gaze on him. "Well, you said you wanted me to tell the truth."

Jakob chuckled, cradling her cheek in his palm. "That I did. And here's another truth—I'm more than happy to comply."

"There you two are."

They jumped apart as Quinn, wearing a white cape around her beautiful dress, stepped outside. "I've been looking all over for you two."

"We've been out here—" Jakob started.

"Talking," Mary finished.

"Uh-huh." Quinn tilted her head and gave Mary a wink. "We're about to cut the cakes, and I don't want either of you to miss that." She turned and headed for the door, then called over her shoulder, "Just remember to invite Tanner and me to your wedding next year." She opened the door and disappeared inside.

Mary looked at Jakob, and their gazes locked. "She's putting the cart before the horse, don't you think?"

He took her hand, then gave it a squeeze. "Maybe. But I have a feeling she might be right this time." His expression grew serious. "What do you think? Are you willing to give us another try?"

She knew what he was really asking—whether she was willing to give him her heart. This time she didn't overanalyze or worry or let fear get in the way of her decision. Instead, she reached up on tiptoes and kissed him, not caring if anyone saw. "I'm more than willing."

EPILOGUE

December twenty-third, one year later

As the snow softly fell, Mary waited for Jakob to unlock the oak door. Then when the door gave way, he took her hand. "Ready to *geh* inside?"

She nodded, filled with excitement. She and Jakob had married a week ago, then visited family and friends as was customary for Amish newlyweds. Now, two days before Christmas, they were finally staying in their own home. Jakob and his father had built it, two houses down from her parents' place. She and Jakob would join her family tomorrow night for their first Christmas Eve as a married couple, then go visit with his. But tonight they'd be alone.

As soon as she started to step over the threshold, Jakob put his hands over her eyes.

"What are you doing?" she said, letting out a little giggle as he gently pushed her forward from behind. Then she heard him manage to shut the door behind them, she guessed with his foot.

"I want this to be a surprise. Do you smell something?"

She took in a deep breath. "Pine boughs. Cinnamon." She breathed in again. "Apples!"

He removed his hand, and she gasped as she looked around the living room. It was decorated for Christmas—pine boughs, red ribbon, small packages of potpourri, and a large pine wreath above the simple stone fireplace. A beautiful wood coffee table she'd never seen was laden with cookies, a glass pitcher of apple cider, and a tray of cheese and crackers, and three candles sat on the deep sill of the large picture window. Jakob walked over and lit them.

"I asked *mei daed* to come over and turn on the gas lamp, but we don't need it now," he said. Then he lit a couple more candles placed around the room before turning off the lamp.

They sat down on the couch in front of the table. She turned to him. "You did all this?"

"With Quinn's help. She wanted to scatter a few glittery ornaments around, but I talked her out of it."

Mary smiled. "That doesn't surprise me."

He poured her a glass of cider. "I know you wanted a Christmas wedding—"

"We got married on the seventeenth. That's close enough."

"But it wasn't Christmas." He handed her the cider. "Still, tomorrow we'll be around *familye* and friends, which I know you enjoy."

"You do too."

He nodded. "But I wanted a little special something between us for our first Christmas together."

As he held her gaze, a shiver traveled through her body. They had spent many Christmases together, but this one was the most special. She took a sip of the cider, then set the glass on the table. "Where did this gorgeous table come from?"

"I just finished it, right before the wedding." He reached down under it. "I also finished this."

He handed her a small wooden box with apples carved on the lid. It was a miniature version of the hope chest he'd made for her last year, then given her the day after Christmas. He'd been finishing it when he fell asleep before Quinn's wedding. That seemed so long ago, when her fear and doubts had clouded her decisions. Now she couldn't fathom either one in her life.

"Open it," he said.

She lifted the lid, and inside was a small sprig of mistletoe. "Why is this in here?"

He took it from her. "The Yankees have this custom," he said, fiddling with the red bow at the top of the sprig. "If someone holds mistletoe over *yer* head, you have to kiss them."

"Have to?" she said, smiling.

"It's mandatory." He lifted the sprig above them.

She leaned close. "I guess it's okay, *yer* being *mei* husband and all." She tilted her face to his and kissed him. "Merry Christmas," she whispered. "I love you."

"I love you too." He took her in his arms. "Merry Christmas, *lieb*."

Acknowledgments

Thank you to my editors, Becky Monds and Jean Bloom, for their suggestions, edits, and support. A big thank you to my agent, Natasha Kern, who is always there for me.

Discussion Questions

1. Mary and her family had special Christmas Eve traditions. What Christmas traditions does your family have?
2. Christmas gifts are often special surprises, but Mary's father wanted her mother's gift to be extra special. Have you ever surprised someone with a gift they didn't expect but treasured? What was their reaction?
3. Because Mary liked to do things for other people, she often overextended herself. Jakob's favorite saying was "One day at a time," and Mary tried to take that advice when she felt overwhelmed. How does that phrase help you when you feel stressed?
4. Even though Mary and Jakob were friends, she had difficulty trusting him with her heart. Was there ever a time when you had difficulty trusting someone, or even trusting God? Discuss.

A Christmas Prayer

Vannetta Chapman

For my students

While they were there, the time came for the baby to be born, and she gave birth to her firstborn, a son. She wrapped him in cloths and placed him in a manger, because there was no guest room available for them.

—Luke 2:6–7

Love is, above all, the gift of oneself.

—Jean Anouilh

1

December 1
Shipshewana, Indiana

Micah was headed home after visiting a friend when the snowfall picked up in earnest. In no time at all, the ground was covered, and he had to lean forward for a good view of the road. Then something stumbled in front of him—white against white and low to the ground. He pulled on Samson's reins, certain he would hit whatever it was.

But he didn't.

He sat there in the middle of the blessedly empty road. The last thing he needed was to be rear-ended by another buggy or an *Englisch* car. But Shipshewana was a small town of barely six hundred residents, and although tourists swelled their ranks to thirty-five thousand at times, on this cold December evening he had the road to himself. Everyone else was snug in their houses.

Something had run across the road, though. What would be out in this storm? Any animal with a lick of sense would be bedded down.

On the other hand, if it had been a child . . .

He craned his neck for a better look at whatever was out on such a night. There it was, at the edge of the streetlight's glow, headed down into the ditch. Micah whistled once—a short, sharp sound. Four-legged, limping, and nearly the same color as the snow accumulating on the side of the road, a dog turned, then sat and stared at him. Micah's first inclination was to drive on. The temperature was dropping, and the snow was coming down hard for an early December storm.

He didn't follow that inclination.

Micah had recently turned sixty. He was tall and thin, with streaks of gray in his hair and beard, and not particularly good-looking. He didn't mind any of that. As an old bachelor—a widower, to be more accurate—he didn't really care what he looked like. But his actions? He'd learned the hard way that the wrong choices would most certainly haunt him at night.

Nein, he wouldn't be leaving the injured animal in the ditch.

He called out to Samson, who tossed his black mane before trotting to the side of the road. The horse stopped, head down, one forefoot stamping three times to convey his displeasure.

"I know, Samson, but we can't just leave it out here to freeze."

As he dropped to the pavement, he thought the dog might not come to him, that it might be frightened or bad-tempered or poorly trained. But another whistle from Micah, and it trotted within ten feet of him, then cocked its head and again sat. A female, the dog seemed too well trained to be a stray.

Stepping closer, Micah offered his hand for her to smell. When she didn't snarl or snap, he squatted, his trouser legs immediately soaking up the snow, then ran his hand down her coat to the offending back leg. His fingers came away red. The wound was bleeding but not vigorously. It must have clotted in the cold. The dog whined softly, looking at Micah with eyes that appeared to understand what a fix she was in.

"Come on, girl. Let's get you in the buggy."

Micah slowed when they reached Samson, who sniffed the dog thoroughly, then tossed his head as if to say, *Go ahead. Put her in.* Then he glanced back at Micah.

"*Ya*, I know we can't take her home. You don't have to look at me that way."

His house wasn't an option.

The animal shelter was closed at this hour.

Bishop Simon was out of town for the week. He'd taken a bus to visit family in Pennsylvania.

That left only one choice.

Micah checked the road in both directions, then turned the horse back the way they'd come. The drive took less than twenty minutes. He and Samson were both accustomed to the route since they took it five days a week. Rachel King served tea to the *Englischer* tourists he ferried to and from her house. She was always kind to strangers. He only hoped that kindness extended to the furry kind.

Who was he trying to fool? He thought of Rachel because she was on his mind more often than not. Micah's wife had died five years earlier. He still missed her, but now his mind brought up only the good memories. And speaking of minds, Inez had never had trouble speaking hers. One of the last things she'd said to him was that he would need to move on. "Don't sit around feeling sorry for yourself, Micah. Live every day of the life *Gotte* has given you."

Did that mean courting Rachel? Did sixty-year-old men court women? Or was it called something different? Regardless, he no longer felt it was unfaithful to have romantic thoughts about another woman, and the only woman he felt that way about was Rachel.

As he pulled into Rachel's lane, he wondered how he would present the idea of taking in an animal to her, but nothing terribly inspiring came to mind.

"Guess we'll have to depend on your charm," he said to the dog, who didn't respond but did nail him with her large brown eyes. In Micah's opinion, Labradors could win someone over with only a look.

"Let's hope Rachel sees you the same way."

An image of her formed in his mind. She was a good six inches shorter than his six feet and round in the way of older women. Like his, her brown hair had a liberal sprinkling of gray, though he'd seen glimpses of it only once or twice in the two years he'd known her. They both had brown eyes too. Rachel always dressed neat and proper—her dress a conservative color, her apron clean and pressed, her *kapp* covering her head.

As he parked the buggy, he realized he'd brought the dog here for another reason. Something seemed to be eating at Rachel. She had a layer of sadness about her, just below the polite face she wore for everyone to see. He couldn't claim to understand women, even though he knew intelligent and kind—and pretty—when he saw them. Rachel was all those things.

He suspected she was lonely now that her elderly parents had passed, with no extended family at all as far as he knew. She'd never been married. She also had no brothers or sisters—no nieces or nephews or grandbabies to remind her of the miracle of new life.

He'd seen the expression on her face when his granddaughter Betty's brand-new baby was passed around at a recent gathering. Little Nathan had a head full of dark-brown hair, eyes bluer than the summer sky, and a disposition confirming he was a Miller—meaning he was demanding and not afraid to show it. Already he'd won Micah's heart and the hearts of everyone who'd held him.

But then he saw the look on Rachel's face when he suggested she hold the infant. Suffice to say, her mask slipped for a moment, and what he saw tore at his heart. Not just loneliness but something like remorse and desire too. They all seemed to be mixed into that one expression.

It didn't last long. Rachel was good at keeping her true feelings covered.

Then there was the day the week before last. He'd returned to her place because an *Englischer* had left her cell phone there. Rachel hadn't answered his knock, so he walked around to the back porch while the woman waited in the buggy. He'd found Rachel sitting in a rocker, staring at a handwritten letter, tears streaming down her face. She insisted it was allergies, but he was pretty sure he could tell the difference.

Perhaps she would let the dog into her home and life, especially since he'd focus on presenting his case as the dog needing her. Despite her reluctance to hold his great-grandson, Rachel was a nurturer. He'd seen it in how she served the tourists, cared for her buggy horse. And he'd heard how faithfully she'd cared for her aging parents.

Hopefully that instinct extended to injured animals.

Rachel King opened her front door, light spilling out from the sitting room. She was surprised to see Micah Miller standing on the porch. Her surprise switched to alarm when she saw the ragged dog sitting beside him.

"Sorry to bother you." His hand went to the top of the dog's head.

"Why are you here?"

"Just rescued this gal, and she . . . well, she needs a place to stay. She seems lost, and she's injured her leg too."

"So you brought her to me?" Rachel fought to lower her voice. She prided herself in remaining calm, practical, logical. "I don't want a dog. I've no use for one."

Micah took off his hat and twirled it in his hands, a sure sign he was at a loss for words. She peered past him, surprised to see how much snow had built up in the last hour. The wind was beginning to blow, and the temperature was dropping. Not a night for man or beast to be out if they could help it.

Do not forget to show hospitality to strangers, for by so doing some people have shown hospitality to angels without knowing it.

The verse slipped into her mind unbidden. Micah wasn't a stranger, and the dog didn't look like an angel. Still, the night was terribly cold.

"Come in. No use in your freezing while we figure this out."

Micah stepped through the doorway, but the mongrel hung back. Rachel looked at the mutt, really looked at it for the first time, and wished she hadn't. A person could lose their common sense in those brown eyes. As Micah hung up his coat and hat and stomped the snow off his wet shoes, she motioned toward the kitchen with her head, and the dog, limping, quietly padded inside.

"Someone has house-trained it," she muttered as Micah followed.

"Mind if I put down a bowl with some water?"

"The least we can do." After pointing to the right cabinet, she went about putting a kettle on the stove, turning on the burner's flame and adjusting it just so, then slipping decaffeinated tea bags into two mugs. The actions helped calm her. She'd never been the nervous type, but lately she grew flustered when Micah was close. Some days she even heard herself giggle like a schoolgirl, and then she quickly wondered if she'd lost her mind.

She needed to focus on the problem at hand.

Micah liked his tea with cream and sugar, so she set them on the table, where the man had just settled into a chair. While she was pulling cookies from the pantry, she thought of at least half a dozen reasons why she could—and would—refuse him.

She glanced at the dog again, who was definitely a Labrador. She'd curled up next to the stove—head on paws, eyes locked on hers.

"Don't look at me that way. You're not staying."

The dog didn't even blink.

Micah pulled three gingersnaps off the plate she placed between them, then stuffed one in his mouth before washing it down with the tea. "Hits the spot. *Danki*."

"Gem gschehne." She sipped her own tea, and after setting the mug just so on the place mat she'd sewn and quilted, she forced herself to meet Micah's gaze. "I can't keep it."

"Okay."

"I don't know a thing about caring for dogs."

"There's not really much to learn."

"We're Amish. We don't keep pets in the house."

"Some do. Widow Lapp keeps one of those little yippy things in her home. I think it's some sort of terrier."

Rachel resisted the urge to roll her eyes. Widow Lapp also knitted sweaters for the little dog. She was growing more eccentric with each year.

"You'd be unique, having a big dog living with you."

"When we were growing up, such a thing was unheard of. My *dat* had a hunting dog once, but it stayed outside."

"I could take her to your barn."

Rachel dismissed that idea with a flap of her hand. She could count on Micah to try the sympathy card. He knew she wasn't a coldhearted person, that she wouldn't put an injured animal in the barn. She had a heart for lost things. To prove it, she stood and fetched two clean rags. She soaked one in warm water, then set about tending the animal's leg.

Micah's knees popped as he squatted beside her. "Looks like it might have been scraped on a fence."

She caught the scent of snow and under that the soap he'd used. She closed her eyes, breathed deeply, then refocused on the dog. "Why don't people take better care of their animals? It's a responsibility, you know. Dogs shouldn't be running around in the snow with injured legs."

"No ID tag, no collar, and her ribs are plainly showing. I don't think anyone has cared for her in a while even if she has an owner. But I'll check around."

They were both sitting on the floor now.

Micah held the dog's head in case it resisted Rachel's doctoring, but she sat quite patiently while Rachel cleaned and then bound the wound. Once she was done, Micah carried the wet rag into the mudroom to spread it out on the gas-powered washing machine.

Rachel washed and dried her hands, stepped to the refrigerator, and took out a chicken breast she'd planned to eat the next evening, then cut it into small chunks. After fetching the loaf of bread from the bread bin, she cut off a good-sized slice and pulled it into pieces. Then she mixed it in with the chicken. The dog's tail thumped a rhythm against her floor the entire time. When she set it next to the water bowl, the dog looked at the food, then looked at her and waited.

"Go ahead," she said softly, which was all the encouragement needed.

The bowl was licked clean in record time.

The dog stood and shook herself before limping over to Rachel. She sniffed her hand once, then returned to her place by the stove. Turning in a circle three times, she flopped onto the floor with a heavy sigh and closed her eyes.

Micah snapped his fingers. "I've got it."

"Someone who needs a dog?"

"*Nein*, her name. You can call her Chloe."

"Why would I do that?"

"Because she looks like a Chloe. It's a *gut* name."

"Listen, Micah, I appreciate your tender heart. I do." She glanced at the sleeping dog, the stove, anywhere but into the eyes of this man she was beginning to care for—deeply.

"I hear a *but* coming."

"But I don't want a dog."

"Are you sure you don't?"

"*Ya*, I'm sure. What kind of question is that?"

"Sometimes something is missing in people's lives, but they don't know what it is. Then *Gotte* provides for that thing in unexpected ways."

"So *Gotte* brought me this dog?"

"*Nein*. I brought her."

They both sidestepped *what* could be missing from her life. Just as well. Micah might have guessed just how lonely she'd become, but she wasn't about to affirm his guess or reveal any of her regrets. She only hoped his friendship wasn't based on pity. She didn't think it was.

"Why can't you take her home?"

"Three of the family are allergic, and then there's the new great-grandbaby. I don't think Betty would be sympathetic to the idea."

"Surely you at least suspected I wouldn't be sympathetic, but that didn't stop you."

"What if I provided the food? I could even help with the cost of vaccinations and vet visits, if that's what you're worried about."

Rachel waved away that idea. "It's not about the expense."

"Then what is it?" Micah leaned forward, and she dropped her eyes. He said nothing until she looked at him again instead of staring at her half-empty mug. "What are you afraid of?"

"Who says I'm afraid of anything?" Rachel stood to rinse out her mug, irritation building like steam in a kettle. She would not become emotional in front of this man. He was a dear friend, but he didn't know her *that* well. He couldn't possibly understand that although she was lonely, she found comfort in her life's predictability and stability. Adopt a dog? She didn't need to develop feelings for this animal. It would probably be gone as soon as the storm ended.

Then again, how could she send her back out in the snow if Micah truly had nowhere else to take her?

Maybe someone was looking for the dog. Micah had offered to check around. If she stayed only one night or even a few days, perhaps she wouldn't become attached to the animal.

Pulling in a deep breath, she turned to face Micah. Lines creased his face in a map familiar to her. If she was honest with herself, she'd admit she didn't want him to think less of her.

"She can stay the night. In the mudroom."

"I'll fix her up a bed."

Rachel nodded once, knowing he'd find what he needed out there, then set to washing their mugs and covering the rest of the cookies.

Minutes later she'd joined Micah at her front door. Once again he was turning the hat in his hands.

"See you in the morning?" he finally said.

"Of course. Be safe in this weather."

He nodded but still looked as if he wanted to say more. Micah often had that look on his face. But he stayed silent, which she appreciated. That was one of the things she respected about him. Not only did he not pry, but he never gave his opinion unless she asked for it—except about the dog.

As she walked through the house turning off lanterns and tidying for her guests the next day, it occurred to her that was probably the real reason she'd agreed to keep the dog. She didn't want to disappoint Micah Miller.

2

RACHEL WOKE THE NEXT MORNING WITH THE FAMILIAR—and ever-increasing—dread and hopelessness pinning her to the bed. During the day, when she was busy, she could forget her troubles. In the evening, when she collapsed into bed, she was often too tired to wrestle with them. Mornings were difficult.

How had she arrived at this point in her life totally and utterly alone?

What could she have done differently?

What *should* she have done differently?

The questions pressed in as she contemplated another ten, twenty, even thirty years alone. She might have given in to self-pity and pulled the covers over her head, which would have been a childish and useless thing to do, but she heard a soft whine. At first she couldn't imagine what animal might be outside her door.

Then she remembered Micah appearing out of the snowstorm, the Labrador waiting patiently at his side. She remembered the trusting gaze the dog had settled on her. She realized the animal wasn't outside her house but in her mudroom.

Swinging her feet over the side of the bed, Rachel found her slippers, then snatched up her robe.

It was barely dawn, but no doubt the dog needed to be let out. What had she been thinking? With any luck, it would take the chance to run back to its owner—if it had one.

She half expected to see a mess when she opened the door to the mudroom, but everything was in the same condition. The dog padded to the outside door and whined softly.

"Sure. *Ya.* I understand."

For a moment she watched it wade through the snow, still limping a bit. The accumulation had been several inches, but Rachel expected it would melt off by midmorning. Her chestnut gelding was already out in one of her fields. Josiah Troyer leased her other fields. He paid her only a small amount, but he also took care of Penny, for the most part. Her buggy horse's coat was a lovely reddish brown, and with the rising sun already shining on her, she definitely resembled her name.

That image—the dog and the horse and the snow—lifted her spirits. The tightening in her chest lessened, and she laughed as the dog maneuvered to the right and left, trying to chase something Rachel couldn't see. She backtracked into the kitchen, then made herself a strong cup of coffee before returning to the back door.

Chloe had not trotted off to find her owner.

Instead, she was waiting patiently on the back porch.

When Rachel let her in, she went straight to the water bowl

and drank her fill, then sat, tail thumping, brown eyes focused on Rachel.

"I suppose you expect me to feed you breakfast too."

Thump.

"You ate all the chicken."

Thump, thump.

"But I usually make myself an egg, and I have plenty of those."

Rachel stepped to the sink, then wondered if Chloe had followed her and tracked snow across the kitchen floor. She turned to admonish her but found the dog was already lying next to the stove. She really was exceptionally well-behaved.

Rachel had prepared for the morning's guests the evening before, just before Micah and Chloe arrived. It was a full group of twenty today. As the last group was leaving, Micah always shared the numbers for the next day to help her plan correctly.

On one counter sat twenty cups and saucers with a tea bag in each cup. Next to them sat five small sugar bowls, and in her refrigerator she'd placed five small pitchers of cream. Five plates of cookies waited on the opposite counter, each covered with a dishcloth to keep the treats fresh. Finally, she had five teapots. She was also prepared to serve Micah and the other drivers.

"Our *Englisch* guests arrive at ten. You'll have to be back in the mudroom by then." It didn't occur to her to feel silly talking to the dog. She'd never been one to doubt they could understand every word. Her mind flashed back to the blue heeler she'd had as a child. Though it was technically her father's hunting dog, she'd grown quite fond of it. She remembered brushing its coat and how it would trot next to her down to the pond. Roxie had been a good dog. Why had she never had one since?

Of course, they were expensive to keep.

And could sometimes be a behavior problem.

They most certainly shouldn't stay in the house. Her *Englisch* guests would sometimes pull out their phones and show her photos of their homes, grandchildren, or pets. She'd seen more than one dog sitting proudly on a couch or in the middle of a bed. She couldn't imagine such a thing, though she supposed the mudroom might be all right.

If she were keeping this dog, which she wasn't. But she did change her bandage, the old one now wet from the snow. Then she scrambled three eggs, two for Chloe and one for herself. Like the night before, after Chloe had eaten, she padded over to Rachel and sniffed her hand. This time, though, she sat next to Rachel's chair and leaned against her. It was a comforting thing, the dog's weight ever so slightly pressing on her side as she ate her breakfast.

A person could get used to such things.

It might even help with the loneliness.

Stranger things had happened.

She'd never married and had children. Some days she regretted that. Most days she regretted it. And she didn't have any family in the area now that her parents had passed—another reason she'd come to feel her aloneness so keenly.

Her mind jumped to the box of letters she'd recently found. Her *mamm* had written them to her *aenti*, yet they were not only never mailed but unaddressed. So, then, she had no idea where her *mamm*'s only *schweschder* was. She wished she knew how to contact Deborah, her single chance for extended family, since her father, like her, had been an only child. All she knew was that her maiden name was Byler and her married name, Glick.

Those were common Amish names, and she didn't know where to start looking for her. She didn't know how to start looking.

And to complicate matters even more, she didn't understand her feelings for Micah. Some days he seemed like more than a dear friend—like the days she was flustered or giggled around him. But other days she thought she was imagining such a thing. Then again, *why* did she often become flustered and silly around him? And she certainly looked forward to seeing him. She thought he even understood her better than anyone else. Was that love? Could it be possible that at the age of fifty-six she was entertaining romantic thoughts?

She glanced at the dog, who offered no answers. Perhaps that was a bit much to expect from a Labrador.

Micah had been a farmer all his life, but the heart bypass three years ago had ended those days. When he'd fully recovered, his son, Tom, insisted he sell his place in Goshen and move in with his family in Shipshewana. Some mornings he'd felt strong enough to work in the fields, but Tom and his wife would hear nothing of it. Even the *grandkinner* had chimed in with "Just play with us, *Daddi*. It's way better than working."

He did enjoy playing with the littlest tikes—though calling them tikes now might be a stretch. They'd grown so. And his oldest granddaughter, Betty, had just had a child of her own. These days it would be a great-grandchild who'd most want his company.

Nein. He couldn't sit home all day, playing checkers and

whittling. That was a bleak future indeed, as much as he loved his *grandkinner.* He needed to feel useful, needed to contribute, same as anyone else.

While sitting at the Blue Gate one day—enjoying a piece of pie and cup of coffee, staring out the window at the crowds of tourists walking up and down the sidewalk—he'd come up with the idea of ferrying *Englischers* on a tour. It hadn't taken long for the notion to grow. Before he could fashion another turkey call, some other Shipshe folks were expressing interest in the new venture. He hadn't wanted to rush into anything, though.

So he'd written to his *bruder,* who did something similar in Ohio. He'd also called an old friend in Goshen who had recently started offering tours of his farm. Finally, he'd spoken with Bishop Simon to be sure that what he was considering wouldn't be at odds with their *Ordnung.*

He learned that his idea was not only doable, but in every case it was profitable. Then the key was to think it all through properly. What was it his own *dat* always said? *You get what you pay for.* He certainly wanted the *Englischers* to receive a unique experience since he expected them to pay for it.

Many people from the city seemed fascinated by their Plain life; yet for most Amish, plain was all they'd ever known. There was nothing unusual about living without electricity and not owning cars and computers. Micah suspected, though, that the way they lived was not just unfamiliar to the average American but strange. However, he also understood that the people who spent their vacation in places like Shipshewana were seeking a way to simplify their own lives. But first they had to believe it was even possible in this current day and age.

So how could he help them along that journey?

He'd jotted his notes on a sheet of paper that he still kept in his top dresser drawer.

> Some sort of tour that would last from nine in the morning to noon.
>
> A unique look into Amish life.
>
> A business that would benefit Amish families trying to supplement their farming income.

By that time the others weren't just interested but were eager to join him. Emily Yoder had a yarn shop in downtown Shipshe, and she was more than happy to offer her place as a pickup spot. Joseph Schrock wanted to offer free samples for groups visiting his cheese shop. And Claire Beiler had every sort of animal on her small farm that a tourist might want to see, owing to the fact that her husband, David, was the restless sort who was always moving on to the next great thing. That meant the Beiler family had not only cows and chickens, but goats, alpacas, and camels. And most recently, they'd acquired rabbits.

What surprised him the most was Rachel King pulling him aside at church one Sunday to say she'd like to offer tea to the tourists. "And perhaps they'd like to see my quilts."

In fact, they clamored to see her quilts, and that opportunity was now in the top spot on their brochure. "Amish quilts for sale" brought in tourists faster than yarn, cheese, or farm animals—especially the closer they came to Christmas, it seemed. But the groups appeared to enjoy all aspects of the tour, even in cold weather. It had been more than a year since they'd started their venture, and everyone was happy with the results. Recently they'd been featured on the Shipshewana web page, which prompted Emily to purchase a laptop and hire an *Englisch* teenager to manage online reservations.

Yes, they had a booming business for sure and certain.

And Micah was happy to be busy.

But he'd never have guessed he'd come to care for the little group of entrepreneurs as if they were his own family. And what he felt for Rachel . . . Well, he believed their friendship could turn into something more, but she seemed to maintain a barrier between them. Yet the first thing that crossed Micah's mind when his eyes popped open that morning was the limping dog followed by Rachel's look of dismay at being asked to keep her.

He had been so sure the Labrador could lift the heaviness plaguing Rachel of late.

But what did he know of a woman's burdens?

"Ridiculous," he said aloud, snorting as he combed his hair and prepared for work. "Problems are problems—whether they belong to a woman or a man."

He was still hoping Rachel would decide to keep Chloe. Perhaps now that she'd slept on the idea, she'd be more receptive. Maybe Chloe had worked her way into Rachel's heart. He decided to be optimistic about it.

"Where are you going so early, Pop?" Naomi asked. It was hard to believe Tom and his wife were both forty. Naomi was short and round, and she possessed the sweetest personality he could ask for in a daughter-in-law.

"Need to stop by the dry goods store before I pick up my group."

"I hope you have a backup plan for that dog."

The night before, he'd told her and Tom about finding the dog and leaving it with Rachel.

"Actually, I don't."

"Chances are you're going to need one. I've never seen a cleaner house than Rachel King's, and dogs are never conducive to a spotless house."

"But she could leave it outside."

"*Ya*, most folks in our community do that, but dogs are still a lot of work. And I think your Chloe would get lonesome with just Rachel there."

"Maybe." Micah thought the dog was lonelier in the ditch where he'd found her, but he didn't argue with Naomi.

"Then again, Rachel might be lonely herself since she lives there all alone." Naomi glanced at him, a smile forming on her lips.

"Tell me you're not matchmaking, especially this early in the day."

"*Nein.* I wouldn't think of it."

"That's *gut* to hear."

She handed him a bowl of hot oatmeal and nodded toward the raisins, sugar, and walnuts on the table. "Some days I'm tempted to, though."

Without responding, he downed his breakfast and then took off before the deluge of children hit the table. As he drove into town, he considered ways they might look for Chloe's owner, assuming she had one who wanted to be found. They could put up flyers, but that would be expensive. They'd handwrite one since Amish folks didn't have computers, of course, but then they'd have to make copies in town because Amish folks didn't have copy machines either.

They could also check with the local animal shelter and vet. Those would be *gut* places to start.

With a plan in place, Micah turned his thoughts to the day's business.

They had another large group scheduled for the day. Micah could fit only six people into his buggy with him, so on days like today, they asked Emily's son, Paul, to drive a second buggy. They also called on an *Englischer*, Bill Harris, for big groups or when they had tourists who'd rather travel by automobile. Bill was well-known among the Amish community and had recently retired from an office job. Now he was supplementing his income by giving Amish rides in his new van.

Micah arrived at the dry goods store just as they were opening for business. He purchased dog food and treats, as well as a shampoo that claimed to "kill fleas and restore your pet's coat to a healthy shine." He placed the supplies in the chest attached to the back of his buggy. Their first stop was the animal farm, and their second stop was Rachel's. By the time they made it to her place, their groups were ready for cups of hot tea and a midmorning snack.

For Micah, visiting Rachel's was the highlight of the day—which said something about the depth of his feelings for her. But he wasn't quite ready to examine just how deep they were. Not with that barrier between them.

3

RACHEL HAD MEANT TO CLOSE CHLOE UP IN THE MUDroom, but the dog was so quiet—maybe from exhaustion after her morning romp—that she completely forgot about her.

The tour arrived promptly at ten. Micah was good about keeping to the schedule, and she appreciated that. The teakettles had just begun to whistle when she heard Micah's buggy pull up, followed by Paul's buggy and Bill's van.

The *Englisch* women on the tours—and ninety percent of the tourists in their groups were women—reminded Rachel of the time she'd visited an aviary with her parents. Like the birds, the women represented so many different colors and types, all chattering excitedly to one another. She'd become accustomed to their looks of surprise at seeing a house not so different from their own. She had the same pieces of furniture, the same appliances in the kitchen—though gas powered—and the same sunshine coming through the window on a bright December morning.

In fact, a glance at the calendar had reminded her that today was the second of December. Perhaps that explained part of her glum mood on waking. This wasn't the easiest month for someone living alone.

How do you celebrate Christmas if you're the only member of your family? More than two years had passed since her parents had died in the buggy accident, but she still didn't know how to handle holidays. What's the point in cooking a special meal when there's no one to share it with? And was she supposed to give herself a Christmas gift?

She pushed those thoughts aside as she poured boiling water into the teapots. Then she listened to her guests' comments as she greeted them in her sitting room.

"Your house is lovely."

"It's so uncluttered. I read a blog post about that last week."

"No television either. I ask Earl to turn off that noisy thing every day, but he just sits there flipping through channels."

Rachel cleared her throat, and the guests immediately grew quiet. "Welcome to my home. I'm so pleased that you've chosen to spend part of your morning with me. We'll have tea, and then I'll answer questions about the Amish lifestyle. Finally, I have some quilts you might be interested in."

The response was immediate—nods and murmurs of agreement.

"I have seating for a dozen of you in this room. The other eight will fit around the kitchen table. If someone would like to help me with the trays . . ."

One or two women always jumped up at the idea of helping. These were the ladies with whom Rachel felt the most kinship. Amish or *Englisch*, some people immediately lent a hand while others seemed unsure what was expected of them.

Two of the women followed her into the kitchen—one tall and thin with dark skin and the other shorter with light skin and red hair. Rachel selected a tray from the counter and handed it to the first woman. "I'll bring in the teapots."

She'd just turned to pick up another tray when she heard a squeal. "You have a dog—a Labrador. Do you mind if I pet her?" The redheaded woman was kneeling in front of Chloe even as she asked the question.

"She isn't really mine. Micah found her last night and brought her here."

"You bandaged her leg?"

"Yes. We think she injured it on a fence. And it seems she's not been eating well."

"She's still beautiful."

The woman's squeal had prompted several other guests gathering in the kitchen to turn toward the dog. Three more hustled over to pet and coo over Chloe, who withstood the attention surprisingly well. Then Micah came in, his face wreathed in a smile.

Standing close enough to Rachel to practically whisper, he said, "Our guests seem to be enjoying Chloe."

"Maybe one of them will take her home."

"She hasn't won you over yet?" His eyebrows knit together in mock surprise.

Another thing she liked about Micah was that he didn't rattle easily, and she knew in her heart that he wouldn't judge her regardless what decision she made about the dog.

"She's well-behaved, I'll give you that."

"And like I said, it's unique—having a dog in an Amish house."

Unique was one of Micah's favorite words.

Leaning closer, he lowered his voice even more. "Helps dispel those with an idea that we all run puppy mills."

Rachel tsked at that. The last person she'd known to try to run anything like a puppy mill—which was actually three beagles he'd bred multiple times—had received a prolonged lecture from Bishop Simon about the proper way to care for *Gotte*'s animals. The next week all the beagles had been adopted, and the man had moved on to keeping bees, which he was much more adept at doing.

Word spread through their group, and over the next twenty minutes each woman seemed to make her way into the kitchen to see Chloe. The dog certainly did help put people at ease. Everyone was smiling by the time Rachel called them all into the sitting room. Micah and Paul brought in the kitchen chairs so everyone would have a seat.

Rachel stood next to the woodstove. When everyone quieted, she let her eyes scan the group more thoroughly, most of the women evidently enjoying the tour in pairs or groups of three or four. Though she did notice one woman sitting a bit off by herself. She was gazing around the room as if she needed to drink in the sight of it. When she turned her eyes to Rachel, something in her expression caused Rachel to cock her head and pause.

But then someone commented on how the tea had really hit the spot and someone else murmured that she couldn't wait to see the quilts. Those snippets of conversation brought Rachel's attention back to the matter at hand.

"*Gudemariye.* That means good morning in Pennsylvania Dutch, the language Amish folk speak with one another."

The ladies attempted to reply in kind, which brought a lot of laughter from the group—from everyone except the solitary woman who smiled as if the word pained her in some way.

"We strive to live a simple life, a life apart, and yet we welcome you to our community. We understand that in today's world, life can be hectic, and many are seeking a quieter, calmer place."

"It's certainly calm and quiet here. I don't miss the traffic noise one bit."

"For certain there's not a lot of traffic on an Amish farm."

That brought more laughter. It was obviously a good-natured group—at least most of it.

"The Amish life isn't for everyone, but perhaps you'll see something here to take back to your own world, something that will calm your spirit and bring you into closer fellowship with our Lord."

That brought more nods and murmurs of agreement.

"I'll tell you a little about our community and faith, and then I'll answer whatever questions you have."

Rachel had been surprised to find that she liked speaking to these groups. She was always impressed by their interest and politeness. To her, the Amish life seemed simple and the things they did on a daily basis—baking bread, hanging out the laundry, planting a garden—uninteresting. Though most of her guests lived in urban areas, she knew many of them had grown up with grandparents who did those same things. Visiting her home was like a trip back to their own childhood.

She'd become accustomed to the questions, which were usually at least similar.

"Why do you hate technology?"

"We don't hate it. We only strive to limit its intrusion in our lives."

"Is it hard living without electricity?"

"For me, it's what I've always known. It's no harder than it was for my parents."

"Why don't you own cars?"

"Automobiles are quite expensive and don't last as long as a horse. Also, we can grow what the horse needs to eat versus purchasing gasoline, which fluctuates in price with each season and year."

"Do most Amish women really have ten children?"

"Many do. We believe children are a gift from God." She glanced at Micah. He once mentioned that he and Inez had hoped for more children, as had his son and daughter-in-law. But *Gotte* knew best.

"Why do the children attend school only through eighth grade?"

"Because that's all the education they need to acquire a job in the Amish community. In fact, most teens enter apprenticeships so they can try several different jobs before deciding on their life's path."

"Are women treated equally with men?"

"The Bible commands us to treat each other with compassion and respect regardless of gender or race. Although Amish women fill more traditional roles in an Amish community, they have an equal say in the running of their homes and schools."

"Is the Amish faith a cult?"

"My understanding is that a cult follows a particular man. While we have a bishop in each community to lead us, when he moves or dies, another is randomly selected."

Most of the women listened intently, speaking softly to one another between questions.

Micah signaled that they had fifteen minutes left.

"Now I'd like to tell you about our quilting. We still hand-sew each quilt—both the piecing and the quilting itself. We use traditional colors for quilts to use in our own homes, which you'll see with the quilt on my bed in a moment. However, for quilts we sell, we use all types of colors and patterns."

A woman sitting closest to her with reading glasses on a chain around her neck raised her hand as if she were a *youngie* in school. "I heard Amish women put a mistake in each quilt to help them remain humble."

"Trust me, that's not necessary. Every quilt I've made already had a mistake in it. No need for me to put one there."

That brought more laughter, and some of the women again nodded in agreement. A few quilters were always among the women who came.

"Did your mother teach you to quilt?"

This came from the woman sitting a little apart. Like Rachel, she was around five feet, six inches and a bit thick through the waist and hips. Her hair was also brown—though it was cut short and seemed to curl naturally. Something besides her physical appearance seemed familiar, though. Yet that was impossible. Rachel was sure she'd never met her before.

"My late mother did teach me, and her mother taught her. If Micah thinks we have time, I'll tell you a story about my mother and her sister."

The lone woman sat up ramrod straight, then proceeded to worry her thumbnail.

The other women turned as one toward Micah, who raised

his hands in a palms-out gesture. This brought more laughter. They were certainly a pleasant group—other than the woman who had asked the question. Her expression was serious. Troubled, even.

Rachel went on.

"They were teenagers at the time. *Aenti* Deborah was pledged to be married, and the two of them decided to make a quilt in the traditional double wedding ring pattern. You may have noticed that Amish don't wear jewelry, not even a wedding ring. But the quilt pattern is said to symbolize a never-ending bond between the bride and groom. My mother and aunt misjudged how long it would take to make a queen-sized quilt, though. In the months and then weeks before my aunt's wedding, they found themselves often staying up late at night, sewing by lamplight. Perhaps that's why they didn't see the mistake until they placed it on the bed in my aunt's new home."

Now the strange woman was staring at the floor, but the others were leaning forward, completely caught up in the story. It was a bittersweet memory for Rachel, as many memories of her parents were. She still hadn't quite recovered from their sudden passing.

"Can any of you guess what mistake they found?"

No one ever answered that question. In fact, Rachel barely paused before giving the answer. Today was different. The woman sitting alone tentatively raised a hand and said, "One of the panels was upside down."

Everyone turned to stare at her, but the woman kept her eyes on Rachel.

Rachel was completely taken aback. The answer was a statement, not a question as if the woman was guessing. How was that possible?

Clearing her throat, she glanced at Micah, who shrugged his shoulders in surprise.

"Exactly." She needed to wind up the speech quickly so the women would still have time to visit what had been her parents' room and view the quilts she'd placed on the bed. "And the quilt remained as it was, a reminder that no person and certainly no relationship is perfect."

The mysterious woman followed Rachel and the rest of the women into the bedroom, staying just long enough to stare at the quilts and then glance around. Rachel had removed her parents' personal effects, so there wasn't much to see.

By the time Micah had herded everyone outside, she'd sold three quilts. But she was less interested in the money than in the woman who'd known her *mamm*'s story. She hurried outside to search for her, but she wasn't among the guests in the buggies. She must have come with Bill, whose van was already driving away.

Rachel supposed how the woman had known about the quilt would remain a mystery.

4

MICAH HAD BEEN LOOKING DIRECTLY AT RACHEL WHEN the *Englisch* woman answered her question. He'd seen the look of shock, which she'd tried to cover with a smile. It was as plain as the sunshine melting the snow on the side of the road that the response had upset her. He'd thought it was strange too.

So after lunch, though he'd already unloaded the dog supplies, he decided to swing by to check on her, maybe tell her what he'd learned about the woman. But only if she brought her up.

"Come to retrieve your dog?" Rachel was outside sweeping the already clean porch when he pulled up. Chloe was curled up in a corner watching. Her tail beat a pattern against the wooden floor as he bent to pet her.

"*Nein*. I haven't had time to ask around about her."

Standing on her porch steps, he turned and glanced out over the fields she leased to the Troyer boy. Though he was hardly a boy, and he had a family of his own. Josiah had made Rachel an offer for both her fields and the house last summer. Micah had been there the day he'd suggested buying the place. That had been one of the first times Rachel invited him to stay for tea when he'd brought her some news about the business. She'd turned Josiah down with a tight smile. When Micah asked her why, she simply replied, "And where would I go? This is the only home I've known since my family moved to Shipshe years ago."

He thought of that now as she swept the clean porch.

It was a beautiful winter's day, and something told him Rachel was feeling a bit restless.

"Care to go to town for a pretzel?"

She leaned the broom against the wall, crossed her arms, and gave him a pointed look. "Micah Miller, when do you take off in the middle of the day to eat pretzels?"

He glanced at Chloe, who simply stared at him with her large brown eyes, then looked back at Rachel. Apparently Rachel hadn't caught on to the fact that they were semiretired and could pretty much do whatever they wanted in the middle of the day. He needed a valid excuse for getting her out of the house, and Chloe looked like a good candidate.

"We could take Chloe by the vet and the shelter—see if anyone is missing a dog."

"Now that's a *gut* idea. Let me grab my coat."

Ten minutes later, Chloe was in the back of the buggy, curled on a blanket on the floor, and Rachel was riding by Micah's side. That seemed good and right to him, and in that moment he realized he was lonely too. Yes, it was possible to be lonely even when you lived in a house full of people. He would always miss Inez. They'd had a long and happy life together, but she'd been gone five years. Perhaps he was ready to move on with his life. Perhaps he was tired of being alone.

He and Rachel had ridden together half a dozen times in the past year. After she'd invited him in for tea that day, occasionally he'd offered to pick her up for church, especially if the weather was bad. It wasn't courting, and they certainly didn't need a chaperone at their age. Still, she often seemed a bit tense the first few miles. This time Rachel seemed to relax as soon as she settled in the buggy. Her posture was less rigid, and she'd stopped worrying her *kapp* string.

"Your buggy horse seems to enjoy this weather."

"*Ya*, Samson is good-natured enough."

"Had him long?"

"Let's see. Tom was twentysomething when I purchased Samson from an *Englischer*."

"And now Tom is forty?"

"He is."

"So Samson is probably fifteen years old."

"A *gut* guess."

"It always makes me laugh when *Englischers* ask why we don't drive cars. I imagine most of them haven't kept their vehicles more than the four years it takes to pay them off."

"The other night Tom told me many car loans are for six years now."

"No kidding?"

"Cars have computers in them, backup cameras, all sorts of fancy technology. The cost has nearly doubled in the last twenty years."

"Horses haven't changed much."

"Indeed."

Rachel smiled, and Micah wondered at how comfortable he felt with her. The rest of the ride passed in silence as they enjoyed the bright sunshine.

Their first stop was the animal shelter. No one had reported a Labrador missing, though the girl who worked the front desk took a photo of Chloe and promised to post it on the board in their waiting area as well as on their website. "She looks like a real sweetheart."

"Do you have space to keep her?" Micah hated asking the question. He could feel Chloe's accusatory eyes on him, but at the same time, he *had* rather sprung the dog on Rachel with no fair warning.

The girl was already shaking her head. "We're full at the moment, but we can send her to the shelter in Middlebury."

"No need to go to all that trouble." Rachel wrote the number for the phone shack closest to her home on a piece of note paper. "Call me if anyone shows up looking for her."

"Sure thing."

As they walked back outside, Micah tugged on her sleeve. "You know the likelihood of that happening is practically zero. If you don't want to keep Chloe, I understand. I just thought . . ."

She didn't fill in the pause for him.

"Well, I thought she might be *gut* company for you."

Instead of responding to that, she walked around to her side of the buggy and said, "Best go on to the vet's and see if she can tell us anything."

Doc Staci gave Chloe a thorough examination.

After Micah explained how he'd found the dog wandering in the snow with an injury, Staci ran her hand down Chloe's leg, took off the bandage, and declared that they'd done as good a job as she could have. She applied antibiotic cream and wrapped a new bandage around the leg, with instructions to change the wrap once a day for three days, then leave it open to the air.

Once the leg was taken care of, she ran a handheld device over the dog's neck. Staring at the screen, she said, "I thought she looked familiar. This is Josh Cramer's dog, Sister."

"Can't say I've heard that name." Micah glanced at Rachel, who shook her head.

"Josh was in his eighties—lived on the northwest side of town. He passed about six weeks ago. The good news is that she's up-to-date on her shots, but the bad news . . ."

"No one's going to claim her," he finished.

"I'm afraid not. His family doesn't live around here."

As she walked them out to the waiting room, she turned to her receptionist and said, "No charge."

"But . . ." Rachel looked flustered at the idea of accepting this act of kindness.

"I insist. You did a very good thing—both of you did. Some people will stop if they see a puppy, but few will for an old gal."

Rachel looked at the dog and blew out a breath. "Looks like we're stuck with each other, Chloe."

Micah wasn't sure if she meant they were stuck together temporarily or permanently, but he noticed she used the dog's new name. Maybe it was her way of giving it her blessing.

"Why are you smiling at me like that?"

"You used the name we came up with together."

"Oh. Well, I don't suppose we can ask her which she'd rather we use."

"Actually, you could." Doc Staci knelt in front of the dog. "Which is it going to be? Sister?"

No response, other than the dog continuing to stare at her.

"Chloe?"

Now the dog's ears perked up, and she leaned forward to sniff her hand.

"I'd say she's taken to the new name. Dogs will do that sometimes."

"How old is she?" Micah asked.

"Seven, according to my records. That's a senior dog when you're talking about a Labrador. She's fairly healthy, but you'll probably notice her limping slightly, even with her leg fully healed, and walking a bit stiff. She may occasionally have trouble standing up."

Rachel's hand went to the top of the dog's head. "She has arthritis?"

"Most older dogs do. You might provide padded bedding."

"Old blankets?"

"That will work if you fold them up about four inches thick. And the effects of arthritis will be less noticeable once the weather warms. As you can see, she also could stand to put on a few pounds. Call me if you need anything."

As they walked back outside, Micah wasn't sure what to say. He helped Chloe and Rachel back into the buggy, but he didn't immediately call out to Samson.

Had he overstepped by bringing the dog to Rachel?

Did she feel backed into a corner?

And would she hold it against him?

He was surprised when she set her purse on the floor of the buggy and said, "I suppose I'll take that pretzel now. And a cup of hot tea."

The sun was shining warmly through the buggy windows,

and Chloe curled up on the blanket again. She didn't seem to mind one bit when they parked outside the Davis Mercantile and left her sleeping in the sunshine.

"She's out of the wind, and your little heater has warmed up the buggy tolerably well." Rachel pulled her purse strap over her shoulder. She looked as if she wanted to say something else, but if she did, she held it back.

Not until they'd ordered—cinnamon pretzels for both of them, coffee for Micah and Rachel's hot tea—did she share what was on her mind.

"I've decided to keep Chloe."

"I'm real happy to hear that. What changed your mind?"

"Doc Staci—when she said most people wouldn't stop for an old dog. That's just sad, Micah. Chloe was a *gut* dog to someone—"

"Cramer."

"Though apparently his family, for whatever reason, didn't see fit to take her with them."

"Or perhaps she ran off, and then they didn't know how to find her."

Rachel sipped her tea, then popped a piece of the cinnamon pretzel into her mouth. "You have a habit of assuming the best about people."

"You say that like it's a bad thing."

"Regardless, old things are valuable." A frown formed between Rachel's eyes. "We don't throw away people or animals or things simply because they've aged."

"True."

"Besides, Chloe and I have a lot in common."

"Such as?"

"We're both old."

"Fifty-six is not so old, Rachel."

"We both have arthritis."

"I suppose most people do at our age."

"And we're both alone. At least I am." Micah started to protest, but Rachel stopped him with a firm shake of her head. "Don't try telling me I'm not alone. I know my life is . . . well, my circle has become a bit small. I suppose it always was, being an only child and all."

"Must have been hard."

"I don't know how it happened." She met his gaze for the first time since they'd sat down, and Micah saw such misery in her eyes that he almost reached for her hand. As if suspecting he might, she jerked both hands off the table and fiddled with her purse. "I suppose I thought I had all the time in the world, and then I didn't."

"All the time to do what?"

"Make plans. Start my own life. Prepare for the future."

"Why did you never marry?"

"I liked my alone time."

"Unusual for an Amish woman."

"I know it is, but remember, I had no siblings. Can you imagine what that was like?" She didn't pause long enough for him to answer, simply pushed on with her confession. "But I liked the hours alone. They gave me time to design and sew quilts, the one thing I could do well."

"You're a gifted quilter."

"One day I looked up, and everyone else was married." She laughed, though he heard little joy in the sound. "Then came the second wave."

"Second wave?"

"Widowers and the occasional awkward man who had never found a *fraa*. It was all . . . well, it was uncomfortable the way people looked at me. So much so that it was almost a relief when I turned forty and everyone seemed to accept that I was never going to wed."

"Do you wish you had?"

"What difference does it make?" She took another bite of the pretzel, chewing thoughtfully. "Then my whole life became my parents as they aged. Taking care of them kept me quite busy. They were older when I was born, so by the time I was forty, they were in their seventies."

"And then the buggy accident."

"Ya."

"Their life was complete."

"I believe so, but mine?"

"Your life is what it should be. *Gotte* has a plan for your life, Rachel. Same as He does for every life. He hasn't forgotten you."

"Well, be that as it may, you were right. Having Chloe around will be *gut* for me. It's time I stop focusing on myself and start thinking about someone else. The problem is I'm not quite sure how to do that. Perhaps Chloe will be a *gut* first step."

They were nearly back to her place when Rachel brought up the mysterious woman from the tour that morning.

"Do you know her name, Micah?"

"*Nein*. I wondered about her, too, and I asked Emily to check her reservation. She paid in cash, and the name was Farver. No first name, no address."

"How could a stranger know about my *mamm*'s quilt?"

"Might have been a coincidence. Maybe someone she knows

made the same mistake. Or maybe she knows someone who took the tour and heard your story."

"Maybe. Did you notice how she sat off by herself a little?"

"I did."

"And the look she gave me. It was as if she wanted to say something but couldn't bring herself to utter the words."

Micah rubbed at a spot on his forehead.

"I'm giving you a headache."

"Not at all. I just remembered . . . She asked about you."

"I don't understand."

"When she was waiting for the tour to begin, she asked Paul Yoder about you."

"Paul told you this?"

"*Nein.* I heard her. I didn't put it together until now."

"Can you remember what she said—specifically what she said?"

"She said, 'Is this the tour that goes to Rachel King's, the woman who quilts?'"

"Most Amish women quilt."

Micah rubbed at his jaw, which suddenly felt like he'd developed a cramp there. "I suppose that's true, and your name is at the top of the brochure."

"Still seems a bit odd."

"Indeed."

"As if I have my own *Englisch* stalker."

"As stalkers go, she didn't look very dangerous."

"Nothing I can do about it now, I suppose."

To Micah, the woman had seemed like she was searching for something, but then that was often the case with *Englischers* who came on their tours. How many had he heard confess that they were burned-out, exhausted, at their wits' end? Too many. "Did she purchase a quilt?"

"Nein." Rachel drew out the word. "But she glanced around the bedroom as if she couldn't imagine how she found herself in an Amish home. And then she left."

"It's a mystery for sure and certain." Which was all he could think to add on the subject.

As he drove Rachel the rest of the way home, his thoughts were less on the mystery woman than on Rachel's confession over their afternoon snack. What would it be like to wake one morning and realize you were on a path you hadn't meant to take? And how did you correct it at their age?

Many things about his life had been hard. He and Inez had suffered through one stillbirth and one miscarriage. Through it all, though, he'd never doubted that their life together was what it was supposed to be. And his family was everything to him. Without them, what would be the point? Was that how Rachel felt? Was she wondering what the point of her very existence was with no family now?

He dropped Rachel and Chloe off, then turned Samson toward home. But he didn't notice much about the countryside. Instead, he prayed that *Gotte* would help Rachel find her way—and that somehow he could be part of that journey.

5

NEARLY TWO WEEKS LATER, RACHEL'S WASH DAY WAS INterrupted by the clatter of buggy wheels. She had happily hung her clothes, towels, and bedding outdoors, even though it was quite cold. The temperatures had fallen into the teens the night before—if she could believe the thermometer on her back porch. Yet sunshine had soon melted the light frost, and she actually felt a bit too warm in her coat.

She'd just picked up the clothes basket when she heard the buggy and spied Micah driving up her lane.

Chloe whined softly, looking to her for permission.

"*Ya.* Go on now. I know you miss him."

Rachel admitted to herself that she also missed Micah the two days with no tour group. Mondays were solitary affairs, but at least she was busy giving her house a good cleaning and taking care of her laundry and baking. On the Sundays they had church, she saw Micah there, but seeing him gathered with the other men just wasn't the same. On their off weeks, when they met as families instead of worshiping in a group, someone always took pity on her and invited her over. On those Sundays, she tried to arrive early to help set up the food and tables, but she inevitably left early because she felt so out of place. Even when the invitation came from Micah's family.

It seemed now that she'd spent her entire life feeling out of place, as if she didn't belong. She was growing tired of wallowing in that feeling. Perhaps if she didn't fit here, it was time to find where she did. But how?

Micah waved as she waited for him. He was carrying a rather large box under his left arm. His right hand sat on top of Chloe's head, and she looked up at him as if he'd caused the sun to rise over the fields.

"Come on in. I baked fresh oatmeal bars this morning."

"I see no reason to turn that down."

When Micah smiled at her like he was now, Rachel's worries seemed to evaporate like the frost in the fields. She wondered how he could have that effect on her. Had their friendship grown that close over the last year? *Were* her feelings for Micah growing into something more?

Chloe followed them into the house and assumed her position by the kitchen stove.

"She seems to have adjusted well."

"Would you believe she's never attempted to lie on the couch or walk through the other rooms? It's as if she knows she's allowed only in the mudroom, and if she stays by the stove, in the kitchen."

"And she's put on a few pounds."

"I think so. The padded bedding has helped too. Some

mornings she's as stiff as I am, but we manage." Gratitude swelled in her heart for the dog. She hadn't realized how far she'd sunk into despair until she'd climbed partially out of it—and Micah and Chloe were two of the reasons she had.

Though she was well aware she still had a ways to go.

Just the thought of Christmas was enough to send Rachel ducking under the covers. Another holiday alone. Another family gathering with no family to gather around. She was trying not to dwell on it, though the big day was now less than two weeks off.

She made them hot tea and set the plate of oatmeal bars on the table. Apparently Micah wasn't going to bring up the box he'd set on the chair between them, so she'd have to ask.

"Is it for me?"

"It is." He smiled at her and wiggled his eyebrows.

It was such a ridiculous sight, more like something he would do for the *bopplin*. She couldn't help laughing.

"It was mailed to our tour company, care of Emily. That was so unusual I thought I'd bring it on out. Could be something you've been waiting on."

"But I haven't ordered anything."

Instead of answering, he nudged the chair toward her with his foot.

"But it's for me?"

"*Ya.* Your name is on the label."

She went to her small desk in the sitting room and retrieved her reading glasses, then peered at the return label.

"I don't know anyone in Berne, Indiana."

"Apparently someone knows you. Open it." Micah reached into his pocket and withdrew a pocketknife. After pulling the blade open, he turned the knife around and handed it to her.

"Danki."

"Gem gschehne."

She slit the flap open and removed an envelope, which she sat on the table, then folded back the tissue paper.

Why would someone send her a quilt?

And not just any quilt but a very old one.

She ran her fingertips over the hand-sewn squares, admiring the stitching and double wedding ring pattern. Pulling the quilt out, she partially unfolded it, enough to reveal the bottom corner. And now her heart was racing as if she'd chased a rabbit just as Chloe had earlier that morning.

She stared at the quilt in her hands for a moment—disbelieving—then plopped into her chair.

"Oh my . . ."

Micah was at her side in a second. "Are you okay? All the color has left your face."

He squatted beside her, and she clutched his hand.

"Take a deep breath. Don't pass out on me, Rachel."

"Nein." She closed her eyes, then opened them, staring at the quilt and then at Micah's concerned expression. "I just can't believe my eyes. Help me unfold it."

She stood and motioned for him to pick up one end of the quilt. It couldn't be what she thought it was. But when Micah took his end and stepped back, she saw the entire thing—the double ring pattern set against the ivory background, with colors just as her *mamm* had described it. And in the corner, the single block turned the wrong direction.

"Is this the quilt you . . ."

She knew Micah was trying to catch up with what she'd already realized.

"It is. I don't know how, but it is."

"Perhaps you should open the envelope."

They carefully refolded the quilt, this time with the upside-down block facing toward the outside. Micah placed it gently across the back of a chair as Rachel picked up the envelope. He moved to sit down across from her, but she shook her head and pulled out the chair on her right side.

"Read it with me."

"But it might be personal."

"Please."

For reasons she couldn't describe, she didn't want to face this alone. She'd faced her whole life alone. But now, at what could be an important juncture in the road of her life, she wanted Micah beside her.

Her hands shaking, she slit the envelope with Micah's pocketknife and pulled out a letter.

Dear Rachel,

I'm your cousin, Savannah Glick Farver, and I have been looking for you and your parents the last year. That's how I ended up in your home on the tour a couple of weeks ago.

My mother, Deborah Lehman—you would know her as Deborah Glick or even by her maiden name, Byler—passed eighteen months ago. Lehman was my stepfather's name, the man she married after my parents divorced and my mother and I left Nappanee and moved to Berne. We also left the Mennonite church, of course. (You should know that I, however, returned to the Mennonite church as a teenager and married a Mennonite man.)

It took me a few months to go through my mother's

things, but then I found letters she wrote to your mother when your family still lived in Nappanee. I won't go into the contents, as that would take many pages. Suffice to say, the letters were all mailed back unopened with Return to Sender penned on the outside.

Of course, Mother shared the story of the quilt with me. She kept it on her bed all these years. But otherwise she rarely talked about your family. She rarely talked about her past at all. I think it was too painful.

A year ago, then, I learned your family had moved from Nappanee—do you remember our playing together there as young children?—but I didn't know where you'd gone. Still, I needed to know what happened to this lost branch of my family. I finally found someone in Nappanee who thought you moved to some other Amish community in northwest Indiana. But the name King and your parents' first names are common in Amish communities, so finding you wasn't easy. I wasn't even sure your last name was still King. When I did find you, I learned your parents have also passed, and I'm so sorry.

I want to apologize for the way I behaved when I was in your home that day. I was experiencing so many different emotions—disbelief, joy, relief, and even fear. I simply froze and didn't know how to tell you who I was, even after answering your question about the quilt. And since my return home, I've been praying for the words to explain why I was looking for you and how much it means to have found you. Perhaps our mothers' quilt will help. I hope it was all right to send it where I did, but I failed to note your address when I was there.

As you can tell, I'm still stumbling over my words. I'm

also still coming to terms with the fact that I, an only child, might soon have more family in my life. I'm just not sure how you'll feel.

I'm enclosing my phone number and address. If you could see your way to respond to this letter, I would be quite grateful. I still don't understand all the reasons our family remained torn apart, but certainly it's time to build a bridge across the divide.

Blessings,

Savannah

Rachel read the letter twice. She had at least a dozen questions, and the expression on Micah's face told her he did too. Chloe was watching them closely, as if she could sense that something was amiss.

Finally, Rachel folded the letter and placed it back in the envelope. Glancing again at Micah, she saw such patience and concern that she felt tears prick her eyes. She looked left and right, anywhere but directly at this dear man.

"Perhaps we could go for a walk," she said.

"*Ya.* A fine idea."

He helped her into her coat, then shrugged into his own, and called out to Chloe. She didn't need to be asked twice. They walked down the back-porch steps and into a December day so bright and crisp that Rachel felt pierced by the beauty of it.

They were halfway across the field before she found the words to begin.

"I barely remember my *aenti* Deborah. A few years after she married, she and her husband left the Amish church and joined the Mennonites."

"What year was this?"

"I hadn't begun school yet, so it must have been more than fifty years ago. I didn't understand what had happened, why they weren't around anymore. I only knew that I'd lost my playmate."

"Savannah."

"Ya." Rachel smiled at the memory. "Even her name was different. According to my *mamm*, her *schweschder* never quite settled into our Plain life. She wanted to continue her education, even after she'd had Savannah, and that wasn't allowed. Also, she and her husband questioned parts of our *Ordnung*. I don't know the entire story, only what I've managed to put together. You see, a few weeks ago I found a box of letters *Mamm* wrote to Deborah."

"The day I surprised you on the back porch, you'd been crying, a letter in your hand."

"*Ya. Mamm* never mailed the letters. They weren't even addressed, probably because she didn't have an address. I think she always intended to send them if she could ever learn where Deborah was, believing in her heart they would somehow reconcile. But apparently she and my *dat* were killed in the buggy accident without her ever discovering Deborah's whereabouts. I doubt she knew how to try. I didn't."

"Did the letters explain what happened?"

"*Mamm* talked around it a bit. Apparently my *aenti*'s husband had a *schweschder* who'd been abused by her husband. The man left the church and divorced her, but as you know . . ."

"Under our *Ordnung*, she wouldn't be allowed to remarry."

"That seemed the final straw that pushed her family into the Mennonite faith, where women who've been abused aren't under the same restriction."

Micah picked up a stick and threw it for Chloe, who dashed across the field the best she could. She might be an old dog, but she still enjoyed playing. There was a lesson in that.

Micah stole a glance at Rachel. "Fifty years ago . . . Many communities still practiced shunning then."

"Many still do, but *ya,* at this time it was still our practice to sever ties completely with someone who left the church. I suppose my parents thought they were doing the right thing. They thought by cutting off all communication, Deborah and her family would come home, but they never did. I suspect *Mamm* regretted that decision once she had no idea where her *schwesch-der* was. According to one of *Mamm*'s letters, she'd somehow learned Deborah and her husband divorced, apparently without abuse involved, and that's why Deborah left the Mennonite church too. She had no choice. And then she moved away from Shipshe."

"So they lost touch, your *mamm* and Deborah."

"We never spoke of it, and I regretted that after *Mamm* and *Dat* passed. I tried looking through their things, but I found nothing except Deborah's and Savannah's names penned in the family Bible. Later I found the letters."

"Apparently she and Savannah settled in Berne, assuming that's why Savannah lives there now."

"So it would seem."

They continued to the far side of the field where Rachel's *dat* had long ago set a picnic table under a tall maple tree. Chloe moved to sniff around the tree. Rachel and Micah sat.

"Will you answer her?"

"I suppose I will, after I've given it some thought and prayed on what exactly to say."

Micah didn't push. They sat in the sun, Chloe now sprawled at their feet, and enjoyed the peacefulness of the day.

Finally, Rachel pulled in a deep breath. "This is all so new to me, but it's what I've prayed for lately . . . that *Gotte* would bring more people into my life." She hesitated and then added, "As he brought you."

Micah reached for her hand, then cupped it between his own hands and ran his thumb over hers. "I haven't told you how much you mean to me, Rachel, but I'd like to sometime. When you're ready to hear it."

Her mood lifted at his words. She'd hoped. Of course she had, and then she'd called herself an old fool for daring to dream such a thing. It wasn't just Micah's affection for her that tugged at her heartstrings; it was that he was in no hurry. He was willing to give her the time and space she needed.

She squeezed his hand and smiled her thanks. Then they walked back across the field. Perhaps that was how you knew when you were truly comfortable with someone—when you didn't need words to fill the silence.

When they reached Micah's buggy, he crossed his arms and leaned his backside against the door.

"Christmas will be here soon."

"Eleven days."

"I would love for you to spend it with me, with my family. They care for you as I do."

"Danki."

"Will you, then?"

"I'll think on it." An idea was forming in the back of her mind, but it might be too preposterous to voice, even to herself.

"Gut."

Micah's smile eased part of her worries. Somehow his presence added a solid feel to her world. She stood with Chloe on the porch, watching him drive away and considering just how much her life was about to change. And beneath that she wondered if she was ready for it.

6

MICAH THOUGHT PERHAPS OLD MAN WINTER WAS TRYing to make up for a temperate start. The last week had brought ten inches of snow with two different storms. The north wind was strong enough to knock a man out of his coat, and the sun barely managed to pierce the clouds at all.

The weather didn't slow down their business a bit. *Englischers* from the south *oohed* and *aahed* over the snow. Those from Canada declared the weather in Indiana was a delight. He supposed it might seem that way to them. Their home country had received record snowfall and below-average temperatures for several weeks.

If he was worried that the weather would have an ill effect on Rachel, he shouldn't have. In fact, she reminded him of a beautiful crocus, pushing through the last of winter's snow. Rachel had literally blossomed before his eyes.

She'd begun taking daily walks with the dog—even in the snow.

At their church meeting yesterday, he saw her singing with her eyes closed and a smile creasing her face. And at a gathering after, she didn't escape as soon as it was acceptable to do so, instead choosing to stay and sit in a circle with the others—even rocking someone's *boppli*.

The day he visited her for afternoon tea, she'd greeted him waving an envelope postmarked Berne, and she insisted that he sit and read the letter with her.

The wound that had splintered her family so long ago had begun to heal. But he'd been surprised Savannah invited Rachel to spend Christmas in Berne—and astonished when she'd agreed.

"I'm glad you're going, glad you have this chance to get to know your family, but we're going to miss you here."

"Danki."

"I mean it, Rachel." He reached for her hand, intertwined his fingers with hers. They were sitting in the kitchen, the dog asleep by the stove, and he marveled that he felt so comfortable here. "I was looking forward to spending Christmas with you, but there will be other Christmases for us."

"There will?"

"Indeed." He squeezed her hand. "Family is important. I'm very happy that you're reconnecting with yours."

"I'll be there less than a week, so you and our tour partners won't have to cover for me too long."

"Back before Old Christmas, then?"

"I'm sure."

"My granddaughter Nancy asked me about Old Christmas this morning."

"She's seven?"

"Right. And she remembered us celebrating it in the past, but she couldn't remember why it's on January sixth."

"Holidays and calendars can be confusing for *kinner.* Remember how long it seemed from the last day of school to Christmas? And yet it couldn't have been more than three or four days."

"Exactly. Well, I explained to Nancy that the wise men visited the Christ child twelve days after his birth—at least that's when we celebrate it."

"And what did she think of that?" Rachel leaned forward. She always seemed so interested when he spoke of the *grandkinner.* He could easily imagine her being their grandmother.

That temporarily derailed his train of thought. He got caught up envisioning her rocking the *boppli*, helping the older *kinner* with their homework, baking cookies . . .

Rachel patted his arm. "Lost you for a minute."

"Sorry about that. My mind wanders at times."

"You were telling me about Nancy and the wise men."

"Right. She's a smart one. Right away she starts singing 'The Twelve Days of Christmas.'"

"An *Englisch* song if there ever was one."

"I have to agree with you on that. Can't say I've ever seen ten lords a-leaping. Nancy immediately insisted on going outside to look for a partridge or a pear tree. I didn't have the heart to tell her she wouldn't find either."

Rachel sat back and sighed, apparently satisfied with the story.

"I'll look forward to being home in time for Old Christmas, then. Perhaps we can read the story of the wise men with Nancy."

"That's a fine idea."

He was actually quite disappointed that Rachel wouldn't be home for Christmas, but he could see she'd already made up her mind. Plus, he honestly was happy for her. It was only that he looked forward to the day a little less, knowing she wouldn't be there to share it with him.

As long as he'd known Rachel, she'd never spent a night away from her farm. But in that blossoming, she was a new woman, or perhaps she was becoming the woman she might have been if her life had taken a different path. Her demeanor had changed from caution bordering on sadness to one of confidence and optimism.

Perhaps by reconnecting with Savannah, she'd realized she was no longer alone. Or now she was too busy living life to worry about it. Regardless, he saw a lightness to her step and a sweetness to her smile previously missing. A time or two he'd thought of the woman he'd found weeping on her back porch, and when he did, he said a silent prayer thanking *Gotte* for his provision and care.

But was he part of that provision? Did he want to be? He'd prayed to be part of her journey, but was he ready for big changes in his life?

He didn't have answers to those questions, but he'd think about them over the next few days.

As Micah shrugged into his coat on Christmas Eve's eve, ready for the children's Christmas play, he saw Tom and Naomi exchange a knowing smile. He might have ignored it, but Tom tossed the dish towel he was using over his shoulder and slapped him on the back.

"Going to pick up Rachel?"

"I am."

"That's *gut*. I was worried she might not come to the play."

"Everyone comes to the school play."

Tom stepped closer. "You know, *Dat* . . . it's all right if you have romantic feelings for her."

"It's all right?"

"What Tom means is that we all like Rachel." Naomi stepped closer and brushed some imaginary lint off his coat. Then she stood on tiptoe and kissed his cheek. "We want you to be happy."

"I didn't realize I was unhappy."

Tom's expression turned from teasing to serious. "We miss *Mamm*. We all do, and we always will. But we also understand that *Gotte* doesn't mean for any of us to be lonely."

Micah didn't realize he'd been worried about his son's opinion on the matter of Rachel, but perhaps he had been. Suddenly a weight that had been holding him back was gone.

"*Danki*, son. I appreciate that. I appreciate both of you telling me how you feel." He ran his fingers through his beard, attempting to maintain a serious expression, but it was impossible. Grinning, he added, "*Danki* for your permission to court."

"Ha! As if you needed my permission. But you know, *Dat*, you're not getting any younger."

"Indeed."

"Might want to keep the courting period short."

Micah didn't answer that. He wasn't sure how to.

"I'm just saying, if you're sure of your feelings, and if you've had them for some time . . ."

"And of course, if Rachel shares your feelings . . ." Naomi added.

"Then now might be a *gut* time to ask her."

Micah raised his eyebrows, as if he had no idea what his son was talking about. Naomi laughed and shook her finger at him. "A Christmas wedding would be real nice."

"You expect me to ask Rachel to be my *fraa*?"

"Ya." Naomi and Tom nodded in unison.

"And then we should marry . . . in two days."

"Might be a bit rushed," Naomi said, admitting that reality. "But Old Christmas? Now, that would be doable."

"Well, thank you both for your blessing, but Rachel is quite busy at the moment reconnecting with her family. I won't be adding to that by asking her to be my bride."

"You think the timing is bad?" Tom stepped closer to Naomi and slipped his arm around her waist. "Because personally, I'm not sure there is a bad time to tell someone you care for them."

"When did you become so wise?"

"Guess I got it from my old man."

Micah laughed at that. He remembered when he'd first called his own *dat* an old man. His *dat* had insisted on challenging him to a wood-chopping contest, and Micah had lost. Still, he understood it as a term of affection, so instead of being offended, he told Tom and Naomi he'd think on what they'd said and hurried to his buggy.

"Come on, Samson. We've a lady to pick up."

Rachel was ready when he arrived, needing only to put on her coat and wrap a bright-blue scarf around her neck.

"That's pretty. I don't think I've seen it before."

"I believe I've been holding on to a deep sadness for the last few years, maybe for my entire life. Even deeper lately. But now . . . well, now it's time for color."

Micah couldn't have resisted if he'd tried. He stepped closer, put his hands on her arms, and kissed her softly on the lips. A deep contentment filled his heart in that moment, and any worries he might have had fled.

Rachel felt right in his arms. She felt as if she belonged there.

Color blossomed in her cheeks, and they both laughed when Chloe sighed heavily.

"That dog looks mighty content."

"As she should be. We shared a bacon sandwich for dinner."

She returned to the kitchen to be sure she'd turned off the stove. Micah followed her and looked around. The place had none of the Christmas sparkle his son's home had. Of course, she wouldn't be there for the holiday, so why would it?

As if she could follow his thoughts, Rachel glanced around the room. "It was different, I think, having Christmas in such a small family. But my parents did what they could to make it special."

"Ya?" He took off his hat and twirled it in his hands. Rachel had spoken little of her past in all the time he'd known her, but since reconnecting with her cousin, it was as if she was also coming to terms with what had been.

"*Mamm* made gingerbread cookies, and then I helped her decorate them. I remember standing on a stool in front of this counter, putting little raisins into the still warm dough so the gingerbread people would have eyes."

"Special memories."

"Indeed." Rachel turned in a circle, a smile playing across her lips. "She'd spread pine boughs in the windowsills, then set a small candle in the midst of them."

"Battery powered?"

"Of course. *Mamm* always had an eye out for fire hazards. *Dat* said we'd break him with the cost of batteries, but then he'd laugh and say the place looked nice."

Rachel's gaze seemed to reach far beyond the room they were standing in, into the past, to pull forth sweet memories.

"We'd have one for every window. I'd help *Mamm* pull out the box where we kept them . . . I knew Christmas was close when we'd unbox them and check each battery, dust off each one, and set them carefully in the center of the windows."

"Seems to me it's the small traditions that matter so much as we get older."

"We'd make paper chains from bright construction paper and decorate the table for Christmas dinner." She laughed at the memory. "Our gifts were always wrapped in plain brown paper, but *Mamm* would tie bright hair ribbons around mine. I used them for bookmarks."

"Sounds to me like you had a *gut* childhood."

"You know what? I did."

As they walked toward the front door, Rachel pulled her gloves out of her coat pocket. She slipped her hands inside them, wriggling her fingers just so. She laughed again when she saw him looking at the holes revealing her index fingers. "I've been meaning to mend these, but then I forget about it as soon as I take them off."

They spoke of her upcoming trip to Berne as they traveled the short distance to the schoolhouse. Micah wished there was a longer route to get there. He wasn't ready to share Rachel with a room full of people.

"Are you looking forward to your trip?"

"*Ya.* But I've never traveled during the holiday before. To tell you the truth, I've never traveled at all."

"You'll enjoy the ride to Berne. It's only a few hours, and since you switch buses in Fort Wayne, you'll have a chance to stretch your legs."

"The thought of meeting so many new people, all related to me . . . Well, it's one of the best gifts I could receive. It's a real Christmas gift."

"Indeed. Family is a blessing."

They'd pulled into the yard of the schoolhouse, already filling up with buggies. Rachel stayed his hand when he made to open the door.

"It occurs to me that I have you to thank for this—for bringing Savannah and me together."

"What did I do?"

"If you hadn't started the Amish Tour Company, if you hadn't allowed me to be a part of it, she might never have found me."

"You give me too much credit."

"I don't think so. *Danki* for the Christmas gift I'll never forget."

He almost asked her to marry him then, with her face turned toward his and a smile on her lips. But suddenly little hands were knocking against his buggy and they were surrounded by *grandkinner.*

The schoolroom was filled to capacity. With the stove throwing off heat and friends and family pressed in around, it was easy enough to forget the cold, wintry night outside.

But it was the look of delight in Rachel's eyes that captured Micah's attention. He caught her staring at the paper-chain garland made out of brightly colored construction paper, then stepped closer so he could whisper, "Like from your childhood."

"Exactly what I was thinking."

"Did you make paper snowflakes too?"

"Only at school."

The children sang carols, read the Christmas story, and performed a short play about the Christ child and the wise men—only these wise men had a sheepdog instead of a camel. Micah and Rachel exchanged a look, and he knew she was thinking of Chloe and how Micah had shown up at her front door with the pitiful-looking dog. It seemed that Chloe had marked the beginning of something new for Rachel, and it occurred to him that Naomi might have been right. Perhaps Old Christmas would be just the time for him and Rachel to begin spending their lives together.

Rachel was pleasantly surprised when Micah's two youngest granddaughters, Melinda and Nancy, threw their arms around her legs. The girls were in first and second grade, but they could have easily passed for twins—blond hair, blue eyes, and a smattering of freckles.

"You came."

"We knew you would."

"We hoped you would."

"Did you see me rocking the baby Jesus? It was only a doll."

"And did you like my poem?"

Rachel returned their hugs. "You both did a fine job. Are you excited about Christmas?"

"I asked for a new doll."

"I asked for a book."

"In the morning we each get to read a part of the Christmas story."

"Are you going to be there, to read with us?"

"*Nein*. I'm going on a trip." Rachel's heart twisted at the look of disappointment on their faces. No doubt they missed their grandmother—or rather they missed having a grandmother around. Naomi's parents lived in Ohio and visited Shipshe in the summer. Micah's wife had passed when the girls were quite young.

"We were hoping you'd spend the day with us."

"I would have liked that very much." She squatted so she could look them directly in the eyes. "I'm afraid I can't, though. I'm going to visit my cousin."

"She's your family?"

"Ya." A lump formed in her throat. She swallowed past it and pulled in a deep breath. "She is."

"What's her name?"

"Savannah."

"That's pretty, but we're going to miss you."

"*Ya*, we're going to miss you."

Both girls snuggled in close and threw their arms around Rachel's neck. She smelled in the goodness of them—the innocence. Did such qualities have a scent? She thought maybe they did. Standing, she turned them toward the back of the room. "I believe I heard someone is serving cookies and punch."

Which was all the girls needed to peel off and join their friends.

While visiting with her own friends and neighbors, Rachel found herself scanning the room for Micah. When she found him, he winked and smiled—almost as if he somehow knew she'd been looking for him.

Rachel enjoyed a cup of punch as she congratulated the teacher on a fine Christmas program and then answered Naomi's questions about her trip.

"Micah mentioned you found some letters."

"*Ya*, that my *mamm* wrote. I think she planned to send them someday, although perhaps she simply wrote them to ease the pain in her heart."

"But they were to her *schweschder*, your cousin's *mamm*?"

"They were. I've wrapped them, and I'm giving them to Savannah for Christmas."

"What a perfect gift." Naomi reached out and squeezed her arm. "We're so happy you're having this time with your family, but we'll miss you at Christmas dinner."

"Danki." Rachel had always thought Micah's family merely tolerated her presence at the occasional dinner, but with a start, she realized they actually liked her. Why did that surprise her so much?

Micah took the long way back to her house, and the scene outside her window was like something from an *Englisch* fairy tale. Snow covered the fields. Streetlights glowed softly. Bright Christmas displays decorated *Englisch* yards, and candles shone from Amish windows.

When they reached her house, Micah said, "Before you go

in, I need to ask you something . . . although I know you leave tomorrow and probably have things to do."

"I do have a lot on my mind. Mainly I'm worried about Chloe. And Penny, too, but Chloe is more used to my company."

"Both your dog and your horse will be fine. I'll check on them every morning."

"And Josiah said he'd walk the dog in the evenings, or at least let her out to run as he cares for the horse."

"It's only for a few days."

"Ya." Her heart fluttered at the idea of being away from home. Why had she felt trapped there for so long? Looking at her snug little house from Micah's buggy, she realized she would miss the place if . . .

"I should tell you something." She wanted to stare at her hands or pretend to look for something in her purse, but she owed Micah more than that. She raised her eyes to his. "I've spoken to Josiah about selling to him after all."

"Your fields?"

"And the house."

"Oh." He looked about to say more but ran his fingers through his beard instead.

"That's not all. It's early yet, and I haven't made a decision, but Savannah has suggested I move to Berne. She's invited me to live with her and her husband."

"Move?" Now Micah's eyes widened as if she'd said she was relocating to Indianapolis.

"There's an Amish community there now." She paused for a moment, searching for the right words. "I should have mentioned this when we spoke about spending Old Christmas together, but I didn't know how to bring it up without spoiling the moment. Of course, a move wouldn't happen right away. These things take time."

Micah stared out the window for a moment, suddenly more serious than she'd ever seen him, except perhaps when he'd first brought her Chloe. Then he shook his head, as if he could dispel whatever worried him, and turned back toward her, smiling once again. "Then I'll pray that you'll know *Gotte's wille* for your life, Rachel, and that if Berne is where you're supposed to be, your path there will be smooth."

She started to say how much she would miss him. Hadn't he just kissed her in her sitting room? But kissing was one thing. Marrying was another. Micah hadn't asked her to marry him, hadn't really hinted at such a thing. And if the last few years had taught her anything, it was that people should live the life they had, not the life they wished for.

"You wanted to ask me something?"

"It can wait. I shouldn't keep you any longer."

"You're sure?"

"I am."

"Now I'm going to wonder what it was about."

"At least you'll be thinking of me."

Leaning over, she kissed him on the cheek. "*Danki*. For everything." Tears stinging her eyes, she hurried up the porch steps and into the house. She *would* miss him—of course she would. But for the first time since her parents passed, she was looking forward to the holidays. She wouldn't be depending on the kindness of friends. She'd be with family, and that meant more to her than she could even explain to herself.

So instead of dwelling on how much she'd miss Micah, she spent an extra few minutes brushing Chloe, then readied for bed before sinking beneath the covers. She'd worried that she'd be too excited to sleep. But as she said her evening prayers, she did something she hadn't done in a long time. Somewhere between asking *Gotte* to watch over Chloe and thanking him for Micah, she began to drift off, much like a child falling asleep in her father's arms.

7

Rachel kept in touch by phone with both Josiah, who assured her the farm was fine, and Micah, who insisted that he, Chloe, and Penny missed her terribly but were somehow managing.

She'd called Micah the first night she arrived in Berne, ostensibly to let him know she'd arrived safely. In truth, she simply needed to hear his voice, needed that connection with home.

"Still snowing here," Micah reported when he returned her call after hearing her voice mail message.

"Is it now? There's no snow in Berne, though they said an inch fell last week."

"And you've met the entire family?"

"Only Savannah and her *mann* so far. They're awfully nice."

"Are they, now?"

"But different." She glanced around the guest room she was staying in. "I've never stayed anywhere with electricity."

"Well, they are Mennonite, not Amish."

"True, and it's not as different as you'd think."

But it was different, and just talking with Micah helped settle her nerves. Over the next few days, she grew accustomed to the electricity and television—though the TV was rarely on—and even Savannah's car. It was indeed more convenient than a horse and buggy. But Rachel found herself missing the farm and Chloe and even her mare. Although she'd often grumbled about the chores associated with Penny—the ones she managed without Josiah—she realized now that they helped keep her physically fit.

She was surprised by how much she missed Micah. Perhaps she hadn't admitted, even to herself, how much he meant to her.

Each evening she looked forward to their phone call.

"Must be awfully cold, sitting in that phone shack."

"Oh *ya*. I think I have frostbite."

"You're teasing me, but it must be inconvenient."

"It's just at the end of our lane. Besides, you're worth any inconvenience."

A silence settled over the phone call, one full of possibility and promise. Could a silence hold those things?

She proceeded to tell him about visiting a local shopping mall, seeing a production of *The Nutcracker*, and eating at a local steak house.

"Fancy?"

"It was. I felt a little out of place in my Plain clothes, but the steak was delicious."

"They're spoiling you."

"It's true."

"I miss you." The suddenness of his confession caught her off guard, that and the earnestness in his voice.

"I miss you, too, Micah."

She hung up the phone that night realizing she'd never before felt what she felt for Micah. She didn't know if it was love—though she hadn't minded that kiss—but she did know she was grateful he was in her life. The question was where they would go from here.

Rachel stayed in Berne longer than she'd planned, the visit both wonderful and memorable. And even though it was exhausting at the same time, she could hardly wait to visit Savannah again.

But she was also eager to be home.

Since she'd never been away from her hometown before, she'd never had the joy of returning. She had the urge to press her nose to the window of the bus as it drew closer to Shipshe. So many familiar sites—Howe's, the Auction and Flea Market, Yoder's, and finally the Davis Mercantile. Before she knew it they were pulling into the station, actually just a drop-off site in the middle of town. It was late on Monday afternoon, and she spied Micah standing outside, holding two paper cups with steam rising from the slits in the lids.

His eyes sought hers, and she felt her pulse jump.

She'd missed him terribly.

She'd also missed the white Labrador waiting patiently at his side.

Their reunion was a flurry of hugs, barks, and laughter. Finally, Micah pushed both cups—and now she could smell hot chocolate—into her hands. "Hold these while I fetch your bag."

"There's a box too. Savannah insisted on sending tea cakes

for the tour tomorrow so I wouldn't have to bake late into the night."

He returned with the box under his left arm, her suitcase in his left hand, and with his right, he steered her toward his buggy.

"Tell me all about your visit."

"We talked every night. And no matter what you say, you must have frozen sitting in the phone shack."

"I enjoyed those talks."

"As did I, but as far as my visit, I think I've already told you everything."

"I'm sure you didn't."

So she went back over it. Savannah's children, grandchildren, and husband. The evenings spent sharing stories, knitting together the two families that had been torn apart. How she'd enjoyed their worship service. How Christmas morning was a flurry of gifts and carols and reading of the Christ child's birth.

"So much of what we do is the same," she told him.

"When you say *we*, you mean . . ."

"Amish and Mennonites. I suppose it's the same with many *Englischers* as well. Our faith is centered around the Christ child, so at Christmas in particular, the ways we differ seem unimportant. What we have in common far exceeds our differences."

"*Ya*, it's true." Micah reached over and squeezed her hand. "Though I hope you're not thinking of converting."

"*Nein*. I'm happy with my Plain life."

Her mind brushed back over the last ten days and what it had meant to reconnect with Savannah. "The visit also helped me in other ways. Helped me put some things in perspective."

"How so?"

"Being around other family helped me truly understand the value of relatives. We're family no matter what our choices in life might be, and we'll always be family. After reading my *mamm*'s letters, I think she realized that in the end. Savannah's *kinner* are all grown and have families of their own now. But as Mennonites, they're all still Plain in many ways. It's so obvious how much they value their family and faith."

"Not something the Amish have cornered."

"Certainly not. I'm saying this badly, though. What I mean is, it makes a world of difference to know I have family in Berne, relatives I can visit or call or write a letter to. It also made me realize the limitations of family, though. After all, they all have their own jobs and homes and activities there in Berne, and I have mine here."

"Unless you move to Berne. Then you'd have those things there."

Micah seemed to be waiting for her response, and she couldn't blame him.

She'd put off sharing her decision because she not only wanted to tell him in person but explain the why of it. And now was the time. The bus had arrived later than scheduled, and darkness was already falling. They had a tour the next day, then a day off for Old Christmas, and then three more days of tours. It would be a busy week. So she cleared her throat and cornered herself in the buggy.

"Savannah and her family assured me they would love for me to live with them."

"You told me as much before you left."

Micah's tone was neutral. It was plain that he didn't want to influence her decision, and she loved him for that. Yes, she'd finally admitted to herself that she loved him. Being away from him for ten days had helped her understand how much she'd come to care for him. They weren't *youngies*, and she didn't even know if he felt the same way. She was no longer afraid of her feelings, though. Life was too short for that.

Micah was still patiently waiting, so she began again.

"I can't tell you how much it means to me to have people who are my own flesh and blood. To have a connection, a living connection, to my parents."

Micah quickly glanced at her, then back at the road. Following his gaze, she noticed it looked as if it might snow any minute.

"Until just now, I hadn't realized how hard that must have been for you," he said. "To think you were the last in your family."

"We'll surely all be reunited one day, but it helps to have folks on this side of heaven." Her heart had begun to beat faster. Chloe sighed heavily and gave her a look that seemed to say, *Get on with it*. So she did.

"As much as I love my family, though, I've decided to stay in Shipshewana."

Micah's expression broke into a wide grin. "Now, that's the best news I've heard in some time."

"You thought I wouldn't stay?"

"I worried you might not, though if going was what you decided, I would have tried to be happy for you."

"This is my home." They were nearly to her farm now. She knew every street corner, every field they'd passed. She had fond memories of her life here. She had more friends than she'd realized, and she had Micah. Why would she leave all that?

"Of course, I'll still want to visit Berne regularly. It's a *gut* thing I like to knit, since I'm going to spend that much time on a bus. But my life is here."

Micah turned down her lane, and she was surprised to see candlelight coming from her sitting room window.

"Chloe and I have a few surprises for you."

"Do you, now?"

"I hope you don't mind. The *grandkinner* helped too."

Besides the candlelight, Rachel couldn't imagine what he was talking about. Then he led her up the porch steps, told her to wait, and hurried to the buggy to retrieve her suitcase and box.

Setting them just inside the door, he then blocked her way and said, "You might want to close your eyes."

"Close my eyes?"

"It's better if you see it all at once."

"Okay." She drew out the word. She'd thought Micah might have a Christmas gift for her. In Berne she'd knitted him a scarf out of the softest gray yarn she could find. But this . . . this was something different. She could tell from the way Chloe stared up at her and Micah waited that this was somehow bigger than simply a wrapped present.

She closed her eyes and allowed him to lead her inside, then through the sitting room toward the kitchen. When he stopped, she knew they were standing in the doorway between the two rooms.

"I think I smell . . . gingerbread."

"Do you, now?"

"And pine . . . some sort of pine needles."

"You can open your eyes."

Slowly, Rachel did.

She felt like it was the first time she'd really seen her home in many years.

Chloe barked once, and Micah said something about Naomi and Tom buying Chloe a new bed. But she barely heard him. She was busy taking in the pine boughs in every window, accented with a single candle. Then she turned around and saw the same in her sitting room window. That's what she'd seen from the road.

Paper chains made from bright construction paper adorned the kitchen counters. On the table was a plate of freshly baked gingerbread cookies, and beside it a single long, thin box wrapped in brown paper and fastened with a bright-blue hair ribbon.

"How . . . how did you do all this?"

"I told you. I had help." Micah led her to the table and pulled out a chair, and after she sat, he perched on the one next to her.

Rachel pulled off her outer bonnet, still staring around in disbelief. "Everything is just like . . . just like my *mamm* used to do."

"I know. You told me." Micah reached forward and tucked a stray strand of hair into her *kapp*, then allowed his fingers to linger on her cheek.

"The *grandkinner* made the paper chains. My grandson Raymond helped me cut pine boughs and arrange them. Yoder's had a sale on the candles."

"I can't believe you did all this."

Micah's eyes sparkled. "I was hoping you'd be pleased, and I wanted your homecoming to be special. Naomi and the girls made the cookies, and the gift . . ." He picked up the box and placed it in front of her. "The gift is from me."

"Oh. I have something for you too." She hopped up and rummaged through her suitcase in the sitting room. Finally, she pulled out the scarf, carefully wrapped in tissue paper. It wasn't much, but it was the best she had to give.

Micah wanted to tell Rachel her gift for him could wait, but when she returned and sat down, he understood from the way she peered at him, then glanced quickly away, that this meant a lot to her. The tradition of gift-giving was important—not in the quantity or cost of the gifts but in the sharing. He was only just beginning to grasp how much she'd missed out on in the last few years. He wouldn't hurry her through this. Better to savor each moment.

"For me?"

"*Ya*. Of course it's for you. Though, honestly, I made something for Chloe too. I think she can wait until tomorrow, though."

As if in answer, Chloe sighed and rolled over on her new bed.

"I can't think what I've done to deserve this." He'd meant it as a joke, but Rachel's expression was suddenly serious.

"You saved me, Micah Miller. You literally saved me. I might have become a bitter, lonely old woman, but you opened up a new world to me. The tours you started saved me. When you brought strangers into my house, it's as if you woke me from a long nap. And then to find my family . . . I can't thank you enough."

She placed the gift in his hands. "But I wanted to try."

"Then I say *danki*."

"You haven't opened it yet."

"I'm sure I'll love it, though."

He pulled away the tissue paper, revealing a winter scarf that had been meticulously and lovingly knitted. "You did this?"

"*Ya*, of course."

"You knit as well as you bake and quilt." He wrapped the scarf around his neck and tossed the end of it over his shoulder. "How do I look?"

"Warm."

He was trying to appear lighthearted, but in truth, the gift touched him to the core. He'd fully understood how much he cared for Rachel while she in Berne. He loved his family, and they loved him, but he wanted to live his life with the woman sitting next to him. While Rachel was away, the days had stretched out in front of him like long shadows.

He reached for her hands and squeezed them. "*Danki*. For taking the time to make this for me, and for caring so much."

"Gem gschehne."

"Now open yours."

She pulled off the ribbon, first fingering it, then placing it carefully next to the package. "Blue is my favorite color."

"I guessed it might be."

"I'll hold my place in my cookbook with it."

When she opened the box, a gasp escaped her lips. "Micah, you shouldn't have. These are much too expensive."

"See if they fit."

She pulled one glove over her left hand, running the fingers of her right over the soft brown leather. "It's a sin to be proud."

"*Ya*, but it's not a sin to be warm. And these will last you many years."

"Indeed they will."

She pulled off the glove and set it gently in the box, then clasped her hands together on the table and looked around the room. Finally, she turned her gaze to his. "This has been a fine Christmas."

"For me as well."

"It's *gut* to be home."

"It's *gut* to have you home."

Micah scooted toward the edge of his chair and covered her hands with his. "I want to ask you something, Rachel."

"You do?" When she looked up at him, tears had pooled in her eyes. He knew that she knew, and yet the asking was important. This was a moment they would remember and cherish all their years together.

"Will you marry me?"

"Ya."

He pulled back in surprise, and she laughed.

"You thought I'd say no?"

"I thought I might have to talk you into it."

"But I love you. Why would you have to persuade me to live a life I've dreamed about for some time now?"

He stood and pulled her into his arms, then lowered his face to her head, smelling the scent of her freshly laundered *kapp* and beneath that some kind of strawberry shampoo. She felt so good, so right in his arms, that he didn't want to let her go.

Rachel pulled back and gently placed both her hands on his face. "Do you love me, too, Micah?"

"I do." His voice was low and gruff, and he swallowed past the lump in his throat. Why did he feel the urge to cry? He was becoming a sentimental old fool, but perhaps there were worse things to become. "I do, Rachel."

She entwined her fingers with his and pulled him into the sitting room. When they sat down on the couch, Micah pulled her into the crook of his arm. They stayed that way for some time, the candles still shining in their nests of pine boughs and snow falling outside the window. She enjoyed the quiet and rightness of being together, and she knew Micah did too.

For several minutes they spoke of nothing at all, and then well into the night, they spoke of the future they hoped to share.

8

If Micah had to choose a favorite holiday, it would without a doubt be Old Christmas. Perhaps because it reminded him of his parents and grandparents. Or maybe because it spoke of the real cost of giving things of immeasurable value—especially intangible things—since they were celebrating the gifts the wise men from long ago gave the Christ child.

He was thinking about that just after waking on Wednesday morning. Then as he lay there in bed, stretching, he stared at the ceiling, marveling at how his life had changed over the last year.

He thanked *Gotte* for his blessings, which were many.

The Amish Tour Company had established itself as a *gut* business. Their tours earned much-needed income for Emily and Paul Yoder, Joseph Schrock, and the Beiler family—not to mention for him and Rachel. More than that, the tours provided *Englischers* a glimpse into a simpler world, one they could pursue in their own lives if they chose to. At the very least, their guests received a respite from the noisy and demanding world of their time.

But *Gotte*'s blessings didn't end there.

Micah's family was whole and healthy. Yes, he still missed Inez. She had been such an important part of his world for so many years. But he understood that she wanted him to live his life fully, and to do it with the help of people he cared about and people who cared about him. Rachel certainly was all that and more.

And how he thanked *Gotte* for Rachel. She'd brought a youthfulness and tenderness to his life. She needed him, and he needed her. Weren't most relationships based on that? There was real affection between them, and he found himself looking forward to the years that lay ahead rather than dreading them. He had a purpose—he would do what he could to make up for the loneliness of Rachel's past years.

As he stood to dress, he chuckled at the thought of the day ahead. It was Rachel's idea to share their plans after the Old Christmas celebration.

He walked downstairs and entered the kitchen, gratefully accepting the cup of coffee Naomi pushed into his hands. Coffee for the adults and milk for the children would be their breakfast, and then they would fast until the afternoon meal.

"But why are we fasting?" Raymond dropped his head onto his hands. He'd recently turned ten yet had the appetite of a teenager.

"It reminds us of Christ's sacrifice." Tom shared a smile with Naomi. The children often preferred the gift-giving and celebration of Christmas Day to Old Christmas.

"This is the day the wise men brought gifts to the baby

Jesus," Melinda offered, her small hands clutched around her glass of milk.

"I would have brought the baby Jesus a pacifier." Nancy yawned, remembering at the last second to cover her mouth. "Jenny's little *schweschder* has one, and every time she starts crying they stick it in her mouth. It works too."

The morning passed quietly. By noon they'd gathered in the sitting room to read from the family Bible. The verses, of course, were from the book of Matthew and focused on the visit from the magi. Tom could have read the story—it was his home and his children gathered around. But he didn't. He passed the worn Bible to Micah and said, "Would you read for us?"

"*Ya.* Of course."

Micah was again humbled that he had a valued place in this home. He wasn't just an old thing everyone put up with. What had Rachel said? *"Old things are valuable. We don't throw away people or animals or things simply because they've aged."*

So he took his time turning to the passage in Matthew, waited until he was sure everyone was listening, and then began to read. "After Jesus was born in Bethlehem in Judea, during the time of King Herod, Magi from the east came to Jerusalem . . ."

The poignant story stirred their hearts.

King Herod's inquiry.

Following the star, then finding Mary and the Child. Bowing and worshiping the creator of all things. Offering their gifts of gold, frankincense, and myrrh.

The warning that came in a dream.

When Micah finished, he closed the book, resting his hand on the cover, so cracked and worn from many years of reading. The sitting room was full of his family, and for a moment no one moved or spoke, each imagining the wise men, their journey, and the gifts.

Finally, Tom asked if anyone had questions.

"You explained about the twelve days of Christmas the other day, but what's myrrh again?" Nancy scrunched up her eyes. "Is that the spice *Mamm* uses in potatoes I don't like?"

Melinda hooked her arm through her sister's. "I don't get it either. Who wants frankincense for a Christmas present?"

"Technically, I think it was a birthday present," Raymond said. "I mean, they were celebrating his birth, right?"

They spent the next few minutes discussing the details of the story. When he thought they were done, Melinda raised her hand as if she were in school.

"Why is it called *Old* Christmas?" Melinda ran her fingers up and down her *kapp* strings. "I mean, the story is old, but . . ."

Betty answered. She was holding baby Nathan, who had fallen asleep during the Bible reading. Adam sat next to her, an arm around his wife's shoulders. "It's called old because in 1582 Pope Gregory XIII decided to change the calendar."

"You can't change a calendar," Raymond said.

"But he did." All eyes turned toward Micah. "He wiped away ten days, eleven minutes, and fifteen seconds."

Nancy collapsed back onto the floor, giggling. "You can't wipe away days . . . or minutes or seconds. Sometimes I want to, though. Especially during arithmetic class."

"So someone went to sleep on one day and woke up ten days later?" Raymond stared up at the ceiling, then added, "It would be terrible if your birthday was during those ten days."

They went on to speak of how the Christ child had changed the world, and how things were never the same after that—not even the calendar. By the time they'd finished, Naomi declared she could use some help in the kitchen, and for once she had more volunteers than she needed. "They all want to help when they're hungry."

"I can certainly lend a hand," Micah said, but Tom pointed to the window.

"Rachel's here."

That put an end to any idea of helping in the kitchen. Raymond came outside with Micah to take care of her horse and buggy. The air had once again turned cold, and Micah wanted to get Rachel inside. The sky was gray, too, and he wouldn't be surprised at more snow before evening.

As they walked toward the house, he reached out and snagged Rachel's hands.

"Do you still want to do this today?"

"If you do."

"I'd have done it Monday evening. Don't be surprised if I put an announcement in the *Budget*."

Rachel cocked her head and studied him.

"I'm a bit excited," he admitted.

"As am I."

"Then let's go tell the family."

Everyone was gathered around the table. It was a crowded affair, but no one complained. Chairs were brought in from other rooms, and the children sat shoulder to shoulder on the long bench positioned on the far side of the table, next to the wall.

After they'd silently prayed for their meal, Micah stood to get everyone's attention.

"Rachel and I have news." He noticed Tom and Naomi exchanging a knowing glance. Well, it *had* been their idea to do something about a wedding on Old Christmas. "I've asked Rachel to be my *fraa*, and she's agreed."

He wanted to say more, but suddenly everyone was talking and reaching to hug Rachel and declaring the new year to be a fine one. He waited for the general pandemonium to settle down before he added, "And she'd like to say something before you all dig into this awesome meal Naomi prepared."

All eyes turned to Rachel, and she took a big breath before speaking.

"Only that I love you all, and *danki* for allowing me to be a part of your family. I know I can never replace Inez, and that is certainly not my intent. But Micah has become a treasured friend over the last year, and we care about each other very much."

Silence settled on Micah's family until Nancy looked up with a smile. "Does this mean Rachel and Chloe will come to live with us?"

That started everyone talking again. Micah heard several amens and "We love you both" comments, and then he thought he heard someone say it was about time they admitted they loved each other. The dishes were being passed around with many smiles and a few tears and predictions of many years of happiness for the new couple.

Rachel should have felt worn-out by the meal and commotion. But strangely, she didn't. Instead, the family's reaction to their announcement had energized her. The clouds continued to press down, but the snow had held off. After she helped Naomi and the girls clean up the kitchen, Rachel and Micah walked out to the barn after she helped Naomi and the girls clean up after the meal.

Penny and Samson were in adjacent stalls.

Rachel thought they looked good together—her chestnut mare beside Micah's coal-black gelding. They reminded her of Chloe snuggled in her mudroom at home and Nancy's question.

"What will we do about Chloe?"

"She's our dog. We'll keep doing what you've been doing."

"*Ya*, but I mean your family is allergic—or some of them are."

Micah pulled two carrots from his pocket and handed one to her. Rachel fed hers to Samson, and he walked over to Penny and stroked the mare's nose. She was a fine animal.

"I think the question you're asking is where we'll live."

"Where will we live?" She turned toward him, a smile playing on her lips.

"Wherever you want. If you'd rather stay in your house, we can."

"And if I want to sell it to Josiah?"

"Tom just pulled me aside and offered to build us a *dawdi haus*." He grabbed her hand and pulled her to the door of the barn, where they could see across the property. "There, to the north of the main house."

"Our front porch would be perfect for watching the sun rise."

"And the back porch would be shaded by those maples, but we'd still be able to see the sun set."

She turned toward him and placed the palms of both hands on his chest. "If we had a *dawdi haus*, Chloe could stay with us, and Nancy and Melinda could play with her."

"But she wouldn't be in the main house, so the others wouldn't suffer from their allergies."

Rachel turned back toward the open door, toward the view of their future. Micah stepped closer and put his arms around her, drawing her back against him.

She let out a contented sigh, then said what had been troubling her since he'd asked her to wed. "It almost seems too *wunderbaar* to be true."

He took a moment answering. Then he kissed her cheek and asked, "Do you believe that? Do you believe *Gotte* doesn't want you to have the very best?"

"When you put it that way . . ."

"Ya?"

"I'll try to stop worrying and instead appreciate the direction my life has taken. Especially all the people *Gotte* has seen fit to put into my life. After all, I prayed for more people in my life. I'd say it was my Christmas prayer."

"Sounds like a fine idea."

"It does, doesn't it?"

"You know what else sounds like a fine idea?"

"Shoofly pie and a cup of coffee?"

"Exactly."

Rachel loved the feel of her hand in Micah's as they walked back to the house, toward the life they would share.

Acknowledgments

This book is dedicated to my students—both present and past. I've had the pleasure of being an educator for twenty-two years in a variety of settings (public school, private universities, public colleges), and in each of those I've been amazed at the energy, optimism, and work ethic of my students. They inspire me in so many ways, and it's a pleasure to teach them the fundamentals of both reading and writing.

I'd like to thank Heather and Eric for allowing me to use their sweet Labrador, Chloe, in this story. As is always the case, I want to thank my pre-readers; Kristy and Janet have been with me for so many years that I've lost count. Writing and publishing a book is definitely a team effort, and I appreciate every single person who helps me in that endeavor. My family is also a constant source of encouragement; plus they bring me things like coffee and pizza to sustain me throughout the process. Thank you also to my agent, Steve Laube; my editor, Kimberly Carlton; and the staff at HarperCollins Christian Publishing.

Christmas among the Amish is very different from what most of us experience. Minus the trappings of elaborate gift-giving and holiday travel, they have maintained the simplicity and poignancy of this special season—celebrating the birth of the Christ child. My hope is that this story will remind you, dear reader, of the same.

> And finally, ". . . always giving thanks to God the Father for everything, in the name of our Lord Jesus Christ."
>
> Ephesians 5:20

Discussion Questions

1. At the beginning of this story, Rachel thinks of the Bible verse Hebrews 13:2: "Do not forget to show hospitality to strangers, for by so doing some people have shown hospitality to angels without knowing it." What do you think this verse means? How should it affect our actions?
2. Rachel struggles with how to celebrate the holidays alone. What can we do for those around us who might not have family or close friends to celebrate with?
3. Rachel tells Micah, "Old things are valuable . . . We don't throw away people or animals or things simply because they've aged." What can we do in today's world to show that we value what has aged?
4. After Rachel explains how she ended up alone, Micah says, "*Gotte* has a plan for your life, Rachel. Same as he does for every life." What Bible verses assure us of this truth for ourselves?

About the Authors

Amy Clipston

Photo by Dan Davis Photography

Amy Clipston is the award-winning and bestselling author of the Kauffman Amish Bakery, Hearts of Lancaster Grand Hotel, Amish Heirloom, Amish Homestead, and Amish Marketplace series. Her novels have hit multiple bestseller lists including CBD, CBA, and ECPA. Amy holds a degree in communication from Virginia Wesleyan University and works full-time for the City of Charlotte, NC. Amy lives in North Carolina with her husband, two sons, and five spoiled rotten cats.

Visit her online at AmyClipston.com
Facebook: @AmyClipstonBooks
Twitter: @AmyClipston
Instagram: @amy_clipston

Kelly Irvin

Photo by Tim Irvin

Kelly Irvin is the bestselling author of the Amish of Big Sky Country, the Every Amish Season, and the Amish of Bee County series. Her novel *Upon a Spring Breeze* was the Reader's Choice Award for long romances. *The Beekeeper's Son* received a starred review from *Publishers Weekly*, who called it a "beautifully woven masterpiece." The two-time Carol Award finalist is a former newspaper reporter and retired public relations professional. Kelly lives in Texas with her husband, photographer Tim Irvin. They have two children, three grandchildren, and two cats. In her spare time, she likes to read books by her favorite authors.

Visit her online at KellyIrvin.com
Facebook: @Kelly.Irvin.Author
Twitter: @Kelly_S_Irvin
Instagram: @kelly_irvin

Kathleen Fuller

With over a million copies sold, Kathleen Fuller is the author of several bestselling novels, including the Hearts of Middlefield novels, the Middlefield Family novels, the Amish of Birch Creek series, and the Amish Letters series as well as a middle-grade Amish series, the Mysteries of Middlefield.

Visit her online at KathleenFuller.com
Facebook: @WriterKathleenFuller
Twitter: @TheKatJam
Instagram: @kf_booksandhooks

Vannetta Chapman

Vannetta Chapman writes inspirational fiction full of grace. She is the author of thirty-two novels, including the Pebble Creek Amish series, the Shipshewana Amish Mystery series, and *Anna's Healing*, a 2016 Christy Award finalist. Vannetta is a Carol Award winner and has also received more than two dozen awards from Romance Writers of America chapter groups. She was a teacher for fifteen years and currently resides in the Texas hill country.

Visit her online at VannettaChapman.com
Facebook: @VannettaChapmanBooks
Twitter: @VannettaChapman